the
centurion's
empire

Sean McMullen

the
centurion's
empire

A Tom Doherty
Associates Book
New York

Sean
McMullen
(SF)

THE CENTURION'S EMPIRE

Copyright © 1998 by Sean McMullen

This book is printed on acid-free paper.

Edited by Jack Dann

A Tor Book
Published by Tom Doherty Associates, Inc.
175 Fifth Avenue
New York, NY 10010

Tor Books on the World Wide Web:
http://www.tor.com

Tor® is a registered trademark of Tom Doherty Associates, Inc.

Library of Congress Cataloging-in-Publication Data

McMullen, Sean
    The centurion's empire / Sean McMullen.—
1st ed.
        p.   cm.
    "A Tom Doherty Associates book."
    ISBN 0-312-85131-6 (alk. paper)
    I. Title.
PR9619.3.M3268C46   1998
823—dc21   98-10257
                                                      CIP

First Edition: July 1998

Printed in the United States of America

0 9 8 7 6 5 4 3 2 1

8\20

For my daughter, Catherine

prologue

The Tyrrhenian Sea: 22 September 71, Anno Domini

Vitellan's journey to the twenty-first century began on the Tyrrhenian Sea, during an equinox gale in the autumn of the year 71, Anno Domini. In that year, in that century, his name was still Vitellan Bavalius.

The *Venator* was not a big ship, and because of that the sturdy transport vessel handled storms well. One of the severe gales that lashed the Campania coast around this time of year had boiled into life, and the *Venator* ran steadily with a northeast wind, its mainsail and foresail trimmed to storm-rig as it rode the rolling procession of huge waves.

Captain Metellus cautiously worked his way forward along the railing. At the bow, the great iron and timber anchor was loose in its lashings and rocking back and forth with every movement of the ship. The *Venator* had survived more than its share of storms because Metellus took nothing for granted, not the rigging, nor the packing of cargo, nor anything else. He always bought new sails and ropes long before renewal was due, and he personally inspected the hull with the carpenters—not merely to check that the leaks and seepages were under control, but to make sure that there were no leaks or seepages at all.

From a distance the anchor looked loose but safe, yet that was not good enough for the *Venator*.

Metellus stopped amidships, beside the mainmast. One of the new deckhands was holding on to the railing and was looking out to sea.

"Don't worry, it only gets worse," Metellus shouted to the youth above the wind.

"I'm not sick," Vitellan shouted back. "I'm here to see the storm."

Metellus laughed. "You're mad. Every one of the men on deck would give a week's pay to be below and dry."

"This is my first storm. How can I talk about it to my grandparents if I've been cowering below? I'd miss the huge waves, the sailors struggling with the steering oar, and the danger."

"Hah, there's not much danger on the open sea for a well-rigged, tight ship, Bavalius," shouted Metellus proudly. "Danger comes from stopping suddenly on rocks or a shoal. Turning beam-on to the wind and waves could sink us too, but I won't let that happen. Your family chose well when they—"

Vitellan saw it first. He pointed ahead and shouted a warning to the captain. Another ship, a very large vessel, was directly ahead of the *Venator*, lying on its side with its masts and rigging smashed and tangled. Captain Metellus turned and stumbled aft across the rolling deck, shouting to the steersmen above the wind. The five seamen working the steering oar frantically tried to turn the *Venator* to starboard, but even such a small ship does not turn easily. The *Venator* struck the wreck nearly square-on.

The shock snapped the mainmast, bringing down a tangle of rigging to snare those on deck. The hull split as thousands of mortise and tenon joints ripped apart, then the *Venator* slowly swerved about until the wind had it pinned beam-on to the waves against the wreck of the other ship. The two vessels crashed together amid the mountains of water, rupturing their hulls further.

The *Venator*'s bow was underwater scarcely a minute after the impact. Vitellan was still clinging to the rail, paralyzed with shock, as the legionaries that the ship had been taking to Egypt began struggling out of the main hatch amidships and crawling aft. The *Venator's* newest deckhand seemed to wake from a dream and he realized that death was very close. The ship was doomed, and in a matter of minutes the only living men would be those with wreckage to cling to. Best to have first choice of the wreckage, he decided.

Vitellan could hear muffled screams beneath his feet as he slid down the deck to the water amid fallen ropes, sails, and spars. Part of the pinewood foremast spar was floating nearby, and he waded in and swam to it. Groping under the water he blindly hacked and cut the hard, strong ropes trailing from the spar. This thing had to be his vessel when the ship was gone, and long ropes that trailed away into the water still might be attached to the ship. They would drag him down when it sank, he kept reminding himself as he frantically hacked at the ropes. How long before—Vitellan looked about to find himself alone amid the waves and debris. The ship had already sunk but the spar was still floating.

In sheer relief the youth nearly let go of the spar, then he hooked a leg over it and rested as well as he could. He would not drown for a few moments at least, but even hanging on was exhausting work in the storm. Minutes passed, and he began to tire quickly. Knowing that rescue would be days away if it came at all, he bound himself to the spar while he still had the strength to do it properly. After that it was all he could do to snatch breath while his head was above water. The worst of the squall passed after some hours, but Vitellan was insensible by the time the wind shifted again and began to drive him back toward the coast.

The Campania Coast, Italy: 27 September 71, Anno Domini

A jagged piece of wreckage tumbled ponderously amid the waves breaking on the beach, too heavy to be washed in any farther. Antonius stared at it from the seat of his cart, noting that it was part of the decking of quite a large ship. Further along the beach his children searched the flotsam and wreckage that had been washed up by the choppy autumn waves. The sky was heavy with gray clouds, and the wind flung sand and spray at his face in stinging gusts. It was the season for shipwrecks, and thus it was his family's time of prosperity. Antonius shuddered, recalling that it was almost ten years to the day since he had been washed ashore clinging to the wreckage of his own vessel.

His son Tradus called to him in a shrill voice, but Antonius did not look away from the shattered section of decking. A few days ago it had been part of one of the finest ships in all of the Roman Empire, he thought as another ragged wave burst over the wreckage. Tradus called out again, and this time Antonius did turn. His son was waving and pointing to a shape in the sand. A flick of the reins set his horse plodding along the beach.

"Part of a spar with metal fittings, and a lot of rope tangled around it," Tradus said as he drew near. "A good find, Papa?"

"Not as good as a bag of gold, but better than firewood. Here, take the axe and chop the metal free, then untangle the rope and coil it neatly. Ah, now Domedia is waving too. I'll leave the cart with you and see what she has."

The girl was standing over the naked body of a man in his early twenties. It was chalk white and bloated, already in the early stages of decomposition. Using his staff Antonius pointed to a well-healed scar high on one shoulder.

"That's a spear thrust, and it's at least a year old," he explained. "See the marks here and here on his chin, and the calluses on his left arm? He once wore a helmet and used a shield."

"So he was a legionary?"

"I'd bet my right hand on it," he said, holding up the hook on the stump of his right wrist. "He was probably from one of those troopships from Neapolis that sank in the storm last week."

"He smells," Domedia complained, then moved upwind.

"He's been in the water five days, and been dead for about the same time. A pity that he's naked, there's nothing for us."

As they started back toward Tradus, Domedia's sharp eyes picked out something in a mound of seaweed and she skipped away to investigate.

Antonius scratched at his beard with his iron hook. It was just past the autumn equinox, a dangerous time to be on the Tyrrhenian Sea. The captains of the troopships had taken a chance and had lost their gamble with fate, Antonius thought as he looked out to sea. Then again, perhaps they had been under orders: some new rebellion against Roman rule, troops needed urgently somewhere.

Antonius brandished his hook at the sea as if in defiance, then let his arm drop to his side. He had gambled too, putting his savings into the price of a fishing boat and sailing late in the season when others did not dare. A storm finally, perhaps inevitably, claimed his boat and the crew of five. He had struggled ashore with his hand so badly mangled that it had to be cut off. Fate had been cruel to his family that year. They were reduced to wretched poverty, and two months later his wife had died in childbirth. Ever since then he had lived off the folly of others who had also given the Tyrrhenian Sea too little respect.

"Garum, there's garum in this!" called Domedia.

Antonius strode over to where she was pulling seaweed away from a large amphora tied to a wooden framework by its handles. He cut it free and hefted it.

"From the ship's kitchen, not the cargo," he said as he licked the fish sauce from the cork seal. "It's nearly full."

"Lucky it was tied to that beam or it would have sunk."

"The cook probably secured everything in his kitchen when he saw the storm coming. The beam it's tied to was once part of a wall. This will fetch a good price, a very good price."

Tradus began shouting and waving in the distance. Antonius stood up and beckoned to him. "Forget the spar, Tradus, bring the cart over to us," he called back.

"There's a man here, alive!" Tradus replied.

They ran across to him at once. A youth was lying unconscious under a mass of seaweed and rope. He wore a ragged tunic and had apparently bound his arms to the spar before he became too weak to hold on. A small purse was at his waist, tied to his belt by its drawstrings. Antonius dropped to his knees and drew his knife. His two children stared at him intently as he knelt in the sand. Waves thundered raggedly onto the beach behind them, and a spatter of rain stung their faces.

"He may be from a rich family," Domedia said at last. Antonius sighed, then nodded slowly and began to cut the youth free. His skin had been chafed and torn by the rope, and was cold to the touch. Domedia brought sacks from the cart to cover him.

"Five days in the water, five days without food or drink," muttered Antonius as he uncorked a waterskin. "It's amazing. He's young, but he must be tough."

"About seventeen," ventured Domedia. "No more."

Antonius forced a little water past the youth's swollen tongue. "And fair of face, eh daughter?"

"You gave him only a trickle! Give him more."

"Too much water after so many days of thirst would kill him. Just a little more now. Domedia, take your brother over to the amphora and load it onto the cart. After that, check the rest of the beach. I'll stay here with the boy until you get back."

"But we must take him straight home. He'll die otherwise."

"If he dies he dies. If we don't search the beach for what the sea offers us, we'll die too." He held up his hook-hand. "I've been a sailor, I know how to tend the like of this one."

The youth did not die while they finished searching the beach, and he survived the cart ride back to Antonius' cottage. That evening he revived for a short time as they tended him beside the central hearth, and he began to babble a disjointed account of what had happened. He had been aboard the troopship *Venator*, which had foundered after a collision during a squall.

"Cold, so cold," he concluded. "Cold caressed me, cold sustained me . . . cold was my lover."

"The cold should have killed you," said Antonius. "You say your grandparents have a small farm near Herculaneum?"

"At Boscoreale, near Herculaneum. Find them . . . say Vitellan Bavalius survived."

"Vitellan? A curious name for a Roman?"

"My mother . . . Egyptian . . . named me after . . . someone."

"I see. And who is your father?"

"My father, Marcus Bavalius . . . centurion in legions. Legions dangerous, he said. Join a ship, he said. Safe, safe . . . he said."

"Where is your father?"

"At Alexandria . . . princeps prior. Warm there, too warm . . . heat kills, cold gives life."

"He's raving," grunted Antonius. "Still, he speaks as if educated, and his father has a middling good rank. His family may reward us well for his return. Tradus, take the horse and ride to Boscoreale in the morning. Ask at the farms if anyone has a grandson named Vitellan Bavalius. Tell them he was rescued by a poor crippled sailor."

Antonius sat by the fire and began to carve tenons from driftwood to sell to the boatbuilders. Outside the wind howled and rain pattered on the roof. Tradus thought of his journey the following day and glanced resentfully at Vitellan before climbing into bed.

". . . waves washed over me, chilled away my pain," Vitellan mumbled. "Beware fire, fire is death."

"My fire is bringing you back to life now," Antonius said as he fed wood shavings to the flames. "You should have died out there. How did you endure five days in the water?"

"The cold is my friend, kept me alive . . . the cold is my lover, in her embrace I'll live forever."

Domedia shivered as she sat beside Antonius, splicing the lengths of rope that they had salvaged. "Are the gods immortal because their blood is cold?" she asked.

Antonius frowned at her. "Vitellan here is no godling. He's just a tough—and very lucky—boy. I know what you're thinking, Domedia. Just remember how your mother died and stay out of his bed."

"But how did he survive so long in the cold sea?"

"Why are some men stronger than others? Why are your eyes so keen that you can see flotsam on the beach at twice the distance your brother can? The talent to endure cold is Vitellan's particular blessing from the gods. It has already saved his life once. Perhaps it will do so again."

Vitellan recovered and was soon reunited with his grandparents. They rewarded Antonius by making the former captain an assistant overseer of the dozen slaves on their little farm. Antonius and his son died when Vesuvius erupted and destroyed Boscoreale eight years later, in an odd vindication of Vitellan's delirious warning. Domedia escaped, having married a boatbuilder by then and gone to live in Naples.

Two months after his ordeal Vitellan decided to join the army rather than return to the sea. Some months after that he was put aboard a ship to Egypt, much to his horror, but this voyage was free of disaster. He was to travel widely in the years that followed, and he served in Mauretania, Gaul, the Germanic frontier, and the north of Britannia. It was in Britannia where he learned that by embracing coldness he could indeed live forever, and in an act of petty revenge he designed and built the world's second human-powered time machine.

1

venenum immortale

Rome was near the height of its power in the second year of Vespasian's reign as emperor, and nobody would have suspected that the Empire's fate hung by the life of a five-hundred-and-eighty-year-old Etruscan. Celcinius lay with his ears and nostrils sealed with beeswax plugs, and his mouth bound shut. His body was frozen solid in a block of ice at the bottom of a shaft two hundred feet deep.

Regulus held his olive oil lamp high as he entered the Frigidarium Glaciale. He shivered, even dressed as he was in a coat of quilted Chinese silk and goosedown. The sheepskin lining of his hobnailed clogs did no better to keep out the cold, and the fur of his hood and collar was crusted with frost from his own breath. Wheezing loudly after the long trek down through corridors cut through solid ice, he paused for a moment.

"There'd be something wrong were it not so damn cold," he panted to himself as he leaned against the wall, watching his words become puffs of golden fog in the lamplight.

The Frigidarium Glaciale was a single corridor cut into the ice. It stretched away into blackness, as straight and level as a Roman road. On the walls on either side of him were rows of bronze panels, each two feet by seven and inscribed with names and dates. After a minute Regulus reluctantly heaved himself into motion again, shuffling down the corridor and leaning heavily on a staff that bore the Temporian crest of a winged eye. Its other end was tipped with a spike, so that it would not slip on the ice of the floor.

He paused again by a panel marked with his own name and bearing twenty-six pairs of dates. There was something strangely alluring about this cell cut into the ice, where he had spent 360 of the 437 years since his birth. Following his own private ritual he knocked out the pins securing the top of the panel to retaining bolts set into the ice, then levered it down with his staff. The hinges creaked reluctantly, shedding a frosty crust. Behind it was an empty space six feet long and two feet deep.

Regulus stared into the little chamber, holding the lamp up and running his gloved hand along the surface of the ice. He had been in there when Plato had died, and for the whole of Alexander the Great's short but remarkable career. Regulus had, of course, been awake to attend the Temporians' Grand Council, the single time when all his fellow Temporians had been awake together. That was when they had decided to abandon their Etruscan heritage and support Rome. The Punic Wars and rapid expansion of Roman power and influence had followed, and Regulus had been awake to earn scars in the fighting against Hannibal. There had been more years in the ice after that, until he had been revived in time to cross the Rubicon with Julius Caesar. That time he had stayed awake for two decades, until after the defeat of Antony and Cleopatra. He had returned to the ice again by the time Christ was born.

The old man was secretly a little claustrophobic, and disliked both being in the Frigidarium Glaciale and the prospect of some day returning to his assigned cell there. He heaved the bronze panel back into place. "Never again," he promised himself as he scanned the dates in the dancing lamplight, then he turned and shuffled farther down the corridor of the Frigidarium Glaciale like a short, arthritic bear.

At a vacant cell he took a metal tag from his robes, slid it into a bracket and sealed it into place. He studied the entry for a moment before moving on.

"Vitellan Bavalius, eh?" he chuckled softly to the name on the panel. "You're the lad who survived five days in a cold sea after that troopship sank last September. You don't know about us yet, lad, but you are destined to join us and sleep in this hole. We're watching you now, and you are very promising. You're a strong, natural leader, and you have great resistance to the cold. Those are perfect qualifications to become a Temporian and live for a thousand years."

Regulus patted the tag with Vitellan's name like a teacher encouraging a good student, then walked down to the very end of the Frigidarium Glaciale. The panel bearing Celcinius' name was alone in the wall at the end of the corridor. Regulus turned and glanced behind him, more through habit than paranoia. The entrance had now faded into blackness, but the corridor was empty as far as he could see. He released the pins and pried the panel out to reveal a block of rammed snow, from which emerged leather straps bound with a wax seal. He allowed himself a little smile: the imprint in the seal was his own: 217 years earlier he had been acting as the Frigidarium Glaciale's Master of the Ice for the first time when Celcinius had returned to the ice. Satisfied, he swung the plate back and checked the dates inscribed in it. Celcinius was ninety-four in terms of years awake. That was bad. It would be a difficult revival.

Regulus slowly made his way back down the length of the Frigidarium Glaciale, past the 370 other bronze plates, and stopped at the thick, metal-bound oak door. With a twinge of shame he realized that he had not checked the reading in the lock when he had entered. "Memory's going too," he muttered, taking a stylus and wax tablet from the folds of his heavy robes and peering through a slit in the lock's housing. Three numerals were visible, and Regulus noted them. He was about to pull the door shut when he realized that he had not locked the door behind him while he was inside the Frigidarium Glaciale. "Lucky nobody's here to see all this," he said, pulling the door shut. Taking an iron key nearly a foot in length he locked the door, unlocked it, then locked it again. The lock's mechanism was the most advanced in existence, and had been installed only five years earlier. It incorporated a counter-wheel that recorded the number of openings and closings, and could not be reset. He noted down the second—and now correct— reading.

"If my memory's as bad as that I'll not get out alive," he muttered as he pulled his fur-lined mittens back on.

The Frigidarium Glaciale was not located in a glacier, but was cut into unmoving, stable ice in a deep ravine between two mountain peaks. Regulus cautiously walked down a flight of steps carved out of the ice and along another passage. At the bottom was a door, in fact every twenty feet there was another door to seal in the cold air. There were no guards down here, but it was still a dangerous place for intruders. One door opened onto a walkway above a deep pit with long, sharp spikes at the bottom. The walkway was designed to tip unwary visitors off if they did not reset a group of levers in the right sequence at the halfway point. Beyond this was a vault of ice blocks that would collapse unless a lever back at the previous door was moved to the correct notch first. Finally there was a cage of metal bars, and beside it three wheels with numbers engraved on the rims. Set the wrong code on the wheels and the lower passage would be automatically flooded with water piped from a heated cistern two hundred feet above. The right code alerted a slave in the palace to start his horse turning a windlass to raise the elevator cage. Regulus entered the cage and pulled the door shut. He reached back out through the bars and set the wheels to the correct code.

After an interval that never failed to unnerve him the cage jerked slightly, then began to move upward. He leaned back against the bars and sighed a long plume of condensed breath. Perhaps his memory was not so bad after all, perhaps his lapses in the actual Frigidarium Glaciale had only occurred because his life had not been at stake down there. The olive oil lamplight showed stratified layers in the ice and occasional stones as he made the slow journey upward. He had a name for every embedded stone that he passed, he had made the trip hundreds of times.

All that seemed to change was the intensity of the cold. For the last few feet the shaft was lined with marble blocks.

The cage emerged into a torchlit stone chamber, then stopped. A woman in her late fifties was waiting for Regulus, shivering within several layers of pine marten fur. She unlatched the cage door while the slave in charge of the windlass threw the anchor bolts at the base of the cage. Regulus was trembling almost convulsively as she led him to a little alcove that was heated by air piped from a distant furnace. The warmth slowly eased his distress.

"I *told* you to take an assistant," she said as she poured him a cup of warm, spiced wine from a silver flask on an oil-burner stand.

"The rules are the rules," he replied between chattering teeth.

"Do you know how long you were down there?"

He ignored the question. "Well Doria, the seal on Celcinius' body is intact," he reported, then gulped a mouthful of wine. "Everything is as it was during my previous inspection. I can authorize his release if the Adjudicators vote for it."

"He was eighty-nine last time he was revived," said Doria, putting a pan of wax on the oil-burner. "According to the Revival Ledger he hovered near death for six days. I'll not vote for revival. Not just now, anyway."

"The last unpaired date on his panel shows that he was ninety-four at the time of his last freezing."

"I know, I know. It is in my own records." Doria closed her eyes and took a deep breath. "Surely we can make our own decisions by now. We don't need his sanction."

"Perhaps not, but the Adjudicators are still calling for his sanction," Regulus said as he rubbed the circulation back into his hands. "That's why they want him revived."

"If he dies, what then?" asked Doria.

"If he dies we have lost our founder," he replied with resignation.

"Precisely," she said with some vehemence, now leaning forward and tapping the heated stone bench. "We lose our greatest unifying symbol."

"Doria, please—there are complex issues here. The Adjudicators cannot be forced to rely on their own authority and judgment when they rule on Vespasian making himself Emperor."

She sat back, shaking her dyed black curls. "With Celcinius frozen, at least we still have our founder symbolically alive. The Adjudicators must learn to make their own decisions without a nod from him."

Regulus slowly picked up his cup and took another sip of wine. "I'm confused. Would you have Celcinius frozen forever? What is so bad about such an old man's death?"

Doria sat watching the condensation of her own breath as she considered her reply.

"It is bad for the woman in charge of the revival team that fails to restore Celcinius to life, and I am that woman," she said slowly and clearly, then closed her eyes.

"So, a hidden agenda."

"In the ice he is at least not dead, but if we try to revive him he will almost certainly die. Why bother, why not leave him alone? What is *your* hidden agenda, Regulus?"

The slave appeared at the door of the alcove, bowed and entered.

"We shall continue this later," said Regulus with some relief.

The slave reported that the cage was secure for his inspection. Regulus grumbled, but got to his feet, pulling himself up hand over hand with his staff. The slave bowed again and backed out of the alcove, and Doria followed them with the pan of hot wax. Regulus gave the cage a cursory check, tapping bars, pins, and gears with his staff, then he gestured to Doria. With a practiced flourish she poured the wax over the master lock pin of the windlass, and after a moment Regulus pressed his ring seal into the soft, warm wax. The heat was welcome on his chilled fingers, and he withdrew the ring with reluctance.

"Did you attach the tag plate for young Vitellan Bavalius?" Doria asked as they walked through the blackstone access corridor.

"Yes, yes, yes, I'm not senile yet. When is he due to be initiated?"

"In a few months. He was to be sent to Egypt, but I had him sent instead to the Furtivus Legion that guards the approaches to this palace.

He is stationed in Primus Fort, and Centurion Namatinus has been sending me reports on him—in fact he is due to be part of the escort for our next mule caravan of supplies."

"How has he reacted to being in a secret legion?"

"Extremely well. He is our first Christian recruit, did you know that? The Christians have a strong sense of discipline, dedication, and duty, and they teach their children to keep secrets almost as soon as they can talk. They could well become a prime source of new blood for us Temporians. Vitellan is certainly a model recruit."

Regulus spat and cursed. "Damn cruel, it is, taking a boy of seventeen and freezing him for fifty years. It's killing his friends and family for him, even though they will live out their lives unharmed."

"But he must have all his personal ties severed while he is young and flexible, Regulus. He must become accustomed to living as we do. It may be a sharp wrench for him, but the rewards are great. Our reports certainly indicate that he has the rare combination of qualities that makes a good Temporian."

"He may not want to join us, once he has been told of our existence. He may have a girl somewhere."

"Then he will be killed," said Doria simply. "You know that as well as I do."

They emerged into the palace, but Regulus insisted on going out onto a balcony at once. The winter sky was blue and clear, although the lower part of the mountain was shrouded by mist. The air was still and crisply cold. He breathed deeply, savoring the pure, fresh air and swearing to himself that he would never again drink the Venenum Immortale and sleep frozen in the Frigidarium Glaciale.

An Alpine Trail: 17 December 71, Anno Domini

Gallus was thankful that this was the season's last trek through the Alps to feed the gods. Already the snow was deep, and within a few weeks his mules would find it impossible. An unseasonably heavy fall could easily happen as early as tomorrow, he reminded himself. Vitellan rode the last mule in the line, alert and keenly observing everything. He was young and enthusiastic, like all the other Roman legionaries that had been assigned to escort Gallus' mules over the years. In the spring Vitellan would be transferred somewhere else, but Gallus could look forward to many more years of hauling grain, oil, firewood, and luxuries through the mountains, and leaving it all on a huge altar for the gods to take. Why are my assistants transferred so quickly yet I remain here, Gallus wondered. Have I failed some unspoken test of the Furtivus Legion?

In all his years of travel Gallus had never seen the gods. Their altar was at the base of a sheer cliff whose top was generally obscured by mist. Occasionally a muleteer-legionary would stay back and hide among the rocks to see what took the piles of sacks, bales, amphorae, and firewood from the altar, but the story was always the same. An enormous hand would reach down and snatch away the piles during the night. Some muleteers who stayed back were never seen again.

Gallus was steady and conservative in his work. He displayed no curiosity about the gods, did as he was ordered, and was always punctual. It was a hard but secure life, as there were no bandits to fear in such a remote part of the Alps. Later that day they would meet with the main convoy of seventy mules, and from there it was another two days to the altar.

An arrow thudded into his chest. Gallus stiffened, then toppled across the neck of his mule. His thick butt-leather breastplate had taken most of the impact so that the point barely scratched his skin, but Gallus was not about to let anyone know that. Behind him came shouts and curses from Vitellan and their attackers: "He's hiding!" and "Mind the mule!" The animals were in a panic already, but the snow and their leads prevented them from bolting.

More shouts echoed through the mountains, mingled with the clang of blades. Vitellan was fighting from behind his mule. The mules had value, and the bandits would not risk injuring them. Gallus listened to the voices. Four or five of them. "Grab the lead mule!" That was his cue. Footsteps came crunching through the snow, lungs wheezed that were unaccustomed to the thin alpine air. "Off with ye," said a voice with the intonations of a pleb from the lowlands cities, but as the bandit tried to push Gallus from the mule the old legionary suddenly reached forward with an unthreatening, fluid, even gentle gesture and plunged a dagger into his throat.

Now Gallus slipped from the mule and looked back, the arrow still protruding from his chest. Vitellan had sent one of the bandits staggering away clutching his side and was engaging the other two. Two down. No more than five in total, including one hidden archer. Gallus started back, sheltering behind each mule in turn. An arrow struck a grain sack, fired from the rocks to the side of him. Good, good, nearly past the archer, Gallus thought.

"Keep 'em fighting, Vitellan, they'll tire before we do," Gallus called, but even as he spoke he realized that he was tiring fast himself. With dagger and gladius he engaged a bandit who was working his way behind Vitellan. The man was skilled with his weapons, but was hampered by the thin air, cold, and snow. Another arrow hit Gallus' breastplate, but its point barely pierced his flesh. Somewhere to one side a bandit cursed with pain as Vitellan's blade slipped past his guard.

Gallus was by now all too aware of a lethargy sweeping over him. He tried ineffectually to parry a curving snap and the blade thudded into the side of his head, cutting flesh and bone. Gallus collapsed to the snow, but felt as if he was still falling and falling and falling. In the distance Vitellan screamed, an echoing, fading scream.

Lars scrambled down from his vantage, brandishing his bow and cursing with fury.

"One dead and two wounded!" he shouted. "And from fighting only two legionaries."

"Tough buggers," gasped Vespus, who was draped across a mule's packs.

"You're veterans of the arena."

"Gladiators don't have thin air . . . and snow. These legionaries . . . are stationed here. They're used to it."

The mules were standing still, but were frightened and restless. Lars began to strip Gallus' body.

"Butt leather," exclaimed Vespus. "The old fox wore butt leather under his furs."

"It slowed my arrows and scraped most of the poison from them. No wonder he took a while to die."

Lars tramped over to the edge of a steep drop where the two other bandits sat resting and binding their wounds.

"The other one tried to run, and lost his footing at the edge of the cliff," one of them explained.

"Yes, I saw it all," Lars said sharply. "Now climb down and get his clothes."

The man groaned with dismay. "Master Lars, that's a fearsome drop and we've been badly cut about."

"Do as I say!"

"If we do, it'll take all afternoon. That will make us miss the rendezvous wi' the main caravan in a few days' time. D'ye know the way to the altar without them?"

Lars glared at the black smudge that was Vitellan, half buried and motionless in a snowdrift far below, then tramped back to the mules. "Here's his cloak and a spare tunic," he said, flinging a bundle to the wounded men. "Strip the clothing from this dead one, and that will have to do. What are your injuries?"

"Three broken ribs and a long cut," said one.

"Deep thrust to the leg, but I can ride," said the other.

"Then bind yourselves up and dress as the legionaries. Try to fight like 'em too, if needs be. You will be Vitellan, and you will be Clavius, a new recruit. When you get to the rendezvous tell the trailmaster that Gallus fell ill."

"True enough," laughed the new Vitellan, then winced at the pain from his ribs.

They threw the bodies of Gallus and the dead bandit down after Vitellan, then unloaded two of the mules and flung the sacks over the edge as well. After an hour of frantic labor in the thin air, the line of six mules moved on again. The animals were nervy and cantankerous at being driven by unfamiliar masters. Lars and Vespus rode in padded sacks marked as woollen cloth. The sun was already down when they reached the rendezvous. They found it only because the mules knew the way on their own.

Vitellan revived soon after his fall, but he had the sense not to move until after dark. Deep snow had broken his fall, and beyond a few minor gashes and sprains he was unwounded. He examined the two bodies nearby. Gallus had been stripped, but the dead bandit's body was fully clothed. Vitellan was surprised to find sacks from two mule packs lying in the snow as well. There was costly cloth, fine smoked fish, dried beef and even a small amphora of very expensive wine. With a prayer of thanks to the God of the Christians he crawled under a rock shelter in the face of the cliff, wrapped himself in the bolts of cloth and settled down to a more than satisfactory meal to recover from his ordeal.

"Yet again the cold has saved me," he whispered to himself as he gazed out at the starlit snowdrift that had preserved his life.

The next morning it took five hours for Vitellan to climb back up to the trail with a makeshift pack of provisions on his back. At the site of the ambush there was nothing of any use left behind. He considered his options as he examined the mule tracks. The bandits had continued along the trail right after the ambush, and there were at least four of them. Even if he could catch up with them there was no point in a lone man attacking four. Besides, they had stolen no more than supplies for some temple deep in the mountains where offerings were made to the old gods. As a Christian, Vitellan thus felt no sense of outrage or sacrilege. He would walk back to Primus Fort and alert the centurion. A couple of dozen legionaries would be sent to hunt the bandits down.

Vitellan started walking back along the trail. At first he estimated that he could reach the fort in three days or less at a brisk pace, and provided that no more snow fell. The distance was no problem, as he had plenty of food and warm bedding for the trek. Presently he slowed his pace. Aware that death from bandits, snowslides, or just sheer cold was never far away, Vitellan decided to travel more slowly and cautiously. He had been badly shaken by Gallus' lonely death and his own narrow escape. He had not known the older legionary long enough to be a real friend, but his death nevertheless left a distinct hole in Vitellan's sense of reality. As it turned out his trek was without incident, but he took five days to reach the fort. Had he hastened and made it in three, the course of history would have been changed.

The Temporian palace of Nusquam had been built between two mountain peaks, and the original building was over four centuries old. The walls were carved out of the mountain itself, while the buildings of the palace rose in terraces up the side of one peak. The design was such that it was not obvious to anyone looking up from below. It was divided into the Upper Palace, where thirty Temporians lived, and the Lower, which housed seventy slaves and guards. Three hundred frozen Temporians lay far below in the Frigidarium Glaciale, and the other forty Temporians were scattered throughout the Roman Empire, attending to its business and expanding their control.

Since their early Etruscan beginnings the Temporians had remained a remarkably stable group. Celcinius had been a physician in an Etruscan city north of the Po River. He had been experimenting with medical formulations when he had stumbled across what he named the Venenum Immortale, the Poison of Immortality. Animals treated with it could be frozen, then thawed and brought back to life. If given an antidote straightaway they would thrive and live normally. At first Celcinius thought of the Venenum as an interesting curiosity, but soon after he perfected the dangerous oil's use he discovered a most important application.

He had a nephew named Marcoral who was a brilliant young military commander. Marcoral had fallen in love with a noble's wife, and the two had been sentenced to death when the liaison had been discovered. Celcinius had "executed" them with his potion, then he had frozen their bodies in rammed snow and had them buried in a perennial icefield high in the nearby mountains. Nine years later, when his city came under attack, he brought the couple back to life under the guise of sorcery and magic. The unnaturally young-looking lovers seemed to have been deified, and rumors spread among the troops that Marcoral was now invincible. The city's defenders swarmed out behind him to annihilate the enemy in a brief, one-sided battle.

The broader, strategic significance of what he had done did not escape Celcinius. What good was a brilliant commander in times of peace? Why should the best engineers and masons be idle during the quiet decades of a city's development? Could the best administrators be saved for times of crisis, rather than wasting their years through periods of tranquillity?

Celcinius had a fortified villa built on a mountain in the Alps. Beneath it was a blind ravine filled with ice, and unlike the unstable, fracturing, moving glaciers, the lower layers of this ice were stable and unmoving. It was a perfect site for a permanent, stable ice chamber. He set his apprentices to work, developing and refining his original formulation, then he lay frozen himself for three decades to await results that he could not have normally expected to see until he was an old man. Once the Venenum Immortale had been refined and perfected, Celcinius had been revived. He immediately had all his apprentices killed, and after that its secret was never again known to any more than three Temporian men at any one time.

Other talented men and women began to join Celcinius, and gradually the power and wealth of this strange oligarchy grew. His villa slowly expanded until it became the palace Nusquam. As the centuries passed, social structures grew and evolved among the Temporians—as they began to call themselves. The impressive and secret pool of talent grew continually in influence, yet they never allowed themselves to become kings. They always worked as lesser leaders, and from behind the scenes. When the continuity of Temporian administration was added to the vitality of the emerging city-state of Rome, the seeds of a mighty empire were laid.

The keystone of Temporian power was the Venenum Immortale, and its key ingredients were derived from the bodies of snow-dwelling insects. These were gathered by ordinary farmers and their slaves, along with the other harvests that they took from the land. The makers of perfumes, medicines, and the like already paid good silver for bags of odd roots, insects, and dried animal glands, so the collection of the insects for the Venenum Immortale went unnoticed alongside this trade. Every five years there would be enough to brew up several jars of the Venenum, and one of the three Venenum Masters would be revived to do the work.

Experience was never lost to the Temporians, and they learned to disguise their own existence to the point of near-invisibility. Some senior Romans knew that "gods" walked among them, strange and brilliant individuals who only appeared when particular types of demanding work needed to be done. These people did not seem to age at all. They were known as the Eternal Ones, the Gods of Romulus, the Sons of Romulus, and the Immortal Scribes, and it was also known that exceptionally talented mortals were sometimes recruited to their ranks. Outsiders, even if they were kings or emperors, always died or disappeared if their investigations of the Temporians were too persistent. Julius Caesar, Caligula, and Nero had that in common at least.

Nusquam: 17 December 71, Anno Domini

Doria was the current Mistress of Revival. Just as Regulus oversaw the freezing process and maintenance of the Frigidarium, she was in charge of the delicate and dangerous process of restoring the frozen Temporians to life. Regulus lay on a couch in her comfortably heated chambers, recovering from the ordeal of his inspection tour. He contemplated the frescoes on three of the walls, which ranged in subject from battles with Hannibal to erotic frolics involving naked Temporians in Arcadian settings. Regulus was depicted too, standing beside Caesar on the banks of the Rubicon in the most recent scene to be added to the frescoes.

The fourth wall was lined with shelves of colored glass jars, most containing oils and powders. There was also a large collection of scrolls and various medical instruments. The women who conducted the revivals documented their skills and experience in considerable detail, quite the opposite of the Venenum Masters. Doria sat at a writing desk, working her way through a scroll and frowning.

"I can't think of anything more dangerous," she said after she had been writing for some time. "Celcinius is too old, he survived that last revival through sheer luck."

"Who was in charge of that revival?"

"Rhea. She is the leader of Prima Decuria for this revival too."

"Well, that's the best you can do."

"The whole thing is still dangerous. The question remains, but nobody will answer it: why revive him? Celcinius is worth more to the Adjudicators frozen than revived. He's our symbol, and a very potent symbol."

Regulus turned sadly from her and looked to a fresco of Celcinius experimenting with chemicals in his ancient Etruscan villa. He had been handsome and dynamic when younger.

"It seems wrong that he can be allowed to neither live nor die," he said. "It's so undignified for one so great."

Doria looked up, then tapped her scroll with a char stylus. "He may be more safely revived in another three or four hundred years."

"How so? His condition is unchanging as long as he lies in the bath of ice."

"I've been looking at the records of revivals since the earliest times and compiling figures. We Temporian women are getting better at revivals, Regulus. When Celcinius first began freezing people the revival rate was two in three. Within a century it had risen to ninety in one hundred."

"Nine out of ten, we all know that."

"Not so. Since then the rate has risen to ninety-four in one hundred, and that is in spite of the mean age of Temporians having risen from thirty-five to nearly fifty. Our techniques and skills are slowly improving, and I can see a time when every revival will be a success."

"But that time is centuries away, your own figures prove it. The Adjudicators want Celcinius awake now."

Doria stood up and stretched, flexing her stiff joints. Regulus beckoned her over, patting the couch, but she remained standing beside the writing desk, shifting her weight from foot to foot.

"We are making a crisis where one need not exist," she said, picking up her scroll and brandishing it. "Celcinius can give us no more than his decision, one way or another. I don't see what makes the situation so very special. Vespasian has made himself Emperor of Rome, and Vespasian is one of us, a Temporian! Why are they so worried?"

"It is a precedent of the most alarming kind, it threatens our whole philosophy of controlling Rome from behind its administration. In the 540 years since the Frigidarium was built, not one of us has ever taken the rank of a major public leader."

Doria clasped her hands behind her back and began to pace. "Who is to say that Vespasian's action was not a good thing? You have said as much yourself, many times. Caligula was a monster, Nero was a buffoon, and then we had those clowns Galba, Otho, and Vitellius struggling with each other for control while what we really needed was strong and stable leadership. Vespasian may have a common manner, but he is doing a lot of good. Laws are meant to work, not just be kept for their own sake."

Regulus chewed on a dried fig, then picked at his teeth as he assessed what she had said. Now that he was physically old he needed to think more slowly, and he used little tricks to stall for time in every discussion. He took a deep breath.

"We need the authority of Celcinius to call another Grand Temporian Council. We have not had one since the Punic Wars, and there is much to decide. Perhaps Temporians *should* become emperors if it is appropriate, in fact perhaps *all* emperors should be Temporians. Whatever the case, we need a decision with the greatest authority or there will be division."

"We could deduce his opinion from the precedents of his past decisions. It has been done before."

"No, no, there is also the expansion of the Empire to consider. How far can Rome's reach be safely extended? Some say we should conquer the world. Marcus Bassilius has secretly sent ships to India, to the even more distant Silk Empire, and right around Africa. He wants to lay the foundations of a world governed by Rome, and he wants the Frigidarium expanded to take the extra Temporians needed to govern the larger empire."

"How many does he have in mind?" asked Doria.

"His lowest estimate is two thousand. He has given me a list of preliminary names."

"I've seen it, and I don't like most of the names proposed. They should all be like that young legionnaire Vitellan who survived five days in the ocean. He has wonderful resistance to cold, and he is young enough to be revived dozens of times and remain healthy. Youngsters like him are our future, not the spoiled and sickly sons and daughters of nobles and senators!"

When Regulus did not reply Doria gave a short, humorless laugh, then returned to her desk and wrote down the figure two thousand on a wax tablet. She did several calculations before looking up again.

"That raises another question," she said. "Only three Temporian men know the Venenum's secret, and one of those is Celcinius. Thus two men produce the Venenum Immortale for 370 people. That cannot be allowed to continue."

"Why not? It is a secret of power, the ultimate secret that all Temporian control rests upon."

"I have some figures here, figures about how much time two men would have to devote to making enough Venenum Immortale to allow two thousand people to be refrozen every five years—on average, of course. Two is just not enough. Even ten Venenum Masters would have trouble meeting such a quota. The process should be common knowledge among us."

"But no more than three have ever needed to know it in the past."

Doria walked slowly across to the couch where Regulus lay and sat down stiffly, grimacing at the pain from her arthritis. She handed him the wax tablet and pointed to figures with her stylus as he read.

"Two thousand Temporians would need five times more oil if they are to be frozen and revived at the same rate. Now just think. There are sufficient women in the revival teams to meet the quota. Women could produce all the Venenum that we need."

"Then women would hold a total monopoly on both freezing and revival. The Adjudicators would never agree to that."

"If more Venenum is not made, there can be no extra Temporians to govern a bigger empire."

"There might be if we governed differently."

"As kings and emperors?"

"Exactly. Whatever decision is made, it's going to be a sharp break from tradition, and it will need authority and unity behind it. Only Celcinius can give the Adjudicators that."

Doria returned to her writing desk and sat with her arms folded, staring at her scrolls but reading nothing. It was some time before she spoke, and Regulus was not inclined to disturb her.

"All right then, when do you propose to disturb his rest?" she asked, resigned at last and sounding as if she no longer cared what happened.

"Tomorrow."

"As soon as that?"

"The pressure on us is already great. Can your revival teams be ready?"

"Yes, but Venus is still in the evening sky. Revivals are best done when Venus rises before the dawn, and we shall need the best planetary alignment possible for reviving a ninety-four-year-old man."

By that time you will have passed your office on to someone else as well, Regulus thought to himself as he swung his legs over the edge of the couch and stiffly rose to his feet. "I shall make my report to the Adjudicators this afternoon. If I am any judge of politics they will vote to take their chances with Venus, and break Celcinius' seal on the equinox."

The Cliffs Below Nusquam: 21 December 71, Anno Domini

Lars and Vespus lay hidden in their sacks of cloth on the altar while the light faded. The cliff beside them towered away into gray mist, but they could see nothing of it. The muleteers had unloaded their shipment of grain, dried fruits, and cloth in the mid-afternoon, leaving the sacks in five neat piles at the center of the altar. Now they were gone, and everything lay unguarded amid the snow and rocks. Nobody came to inspect what was there, no thieves appeared to steal even a single sack. Lars and Vespus had no doubt that they were under observation from somewhere, however, and the two thieves lay very still until after sunset.

Nusquam, the ancient palace of the Temporians, could no longer be reached by any path. Centuries earlier, when the palace had been completed, the access path had been systematically demolished, leaving only the sheer mountainside. Food, fuel, slaves, and Temporians all came by mule, to be left on the altar.

The snow had stopped around sunset, and a brisk breeze moaned by the cliff. Somewhere in the distance there was a dull, irregular thumping. Small rocks pattered down around them.

"Something on the way," said Vespus. "Something big. A god's footsteps."

"It's just a noise," Lars snapped impatiently, annoyed at his companion's fright. "The footsteps of a real god would shake the very ground beneath us." He listened for a time. "Something is being lowered from above, and the wind is blowing it against the cliff, knocking loose the stones that are falling around us. It's probably a great basket to carry all these goods."

"Soon it's us who will be thumpin' against the cliff," replied Vespus, still unhappy.

"They'll have some arrangement to keep the goods safe, and if the goods are safe then so will we be. Think of yourself as a bundle of fine garments, Vespus. No harm will come to you."

The thuds grew louder, but they were the hollow booms of a great drum rather than the footfall of gigantic feet. Suddenly it seemed to them that all was darker than before, then there was a soft thump nearby followed by footsteps crunching through the snow. Someone had ridden down on the crane's hook.

"Lupus? Vulpus?" asked a voice with a curiously twisted Roman accent.

Lars hesitated, but those were the codenames that they had been told to use. "Lacerna?" he called softly in turn.

"Yes, yes, where—ah, this pile. Quickly now, out with you for a stretch and a piss. It'll be your last chance for hours."

"But we'll be seen from above," said Lars.

"Impossible," said the slave, laughing. "Take a look."

Lars had the impression of a huge canopy resting on five thick legs. It straddled the altar. The slave was an indistinct shape doing something with ropes nearby.

"The hand of the gods," said Vespus behind him.

"That's it, the mighty wicker and cloth hand of the gods," Lacerna replied. "A hook beneath each finger, and above it all a crane driven by five horses at a windlass. It's made to boom like a huge drum when the wind bangs it against the cliff, and it sends the yokels screaming."

Each of the piles of sacks had been placed on heavy netting, and the slave tied the corners of these to the hooks below each finger.

"How long is the arm?" asked Vespus, looking up the black center.

"When fully extended, about two hundred feet. At night, in the mist, it looks to be the arm of a mighty and gigantic god. When we wind it back up it reaches a spar near the top and is furled like a sail. Now, back in your sacks and lie still and quiet. I'm to whistle in the guards."

"Guards?" exclaimed Vespus.

"Aye, there's four guards been lying out of sight down here since before dawn. Sometimes we let curious muleteers see the arm of the gods to keep the legend going, sometimes we make 'em disappear to show that the gods are dangerous."

The slave blew a shrill, piercing blast on his whistle. Soon they could hear the tramp of feet in the snow.

"Bad hunting tonight, sir?" called the slave.

"Thirty came, thirty went," someone called. "What of the sacks?"

"All in order, sir."

"Then whistle us up. I'd kill for a warm fire and a pot of stew after a day down here."

Lacerna blew another three quick blasts, and almost at once Lars and Vespus felt themselves crushed by the sacks around them as the net was winched up. The wicker hand began swinging as soon as they left the ground, and it hit against the cliff with deep, resonant booms.

"When we get to the top the load will have to be carried into the storehouse in case more damn snow falls," shouted the guard's Temporian leader between booms.

"What say I do the load for a day-ration of wine?" suggested the slave. "I'll not tell my master."

"A day-ration, you say? Done."

"From each of you."

Groans and jeers floated over from the other guards until another boom cut them short.

"I thought your price was a trifle low," said the Temporian. "Well then, those who can't spare a day-ration can stay behind and do their share. Who's for it?"

There were disgruntled curses, but none volunteered.

Each time the load thudded against the cliff the two thieves were wedged even more tightly in among the other sacks. Both began to feel something akin to seasickness, but to throw up would be to alert the guards at once. They breathed deeply and clamped their jaws as the wicker hand and its load swung and bumped. Presently they could hear the clopping of horses around a windlass track, then the bumping against the cliff stopped as the rope grew shorter. The slave shouted directions and the load was swung over the edge and lowered to the ground. As the hooks were detached from the netting, the crane's supervisor locked the gear mechanism and released the horses from the windlass. The guards helped lead the horses back to the palace stables, leaving Lacerna to haul the sacks in under cover. Even after it had been quiet for some time the two thieves remained motionless in their sacks.

"It's me, Lacerna," the slave finally called as he passed near them. "I'm alone again, but wait till I carry your sacks into the store before you get out."

He was strong and efficient, carrying two sacks at a time on a yoke across his shoulders. Within an hour he had the entire load under cover, while Lars and Vespus extricated themselves and unpacked their gear.

"Where do we stay?" asked Lars.

"That bag by the door has a map and some provisions. Follow it to the ruined lookout tower on the far side of this hill. I've left more food there, and hay to sleep under. Stay there, but don't light a fire. Dig a deep privy hole and keep it well covered. Don't let telltale scents give you away, because guard dog patrols are sent out each morning."

"Guard dogs! They could track us from tonight's footprints."

"No, more snow is falling now, and that should cover your scent. Just to be sure I'll carry you both a few hundred paces clear of this place on my yoke."

"How long must we stay in the tower?" asked Lars.

"Some days. I'll come past and tell you when to move."

"Days?" exclaimed Vespus softly. "Why so long?"

"There's a big meeting soon, but I don't know the date yet. The inner area of Nusquam, the Upper Palace, will be sealed while they all get together and debate in some strange language. Every Immortal on the mountain will be in the main hall, so the rest of the Upper Palace will be yours to plunder as you will."

"What about guards?"

"Mortal guards are not allowed in the Upper Palace, only slaves of dull wit—and slaves who feign to be so. I presume that Immortals are on patrol there, but during the great meeting even these will probably be withdrawn. Get past the outer walls, frozen moat, and the guard perimeter, and you'll have a free hand. Now that you're up over the cliff the whole of Nusquam should be open to the likes of you. There's not been one intrusion in all my time here, so the guards are lax."

"And what about this oil that we're supposed to steal? Where is it kept?"

"Oil? How should I know? I've carried load after load of bugs and beetles into the Upper Palace for fifteen years, but never seen what comes out."

Vespus took a tiny glass phial of oil from his pack and uncorked it. "Have you seen or smelled the like of this before?"

The slave sniffed the contents of the phial. "Never," he said at once. "What's it for?"

"We were not told. I presume it's what their physicians brew out of all those sacks of insects that you carry. The man who hired us will pay plenty for a larger supply."

The slave shrugged and shook his head, then began to bundle up the sacks that they had hidden in. "Take these with you and use them for bedding."

"One last word," said Vespus. "Suppose something happens to you, and you can't reach us?"

"In that case, wait seven days then do as best you can." The slave hefted the yoke and placed it over his shoulders. A leather loop hung from each end. "Step into the straps now, and I'll carry you clear of this place."

Nusquam, 21 December 71, Anno Domini

Regulus broke the wax seal behind Celcinius' panel without ceremony, then supervised as two of the younger Temporians scraped away the rammed snow to expose the block of ice in which Celcinius was frozen. The block was mounted on metal skids, and slid out easily once the end was free. Eight blindfolded slaves carried it out on a litter, straining with the weight and taking small, cautious steps on the ice floor of the Frigidarium.

The journey back up to the palace with the awkward and heavy load took much longer than Regulus' previous visit. It was two hours past dawn before the exhausted slaves lowered the block on its litter to the floor of the tepidarium in the women's baths. Already the sides of the block were slick with melting ice, and drips splashed to the flagstones as Doria and Rhea examined the surface. Once she was satisfied that the ice had not been violated since Celcinius had been frozen, Doria signed the Register of Revival. Regulus countersigned, and began to shuffle toward the door.

"Regulus, please stay and watch," said Doria. "It's time that men got some appreciation of what we do here."

Doria had been meticulous in her preparations for the revival once it had become probable that Celcinius would be unfrozen during her term in office. Her teams of women had revived three other frozen Temporians for practice, and all had been men over sixty. None had died.

Four women began chipping the outer ice away, and it did not take long to reach an inner layer of Egyptian linen. Now the body was lowered into a marble bath of tepid water, and the cloth soon came away to reveal the body beneath a thin film of ice.

"Tepid heat," ordered Doria, and Rhea pulled a lever controlling air from a furnace that flowed through the hypocaust beneath the marble bath.

The women ran their hands along the ice as the temperature of the water slowly increased. "Skin, I feel his skin," someone said excitedly. The first hour passed, and the Prima Decuria changed shifts with the Secunda Decuria. Very slowly the heat from the water penetrated the flesh of Celcinius as the women gently massaged him. The temperature of the water continued to rise. "Pump heat," Doria ordered as his limbs grew flexible. The shift was changed again.

By noon the air was heavy with steam. The women were slick with sweat, and their robes clung to them, sticky and uncomfortable. Regulus fanned himself and drank watered wine as he watched. Doria removed the gag that had sealed Celcinius' mouth and held his head up while Rhea removed the wax ear and nose plugs. The water was drained from the bath until Celcinius could be laid back with his face exposed above the surface. Rhea and Doria climbed into the bath with him, and while Rhea blew breath between his lips Doria began the much more difficult task of pounding his heart back into life.

All the while the temperature continued to rise. "Revival heat," panted Doria as she worked, and Rhea's understudy moved the lever controlling the hypocaust flow a final notch. In effect, Celcinius was now just an old man with severe hypothermia.

The procedure was based on experiments with animals and slaves, and through many deaths it had been refined to perfection. A physician of two millennia in the future would have said that they were attempting to get blood flow to the brain established while it was as yet too cold to be damaged by oxygen starvation. The Venenum Immortale that Celcinius had been treated with had both antifreeze properties and a limited ability to carry oxygen.

Other women presently relieved Doria and Rhea, who lay exhausted on wicker couches while lower-ranking assistants dried them. By now it was mid-afternoon. As soon as she could sit up again Doria went to the edge of the bath and felt for the pulse at the old man's neck.

"Very faint," she said. "What I feel is all from the hands that pump at his chest."

"Ninety-four is too old," said Rhea, but Doria only glared at her and shook her head.

They kept working, by now with the bath near body temperature. Food was brought in, and the women who supplied the breath and heartbeat to Celcinius were working in progressively shorter spells. The light behind the mica windows faded and more lamps were lit. Regulus dozed in his chair, emotionally drained in spite of his inactivity.

Abruptly he sat up. All was still, and Celcinius lay pallid and still in the bath with exhausted women sprawled all around, some naked, others in soaking wet robes.

"You've stopped," said Regulus breathlessly.

Doria lifted her head and nodded.

"Have you lost him?" he ventured.

"Why waste effort on a man who can breathe for himself?" she replied.

That was not the end of the ordeal. Another five hours passed before Celcinius' condition was stable. His heart was a problem, for when it was beating at all its action was quite feeble. Gradually he passed into a state akin to sleep and was lifted from the bath and dried.

The women of Prima Decuria carried him on a litter to another room where a bed had been prepared. The flagstones of the floor were warm with the heat of the hypocaust beneath.

"Two women will lie on either side of him for the night," Doria explained to Regulus. "Skin against skin. That will keep him warm, while their breathing will stimulate his body to breathe. If his condition worsens they can take action to revive him at once."

"Lucky Celcinius," cackled Regulus. "I wish two women had lain against me when last I was revived."

"They did," replied Doria. "I was one of them."

He turned and opened his mouth, but at that moment Celcinius coughed. Doria immediately knelt beside the bed and began to massage his temples. He opened his eyes, and his gaze focused on her face.

"Can you hear me, Celcinius?" she asked. His lips moved a little, but he made no sound. "It is the 824th year of the founding of Rome, my great lord, and you have been asleep two hundred and seventeen years."

She drew back a little, and Regulus moved closer.

"Rome?" wheezed Celcinius faintly.

"Rome is now the greatest power on earth," said Regulus over Doria's shoulder. "Temporian rule is still firm."

The edges of Celcinius' mouth lifted briefly into a smile.

The old man managed to swallow a mixture of weak broth and antidote before falling asleep. Regulus returned to the Register to note that the founder of the Temporians had once more been brought back to life. Celcinius was now the oldest man on earth in absolute terms, but of more concern was his age in waking years. Whatever value that could be had from his authority needed to be taken quickly.

The next evening Doria's women were given a great revel by the other Temporians, and even Celcinius was carried in on a litter for a short time. Regulus became quite drunk, and could not speak to Doria without tears welling up in his eyes.

"It was like a long and difficult birth," he kept saying. "Your work requires a thousand times more skill than the freezing process."

"So much so that we should have a place in that process?" she asked.

"You'll have my vote on that. Why, when I saw the skills that you commanded it even made me think to trust *myself* to another leap through time in the damnable Frigidarium. Besides, it would be worth it to have your body against mine again, and next time I might even remember it."

"You need not wait so long as that," Doria replied coyly.

Regulus sat up straight with a crackle of joints. He thought through her words again, just to be sure, then raised an eyebrow and gave a knowing, gap-toothed leer.

On the third day after his revival Celcinius was strong enough to walk. He had already issued a decree that Vespasian had his support in taking on the mantle of Emperor, given the crisis of the time. At his direction the Adjudicators called a preliminary meeting of the Temporian Council, and it was expected that a Grand Temporian Council would result from this. All Temporians currently working throughout the Roman Empire would be called in. Several dozen other key Temporians lay frozen, and these would also have to be revived. Doria drew up rosters for the massive project, yet did not complain. She had brought Celcinius back from the ice, and nothing else could be a problem by comparison.

Primus Fort: 22 December 71, Anno Domini

Vitellan trudged into Primus Fort early in the afternoon of the fifth day after the ambush. He was given hot, spiced wine and clean, dry clothing as he warmed himself in front of a fire. The fort's centurion, Namatinus, soon arrived to question him.

"You say bandits stole the mules?" Namatinus asked, scratching his head. "That's odd. There was little else but food and cloth, it was all sacrificial offerings for the gods."

"They may have wanted supplies for their stronghold," said his optio. "Supplies dragged all the way up here can be worth more than face value."

"There was one thing that did not make sense," Vitellan added after another swallow of hot wine. "Gallus was stripped of his clothing before being thrown over the cliff, yet the dead bandit was flung after him fully dressed. They also threw down the goods from the packs of two mules."

"Even more odd," said Centurion Namatinus, now frowning and rubbing his chin. "They took Gallus' clothing and your cloak, they may have wanted to pass as legionaries."

"It could be, Centurion."

"They may have plans to steal more than the mules they already have," suggested the optio. "They may be planning to find that secret altar and to steal all of the offerings left on it. That would keep them well supplied in their hideout for the whole of the winter."

"You may be right," said Namatinus. "Yet you say that they emptied two mule packs, Vitellan Bavalius—oh no!"

Namatinus suddenly realized that the goods thrown over the cliff left enough space in the mule packs to fit two small men. He seized the optio by the arm and hurried him to the door.

"Get the horses saddled and provisioned, quickly!" he ordered.

"Yes, Centurion, but how many?"

"All twenty, every horse in the fort. Rouse out the eighteen best riders from among our legionaries. Bavalius, you and I are going as well."

Nusquam: 24 December 71, Anno Domini

By the day of the preliminary meeting of the Council, Celcinius had some color back in his face. Although his hair was sparse and his scalp blotched with liver spots, he still had all his teeth and walked without a stoop. Regulus and Doria were sitting in the front row of the enclosed Council Amphitheater as he emerged from the shadows between two pillars. At once everyone rose to their feet, cheering and applauding.

"I'm told that he even mounted a slave girl last night," Doria whispered in Regulus' ear as Celcinius descended the steps to the speakers' dais.

"Hah, but *you* were worth more for *my* centuries of waiting," Regulus replied, nudging her with his elbow.

Celcinius raised his hands for silence, and at once they all sat back down on the cushions of their serried ranks of stone benches. Regulus noted that he moved with great care and deliberation, even though there was much vitality about him. He cleared his throat.

"My friends and colleagues, fellow Temporians, this is a glorious day," he began, his voice a firm, penetrating tenor. "Whatever the problems of Rome, they are nothing but the stings of ants on the feet of an elephant. We have conquered the world. Now we must decide how to govern it."

At this there was more spontaneous applause. Perhaps the Venenum Immortale actually delays aging as well, Regulus found himself wondering. Celcinius seemed in unbelievably good health; he might have been no more than sixty.

The Temporians' founder raised his hands for silence again. "The future belongs to Rome. We need only—"

He gasped, then clutched at his chest with both hands, doubling up with pain. Those nearest to him were already running forward, but they were not quick enough. The heart attack had actually been fairly mild, but his head struck the marble dais so hard that his skull fractured. Doria lifted his head very gently and noticed the blood oozing from one ear. There was no pulse at his neck.

"Celcinius is dead," she said in a firm, calm voice, but her face was chalk white and she suddenly seemed years older.

An Alpine Trail: 24 December 71, Anno Domini

Centurion Namatinus, Vitellan, and his riders met the main mule caravan well south of the secret altar in the mountains, and the bandits calling themselves Vitellan and Clavius were quickly identified, seized and tortured on the trail itself. They confessed to being in the pay of two master thieves from the southern cities, and said that they had left the thieves in mule packs on the altar.

Now Namatinus led Vitellan and the others north, riding as fast as was practical on the treacherous, snow-covered mountain trails.

"There is a—a temple high above the altar," Namatinus explained as they rode. "It is a secret temple, and those two thieves are up there now."

"But two men can carry away very little from such a remote place," Vitellan pointed out.

"They could carry away its secret at the very least. That weighs nothing at all and it would fetch a very high price in the right places. As to treasures, I dare not even *think* about what those two may plunder from the temple."

"How much further until we get there, Centurion?"

"It's far, too far. Our horses are near exhaustion, but if we ride them as hard as we dare, and if we ride in the dark by torchlight, we could reach it some time tonight."

Nusquam: 24 December 71, Anno Domini

Powdery snow drifted out of the blackness above Nusquam. It was designed and built against easy approach and organized assault, but now it was the depths of winter and the weather was its shield. The guards were more concerned with keeping themselves warm than with the prospect of intruders. Lars and Vespus crossed a tripstring field, scaled the outer wall, stole across the frozen moat and made their way to the rooftops of the Upper Palace. They paused to rest, pressing deep into a shadowed corner on the curved terracotta tiles.

"In Rome we would have had our work done by now, and be halfway home," whispered Vespus unhappily.

Lars ignored his words as he massaged the circulation back into his fingers. "Something of a fortress, something of a villa, and something else as well," he said as he peered out over the snow-covered tiles. "Storehouses, workshops, and sharp, strange smells."

"No palace on earth has a layout like this. The slave's map is useless."

"The slave's map brought us as far as we are now. To go further we'll have to earn our one hundred thousand sesterces."

"It's cheap at such a price. 'Find an amphora containing oil such as this' is all that we were told," Vespus said as he held up the tiny phial. "Among all of these rooms, too—and ask the gods how many tunnels and cells lie below. We might as well be looking for a marked grain of sand on a beach."

"Put that away. It cost sixty thousand sesterces and eleven lives."

"Then *you* should carry it. You carry the nose, and one is useless without the other."

Lars frowned, but nodded. Vespus handed him the phial. "An oily, sharp-tasting poison. Who could want such a thing?"

"I followed our go-between and—"

"I know, I know, he met with a man who led you to the house of one who wears the purple stripe on his toga. This still tells me nothing."

"We know that two drops will kill a rat."

"So it's the most expensive rat poison in all of history," suggested Lars.

"Bah. We had to force the stuff down its gullet so vile was the smell and taste, and it died writhing in agony. Hardly a subtle potion to slip into an enemy's wine."

"I cut the finger of a slave and rubbed a little on the wound. It neither stung nor soothed, and the wound healed neither faster nor slower.

The slave is still alive, too. Our employers, and even the slave Sextus, referred to them as Immortals, yet how could a poison make men immortal?"

"Perhaps it has a use in impotence," Vespus wondered.

"Do you wish to rub a little onto—"

"No! No, but, well, perhaps it ensures that boy children will be born from a coupling."

Lars was impressed. For all his trepidation, Vespus had some skill with lateral thought.

"Now *that* could well be a use for it. Wealthy families would pay a fortune to be sure of an heir. If one person controlled the supply of such an oil he would command silver by the barrowload."

The inner area was strangely quiet, and the very lack of guards made them uneasy. Once he had rested, Vespus took off the extra gear that he had been carrying and crawled away across the tiles to explore.

Lars sat alone, longing for Rome, for the familiarity of crowded streets and densely packed buildings, for the roadway of roofs above the streets and alleys that he could run as easily as a cat. Here there was a villa within a fort, but beyond it was nothing but mountains and snow. Once the alarm was raised the pursuers might hunt them down like wild boars; there was no maze of alleyways, roofs, and trapdoors in which they could lose themselves.

He looked about again. A villa within a fort, a palace of sorts. The Upper Palace was isolated by a moat and a high wall, and within that wall were only the Temporians. By day some slaves were brought in to do the cleaning and carrying, slaves carefully selected for dull wits. The guards were never admitted. Lars could make no sense of it, except to deduce that something of immense value was being concealed.

In a hall not far from where Lars crouched, every Temporian in the Upper Palace sat in conference discussing the death of Celcinius. His blood was still on the speakers' dais, and nobody had been willing to either clean away the stain or even set foot on the dais since their founder had died there.

"He died of a failed heart, and the fall which followed cracked his head open," Doria explained wearily, but her audience was not really interested. The death of Celcinius was inconvenient, it forced issues into the open.

"But why did his heart fail?" asked Levites.

"He was ninety-four years old! The shock of revival is dangerous enough for a person half of his age."

If Lars could have seen the hall he would have been even more perplexed. The Temporians sat on purple cushions in concentric ranks of semicircular stone benches. Both men and women wore silk trousers and tunics under a purple-edged toga praetexta . . . except that they were not true togas. They were made of silk, had voluminous sleeves, and were tied at the waist by a pinned silk belt. On their feet were sandals, but of a buckled design, and nothing like those that the Roman mortals wore. It was as if some distant Chinese court was having a costume party with a Roman theme. The moderator stood beside the blood-smeared dais as the rest of the company debated.

"He was our founder," wailed Tullius theatrically. He was one of the more recent recruits, and was barely a century old. "He was the man who transformed Rome from just another walled city into what it is today. Without him we're lost."

"Lost?" sneered Levites. "We have been without him for five years out of every six since we were founded."

"But in dangerous times we always had him to call upon."

"You rave. Was he revived during Caligula's rule? Or that of Nero? The greatest possible insult to Celcinius would be to say that his work was so poor that we could not survive without him. He was one of the three who shared the secret of the Venenum Immortale, but Lucian and his student are still alive and there is a full store of Venenum left, enough to last through many centuries. Celcinius should be given a hero's funeral, then we must go back to maintaining and expanding his empire."

Lucian stood to speak. "Were I to die now the secret of the Venenum Immortale would not be lost. Quintemes has had enough training to brew up usable Venenum, yet I am worried that there are only two of us. We need to have more of our number trained in its preparation. Two extra at least, perhaps as many as four."

"Four?" exclaimed Levites. "Factions would spring up, breakaway groups would tear us apart. No more than three have ever been able to make the Venenum Immortale at any one time. Three has been sufficient for many centuries. Why change now?"

"Were they to die in the same accident, the secret would be lost," said Regulus. "Why not have a whole trusted group sharing the secret? The women who do the revivals, for example?"

There were cries of dismay and jeers, but scattered applause as well. Regulus waited for the commotion to subside before he went on.

"With four sharing the secret we could have three frozen while the other made more Venenum. That means a longer lifespan for all. Factions are formed by conspirators, not by frozen men. Up to now we have had Celcinius frozen most of the time while another was awake one year in five to make more Venenum. Lucian and Quintemes have the skill to make the Venenum, it is true, but we have been lucky until now with having just two trained to make it. Four students must be trained."

"No! Lucian and two students are enough."

"Lucian is sixty-seven years old, and is likely to survive no more than five or ten more revivals. Then what? We must train those who are young, in the prime of life."

"Young men are ambitious, and would use the secret of the Venenum Immortale to seize power for themselves. We cannot afford factions, we are too weak! Gods of Romulus we might be, but we are still mortal. If stabbed we die."

"And we die when our bodies grow old, too," retorted Regulus. "All right then, train only one more new student besides Quintemes, but make him young."

"No, there is no precedent—" Levites began to protest.

"Yes there is a precedent! Our women train *all* their number in the arts of revival."

"Without the Venenum Immortale there could be no revival at all."

Regulus slumped against the cold marble backrest and pouted sullenly, intractable rather than defeated. "I've made enough concessions," he declared. "There must be at least one extra student, and *she* must be less than thirty years of age."

"Below thirty! She! You would have a girl control the destiny of Rome?"

"Why not? It survived Nero."

"We kept Nero in check, and when he defied us we struck him down."

Regulus folded his arms and straightened his back as far as it would bend. A joint popped loudly. Levites began to laugh, but Regulus glared at him angrily until he turned away.

"I'll veto any proposal to train some doddering old goat to make the Venenum," declared Regulus. "This is the time for reform."

Above their heads, at an air vent, Vespus was listening but not comprehending. The debate was in Etruscan, which was the Temporian language for formal and ceremonial occasions. Vespus looked around before moving on. In the distance he could see two guards pacing at the top of a tower at the edge of the Upper Palace. Guards were not permitted into this sanctuary of the Immortals, so what would happen if he were seen? Would the Immortals climb the roofs to pursue them, and how good were they as fighters? He decided that he had seen and heard enough.

"Big meeting, over there," he reported when he had returned to Lars. "They spoke a language that sounded familiar, yet I understood nothing. It might have been Greek."

"A Greek fortress here!" exclaimed Lars under his breath. "Perhaps an attack on Rome is being planned and prepared."

"Some of the speakers were women."

"Women! That's odd . . . but no matter. What of the venendarium?"

"I checked the chimneys, every one of them. There's a cluster down there, to the southeast, where the soot is oily, and has a sharp scent about it."

"Then we should go there at once. Pray that their speakers are long-winded."

Vespus went ahead and Lars followed, carrying their gear. The snow had made the tiles treacherous, even though it dampened the sounds that they made. Suddenly a white shape detached itself from a wall and fell upon Vespus with a hissing yowl. Lars drew his pugio and scrabbled toward the struggling flurry of snow and limbs, but even as he drew near Vespus pushed the big cat's face away with bloodied fingers and stabbed repeatedly at its ribcage. Lars seized it by the scruff of the neck, jerked it back and slashed the dagger across its throat.

For a moment they lay silent, but no alarm had been raised. They had rolled into deep snow between roofs, and this had muffled the sounds of the struggle.

"Are you hurt?" Lars whispered as he rolled the cat's body to one side.

"Mauled my hand," Vespus gasped. "Clawed me here and there . . . but nothing bad."

"Your hand is badly mauled, no more climbing for you tonight. I'll bind it and you can stay on the roof while I go below and force a few doors."

"Strange, it doesn't hurt much. Did it get you?"

"A scratch on the arm. Nothing more . . . but what's the matter?"

"Resting, just a moment."

"Are you sure you're all right?"

"Tired, just tired."

Vespus began to curl up in the snow as Lars wrapped a strip of cloth around his hand. The cat lay beside him, a mound of blood-streaked white about the size of a common dog.

"Not a real killer, it's probably trained to pounce and cause a commotion, raising the alarm," said Lars. "Lucky you didn't cry out. It's as white as snow, I've never seen one like it."

He lifted a paw with the blade of his pugio.

"There's something buckled to its paws—Vespus?"

Vespus was no longer breathing. Shivering, alert for more cats, Lars again lifted the animal's paw on his blade. The sharp metal spikes were coated in something dark and sticky. They too would tear skin when the cat used its claws. The coating of poison had killed Vespus in moments. Lars sank to the snow, clutching his arm, fighting down despair and panic. Minutes passed, his heart pounded—yet he did not become drowsy. The scratch was ugly, but had been from one of the cat's natural claws.

He flexed his limbs. Vespus lay curled up in the snow as if asleep. He patted the dead man's shoulder, pausing for a moment to find words to speak. He had seen death many times and was not used to feeling sorrow in its presence. He spat on the body of the white cat.

"They will regret making the roofs so dangerous," he told the corpse of Vespus as he turned to go.

Lars moved slowly across the roofs with his gladius in his hand. It was a weapon that might keep another cat at a distance . . . perhaps. Nothing else stirred on the snow-shrouded tiles. Across a courtyard Lars could see the chimneys that Vespus had described to him: strange, squat, pentagonal towers of brick.

He was ready to drop to the ground and enter one of the inner buildings when he had noticed a movement in the shadows. A very large dog, perhaps a wolf. So, there were many guards beyond the inner wall after all, but none of them were human. The slave had not known of them, but he had only been there during the day. The wolves and cats were probably let loose at night, and they were undoubtedly trained to distinguish between their masters and mortal intruders. It all made sense. Animals could not be bribed to turn traitor and betray secrets. Lars's skin was smeared with astringent and he had kept some of his clothing in a bag of pigeon feathers while they hid in the tower. Thus his scent was masked, even if he did not look like a pigeon. So far the wolves had taken no notice of him . . . or perhaps he was being stalked and did not realize it.

Fight fear, fear stinks, Lars told himself as he shivered and wedged himself into a corner beside a smoking chimney. He sat massaging his limbs and looking for further movement. The warmth from the chimney revived his spirits as much as the scent of roast that was on the air. So the Immortals did eat, just like everyone else. The voices from below were muffled by the tiles and snow, but were distinguishable as both male and female. The slave had said nothing about women, but perhaps these were mere harlots for the Immortals' amusement.

Lars slowly twisted, pressing his back against the warm bricks. His survey of the roof was done, he knew where he could escape once he had burgled the venendarium, and where he would retreat if seen and challenged. The shapes remained near the door as he began to unpack the bag strapped under his white cloak. His little bow consisted of two short lengths of ashwood which he fitted into a brass sleeve. It had a light draw, but its arrows were poison tipped. The first shot missed, and the wolves started awake at the clink of metal on stone. Lars drew back his bow again, but this time the target was standing and more distinct. There was a snarl as it hit. The wolf was already staggering when its companion was struck, and the second wolf dropped at once. A lucky shot had found its heart, Lars surmised while he waited for the first wolf to stop twitching. He slung the bow over his shoulder and dropped softly to the courtyard. Both wolves were dead, and he dragged them back to where they had been sleeping beside the door. There had been little noise or blood, but he smoothed out the snow anyway.

Now he had no reason to hurry. Lars doubted that the wolves would be checked until morning, and who would want to begin work in the middle of the night? The door had a latch, but was not locked. The wolves had been trusted to keep it secure. Once inside Lars took out a tiny phial of wormglow compound to light his way, then unstrapped a cylinder of butt-leather. A tiny dog licked his fingers, a dog worth at least its weight in gold coin. It was trained to be silent, and it had a sharp sense of smell.

Lars glanced around as he fumbled for his phial of oil. Having negligible experience in the methods of physicians was a hindrance. He knew little of how the mortars and pestles, jars, glassware, tubs of dead insects, oils, and masses of parchments might relate to what he wanted. The slave who called himself Lacerna had never seen a jar of the oil put away, so Lars had no clues to begin with. The dog would not be over-awed by the trappings of arcane knowledge, however: he let it sniff at the oil in the phial, then set it free.

They make the Venenum Immortale here but store it in some unknown place, his informant had said. Perhaps a load had just been sent out, he wondered as he watched the dog wandering about and sniffing. He quickly dismissed the thought, it was too much to bear. The little dog began to scratch at a floorboard. Lars walked over and held his glowing phial near the wood. A trapdoor. He scooped up his tiny dog and returned it to the butt leather roll.

The well was beneath a hinged cover, with a tiny lever at one edge that would, when the cover was lifted, press on a rod that protruded through a hole in the wall. Lars examined the lever, and found that it was on a hinge and held in place with a pin. With the lever safely unpinned, he lifted the trapdoor.

Snow and ice were packed around three amphorae. The oil slowly grew too toxic to use if not stored cold; his employer, Fortunatus, had told him that when he had accepted the contract. How slow was slowly? Thirty or forty years, Fortunatus had replied. It could easily last a few months at body temperature.

One amphora was empty, another sealed and full, and the third was near full and not sealed. He sniffed the stopper, then smeared a little of the contents on one finger and tasted it. Bitter! Sharp, oily and bitter, just like what was in the phial. This had to be it. He unpacked a dozen goatskin pouches and began to pour the viscous philter out into them. If carrying the same amount in a jar he would have barely been able to walk, let alone climb. As each pouch filled he strapped it to his body, arranging them to look as if he had a more corpulent build. The twelve pouches were filled before the amphora's level had dropped by even a third.

Lars checked the door and the courtyard beyond. All was as he had left it. Now he hastily scanned the scrolls that had been kept near the cold store. Some were in Latin, some in a language like Greek. There were notes about the purity of oils and how many tubs of snow insects had been collected by the slaves. *Method and Usage of Venenum:* these were instructions about the philter! Such incredible good fortune, thought Lars, surely some god was smiling on him—a loud clack echoed through the darkened room.

Lars froze for an instant, then rammed the glowing phial under his cloak. No movement, no light. He hastily folded the scroll into his pouch. The clack had come from the ice tub in the floor, yet he had put everything back as he had found it—but not quite. He dropped to his knees and let a little of the phial's glow leak between his fingers. He had not bent the triplever back to its former position, and now the rod that it would have pressed against protruded a handspan from the wall: the accursed device not only warned when the cover had been lifted, it could also be used to remotely check that the lever was pinned in place!

Where was it controlled from? How far away? How soon would they check? How many guards would come? Lars fought down his panic. The rod would be to check if the trap had been set in the first place, it was only a guard against carelessness, he decided. They would come without suspicion, intending to merely reset the trap. He strung his bow and stepped outside. Behind the dead wolves was a column that would cast a shadow from the lamp of anyone approaching. After a minute two figures appeared, both carrying thumblamps.

Lars watched as they rattled at the bolt. Once inside they would see the scrolls that he had not had time to tidy away. The first stepped through the door as he raised his bow and shot the figure behind him. The man sprawled, dead before he hit the snow. The other turned.

"Mind that step—" he began, but was silenced as a second arrow took him in the eye. At such close range Lars's aim was deadly. He dragged the bodies inside and removed the arrows. Perhaps they would soon be missed—he needed a diversion rather than a silent escape. One of the thumblamps continued to burn where it had fallen on the doorstep. Lars picked it up and poured a little olive oil on the scrolls. Sputtery flames blazed up. He dangled a cloth strip in burning oil, then set more fires.

Lars climbed back onto a nearby roof. He took several items of stolen armor and clothing from his pack, and dressed himself to look like an overweight guard. He tried to move quickly; he was aware that the flames would soon be noticed. A tile suddenly broke beneath his weight and his leg plunged through the roof. Somewhere in the distance men were shouting. The security imposed by the Immortals hindered them now. Lars watched as a dozen of them ran back and forth with buckets while the flames spread as if the place had been drenched in olive oil. An explosion suddenly blasted out the side of the venendarium as an amphora of something volatile detonated. The roof collapsed in a spark-studded, swirling cloud.

Lars noticed that guards from outside had now joined the Immortals. He dropped to the ground and went limping toward the gate, waving a bloodied arm for attention as more guards came streaming in.

"Sheepskins, soak sheepskins in water and bring them, quickly!"

The advice was sensible. Several guards turned and ran with him back to the outer part of the palace, then turned off for a storehouse. Lars made for the shadows, scaled the palace wall and clambered down the outer face with the aid of a rope.

The path to the crane was not long, and was by now unguarded. Lars swung the arm out over the edge and chopped the pulley free with his gladius. The rope rattled out to its full six-hundred-foot extension and the wicker hand crashed to the altar below. He began by climbing down hand over hand, but as his fatigue increased he dropped longer and longer distances, until his leather mittens were smoking with the friction. Near the bottom of the rope his hands and wrists were so badly wrenched that he could barely hold on, yet he landed safely on the torn wickerwork of the great hand. Barely pausing for breath, he staggered off through the snow. His way was lit by the glow from the burning venendarium reflected against low clouds.

Sextus, the slave that Lars knew as Lacerna, arrived at the edge not long after the thief was out of sight. Behind him was the glow of the fire and the shouts of those fighting it. Only one set of footprints was visible in the snow, so one of the thieves had been left behind. Alive or dead? The question troubled him. The thieves had seen his face by lamplight, even though he had given them a false name. He came to the disabled crane, its mechanism still locked but its rope chopped free and dangling over the precipice. He touched the severed ends of the ropes that Lars had cut, quivering with fright. Two slaves had been scourged to death for merely allowing the rope to fray more than the overseer would accept, and Sextus himself had been given thirty lashes for allowing the pulley wheels to develop a squeak. The crane was the Temporians' only link with the world below, and they took a dim view of anything that endangered it.

If one of the thieves had escaped down the rope, then he could too. With his hands trembling, Sextus crawled out along the crane and began to climb down the slick rope. The clouds above still glowed red from the fire; blackness yawned below. He was dressed for the heated interior of Nusquam, he wore only sandals and a tunic, and had no gloves. Voices grew louder above him, they were coming for him. His weakening hands began to slip as he tried to move faster. No food, no map, nobody to guide him through the yawning blackness down there. He had come to the Temporians as a child fifteen years earlier. Even that had involved traveling for ten days wearing a blindfold. Burning torches appeared at the edge of the cliff.

"There! On the rope!"

"I see him."

A bowstring twanged and something swished past the slave's head.

"Don't! We want him alive."

"You on the rope! One move and you're dead."

Sextus lowered his gaze from the torches to the blackness below. Why cling desperately to a rope with aching fingers in order to face death by torture, he asked himself. The rope trembled as a guard began to climb out along the crane. Sextus let go and fell without screaming. The distant thud that obliterated his life echoed up the cliff to his pursuers.

"Shit," sighed the archer, and he spat into the darkness below.

"Climb down the rope, follow me," said the tesserarius of the watch.

Namatinus and his horsemen arrived at the altar only a few minutes later. The reflection of the fire from the clouds was so bright that they could ride without torches now.

"Too late, too damnably late!" shouted Namatinus, looking up at the fire. He turned to his men. "None of you will ever mention this again under pain of death. Understood?"

The riders chorused agreement. Namatinus and Vitellan dismounted and walked to the altar where the wicker hand had crashed. The tesserarius and his guards had already descended from the clifftop by the rope and were examining the body of Sextus.

"Centurion Namatinus of the Furtivus Legion, Primus Fort," Namatinus said as he reached the altar and the guards confronted him.

"What is your business here?" asked the tesserarius warily.

"I discovered a conspiracy to breach the security of Nusquam, two thieves were to smuggle themselves up the cliff amid the supplies. I came as fast as I could, but—"

"But you are too late, Centurion—or maybe you are just in time with your men and horses. Did you see anyone on the trail as you approached?"

"No."

"You're sure of that?"

"Positive.

"You mentioned a conspiracy, Centurion. What can you tell me about the thieves?"

Namatinus beckoned Vitellan forward. "Tell him your story, Legionary Bavalius."

"I was with Gallus, escorting some mules to meet with the main caravan. Five bandits attacked us. Gallus killed one, I wounded another, then I fell down a cliff beside the trail into deep snow. The bandits emptied two mule packs, leaving enough space so that two men could hide in them. That is all I know."

Namatinus described how Vitellan struggled back to the fort, and how they rode out and met the mule caravan as it returned from the altar.

"We caught and tortured the truth out of the two imposters," Namatinus concluded. "They said that they left their two leaders concealed in packs on the altar."

"So, there's definitely only two outsiders to find," the tesserarius said with relief.

Namatinus pointed up the cliff. "What happened up there? Are you allowed to tell me?"

The tesserarius shrugged one shoulder and gestured upward.

"A large section of the palace is pretty obviously alight, but nobody is sure how the fire started. At least two Temporians and several guard beasts have been killed. We saw the body of one thief on the roof of a building before it collapsed."

Namatinus looked at the body lying crumpled on the altar in the surreal red glow reflected from the clouds.

"And that one makes two."

"Probably not, Centurion. I know him as a slave from the palace, and he was probably helping the thieves. The second thief has not been found."

"Well as I said, we saw nobody as we came up the trail."

"Good news, the first good news of this terrible night. Maybe he cut the crane loose but stayed above, maybe he climbed down the rope and is hiding nearby. He is armed with a bow and his aim is deadly."

Namatinus turned to his men. "I want you to split into groups of three and search the area for footprints. Never go alone, this thief is very dangerous and he has a bow. Now, I also want three volunteers to ride back to the mule caravan and tell them to guard the trail and let nobody past until I return. Who knows the trail well enough to ride all the way in the dark?"

One of the tesserarius' men stepped forward. "I can guide your men, Centurion."

"Then you will go. Vitellan, you've seen enough action in the past few days. Give him your horse and stay here with me."

The portly guard mounted Vitellan's horse and led the other two volunteers down the trail and into the darkness. It was morning before the tesserarius realized that of the six guards who had climbed down the rope with him, all six were still present. By then Lars had killed Namatinus' two legionaries and was so far away that there was no hope of ever capturing him.

Libarna, Northern Italy: 29 December 71, Anno Domini

Libarna nestled securely in the foothills of the Alps, a prosperous little market town servicing a patchwork of farms.

"The most boring place on earth," Fortunatus sneered as he looked out across the melting snow. "No games, no chariots, no feasts, ugly harlots and sour wine."

Viventius came from a rural family, and did not find Libarna so very bad. "Why not return to Rome, then? I'd gladly stay here and wait for the thief."

Fortunatus ignored him. He sipped a little wine and looked out along the northward road again.

"Five days. We know there was a fire at Nusquam five days ago. Lars Lartorius must have had a part in it. The body of a thief was found on the roof, but it was not he. Lars is known to cover his tracks with fires. He was said to be near the Circus Maximus seven years ago when the fire was started that consumed much of Rome."

They fell silent again, watching children flinging snow at each other and laughing. A farmer drove an oxcart along the road, bringing hay for the stables.

"They barred me from joining them, they deserved to burn," muttered Fortunatus. "I have earned the right to be immortal many times over."

"Any more than Emperor Vespasian?"

"More than he. I began my career while Caligula still ruled, then I helped hold the Empire together during Nero's excesses. Now the Temporians tell me that I'm too old to become one of them. Too old at fifty-one!"

"There could be more to it than that. Gaius remembers how you manipulated the Senate and lost him money on the grain market."

"Gaius is not an Immortal."

"Gaius has friends among the Immortals. He slept with one of their women when he was younger, now he's a senator."

"I believe none of that. The Sons of Romulus are afraid of me. They want me dead but one hundred thousand sesterces more will see the end of their plans. Lars has robbed the Emperor himself, he will not fail me."

"He's a master thief in Rome, but Nusquam is a fort in the mountains."

"Lars is a master of his trade. He will steal what I want as a matter of pride, if not for money."

"I want a great deal of money," said a hoarse voice from somewhere above them.

The two conspirators jumped to their feet, swords in hand. A moment later their lookout, Portulus, was marched in by the thief's two men.

"They arrived in one of the haycarts," he mumbled, his face flushed with humiliation. "The thief wanted to spy on you before talking."

Fortunatus and Viventius sheathed their swords and sat down again. Lars descended from the beams of the roof. He had an ugly scratch on his arm, and he favored one leg.

"Just the sort of entrance I should have expected from a master thief," said Fortunatus genially.

Lars grinned at the deference. "Here is a little sample of what you wanted," he said, handing a small glass phial to Fortunatus. "I have twelve sachets of it."

Lars watched as Fortunatus uncorked the bottle and sniffed at the contents. "I know the scent, an Immortal named Rhea once taunted me with a cup of it." He poured a drop onto his fingertip and licked it. "Pah! Vile stuff. As bitter as gall," he said, squeezing his eyes shut.

"A philter for immortality, according to what was on the scroll beside it," said Lars, "but you will need more than this."

"How much?"

"I have enough for fifteen treatments. It's buried safely at a day's journey from here."

"It smells more as if it would kill me than grant immortality."

"I force-fed some to a rat. It died."

"Not surprising. Did you see any of the Immortals?"

"I saw several. They're not good at fighting fires."

"What were they like, apart from that?" Fortunatus asked. "I have only ever knowingly met one."

"They are not truly immortal. They have merely learned to extend their lifespans, and accidents can kill them as easily as you or me. They do get older, but very slowly."

"The one that I know, Rhea, has not aged in thirty years."

"Not that you would notice but . . ." He reached into his robes and took out a scroll. "Read this. It outlines the use of the 'Venenum Immortale,' as they seem to call it."

Fortunatus snatched the scroll eagerly and began to read. His smile soon vanished.

"This—this is a monstrous trick!" he exclaimed. "This is not immortality at all. It will not renew my youth."

"But it will allow you to cheat death for quite a long time."

"But this says that the Sons of Romulus live such a long time just by freezing each other in ice."

"Yes, they take turns. At any one time four out of every five are frozen, and that means that they are only awake to get older for perhaps one year in five. At that rate the oldest of them may have been born over four hundred years ago. The scroll shows that the women look after the revival process, which is dangerous and difficult. The men prepare a philter which must be drunk before one's body is frozen. It's quite a complex matter, their type of immortality. I was not able to steal the instructions for the manufacture of the oil itself, but I got you a good supply of it. If you follow the directions in that *Method and Usage* scroll, and if you have reliable friends to freeze and revive you, well, you can live as long as there is ice to preserve you.

You might find that reliable friends are harder to find than ice, of course."

Fortunatus sat with his mouth open. "But . . . in effect they 'live' only as long as any mortal. Why do they do it?"

Lars grinned. "You ask me, a mere thief? What understanding of the affairs of state would I have?"

"Don't patronize me, I know about your background."

"Then you know that one hundred thousand sesterces will not buy what I want. You can grant influence and favors: the return of my family villa, and the slaves and artisans to make it prosper."

Fortunatus looked from him to the scroll.

"What about the Relagatus faction that ruined your family? Do you want them punished?"

"Oh no, they are to be left alone. I want the pleasure of dealing with their people myself."

"Granted, granted. Now tell me how the Immortals govern."

"They freeze themselves for, say, eight years, then appear again among mortals as if they have not aged at all."

"Yes, yes, that makes sense. They seem to spend a lot of time away on their estates, or on long journeys."

"Now ask yourself how the Emperor governs. Does he train his troops personally, or pave the roads himself? No, he has trusted minions of one rank or another to run off and see that his orders are carried out. The Immortals work the same way, with some differences. They work as a team, and they recruit only the most highly skilled administrators and leaders to their number. They set schemes in motion, long-term schemes that span decades, and they are unfrozen from time to time to supervise them. They act as if they were gods with lifespans and concerns well beyond those of mortals."

"But the emperors do not disappear for years at a time."

"As far as I can tell, the emperors are never Immortals, Fortunatus. They are their puppets, the same as you and I."

Fortunatus hunched forward, wringing his hands and staring at the phial of oily liquid that Lars had given him.

"This will make me neither young nor immortal," he said in a high, thin voice.

"But you have their secret, and their philter too. Now I want my payment."

"Payment? For something as useless to me as this?" He snatched up the phial and flung it against the wall where it shattered, leaving an oily, golden patch. "I want to know where that Frigidarium chamber is. If I can't share their immortality I can at least break their power. Find the Frigidarium and I'll pay you."

Lars glowered, but seemed to have expected such a reaction.

"That was not in our agreement, Fortunatus. Besides, I burned their villa-fortress to cover my escape. They will have ten times as many guards on everything now."

"If you were stupid enough to start a fire, then that's your business. What you brought me is useless."

"What I brought is what you asked for, even if it is not what you expected. My services don't come free, and I have given you the best of my services."

Fortunatus slowly got to his feet, suddenly smiling and affable. "Lars, friend, we are of a kind. You brought no more than a taste of Venenum here, while I brought no more money than you brought Venenum—"

A sign to Portulus sent him lunging at the nearest thief with a dagger in his hand. The point stopped in hidden mail, and Lars flung a pugio that plunged into his neck. Fortunatus raised his gladius as the second thief leaped at him, chopping it into the side of his head as Viventius' sword messily hacked into the thief pinned under Portulus. Fortunatus closed with Lars, sword in one hand and a stool in the other.

Lars's blade dug into the stool, stuck and snapped. For all the pain in his leg, Lars still managed a heavy kick to Fortunatus' groin, just as Viventius' sword burst through the light mail under his tunic and slid a short way between his ribs. Lars rammed the stump of his blade into Viventius' face, and was rewarded with a scream of pain. The conspirator blundered into Fortunatus, blinded by his own blood, and hacked at him in panic. With quizzical detachment Lars stood watching them fight for a moment, then drew another heavy pugio and flung it. It buried itself up to the hilt in Fortunatus' back. Lars picked up a fallen gladius.

"Fortunatus, is it over?" panted Viventius as the blade descended.

With the room again quiet, the innkeeper entered. He was no stranger to brawls, but the ferocity of the brief fight left him shaken. One of the town loafers peered around the door and stared at Fortunatus' two companions for a moment.

"These be gladiators, sir," he said in awe. "Auctorati, and good 'uns too. Seen 'em fight at Verona."

"These are gladiators too," panted Lars, gesturing to his companions. "Humiliores, and not from Verona."

Nusquam: 29 December 71, Anno Domini

The rubble was cold as Regulus and Doris directed the slaves who were searching for what they already knew was lost. Light snow was falling.

"The work of at least two men, that is for certain," Regulus said as he looked over charred fragments of scrolls that had been collected from the ruins. "If it was a plot to kill the Venenum Masters, they did succeed. The snow cat got one assassin, but died killing him. We found their bodies together on the roof. Nothing outside the venendarium was touched."

"The other assassin was one of our slaves, Sextus Clodius. He fell to his death while trying to escape."

"Or so the report of the guards speculates. I saw the body, but it was not clothed for a long flight through the mountains in winter. He had neither food nor weapons."

"Perhaps he was truly loyal to us, and was chasing another assassin when he slipped from the rope," said Doria hopefully.

"Without weapons? The guards waited until the crane was repaired before descending the cliff to recover Sextus' body. If there was another, then he had a long start, and the new snow had covered his tracks. It all gathers itself into a plot: the vote to train your women to make the Venenum was won, and almost as soon as the meeting ended the only two men who shared its secret were killed and their venendarium was burned. I just don't understand. Many disagreed with the meeting's decision, but who could profit by the loss of the Venenum Immortale's secret?"

"It might have been a monstrous accident," suggested Doria.

"There are too many odd clues that suggest otherwise. Still, we can't be concerned with them. Our immediate problem is the Venenum Immortale. Does any other person know its secret, or know of someone who knows it?"

"Someone who is frozen might."

"If so, then we have a terrible choice. We do not have enough Venenum left to revive, then refreeze, every Temporian in the Frigidarium."

Snow eddied down around them more thickly, and the slaves digging in the distance began to curse. Doria pulled her robes more tightly about her as Regulus examined the charred fragments of scrolls.

"There is nothing in these scraps," said Regulus. "It's not surprising. The instructions for brewing the Venenum Immortale were not meant to be written down."

"Some mortal outside Nusquam knows of us," said Doria. "If another assassin escaped into the snow, might he have stolen a scroll with the Venenum's secret written out?"

Regulus pulled a scroll out from his robes and checked what the guards had found again.

"That man on the roof was a stranger to everyone here. His body had the scars of a gladiator and the muscles of an acrobat. He was probably a thief, trained to leap about on roofs as silently as a cat. I've also been told that a mule column was ambushed on the way here, yet the mules were recorded as reaching here with their loads intact. The thieves were hiding within the packs, according to the accomplices that were caught and tortured. It all adds up to a plot. Someone is out to steal our secret again, one of those fools in Rome."

"They have tried before. Samples of the Venenum Immortale and the antidote have been stolen a dozen times over the centuries. What harm has it done? The Venenum is of no use without the Frigidarium Glaciale, and we Temporians who operate it. Why, it would be like one man trying to steal a battle galley and operate it alone. He could not tend the rowing, the sails, the steering and the catapults all by himself. If the thief drinks some stolen Venenum without proper preparation and antidote, he will die."

"Except that this thief might well have taken us with him. We have limited stocks of the Venenum, enough to last only about two hundred freezings."

"That at least gives us a margin of centuries," said Doria, squeezing Regulus' arm. "Time enough to rediscover the method of preparing the Venenum."

"We have no such margin," he said peevishly. "We have no more than our normal lifespan: seventy or eighty years at best, and a lot less is left for us two. What good is having two or three centuries of life if you lie frozen for most of that time? This is hopeless, I feel so tired."

He shrugged snow from his cape as a slave came running up with more charred pieces of scroll. He glanced at them.

"Pah, the list of new Temporian recruits to be gathered in for initiation, training and freezing. Gollak Paginius, Vitellan Bavalius, Markus Morilian . . . I can't read the rest but no matter. These young Romans will never know the taste of the Venenum Immortale now. There's barely enough to keep us going until . . ."

He stared intently at a large scrap with small, close writing, holding it out at the focus of his eyes.

"Until?" prompted Doria.

He passed the fragment to Doria without saying any more.

"Ah, promising!" she exclaimed. "Part of an inventory of ingredients. That helps. Tallinian and Rhea know some of the ingredients too, and the types of insects used. This could fill in the gaps."

"It may not be enough without the method of preparation," Regulus warned, but he wanted to be optimistic. "The Venenum is a poison, even in its pure form, and if everything is just thrown together it could be really deadly. We must set the slaves trapping live rats and mice to test our trial recipes. You must question all the women, too. Those who have shared beds with the Masters of the Venenum may have heard them let clues slip."

Doria took the suggestion badly.

"Now that it's too late you finally try to involve us women!" she shouted angrily, flinging the charred fragments of scroll to the snow. "You beg us for secrets that you would not give us in the first place!"

"That's hardly fair," sighed Regulus, squatting in the snow to pick up the pieces of scroll.

Doria watched him for a moment, tears running along the wrinkles of her face. "I speak of the menfolk in general," she conceded, kneeling beside him to help. "Take no affront, Regulus. At least we know how to make the antidote to be taken with the Venenum Immortale."

"Small comfort, having the antidote for that which we cannot make. It may take decades to rediscover the Venenum by just blindly mixing batches and feeding it to rats, mice, and pigs. Who would be willing to grow old while experimenting for the sake of those who are lying frozen in the bloom of youth? Our ship has sunk and now we try to rebuild it out of driftwood."

Some rubble collapsed where the slaves were digging, and there were shrieks of pain from a trapped man.

"I'm having a search made for a stranger, a fat guard who was seen during the fire," said Regulus, ignoring the commotion. "He may be a companion to the thief that we know about, and he may be still here on the mountain. The dead slave Sextus might have been in league with them."

"So if one of the Masters did write a scroll of instructions, you think this fat thief might have it?"

"Probably not, but we must try everything." He stood up, leaning heavily on his staff, then helped Doria to her feet. "Our own rigid security keeps defeating us. The method for making the Venenum was never to be written down, under pain of death: the Venenum was our greatest treasure, the base of all our power, so we guarded its secret more closely than gold. Now it is gone, and we seem like such fools."

Libarna, Northern Italy: 7 January 72, Anno Domini

Milos, a Greek physician, had looked upon the wounded man as a challenge to his skills. The sword wound in his chest had been inflamed, yet he was strong and otherwise healthy. The gash in his arm might have been from a large cat, perhaps the exotic pet of some villa's master. His leg had been badly scratched and the knee wrenched, as if from a fall. Perhaps an adulterer caught in the act, who had barely escaped with his life? Perhaps a thief who had not been sufficiently careful and silent?

Lars had arrived at the physician's house at night. He had dropped a small bag of coins into his hand, then collapsed. For days he lay in the grip of a fever, rambling about immortals, a mountain fortress, and a huge white cat. Milos examined the pack that he had brought, and found it to be filled with sachets of a golden, bitter oil. A cylinder of butt-leather contained a tiny dog that frantically lapped water from his cup and was ravenously hungry. A scroll from the pack described the use of a substance called Venenum Immortale, which was used to freeze animals and people so that they could be brought back to life later. It read like an instruction exercise for a student, and Milos wondered at the real intent behind it.

The physician forced a rabbit to drink a prescribed measure of the oil. It died within two hours. He then repeated the experiment, but this time froze the rabbit after one hour. A day later he revived it according to the instructions, and it lived another hour before it too died of the effects of the oil. He fed its flesh to his neighbor's dog, which became violently ill but survived.

By then Lars's fever had subsided. He awoke from a quiet sleep, but had to be fed by hand, and it was several more days before he could get up. Milos remained discreet with his patient.

"I'll not ask too many questions," he said when Lars was at last strong enough to walk, "but I must warn you that soldiers have been asking about strangers in this village. They are particularly interested in wounded strangers."

"And you did not betray me?"

"I considered it . . . but we are of a kind."

Lars said nothing, but tensed himself. The physician noticed.

"Don't consider killing me," said Milos. "It's not worth it. I'm a fugitive too, fleeing a crime of my own in Thessalonica. A stupid, futile conspiracy against Roman rule."

"So, you choose to hide here in Libarna, closer to Rome?" said Lars doubtfully.

"Not for much longer. My contacts tell me that it would be wise to move on soon. You were lucky that I was here to treat you. You were luckier still that I was in no position to go to the authorities about your wounds. What was your crime?"

Lars's face remained blank and he shook his head. "Whatever I might have done, my name is attached to no crime. I'll be returning to Rome whenever you say I'm fit to travel."

"And I to Genua, to be a rigger aboard a merchantman bound for, well, it's no concern of yours. Not a very likely sailor, am I?"

Lars pushed a shutter open and looked down the street. It was covered in muddy snow-slush, but people were walking about without great effort.

"I should return to Rome," he said again, gingerly feeling his partly healed wound. "Does what I've paid already cover your fee?"

"I'm willing to be reasonable. Believe it or not, I have enough money for my needs. A skilled physician is never short of customers. First tell me, though, what is the nature of that oil, that poisonous oil that you brought with you? Is it something you stole?"

Lars pulled the shutter closed and turned fluidly to face Milos. "What do you know of it? Have people been asking questions?"

"No, but by following the instructions in the scroll that was in your pack I managed to freeze a rabbit solid, then bring it back to life again. The trouble was that some antidote appears to be required, otherwise the animals die within a few days, and their flesh is too poisonous to eat. I could build up their tolerance to the oil by feeding it to them a little at a time, but the antidote would be quicker."

Lars began to relax as he realized that the physician had not betrayed him. The rush of alarm had drained his weakened body and now he had to sit down, his head spinning.

"It . . . should be obvious, as to its use," said Lars, too weary to think, longing to sleep again.

Milos remained bright-eyed and eager. "I think that a pig could be thus frozen for the whole of winter, removing the need to feed it from expensive stores. I think that such a process could be worth a fortune to the farmers of Rome, and perhaps even more could be done too. Remote garrisons could be manned cheaply with perhaps a dozen men over winter, while four or five hundred more lie frozen yet alive. A secret worth more than gold could buy, eh?"

Lars nodded gravely at the entirely plausible yet false explanation as he thought out a reply.

"As you say, the process is flawed. The animals die quickly without the antidote and their flesh is poisonous. I stole what I brought here before I realized that the process has not yet been perfected. It brought me no profit for all my injuries. The antidote that they speak of is yet to be perfected."

"How much would you ask for all of your oil and the scroll of instructions? Five hundred sesterces?"

"More like five thousand. What use have you for it?"

"I have some small skill with mixtures. Perhaps I could detoxify the oil, so that no antidote is needed. Do you have the directions for making it?"

"No. All that I have is in that pack."

"In that case, four hundred sesterces."

"Six hundred or nothing."

Milos smiled at last. "Agreed, but only if you tell me of the man who devised the mixture. Give me his name and tell me where to find him. If I can perfect the antidote while I hide in exile, why, it may buy me a pardon when I return."

Lars gave him a fictitious name, but provided accurate directions for finding the villa in the Alps where the Temporians were waging their long war against death. Milos paid the money for the oil and scroll, then set off for the port of Genua that same day. Lars stayed on in the physician's house, as the rent had been paid in advance. He recovered his strength and got to know the area, and with the money he had looted from Fortunatus' room he bought a nearby farm in the name of his wife and five children. He sent letters and money to them under a false name, instructing them to join him. The farm was less than he had hoped for, but with all his other hoarded wealth it would be just enough to begin rebuilding his family's status and fortune.

Libarna, Northern Italy: 25 March 72, Anno Domini

Publius Varlexus had decided upon a squad of two dozen legionaries to capture the Greek physician. The extra men were more to prevent him from escaping than because of any danger.

The house was shabby and nondescript, neither squalid nor respectable. Varlexus' men surrounded it silently, and more men crawled onto the roof from adjoining buildings. Abruptly a dog began to bark, a high-pitched squeak in the gloom. After a moment the barking stopped, replaced by the clatter of hobnails on flagstones and shouted orders. Varlexus heard wood begin to splinter beneath the blade of an axe. A fire blazed up behind the windows, then came the clang of weapons and screams of pain.

His troops on the roof hastily jumped clear of the spreading flames, then amid the dancing shadows a figure leaped from the tiles across the narrow street. He caught the edge of a roof, hung by his hands for a moment then hooked a leg over the edge. Five bowstrings twanged and three arrows hit the mark. The man fell, crashing down onto a cartload of wicker baskets. A tiny dog scrambled clear and vanished into the shadows of the narrow street.

The fugitive was dying as they laid him out on the roadway. The price of capturing him had been high. Three troops killed in a fight in the house, two others injured, and six people trapped and burned in the buildings to either side.

Varlexus put his face near that of his dying quarry and said, "The justice of Rome has a very long reach, Milos."

The dying man blinked, then frowned and whispered, "Imbecile."

Lars's family prospered on their new farm near Libarna, slowly accumulating a fortune from wine, honey, and sheep. Within three decades his son's wealth had even grown to exceed that of Lars's disgraced grandfather. He used it to build a villa that the family lived in until the barbarian invasions of centuries later.

Primus Fort: 5 May 72, Anno Domini

The government official who arrived at the Primus Fort to see Vitellan was of indeterminate age, and seemed distant and preoccupied. Vitellan somehow fancied that he might have been a sad, defeated pagan god out of some tragic legend, setting his affairs in order before his enemies arrived to vanquish him forever. He handed the young legionary a scroll. Vitellan read it, then looked up at the official who would give no name.

"First I am ordered to Egypt, then I am ordered here to the to serve in a legion that does not officially exist, then this arrives telling me that I am to be reassigned to Gaul. What is going on?"

"Young men and women with your skills and talents are no longer required by my masters," the man replied simply.

"May I ask who your masters are, and what skills and talents I am thought to have?"

"No. Remember, too, that if you ever mention the Furtivus Legion once you leave this fort you will be killed."

"Of course, I learned that the day I arrived. So, I am to have no other chance to do . . . whatever else I was to do?"

"That I cannot say, but you have served well in the Furtivus Legion and it has been noted. Important, powerful people have noticed you, and you have been given special advancement within the army, Centurion Vitellan Bavalius."

"Centurion!" Vitellan exclaimed.

The newest centurion in the Roman Empire could do no more than stand with his mouth open while the enigmatic messenger smiled, gave an odd, curt bow, then walked away. Vitellan stared after him, noting that Centurion Namatinus gave him a great deal of deference. Whoever he was, he appeared to have a lot of authority.

"Perhaps he's not joking," Vitellan said to himself in wonder. "Perhaps I really am a centurion."

The Temporians never recovered from the loss of the recipe for making their Venenum Immortale. Stores of the Venenum were adequate but finite, and although Regulus and Doria spent the remainder of their lives together experimenting with the Venenum's known ingredients, they achieved little more than breakthroughs in the preparation of poisons. The Temporians began to keep some of their number frozen for longer periods, while others were kept awake longer to administer the Empire's affairs. These aged and died before the eyes of those whom they ruled, and this eroded Temporian authority. Legends arose that a group of Christian fanatics was killing them, while the barbarians to the north and east became harder to control. When Rome fell to Alaric's Visigoths early in the fifth Christian century, the last of the Temporians fled their faltering empire on an immense, desperate voyage.

The physician Milos sailed from Genua to Ostia, at the mouth of the Tiber. He told port officials that he was going up the river to see Rome, but while the timber and skins were being unloaded from his ship he found another that was about to sail for Valentia. It was still short of riggers, and he was taken aboard. From Spain he worked his way to Britannia aboard a ship taking olive oil and pottery to Londinium. Some years later he met a young centurion named Vitellan Bavalius, a youth with a curious malady that seemed to be treatable with the Venenum Immortale. After a delay of many years, Vitellan was about to share in the Temporians' type of immortality after all.

pax romana

Wessex, the British Isles: 16 February 870, Anno Domini

The villagers of Durvonum worked their way across the gleaming white field slowly and methodically, harvesting the newly fallen snow into blocks. They were in teams of four, two shoveling the snow into square wooden pails, one packing it down with a mallet, and a carrier taking each completed block to an oxcart at the western corner. Although a raid by the Danes on this particular village was unlikely, a dozen men armed with pikes and axes stood guard near the cart. Alfred looked closely at the nearest team. All the workers were armed, both men and women.

"Notice how they stay within a short run from the cart," he said to Bishop Paeder. "If Danish raiders burst out of the woods the snow harvesters could rally together in moments."

"They also have scouts in the woodlands," said Paeder. "The Danes would have a hard, bloody fight, and for nothing better than a cartload of packed snow. Vitellan trained this first village well."

Alfred considered the words, then nodded. "Just as he is training dozens more. I know that he is my friend, but he still frightens me. The man could have this land on a platter if he turned against us. He knows the arts of warfare so well, yet he has no fame or following."

Paeder shifted his weight in the saddle with a rippling jingle of chainmail. "He is on our side, and we cannot do without him. Let's not tempt fate by prying too much." He glanced casually at the men of their escort.

The sight of the villagers gathering snow was unsettling to the soldiers, and some crossed themselves in a nervous reflex. The scene had an uncanny resemblance to a grain harvest, except that this crop was white and cold. There was something here that seemed pointless and unnatural, the very essence of a pagan ritual.

"So not all churls are so stupid, eh Githek?" Paeder called to the captain. The man was caught off guard. He had been fingering the pommel of his sword and staring intently at the villagers.

"I—ah, their guards are well deployed," Githek began.

"Not the guards, the ice!" said Paeder in loud and studied exasperation. "They need no expensive salt or smoking to preserve their meat. Instead they store it in some deep cave with blocks of ice made from snow—which is free for the taking."

At once the mood of the men changed. Some edged their horses closer for a better view, while others talked excitedly among themselves and traced outlines of square pails in the chilly air.

"Best to make this seem like a clever local trick, rather than let it go unexplained," said Paeder quietly, turning back to Alfred. "This way they will talk about the skill itself, rather than where they saw it done."

Alfred nodded. "Yes, Vitellan has always said that he wants the real secret of this place to go no further than us two."

The villagers worked in silence, except for the dull thudding of the mallets on the compacted snow. Over at the oxcart an elder inspected each block before it was loaded. Paeder pointed to him.

"There's Gentor, the Icekeeper," he said. "He's very particular about the quality of the blocks, and the packing of the ice chamber."

"It's one of the few times I have seen him away from Vitellan."

"This snow harvest ceremony is very important to the people here, and nothing would make him miss it. It's old, very old."

"Perhaps as old as Vitellan claims, in fact," said Alfred, frowning. "Do any chronicles give a clue to its age?"

"I once read a chronicle by Augustine of Canterbury describing a village hereabout where they did this—the harvesting of snow into blocks to preserve meat through summer. I'm sure he was talking about this place. It was written two hundred and seventy years ago."

"I would like to see that chronicle."

"That is not possible, my young lord—even if your Latin was up to it. The book was in a library that was burned by the Danes three years ago."

Alfred blew a streamer of breath into the frosty air, and Paeder briefly had the impression of an angry young dragon.

"Vitellan is right," Alfred said in an ominously muted voice. "There is no more dangerous enemy than one who despises learning. Come Paeder, I've seen enough. Show me the village now."

The thumping of the mallets faded behind them as they rode slowly through the woodlands. Durvonum itself was on a hillock in a large clearing. Although the huts were as small and crude as might be seen anywhere in the Kingdom of Wessex, they were arranged in orderly rows behind a low, square stockade. It had earth ramparts with sharpened stakes pointing outward to break any charge by horsemen. As they approached, a squad of villagers was drilling in a pike-wall formation.

The villagers looked around quickly as the riders came into view, but relaxed when they saw the colors of the Royal House of Wessex. As they got closer the churls stared in fascination at the armor and weapons worn by the men of Alfred's escort. The riders in turn preened themselves as they rode past the staring eyes. To a villager they were magnificent indeed, true warriors dressed in leather scale mail or iron chainmail, with helmets of banded iron and leather. Painted round-shields were strapped to their backs, and their axes had never chopped firewood.

"My, but we're pretty," snapped Paeder sarcastically as they stopped before the line of stakes. "Githek, hold your squad of dandies here and make them watch the churls at practice. They may learn something about real fighting."

Alfred had already dismounted and was walking slowly through the maze of stakes. Paeder jumped to the ground in a flurry of snow and hurried after him.

"No wonder they managed to fight off five raids by the Danes," said Alfred, pointing along the line of the stockade. "It's all rough, country work, but under masterful command. In fact there's something almost familiar about the way this stockade is built."

Paeder grinned. "An outline more often found in old Roman ruins, I'm sure, but there are more marvels to see yet. No magic, just simple, practical things that work miracles."

It was the first village in Wessex that Vitellan had trained, and after it had withstood several raids by the Danes, dozens of other villages petitioned for his help. After a year he assembled a force of two hundred churls and razed a Danish camp near Leicester as an example to them. When word reached Alfred he invited Vitellan to a meeting, hoping to dissuade him from setting up a rival state.

Tension had been expected, and the gaunt, enigmatic Vitellan had everyone on edge at first. The discussions began with politics, fortifications, and strategy, then someone mentioned that Alfred could read. The discussions abruptly became a dialogue between Alfred and Vitellan on literature, poetry and history. At the end of the meeting the pale, clean-shaven commander stunned the onlookers by pledging total loyalty to the Wessex throne. He even offered to train Prince Alfred's own men.

The fifteen heads on stakes that topped the gates of Durvonum had by now been stripped down to skulls by the crows. There was arrogance in the gesture, proclaiming to the Danes that these people had slain their warriors and would be pleased to do likewise to anyone else who cared to attack.

Because all the villagers were armed and trained—men and women—the place was a total fighting machine. An attacker would encounter twice as many defenders as would be expected in such a place: *everyone* fought. Children carried weapons, put out fires, and even helped care for the wounded.

"Mind that you walk only between the little poles," said Paeder, taking Alfred's arm and guiding him.

"But you said we have to go across to that hut."

"Follow the path, my lord. They've planted lilies."

"Lilies? You mean there are gardens under the snow?"

"These lilies are small, conical pits with fire-hardened stakes at the bottom. In winter the snow covers them, in summer they conceal them with leaves and a thin layer of dust. Your foot would be guided down to the stake, and the point would skewer it, boot and all."

"Traps? In here, behind their own walls? Where they live?"

"If the Danes breached the wall they would not be expecting to find still more traps. It's cheap, simple, and very demoralizing for an enemy."

"And Vitellan's idea?"

"Of course."

The chief's hut was unexpectedly neat and orderly, with plank benches for visitors and no litter on the earth floor. Hides hung on the wall painted with crude Latin declarations of loyalty to the Christian church and to the Kingdom of Wessex. A crucifix was included for the benefit of the majority of his visitors, who could not read.

Daegryn greeted them in broken Latin that had obviously been learned by rote, then reverted to a Saxon dialect as he earnestly renewed his allegiance to Wessex and cursed the Danes. He showed them around the stockade and they watched the villagers training. Even though he had seen it all before, Bishop Paeder whistled at the teamwork and discipline that the churls showed. At last the prince raised what he thought was the sensitive subject of the Frigidarium. He had expected Daegryn to become suspicious and guarded, but Paeder had already explained that the prince was in Vitellan's confidence. The chief led the way, lighting a reed torch as they left the hut.

" 'Tis a great way to save salt for curin' or wood for smokin', sire," he explained. "Aye, and it's been in our village since the time of Christus. 'Tis true, and when Christus was leadin' his armies against the Pharaoh, so too were my ancestors packin' ice in the very fields that ye just rode through."

"I must make sure that the local priest comes here more often," murmured Bishop Paeder in Latin, and Alfred grinned.

The entrance to the Frigidarium was beneath a stone slab fireplace, and this was lifted aside by a dozen men using two stout poles. Narrow stone steps led down steeply into pitch blackness, and the chief hurried ahead with his smoky reed torch. Alfred counted ninety-two steps before they reached a small anteroom. With some effort Daegryn opened a massive, stone-inlaid wooden door. Cut into the stone lintel was RUFUS ME FECIT in neat, square letters.

"Observe, sire, the stonemason was literate," said Paeder as they entered. "That makes it very old."

"This place is Roman," said Alfred, holding his torch to the stone lining of the chamber while he shivered with the cold. "Look at the arches and stonework. The village must have been built over this chamber after the Romans left. Even the name *frigidarium* is a Latin term for a cold bath."

The chamber was about fifteen feet long and ten wide, and one could stand up straight near the middle of the roof's arches. Each stone block was neatly cut, faced, and fitted, but there were none of the carvings and decorations common in the Roman ruins that were scattered throughout Wessex. The place was built with a clean, solid grace, and had clearly been meant to last a very long time. The air was dank and clammy, and utterly still.

"So this place is where Vitellan, ah, lay?" Alfred asked the chief, kicking at the slush from the previous year's ice.

The man looked anxiously to Bishop Paeder.

"It's all right, Daegryn, tell the prince what you first told me," Paeder reassured him.

"Until two winters ago the great Lord Vitellan slept here, aye. He was a great Christian king, and spread the faith so far and killed so many pagans that Christus said, 'You are too good to go to heaven yet.

You will be kept here in this village, in case the pagans come back.' Us churls were commanded to make fresh ice each winter for his bed and in return could keep our mutton fresh here, without need of salt or smokin'.

"Then came the pagan Danes, and they burned our chapel and took the silver chalice. Aye, and they burned most of the village besides, and killed twenty people—and fifteen sheep, and six pigs, just for sport. They're cruel, godless pagans, says I to the other village Elders, or those Elders as was still alive, that is. It is time that we called on our sleepin' Master. We came down here and we called, and blew horns and whistles, but he did not wake. That's when I sent for Bishop Paeder, who is skilled in learnin' and cures. Gentor the Icekeeper was against me. He said only he had the right to say when the Master should be wakened and he refused to read out the sacred words that was carved on Lord Vitellan's stone bed. He called down all manner of curses from Heaven, but none came so I'd guess that Heaven thought that I was right. Bishop Paeder came—"

"That's enough, Daegryn," said Paeder. He glanced at Alfred, who nodded. "We wish to speak alone. Wait for us at the entrance." Daegryn smiled broadly, took his leave and bounded up the stairs.

"So Gentor is only in charge of making ice for this chamber?" asked Alfred, holding his torch to a row of grooves in the wall.

"He is the Icekeeper, but the position means more than just making ice. In a way he's more powerful than the chief. They sometimes call him Glacicida, as I recall. It's probably corrupted Latin."

Alfred stared at the far end of the chamber. Although some ice from the previous year had become a dark slush around the edges, the main mass was still solid and the meat embedded in it was frozen. Parts of the floor had been worn into deep grooves, where the villagers had carried blocks of packed snow and ice in for centuries. Other grooves were intentional, deliberately cut to carry meltwater into a small reservoir.

"The Romans built well," said Paeder, following Alfred's gaze. "Perhaps this was a cold room or cellar to chill their wine in summer."

"There are no ruins nearby. If I was building a cellar room I would have it right beneath my fort."

Paeder shook his head. "Dig hereabouts and you may well find some Roman foundations. I first heard of this place when the terrible comet-star flew through the sky thirty-five years ago. The villagers here built a whole chapel of packed snow and thatch, then petitioned the bishop to come and offer mass to drive the star away."

"Did he come?"

"Yes, but he took one look at the chapel and decided that the slightest breeze would bring it down on him. The youngest priest in his entourage was ordered in to say the mass."

Paeder shook his head.

"Yourself?" asked Alfred, raising an eyebrow.

"None other. Twenty summers old, and sure that I'd not live to see one more. The chapel did not collapse, though, and the comet-star went away. I had become a bishop myself by the time they petitioned me to come and revive their . . . Master. They may have remembered my supposed miracle with the comet-star.

"When I arrived the chief told me that a mighty Christian king had been sleeping beneath the village for hundreds of years. If we could revive him he would vanquish the Danes. The body was lying down here, packed in ice, amid frozen joints of mutton and pork. The odd thing was that it was soft to touch, while the flesh of the animals was solid.

"I began to have suspicions. I rubbed my fingers along the skin, then sniffed them. There was a faint scent of strong drink. Now any herbalist will tell you that a drunkard caught in the snow will have a better chance of surviving than a sober churl, so could this man have swallowed a massive draught of fortified mead, then had himself placed down here just hours before I arrived? He could then be revived as some ancient hero, with a senior father of the Church as a witness. After all, some priests claim to have the bones of saints in their churches to increase their own importance."

Alfred stared at the concave slab where Vitellan had lain. Chiseled into the rock were the words UT REVIVISCAM, MANE AQUA CALIDA CORPUS MEUM LAVET; POST MERIDIEM ALIQUIS IN SO MEUM SPIRET ET PECTUS MEUM APERTA MANU PERCUTIAT.

" 'TO RETURN ME TO LIFE: BATHE ME IN WARM WATER FOR A MORNING; BREATHE INTO MY MOUTH AND BEAT MY HEART WITH YOUR OPEN HAND FOR AN AFTERNOON,' " Alfred read slowly. "How was that?" he asked, looking hopefully to Paeder.

"You have the words, young lord, but your grammar is awful."

"Nevertheless, it is better than most in the village could do. It all seems too elaborate for these churls to have arranged."

"Vitellan is highly skilled as a warrior, and speaks Latin as well as Saxon."

"He speaks it *better* than Saxon, but we stray from your story. How did you deal with the villagers? Did you reprimand them?"

"Oh yes, I gave them hellfire and brimstone, and I told them that the comet-star might come back and eat them for lying to a bishop. Then I felt the body again. If the flesh was still soft it could only be because he had not been down here for very long. Perhaps he was still alive. He might be saved.

"I made them rig up a shallow bath, a trench lined with oxhide, and this was filled with warm water. Years ago, when I traveled to Rome, I saw a drowned fisherman brought back to life by a man who breathed down his mouth while another punched his ribs. I held Vitellan's head above the water while two of them did this, then ordered hot irons to be struck against his legs to try to shock him into life. All the while I prayed aloud. After perhaps an hour his heart was beating again, then he began to breathe by himself. By the time the sun was setting his eyes were open, and he could move his arms and speak. He spoke only Latin and said his name was Vitellan Bavalius. I gave everyone another warning and left, but when next I returned he was calling himself Vitellan and, and—"

"Rebuilding the Roman Empire. Do you still think it was a hoax?" asked Alfred.

"After what Vitellan has done? The man teaches a whole tradition of fighting that we know nothing of. Where did he learn it? In the Holy Land, or Byzantium? I hardly know what to believe."

Alfred paced restlessly. A brave and clever man might well take such a terrible chance to gain the status of a dead hero brought back to life. A brave and clever man might also attempt some strange and terrible voyage, across centuries instead of oceans.

"I have asked him if he is the fabled Artorius who shattered the armies of my ancestors many centuries ago," said Alfred, running his fingers along the neat Roman letters in the stone shelf. "Each time he has denied it, even though many churls insist that he is Artorius returned to life."

"Understandable," said Paeder. "Artorius was a Briton, and many Britons still hate us Saxons almost as much as the Danes. They would love Artorius to return and conquer the land for them."

Alfred frowned as he wrestled with two distasteful conclusions.

"Roman rule was within living memory when Artorius was alive, true, but this man remembers Rome as a mighty empire at its height."

Paeder wrung meltwater from the hem of his cloak and shivered.

"Perhaps he has been telling the truth for all these months past. Perhaps he really was born in Calleva in Anno Domini 54, when the Emperor Claudius reigned. He may really be Vitellan Bavalius, of the Imperial Roman Army."

They returned to the surface just as the ice cart was being driven in from the field. Gentor was walking slowly ahead of it, carrying the best formed of all the blocks that had been made that day. The team that had made the block walked on either side of the cart, garlanded with mistletoe. Gentor placed the block on a stone platform as the whole village watched, then five solemn children brought cups of hot, mulled mead for the Icekeeper and his chosen team. Those in the other teams were sent down to scour out the Frigidarium before the first of the new season's blocks were stacked in.

"A fine crop this year," said Alfred, inspecting the heavily loaded ice cart.

"It was not always so," replied Gentor, scowling. "There have been years when no snow has fallen."

"No snow? Then how did you get the ice?"

"We scraped frost from the grass and bushes, and we sent our folk far to the north to find snow. Many of us have died to preserve the sleep of our Master."

"I'm sure Vitellan is proud of you—"

"He is! He is! And he will come back to us when he has won your battles for you and killed all the Danes. His place is with us, living forever in the Frigidarium."

"Very good, Gentor, I'm sure Prince Alfred is impressed by your tradition of diligence," Paeder cut in. "Now, my lord, we have a long way to ride before nightfall."

"But, but I . . ."

Paeder led him quickly from the village and across the ramparts to where their escort was waiting.

"Gentor was getting agitated," he whispered. "He thinks that you want to keep Vitellan awake for years."

"And I do. The man is a treasurehouse of learning. Once the Danes are beaten he will be of even greater use, teaching us the lost scholarship of the Roman Empire."

"You do not understand Gentor, my lord. The man . . . well, gains a measure of immortality by being one of the long line of Icekeepers who has kept Vitellan alive. You might take that away from him by keeping his Master awake too long in a dangerous world."

Alfred shook his head sadly. Power came in many forms, yet people continued to pursue it with the same fervor. The Roman was Gentor's talisman, and he would not let go easily. Neither of them said any more on the long and intricate walk past the traps to their horses.

Alfred and Paeder had planned to spend the night in a fortified town to the northeast, then join Vitellan the next day. Their enigmatic ally was planning a new strategy against the Danes, and he wanted the prince to see his churls in action. All that they needed was a nearby raid by the Danes.

The Danes had begun to conduct raids on horseback five years before, riding swiftly down from their northern strongholds, raiding small towns, then retreating before the Wessex footsoldiers arrived. Vitellan's plan was simple: assemble a force of armed and mounted churls three times the size of a Danish raiding party, then post a network of scouts across the shire. The churls could not fight from horseback, but then neither could the Danes. It was only a matter of catching up with them.

The sun was down and the light was fading fast when a messenger brought word that Danish raiders had struck a hamlet some distance to the south, and that Vitellan had tracked them to a wood fifteen miles from where they were staying. It had been a bigger force than he had expected, but he had decided to pursue them anyway, and to attack at night. Alfred was alarmed: the odds were too heavily in favor of the Danes. He ordered his twenty men to mount up, then they set off through the twilight.

It took them two hours to reach the wood, as most of the journey was in near total darkness. The path through the trees was fairly wide, however, and there was a faint glow a long way ahead. When they stopped, the sounds of a distant battle came to them, and they knew that Vitellan was ahead.

"Brave, stupid gesture," muttered Alfred. "Forward, at a canter. Let's hope these local horses know this path in the dark."

It was a blind, headlong ride through the blackness, with only the hint of a glow ahead. Alfred only managed to fight down his panic at riding blind by placing his trust in the horse. The fast canter was a serene, floating motion—"

They slammed into the other group of riders head on, and it was only by the Danish shouts that they knew them to be the enemy. Alfred was thrown through the air into another rider, and when he crawled to his feet and drew his broadsword he found that it had snapped near the hilt. He flung it away, drew his dagger and lunged for a nearby shape in the frantic, struggling mass of men and horses. In such close fighting a short blade is a superior weapon, or so Vitellan had taught.

The fight was near anarchy, often with only the language of the curses as a guide to friend or Dane. Alfred grappled first, then stabbed if he felt sheepskin instead of the Wessex-style armor. A huge pair of hands seized his throat and would not let go no matter how many times he stabbed the Dane's side. Then they went down under a crushing weight that knocked the wind out of Alfred, and his face was forced into a bloody mush of snow and mud. Only two nights ago I was having a quiet mug of beer and reading Augustine's *Confessions,* he thought as the blind melee's din receded.

Gawking churls with torches were milling around as Alfred came back to his senses, and people were dragging the body of a horse off the body of the Dane that was pinning him down. The Dane's hands were still around his throat, but the grip was gone.

I'm a scholar, a patron of learning, I've met the Pope himself, he thought as they prized the dead fingers away. What am I doing in the mud under a pile of dead horses and . . . "filthy savages," he whispered.

"Did you hear that?" came Githek's voice. "The Prince is alive, easy now." Alfred was helped to his feet, and he shivered violently as the cold air chilled his soaked clothing through the mail.

"The Danes?" he asked through chattering teeth.

"All dead, my lord prince, but . . ." Githek's voice trailed off.

"But? But what?"

"It was a mistake. Vitellan's churls annihilated their camp, but were allowing these few to escape. He wanted a few Danes alive to witness that mere churls had beaten them."

Alfred sank to the ground, clutching at his hair.

"My lord?" asked Githek anxiously. "Is it your head?"

"Yes, my head," replied Alfred, almost laughing at the irony. "But it is not serious."

They carried Alfred into the woods, where a bonfire was being lit, and he fell asleep even as they were removing his armor. He awoke well after the dawn to find Vitellan waiting for him, already scrubbed and shaved. The prince studied the enigmatic warrior as they talked, fascinated by the odd frailty of his features. He had large, brown eyes, small but full lips, and a straight nose that was smoothly rounded at the tip. His hair was black and thick, like that of the people Alfred had met in Rome. A few scratches and a bandage on his wrist were the only evidence that he had been in the fighting too.

He cares for his appearance, thought Alfred, he keeps standards that no longer exist. He is so alone, his standards are all that are left of his world. I am alone, because I am a scholar in a world of barbarians, but Vitellan is a soldier from a time when even mere fighters knew more than the greatest of Wessex scholars. Alfred's frustration and longing for the greatness of the past almost blotted out the pain of his wounds.

Gentor had found his way there during the night, and was cooking his Master's breakfast not far away. He scowled at Alfred.

The Danes had raided a small, badly fortified hamlet, then ridden hard for this wood, some thirty miles away. Vitellan had posted a network of mounted scouts, and one of these reported the raid to the main group of Wessex churls while the fires were still alight in the hamlet. They soon found the riders' trail, then rode fast in pursuit. Once they reached the wood the churls dismounted and slipped as silently as foxes through the frosty undergrowth. The Danes were taken by surprise and slaughtered.

"So you led the fighting, Vitellan," observed Alfred. "Is your stomach better?"

"I always lead the fighting," replied Vitellan in slow, heavily accented Saxon. "But yes, the cramps and bleeding have eased for the past week. Thank you for coming to my aid. That was very brave, riding blind through the woods like that."

"I'm sorry to spoil—"

"Please! Say nothing of it. Anyway, that blind fight in the woods has increased the respect of your men for you."

"I'd rather impress them with my grasp of Latin."

"That would not impress the Danes, but it can come later."

After they had eaten they walked through to the remains of the Danish camp. Alfred noted that it was being systematically stripped of everything of value. Not one Dane was alive, and there was a great deal of blood on the muddy snow. Their mutilated bodies were piled in a heap, naked. Many were missing their heads.

Vitellan took him to where two kidnapped women who had survived the fighting were telling one of Vitellan's captains all that they could remember of the raiders' tactics and methods. One carried the head of her recent ravisher by its long, blond hair. She was thin and disheveled, and there was mania in her eyes. Her dress was torn, and there was still blood on her legs.

"This is Prince Alfred of Wessex," said Vitellan, and the bruised, bandaged, and filthy Alfred cringed inwardly as the two women goggled for a moment, then dropped to their knees.

"Please, stand up," said Alfred, taking their hands. "I think we have all spent enough time in the mud. Was, ah, that your own work?" he asked the thin woman, indicating the Dane's head.

"Oh yes, sire, when the attack started he tries to jump up, but I trips him," she said breathlessly. "I snatches up a little cookin' knife, then pulls his hair back and cuts his throat like Lord Vitellan shows me. Oh brave sire, I hears about how ye charged 'em in the dark and was wounded—"

"It will seem less impressive once I have washed," Alfred cut her short in embarrassment. "One day I must visit your village, when it is rebuilt. Mind that you show that head to your people, that all may know how you fought."

"Oh yes, sire, it will sit on a good high pole, I swear. And ye'll always have a welcome in our poor home if the Danes burn your castle or somesuch."

"Have no false illusions," said Vitellan as they walked on. "The Danes fought back fiercely, and two churls died for every one of them. Still, they were wiped out: their heads will grace pikes, and their skins will be flayed from their bodies and nailed to the doors of our churches as a warning."

"That will cheer our people, but it will surely antagonize the Danes in north Mercia as well," said Alfred doubtfully.

"Of course, my lord. Better to have your enemy making stupid decisions through blind rage than to have him planning his raids against you intelligently."

"My brother's vassals said that your churls could never beat Danish cavalry. I wish they could see this."

"These Danes were not cavalry. They used their horses like their longboats, for the fast transport of footsoldiers."

Alfred felt annoyed with himself. This man always went straight to the enemy's weakness and hit him there. If he was a Roman, then this was another legacy of their vast empire. Their armies had fought countless battles in dozens of countries for centuries, and the lessons learned had been preserved and taught. One could do that when the commanders knew how to write reports. How could Rome ever have fallen, with soldiers like Vitellan?

And yet Vitellan had been born three and a half centuries before Rome had yielded to Alaric. Something had changed. Alfred began to think about the ice chamber that he had seen the day before. It was a marvel as well, yet so simple . . . as simple as pursuing mounted Danes with mounted churls. There were costs, however, such as the oil that had to be drunk before he could sleep for centuries in the Frigidarium. It was a corrosive poison, and had injured his throat and stomach severely, perhaps beyond healing. It was strange that the oil that kept him alive for so long should also shorten his life. Even as Alfred pondered the paradox Vitellan stopped abruptly and clutched his stomach, gasping.

"Just a twinge," he said as Alfred steadied him. "The first for some time."

"Shall I call for help?"

"No! No, the men would think that I was wounded, and we cannot have that."

Gentor had noticed, however, and was already hurrying over. He drew a small clay jar from his pouch and unstoppered it.

"The pain is back, Master, yes? Drink this, quickly, you know how it always soothes you."

"Thank you Gentor. What would I do without you?"

"Such a cruel, rough world, Master, full of harsh food to hurt your poor stomach. In the Frigidarium you would be safe, Gentor could look after you so well."

Vitellan swallowed the contents of the small jar, which he could neither smell nor taste. Alfred caught the suggestion of something strong and sweet on the air.

"A few months more, Gentor, that is all I need. Once the Danes have been driven away I shall return to the ice, and I shall be much less of a worry to you there."

"But surely you would not do that!" exclaimed Alfred, alarmed. "You have so much to teach us."

"But I am dying, my stomach is ruined by the freezing oil. If I am to die soon, I would like to take generations to do it." He laughed softly. "Death may be close behind me, but he will freeze his fingers if he tries to take me with too much haste."

"That's just foolishness."

"Horace wrote that it's good to be foolish at the right time."

"But what has the future to offer, Vitellan? The last time you were frozen the Roman Empire passed away. What might happen in another seven centuries? Judgment Day may come in the year of the Millennium."

"You could not understand, it is like becoming a type of god. The star Sirius is blue now, but it used to be red. Red dogs were sacrificed to it in the temples. The sun seems to be colder, too. I remember the summers being quite hot, and the winters mild. There are great cycles in the sky that mortal men cannot see—but I can. Once, in the time of Lucretius, my countrymen thought that mortals like us, rather than gods, live in the sky. If they are very big and very slow, men could not perceive them in a lifetime, yet I could. Empires, religions, I outlive them all in my chamber. The prospect of sleeping there does have an allure, just like that of being king."

He pointed to Gentor, who smiled and bowed, and showed no sign of moving away.

"Here is the faithful captain of my ship through time. The tradition of maintaining the Frigidarium has outlasted even Rome's rule here, and I have more than enough oil left to be put to sleep again. The jar lay beside me in the ice."

"Horace, Lucretius . . . you speak of their writings so easily, yet most of their works are lost to us and all the gold in the world could not buy them back," said Alfred bitterly. "Much of the wisdom of Rome is gone forever, apart from what is in your head. Could you stay just one year more? If your stomach does not worsen you could teach us so much."

"Scholarship is a luxury in such an age as this."

"So teach us more about fighting as well. A land safe for scholars will be safe for your village too, and then churls who tend your ice chamber."

Vitellan put his hands on his hips and looked around at the carnage from the night before, then closed his eyes for a moment.

"I often wish that I could close my eyes and awake in my old villa. Oh, we had wars back then, but at least there were centers of civilization to retire to. All this countryside was peaceful farmland, with towns, stadia, baths, temples, and fine villas. The weather was warmer then, and the harvests were always good. I would spend the mornings reading, then there would be long afternoons and evenings talking with my friends about all manner of things: Virgil's works, chariot races, the price of corn, old battles we had fought, the Emperor's new mistress . . . People like us need some civilized and safe place as a touchstone."

"Then help me build one."

Vitellan turned to look at the battered, filthy Wessex prince. In this raw and savage age he was fighting for literacy as well as his homeland. He was a rare type of leader in such times.

"All right, then, I shall stay for one year more, or until I begin to sicken. Poor Gentor, you will just have to be patient."

Gentor scowled, but dared not contradict his Master directly. The inspection continued, and Vitellan showed the prince how his churls had skirted the sentries with his own berserkers. He had chosen only men who had lost wives and children in earlier raids for the first wave. The Danish and Norse berserker warriors had terrified them for decades, yet here were local churls who also fought in such a frenzy that they felt no pain and seemed to have the strength of two. Alfred was shown one man who was still hysterical and weeping, with his face in his hands. He killed nine Danes before his axe broke, and then dispatched two more with the shaft.

"Then he attacked his fellow churls for not leaving more Danes for him to kill," Vitellan explained.

"You—you trained him to do that? Can you train my men too?"

"Berserkers are easy enough to train, but they have limited uses. I have seen a pike-wall of women stop a group of Danish berserkers by fighting intelligently and staying together. I had trained them too, of course."

"The women killed them?"

"They held them back until the archers came and shot the Danes down, but that is not the lesson. The women fought as a team and held together, and a dozen berserkers had to explain some very embarrassing deaths to Wotan, or whoever their underworld's god is supposed to be."

"Their gods are said to take badly to that sort of death," said Alfred, laughing out aloud.

Later that day Vitellan had another attack of cramps in his stomach, and this time he vomited blood. Gentor begged him to move back near his village, so that he could be frozen quickly if his condition worsened. Alfred compromised: they would stay in a small fortified town nine miles from the village, and would discuss Roman methods of warfare until Vitellan either recovered or was carried off to the ice chamber.

Vitellan had never made a secret of his origins to Alfred or Paeder, although he avoided the subject with everyone else outside his own village. His father had been an officer in the Roman army, and the youth had followed the same career. He had fought in several areas of northern Europe, and was finally posted to the north of Britain where the Caledonians were making sporadic raids. His uncle owned a large estate in the south, and it was while he was on leave and visiting him that he had met Flavia.

She was the daughter of a minor official, and was captivated by the strong, handsome young soldier who already had a reputation for bravery and was rising fast through the ranks. When he returned to the northern forts they had exchanged passionate letters for two years. Vitellan's uncle had also been impressed by his brave yet studious nephew, and when the childless farmer had died in a boating accident, the young soldier was found to be named as his sole heir. He returned south to the estate, only to find that Flavia had married a local farmer a year before. Her letters had all been lies.

The farmer, Drusus, had the advantage of being a neighbor of Flavia, and had played up to her vanity while disturbing her with stories of how hard life was for the wife of an officer. If she and Vitellan went to an African garrison the heat would make her skin dry and wrinkled. If they were sent north, the cold would make her face red and frostbitten. Drusus knew that Flavia's worst nightmare was the prospect of losing her beauty. Although the farmer soon won her over, she continued to write her romantic letters to Vitellan because the young soldier was exciting and dashing by comparison. She reassured herself that some hairy Caledonian would probably kill him and resolve her dilemma. Instead he returned alive, and rich . . . and there could be no accounting for her behavior toward him.

Vitellan bought a release from the army and retired to his estate. At first he could do little more than brood about his lost love. He alternately thought about murdering her or seducing her back from the fat, prosperous yokel who was her husband. It all came to nothing. They were on their guard against him, and their slaves and servants were too loyal to be bribed into letting him near the villa. He searched for distraction in study and in the running of his own estate, but the bitterness remained, eating away inside him.

A Greek physician named Milos began to treat him for melan-
choly, and they became friends after some months. The Greek said that
he had once worked on an estate high in the Alps, to the north of
Verona. The owner had been experimenting with ways of preserving
livestock through winter. They were fed an oil made from an extract of
insects that could live in the snow. This allowed them to be frozen alive
over winter—without the need of costly fodder. Milos had stolen a jar
of the oil when he moved on, or so he had said.

His own experiments were disappointing. The oil was a type of
poison, and if the animal survived the treatment and subsequent freezing, its flesh was too toxic to eat after it had been revived. The Greek had
continued to tinker with the technique, however, and he showed Vitellan a rabbit that had been revived after five years in a deep cellar on
blocks of ice. The rabbit had also survived the effects of the poison because it had been administered in small doses over several weeks.

Milos had wanted to try the ultimate experiment with the oil by
freezing a treated human, but his ethics as a physician prevented him
from merely buying a slave and force-feeding the oil to him. Under-
standably, free Roman citizens expressed no interest in volunteering for
such an experiment, and Milos was too fond of life to drink the oil and
have someone else freeze him. Vitellan listened to his speculations with
interest and sympathy, however. He had been shipwrecked when he was
seventeen, and had spent five days in the water before being washed
ashore. He had an odd fancy that the cold had suspended his life while
he was adrift, preserving him rather than killing him. Milos and what he
called his Oil of Frosts seemed to be another version of the same thing
as far as Vitellan was concerned. A scheme began to form in his mind:
he wanted Flavia dead to smother his own passion for her, yet he did not
want to kill her. Why not suspend his body alive, in ice, until she was
dead?

Milos was delighted at the prospect. He conducted an experiment
with Vitellan, treating him with the oil, then freezing him for five days.
Vitellan had insisted that it be for five days, the same period as he had
spent adrift on the sea. Milos revived him successfully, and shortly after

that Vitellan had bought what remained of the Oil of Frosts and all the Greek's notes. He now set about ridding himself of Flavia by killing her relative to him. He had the Frigidarium built several days' journey to the north, and hired local villagers to maintain it. Finally he pretended to move to Gaul and marry. When word was brought of Flavia's death, he would be revived to come back as his own son. His faithless lover would have lived out her full life and be gone, and there would be nothing left to fuel his obsession with her. Milos was hired as the first Icekeeper, and Vitellan was launched into the one-way river of time.

Something had gone wrong, however. When he was next revived many centuries had passed. Perhaps his steward's successor had betrayed him, and had continued to pay Milos and the villagers to keep the ice chamber functioning long after Flavia died. After a time the payments would have stopped, but the annual gathering of ice had become an important ceremony by then. It had taken a raid by the Danes to break that tradition.

Alfred, Paeder, and Gentor knew the full story, the villagers suspected that he was Artorius returned to life, while the rest of Wessex was told that he was a great Christian general from Byzantium.

Vitellan's latest victory was the cause of much local celebration. For the first time a party of raiders had been wiped out entirely, with not a single survivor. A frame and thatch hall was decorated with holly and mistletoe, and the weapons, armor, and heads of the Danes were hung on the walls while feasters from all the nearby towns honored the brave and brilliant commander.

Alfred spoke in praise of Vitellan, and of the need to support the king against the Danes, then Paeder blessed the food and drink and the feast began. As usual the Roman confined himself to broth and melted snow while the bishop looked on in distaste over his whole roast goose. Gentor stood behind them, tasting his master's food and guarding his back.

"Water and mush," snorted Paeder as he sliced a leg from his goose. "How can you stand it when such a spread is within your reach?"

"My senses of taste and smell have been burned away by the freezing oil. What I cannot taste I cannot miss. Besides, solid food would make my stomach bleed."

Paeder tore the flesh from a drumstick in two bites, then flung the bone to a nearby dog.

"You could be a king in your own right," said Paeder casually to Vitellan. "Why do you help us so much and ask nothing in return?"

"I get order in return, Bishop, and I secure a scholar and builder on the throne of Wessex."

"And when the Danes are gone, what then?"

"Perhaps I shall sleep frozen for a while. That would make me easier to guard, eh Gentor?" he said over his shoulder in accented Saxon.

"Aye master," said the Icekeeper impassively.

"So is that why you want peace, Vitellan?" asked Paeder. "So that your village can gather ice undisturbed? So that you can live forever without really being alive? What about your friends here?"

Vitellan stared at Paeder for a moment, then sipped water from his drinking horn.

"I make friends easily enough."

"You have friends here, now! You can teach us so much, we want to keep you, to honor you."

"I want civilization."

"But we have that."

"You gnaw meat straight off the bone, and not one in a thousand can write or read."

"Well, I—we wash our hands after meals, not wipe them on our clothing like the pagan Danes."

"True, true, and you are good friends. Sometimes I am tempted." Gentor came forward to refill his water jug, but was jostled as the bishop flung another bone to the dogs. The jug rolled from the table and smashed on the floor. A churl came running with another jug and Gentor filled it from his jar, glaring at the bishop as he poured.

"You never met so much as a single Apostle?" the bishop asked hopefully, returning to a private obsession of his. "Did you never meet any who are mentioned in the Gospels?"

"Most were dead by the time I was born," Vitellan explained patiently. "I did once serve briefly in Egypt, but after that I served and lived in the western part of the Empire."

"I know, I know, I've asked this all before," he sighed.

"What is it you want to know, Bishop Paeder? The chronicles of Christus' followers seem fairly complete."

"It would be good to have, oh, just some little detail about Him. The color of His eyes—"

"They were brown."

"What?"

"You never told me what you really wanted to know, Bishop. My father met Christus while garrisoned in Jerusalem."

The bishop's eyes bulged. Although his jaw worked up and down, no words came, so Vitellan continued.

"Father was keeping the peace during a sermon. He was in command of ten soldiers then, but later he got a commission to—"

"Never mind that!" said the bishop in a strangled whisper. "What did Christus say to him?"

"Why, nothing. Father spoke no Aramaic. He said that Christus seemed a kind and reasonable man, though."

"Your father saw the Son of God and noticed nothing more than, than . . . the fact that he was kind and reasonable?" the bishop bellowed in amazement as he rose to his feet. Most of the hall fell silent and turned to watch, though they could not follow his Latin.

"Well, that's all he said, but he did become a Christian himself in later years. It was a dangerous act in those times. He had me christened during the reign of Emperor Nero, you know."

Paeder sat down heavily. "Christus had brown eyes, and seemed kind and reasonable . . ." He sighed and shook his head, then began to laugh quietly. There were tears on his cheeks when he finally raised his head again. "In a way, that's what I wanted to know," he whispered, staring out across the hall. "I need a kind and reasonable God. We all do."

"Much better than that undisciplined Roman pantheon," agreed Vitellan. "That's why I—"

Paeder snapped out of his reverie. "No wait, I must be clearheaded and remember all this. Please, may I?" Paeder seized Vitellan's water jug and drank deeply. "No more than a glance at Christus and your father was converted! Ah yes, I must chronicle this, every word, every detail that you can recall. The devil, there's something sharp in this water!"

"What? It should be melted snow!" said Vitellan, at once alarmed.

"I'm burning, it's burning me up!" gasped Paeder, clutching his throat as he fell forward across the table.

People rushed from all sides to help the bishop, and Alfred's own physician bent him across a bench and forced a finger down his throat to make him throw up some of the poison. Guards ran to seize the serving churls. It was some time before Alfred realized that the poison had been meant for Vitellan. As Paeder was carried out Alfred found the Roman by the hearth, his arms folded behind his back and his head bowed in thought.

"That was meant for you," Alfred began.

"I know. Someone must have placed the poison in the jug before Gentor poured the water from his jar. He drank from his jar to prove it to me just now. He is still alive."

"The Danes must have—"

"Not the Danes." Vitellan reached into his sleeve and took out a square of folded parchment. It was stained and grimy, as if it had been trodden under foot.

" 'Twas I who found it, after the bishop was carried off," said Gentor, looking straight into Alfred's eyes and folding his arms. "It were right under the Master's bench."

"There are two words on this scrap of parchment," Alfred observed.

Vitellan sighed as he returned the note to his sleeve. "After seven centuries, they are still after me. This is their way of claiming the honor of killing me."

He was shivering in spite of the blazing fire. Vitellan had always looked anemic, but now there was a change in his bearing as well. He seemed crushed, beaten.

"Is, ah, there another Frigidarium, Vitellan? Is some enemy pursuing you across the years?"

"I am being pursued," said Vitellan, "but . . ." He paused, unable to find the words that he needed. Perhaps he cannot find words that I can understand, Alfred wondered. They were both being hunted.

"Her hate is pursuing me, although she is long dead." He shook his head suddenly, as if to clear it. "You must spread the word that I have sailed for Rome on a pilgrimage. They cannot know about how I live so long as yet, they will think that I live as other men but just never grow old. A few centuries more, that's all I need. When I'm revived I shall move to Gaul, grow a beard, change my name completely, become a priest. They are looking for a warrior, after all."

His eyes were dull, and his words were slurred and careless. Alfred seized his shoulders and shook him.

"The assassins were Danes, Vitellan, or churls in their pay."

"No. If the tradition of maintaining the Frigidarium could be maintained for centuries, then their hate could as well."

"But who are *they*, then?"

He seemed to relax, slumping against a heavy beam near the hearth. It was as if the fear had gone out of him once he had accepted the threat from his distant past.

"Lucia's descendants, and mine. Those of our child."

Gentor fetched a stool and guided him to it. Vitellan cowered beside the fire, as if anticipating the years to come in the Frigidarium.

"Fear not, Master," crooned Gentor. "None but the Prince and his bishop know about the ice chamber outside the village."

"Lucia's people may find me there, too."

"Then we'll fight them off, Master. Ye can lie safe there until the end of time."

In the days that followed Gentor slipped away to the village to prepare for the return of their Master. He sent back a small jar of golden-colored oil from the store in the Frigidarium, and Vitellan began to drink small measures of it. In small doses it was not lethal, while the beneficial part seemed to accumulate in his body. It burned and convulsed his stomach, and the loss of blood from internal bleeding soon had him too weak to stand.

It was during these long winter evenings, as he lay in his fireside bed, that he told Alfred the part of his past that only Gentor had known about until now. He had actually broken his journey through time twice before that final vast leap. His steward had been instructed to revive him after twenty-five years, not after Flavia's death. Flavia was by then middle-aged, with seven children. Vitellan returned as his own son and resumed the running of his estate. He also courted Lucia, Flavia's eldest daughter.

"Oh, she was reluctant enough to enter my bed," he told Alfred while a distant chant for Bishop Paeder's recovery mixed with the crackling of the fire. "Her mother had told her that anticipation keeps a man ardent, but when I reminded her that Flavia had made my supposed father anticipate, then given him nothing . . . well, it must have been inherited guilt, for she let me have my way with no more ado.

"Flavia had not aged gracefully, I must emphasize. The paint was thick on her wrinkles, and she dyed her hair every day. Her husband Drusus had prospered and she loved to stage great revels for the local landowners and generally play the temptress, but her figure had sagged with twenty-five years and seven children. At any rate, I was invited to one of these feasts, now that her daughter was sleeping with me. After all those years I finally came face to face with Flavia again. She even drew me aside from the other guests to ask if I meant to marry her daughter."

"I see," said Alfred in a hollow, flat voice. "So you killed her while posing as your own son."

Vitellan began to laugh, but was stopped by a coughing fit. Alfred gave him water to drink after tasting it himself.

"Civilized men have more refined perversions, my young barbarian prince," he said.

Alfred bristled for a moment. "We may live in the shadow of Rome's memory, but we do have civilization. Would you prefer a Dane as a patron?"

Vitellan shrugged. "No, I merely stress how different we were long ago. Revenge often had the status of a high art, and I practiced it well. All that I did was tell Flavia that I really was Vitellan Bavalius, the lover that she had jilted as a girl. It was hard, but I was able to convince her. Apart from my appearance, I knew far too much about her and the things that had passed between us.

"Only now did I have my revenge. I told her that I had found a potion that granted eternal youth—which was true in a way. I'd meant to share it with her, but Drusus had seduced her away with his talk of comfortable, secure prosperity so I had kept it for myself. Now she begged me to give it to her, to restore her face and figure. She promised to forsake Drusus and go with me. It was her weakness, she would give the world to be young again. Nothing mattered to her so much as that. I dangled the promise before her then snatched it back, explaining that I could only halt aging, not reverse it, and the prospect of living forever with someone who looked old enough to be my mother did not appeal. Lucia was a different matter, though."

"You do me an injustice," said Alfred. "I find that more cruel than a knife through the heart, for all the barbarian that I may be."

"The details of what happened later that night . . . they would even unsettle a Dane. I departed early, and Lucia left a slave in her bed and slipped away to my estate. While we fornicated our way through the night, Flavia stole through her villa and silently slew her husband and family. Then she had a slave draw her a warm bath and slashed her wrists. Her mind had probably snapped when I told her that jilting me for Drusus had robbed her of eternal youth, but she did her work so quietly that the sun was up and Lucia was on her way home before the slaves realized what had happened.

"I wish that I could have kept silent as I lay there with Lucia, but I had told her everything. I just had to share my triumph, secrets beg to be shared. All that I concealed was the method of keeping myself young, so she never knew about the Frigidarium."

Alfred emptied his cup, then poured more mead from the jar. He drank the second measure straight down.

"The tongue grows loose when there is company in bed, Vitellan. Spies and agents would have a very poor business if it were not for that."

"I know that now. While we lay tangled together she thought it a great joke on her mother, and was starry-eyed at the prospect of living eternally with me. After she returned home to find her entire family and favorite slave dead, all that changed. She tried to denounce me, but the authorities knew that she was obviously deranged with grief so her wild story was given no credit.

"I was badly frightened, and tormented by guilt. I had wanted revenge, but not that sort of horror. I kept to myself, and a few months went by. I learned that Lucia was pregnant . . . then my taster died of a strong, subtle poison.

"At once I hired extra guards for my villa, and I began to sleep armed. Lucia was ahead of me, and had planted assassins among my newly hired guards. There was a frantic, desperate fight in my room one night in which I killed the two assassins and one innocent guard. They had forgotten that I was a trained and experienced soldier, but next time it would be different. I told everyone that I was moving to Gaul again, then I prepared to return to the Frigidarium."

"And something went wrong?"

"No, it went as planned. After fifty years more my steward's son revived me, and I returned as my great-grandson this time. For five years it was idyllic; I have told you about living here at the height of the Roman Empire already. Heaven on earth, yet the old guilt still lingered. My father had had me christened nearly a century before, and I began to pray, do good works, trying to atone for my sins. The priests preached forgiveness for even the worst crimes, after all. The nightmare passed. Lucia had disappeared years before, taking our baby son with her, and few remembered what Flavia had done.

"Lucia was alive, though, and in her seventies. She had been traveling the Roman Empire, seeking the immortal man who had driven her mother to murder and suicide. Every so often she would return to the old estates in Britain, just to check if I had paid a visit as one of my descendants. Suffice to say that I killed an assassin in the year Anno Domini 161 . . . who turned out to be one of my own grandsons. Again I returned to the Frigidarium, planning to sleep until Lucia was dead, then return as somebody else. I would move to Hispania, buy an estate by the Tagus.

"The village elders were told how to revive me, the Icekeeper was reappointed, gold was hidden, and it was arranged that each year a messenger would come from my villa. As long as he told them that Lucia was alive I would be kept frozen. Somehow the scheme went wrong this time. I was not revived for seven centuries." With his story at an end Vitellan sat staring at the glowing coals in the hearth. "After seven hundred years the coals still look the same," he said, shaking his head.

Alfred drained his cup again. "If enough time passes anything can happen," he said. "Lucia may have learned the truth about you, but not where you were lying frozen. She and her children may have bribed your servants to send the message that she was alive for so long that, well, the villagers forgot who you were, or how to wake you."

"Perhaps. At first I thought that I had outlived her hate. I told Gentor the story soon after Paeder revived me, but he said that the message business was unknown to the villagers. As far as they were concerned I was a great warrior, only to be woken in times of dire peril. Thirty generations, Alfred. A living tradition of revenge."

"Now you will flee again in your time chamber." Alfred's words were a statement, flat and neutral.

"The idea sickens me. I have been alive eight hundred and sixteen years, yet have walked and breathed for only thirty-one. What else can I do, though?"

"My physician says that you cannot drink more of that oil without killing yourself."

For a moment he turned his head so that the light outlined his face like that of a skull. The effect startled Alfred, who gasped and drew back. Vitellan turned again, and the light restored his life to him.

"I am a living ghost, and I shall be dying as I am frozen. The idea appeals . . . the dying man who lives for centuries, the living dead."

Alfred flung his cup against the wall as he stood up. It bounced, clattered, and lay dented beside the fire as he began to pace the floor.

"I expect to hear this sort of talk from senile old men on their deathbeds, but not from you. You're young and strong; if you were to stop drinking that caustic oil you would be as healthy as me."

"I have caused great evil. Only my life can be payment in full."

"You played a cruel joke that led to the death of no more than a dozen people. One Dane could do worse in a rampage through a defeated village. Every time we beat the Danes back we save our people from just such a fate, and *you* are our greatest weapon against them. You cower like some ragged churl caught stealing wine, yet all of Wessex hails you as the hero who saved them from the invaders."

Alfred paced back and forth before the fire as he was speaking, his hands behind his back and his head down. He stopped for a moment, raised his foot above the dented cup . . . then reached down and snatched it up.

"A civilized man repairs and builds, no matter what his temper would have him do," he muttered as he bent the rim back with his fingers. "Look at me, Vitellan. I am the most civilized man in any position of power in this entire land. I need your help." He sat on the edge of Vitellan's bed. "Just think, on the night that Lucia and you were bedded together Flavia might just as easily have drunken herself into a stupor and been carried away to sleep it off by her slaves. She would probably have been a fearsome and bitter mother-in-law, but there would have been no terrible evil weighing you down. You would have died surrounded by your children and grandchildren some time in the second century, and would probably never have used the Frigidarium again."

Vitellan closed his eyes. "I went to sleep as a prosperous Roman farmer, and I woke with Rome shattered and overgrown."

"But Byzantium—"

"From what Paeder has told me, Byzantium is just a circus by comparison. I have been just a centurion in the Roman army, but now I am a great commander—yet who am I commanding? If I had seen you and your rabble coming over the hill seven of my years ago I'd have ordered my legionaries to charge just as soon as I could have drawn breath. Now I design your defenses, show your blacksmiths how to make better armor and weapons, train your warriors, play with your children . . . I've always liked children, yet my own child spawned a dynasty that's dedicated to killing me."

Alfred held his cup up in the firelight, then bent the rim a little more. "If I had done some accidental evil, I would spend my life doing good works to atone for it. What is better, my friend: to hide within a lump of ice, or to help me build a secure and prosperous kingdom? Think upon it."

Alfred was studying reports of the latest Danish movements when Gentor arrived to beg an audience with him. The Icekeeper was too fearful of eavesdroppers to speak indoors, so he led him outside, to the middle of a large courtyard. The snow drifted down around them as they stood talking and a chill wind tugged at their clothing. Alfred was attentive and patient as Gentor took a scrap of parchment from his pouch and showed it to the prince.

"The village chief, Daegryn, found it," he said urgently. "It was on the very stone that leads to the Frigidarium."

"Pretty calligraphy," observed Alfred. "The sort that comes from Meath, I believe."

"But look at what it says—sire!"

"*Lucia,* ah, *vivit.*"

"*Lucia vivit,* sire. It says Lucia lives."

"The—is that the message, the coded message? Was that on the note found after Bishop Alfred was poisoned?"

"Yes, yes, those assassins, the Master's own descendants, they're still here, trying to kill him."

"But we knew that from the note at the feast. We know that it's hopeless to escape them. All that Vitellan can do is flee into time again."

"Sire, they know where the Frigidarium is now!" shouted Gentor, and several distant men-at-arms turned to stare at them through the drifting flakes.

Alfred looked at the parchment again, tracing the words with his finger. Gentor stood wringing his hands, his face contorted with anguish.

"Lucia lives," muttered Alfred. "Lucia's hate lives, aye, that's certain. A slight is paid back with a cruel joke, then many murders result. Should it not end here, after seven hundred years? What would you have us do, Gentor the Icekeeper?"

"Post guards at the village, build a fort over it."

"And what good would that do? Vitellan has been in the care of your village ten times longer than I am likely to live. The generations who pursue him need just bide their time and breed until the guards are needed elsewhere, or the fort is abandoned. Then the assassins would enter the Frigidarium and plunge knives through his chilled heart, cut off his head and put it on a pike to warm and rot in the summer sun—"

"No! No more, sire, I beg you," shrieked Gentor, falling to his knees in the snow with his hands over his ears. "We must build another ice chamber, one that is well hidden."

"Your villagers can do that."

"They can't cut stone and build proper walls and arches, but your army has masons and carpenters who could do it."

Seize what is most precious to someone, and you can lead them wherever you like. It took all of Alfred's willpower to hold the smile down. He hoped that the strain gave him a grim expression.

"I don't even have the men to defend this part of my brother's kingdom. This did not worry you when Bishop Paeder was poisoned, and you first realized that the assassins were still in pursuit."

"But we didn't realize that the Master had nowhere safe to hide."

"Well, you shall damn well have to learn to cut stone and build another chamber. In the meantime, Vitellan will stay in my care, and in the service of King Ethelred of Wessex."

"No! He is ours," shrieked Gentor, jumping to his feet in a flurry of snow. "Only we can protect him."

Shouting at high authority was overstepping the mark in itself, and it was time to remind Gentor of it. Alfred unfolded his arms, let a hand fall to the pommel of his sword, then began to advance. Gentor tried to rally his defiance, but failed. He took a step back, caught his foot on something hidden in the snow and fell sprawling. Alfred glared down at his vanquished foe. To the onlookers it seemed as if the Prince had pushed him over by magic.

"You could not protect the Frigidarium from those who have been pursuing Vitellan through time, Gentor. Go now, build a more secret chamber, then Vitellan will return to you. While I guard him he will show us how to fight as the Romans did. We shall impose the Pax Romana on the Danes, and the land will be even more safe for your Master's sleep."

"Lucia's descendants nearly poisoned him while he was in your care," whined Gentor.

"While you stood behind his back. I understand you, Gentor," he said as he nodded and allowed himself a grim smile. "Without him you are just a churl, but while Vitellan is in that chamber you are the keeper of an immortal, you become part of something immortal yourself. I need Vitellan too! I would not exchange him for five thousand men-at-arms. Now go away and dig your chamber, and do a better job of hiding it this time."

Wessex, the British Isles: 7 April 870, Anno Domini

As the winter eased and gave way to spring both Vitellan and Paeder recovered their strength, and both returned to the fighting. The Danish host was trying to advance into the heart of Wessex, but the defenders had fought them to a standstill. It was the Danes' first serious setback in Britain, and there were more to come. Alfred and Paeder sat watching their men prepare an ambush while their horses grazed beside the road.

Tall poplars were being cut almost through, and were already braced with ropes.

"Sometimes I feel like hunting down that Gentor and making him drink some of that poison himself," grumbled Paeder, rubbing his stomach. "Eight months of watered beer and beef soup, and even now the physician cannot say if I shall ever eat solid food again."

"He only poisoned you by accident," replied Alfred. "Even with Vitellan, he fed him only enough of some type of poison to unsettle his stomach and make him think that he was sick."

"He should be punished," muttered Paeder, continuing to rub at his stomach. "If you caught one of your servants doing that to you, why he'd be worm food within the hour."

Alfred felt curiously relaxed, even though a battle was only minutes away. Now that the unseen enemy had been defeated, it was almost a welcome relief to be fighting mere Danish warriors.

"Gentor was fighting for the most important thing in his life, like a priest defending his church from the Danes. Besides, he is the Icekeeper, the hereditary captain of Vitellan's ship of ice, and our Roman friend may want to use it again. Whatever else you could say about Gentor, he is probably the best, most dedicated Icekeeper that the village has ever had."

Paeder breathed deeply, as if fighting down a cry of exasperation.

"But why would Vitellan want to be frozen again? His stomach is better, now that his loyal servant has stopped poisoning him, and we have been able to keep him safe from those assassins. He may well live to be an old man."

Alfred frowned slightly, anticipating that his friend and tutor would one day want to leave. He had faced up to the idea and accepted it already, but he was no happier about it.

"Perhaps as an old man, with his friends dead and not many years ahead of him, he may decide to travel a thousand years into the future to die. I wonder if my family will still rule Wessex in Anno Domini 1870? Perhaps we could leave a tradition to welcome the Master when he awakes."

"How did you come to suspect Gentor, anyway?" Paeder asked. "To me he seemed like a model of fawning devotion where Vitellan was concerned."

"Vitellan's breath. It smelled of strong drink when I was talking to him after you were carried out, yet he had supposedly been drinking water. Gentor probably had a little jar of his poison in his sleeve, to add to his Master's soup and water. Vitellan could taste nothing, but I could smell it. Besides, Gentor was too calm when the note was discovered. Such a terrible threat to his Master should have made him hysterical for Vitellan's safety. I decided on a little test, and had a scribe draw up the secret message. Daegryn delivered it for me—the chief would do almost anything to annoy Gentor."

"A man after my own heart," muttered Paeder. "How did you know that Gentor wrote the first note?"

"I did not. I took a guess about that. They tell me that Gentor is looking for a hidden cave to seal off and turn into a new ice room."

"That will keep him away from us, and good riddance."

The ambush was on a road bordered on one side by a river and on the other by dense woodland. The Danes had taken to raiding in small mounted parties that would meet up to form a much larger group for the trip home, a group so large that no Wessex force would dare attack. Vitellan proposed to divide the Danish force by felling a dozen poplars across the road as they passed. The Danes would fall back toward the river as the Wessex churls and soldiers poured out of the woods, but the Roman had chosen a part of the bank that was all deep mud and marsh. His own men were armed with long spears to pick off the raiders as they wallowed about, trying to regroup.

In the distance a scout with a mirror flashed a brief signal to them, just as the Romans had once done. The Danes were three miles away, with their own scouts riding a short distance ahead. Vitellan rode along the site of the ambush, making sure that no glinting weapons or colored cloth would betray the four hundred men and thirty women who were hidden among the bushes. At last he rode to where Alfred and the bishop were waiting.

"Are all the ropes bracing the trees hidden too?" Alfred asked, more to prove his diligence than anything else.

"They have been smeared with silt from the river, my lord," Vitellan replied. "They blend with the shadows so well that I myself am not sure which trees are ready to drop."

"Splendid, splendid," said Paeder, unstrapping the axe from his back and hefting it. "I'm looking forward to my bowl of soup at the victory feast already."

They laughed, and Alfred took a small, ornate dagger from his belt. He looked at the blade for a moment, reading the letters engraved on it.

"When I was ten years old my father, Aetherwulf, made me custodian of this little family treasure," he said, handing it to Vitellan. "He told me the legend that goes with it, and made me swear to hand it on to another member of the family if I could not do my duty with it during my lifetime."

Vitellan blinked, then looked intently at Alfred after glancing at the little weapon. Paeder looked from one to the other, scratching his beard uneasily, then rode a few steps away and pretended not to listen.

"Are . . . are you sure that you wish to break such an oath, and such a long tradition?" Vitellan asked.

"My oath is sealed still. You are part of my family, after all." He looked down in embarrassment, toying with the mane of his horse. "I am proud to be descended from you," he said quickly and quietly.

The pressure of hundreds of years suddenly lifted. Vitellan straightened, as if he had been relieved of an enormous weight. He wanted to say something in gratitude, yet what words could match events and emotions like these? Like a good tactician, he changed the subject.

"You would have been proud of Lucia," he said wistfully. "A fine, determined, resourceful girl, the sort of person that royal dynasties could grow from when the circumstances are right. Such a pity that—"

His voice snapped off as he saw another glint from the signaler. A cloud of dust in the distance marked the approach of the Danes.

"Time to hide," said Alfred, following his stare.

Vitellan looked down at the dagger again, reading the engraving on both sides of the blade. "Thank you for lifting this shadow from me. I never thought that I would know such a sense of peace again."

"And thank you, too, for giving Wessex the Peace of Rome."

Alfred motioned Paeder to come with him, and they urged their horses across the road and through the dense bushes. They turned to see that Vitellan was where they left him. Suddenly Paeder gasped loudly and exclaimed in Latin.

"You!"

"So you caught on at last. Yes, the Royal House of Wessex is distantly descended from Vitellan and Lucia. Did you never stop to think how I knew what to put in that note that I used to frighten Gentor? *Lucia vivit* and *Romanus immortalis ad mortem ducatur* are engraved on that faimly heirloom's blade."

" 'Lucia lives,' 'Kill the immortal Roman.' " Paeder laughed and slapped Alfred on the back. "As a father of the Church of Christus I cannot praise your forgiveness highly enough. At last, after seven hundred years, the chain of hate is broken."

"It broke long ago," he chuckled, pleased with his own deviousness. "My father thought that it was a tradition of stamping out Roman paganism. He knew nothing of Vitellan."

As they watched Vitellan suddenly flung the dagger out over the river in a long, glittering arc. It struck the water with a small splash, and he watched the bubbles disperse before walking his horse across the road and into the woods. In the distance they could hear hoofbeats as the Danish scouts approached.

"He must stay. He will stay," whispered Alfred to himself as he held his hunting horn ready and the Danish scouts rode past. The main column of raiders was very close. "Wessex is his immortality now, just as he was Gentor's. He would not desert his own flesh and blood."

The vanguard of the Danish column drew level with Alfred and Paeder, and the young prince lifted the mouthpiece of the horn to his lips. *Pax Romana vivit,* he thought as he blew a long, clear note and the trees began to crash into the Danish column.

* * *

In the following year Alfred was crowned king, and although his great victory at Edington was still seven years in the future, the promise of ultimate victory over the Danes had already been transformed from a dream to a real possibility.

Gentor became so obsessed with secrecy that he would not allow anyone else to see the secret cave he had found for the new Frigidarium. He stayed away for weeks at a time, doing his own masonry and woodwork deep underground, and Vitellan was forced to appoint and train a deputy Icekeeper to keep the old Frigidarium in order.

With Alfred and his kingdom seeming more secure, Vitellan began to long for another jump across time. After all, if the steps that Alfred was taking toward civilization were to come to nothing, Roman skills might be needed in the future. He could be a type of weapon himself, to be revived in times of great crisis, but otherwise to be kept frozen. Gentor was delighted when the news reached him, and he set off at once to meet his Master and discuss his plans. All Gentor's work came to nothing, however: the Icekeeper died in a Danish ambush before Vitellan was refrozen, and the location of the new Frigidarium was lost.

Vitellan was refrozen early in 872, after feigning death from his stomach trouble. The village of Durvonum made a show of going into mourning, and within a few years the memory of its ice chamber faded from common knowledge in the surrounding countryside.

The Danes were never decisively defeated, and control of the land changed hands through many battles and treaties. The millennium did not see the end of the world, as many had been predicting, but 1066 saw the Normans' successful invasion. The village survived unscathed, and without having to wake its frozen Roman. By now its name had been changed from Durvonum to Durvas.

The climate was not quite so kind to the villagers. A warm interglacial fluctuation drove up the average temperature. Snow ceased to fall in winter, and even frosts became rare. At first ice was carted across from the highlands of Wales, then a treaty was made with a Welsh landlord to allow a dozen men and women from Durvas to live in the highlands permanently. Vitellan's frozen body was secretly carted there and kept in a new Frigidarium cave.

Not having the Roman sleeper within the village weakened the tradition of tending him, yet that tradition was centuries in dying. Finally, in the late thirteenth century, the strain of maintaining an outpost of Durvas in the Welsh highlands began to prove too much in the face of changing social structures and the continuing warmer climate. As the fourteenth century opened, Tom Greenhelm was appointed Icekeeper, and he immediately called a meeting to decide how best they could serve their Master as the village continued to decline.

After over twelve centuries of operation, the world's second and only human-powered time machine was about to be made automatic.

3

charon's anchor

As the nine travelers stopped to rest, they found that the stone ruins of the great house were still hot from the fire that had destroyed it. Guy Foxtread, the Icekeeper, warily inspected the charred and smoking rubble as the others unpacked their rations of dried meat and nuts. A day earlier this had been a fortified mansion on a prosperous estate, but in the evening ...

The English travelers had been camping in a forest fifteen miles to the west, yet they had noticed the glow of the fire reflected against wispy clouds, a strange and evil parody of sunrise which had persisted for much of the night. The Jacques had been here. It was 1358, two years after King John of France had been captured by the English at the Battle of Poitiers. The whole of northern France lived in fear of the Jacques.

Everything that had not been burned had been trampled, smashed, or looted, and even vines and vegetables had been ripped out of the ground. Guy estimated that about seven hundred villeins had rampaged over the place. Resistance had apparently been minimal. They had seen a few bodies lying near the road as they approached, and six of them were Jacques. The four others, those of the defenders, had been beaten and trampled to a bloody pulp.

Guy was about to return when something in a nearby field caught his eye. A smoking mound of ashes, something that one would not expect in the middle of a field. The ground was trampled and compacted, and had a faint reek of urine. The mob of Jacques had gathered here for some hours. Suddenly apprehensive, he set out for the mound, his heart pounding, his skin clammy with horror. It might have merely been the site of a feast of butchered livestock, yet it did not have the look of a feast. There was a thick, charred stump protruding from the ashes. Crows flapped into the air as he approached.

Someone had been burned at the stake. Guy saw that the stake had burned through near the base, and had toppled into the ashes along with the body. He tripped and stumbled, then realized with a new surge of horror that he had caught his foot on a body so smeared with mud that it seemed no more than a low mound. A woman, stripped naked, plump and middle-aged. Guy stared down, wringing his hands. A day ago he would have been in awe of her, she would have been an important noble, ordering servants about and perhaps scoffing at the danger from the Jacquerie. Stooping, Guy reached out to feel her neck for a pulse. He snatched his hand back and shuddered as he realized that her throat had been cut.

There were bodies of more women scattered around the ashes, stripped and caked with mud. One was of a girl, barely pubescent, with very long hair. Guy checked that all were indeed dead, then sank to his knees and buried his face in his hands, but after one breath the stench of blood and piss on his hands made him retch. He heard footsteps but did not bother to turn. Only one man in all the world walked with the strange, measured march-step of the vanished Roman legions.

Vitellan stopped beside Guy and looked about. For a long time they were silent and still. Crows were circling impatiently.

"I have seen some horrors in thirteen centuries, but . . . if I have seen worse than this I cannot force myself to remember it." His English was stiff and halting, he had been learning it for barely eighteen months.

"Look at her, Master, she can't have been but thirteen," Guy blurted before his voice cracked into sobs.

"Who could do this? The Jacques?"

"Folk such as I be, Master, though they be French and all," gasped Guy, his voice faint and hoarse as he fought to control his breath. "Common folk."

"Such cruelty, such evil . . . it hangs over this place like a cloud, chilling me though the sun shines brightly."

The crows were circling lower, inky blots on the bright, clear sky of late spring. Some landed close by. They cocked their heads and stared at the humans, both living and dead.

"The French nobles don't treat their common folk as well as do English. They treat 'em as pigs, aye, and now the pigs have turned to bite."

Vitellan helped Guy to his feet, then flung a clod of soil at the crows. "Just look at that, first the Jacques, now crows. These folk must be buried."

"Master, there's eleven women and the burned lord here. Then there's those brave men as died defendin' the house, so that's four more. Sixteen graves is a day's work for nine men such as us."

"We can't leave them in the field for the dogs and crows. Gah, such a filthy way to die."

"Death be filthy whatever its form, Master. Still, if ye think we can spare a day from our journey, then we can spit in the devil's face and give these folk a Christian burial."

Guy walked into the ashes and examined the charred corpse. "Nailed to the stake by his hands. That's how he stayed with it until it burned through."

"I've seen pagan Romans kill for sport in the arena, but this has happened after thirteen centuries of Christ's Word. Death was quick in the Roman arenas, at least as I saw it."

"I fought at Crécy, I saw whole fields piled deep with bodies, a thousand times more than this. Why is this worse now, Master?"

Vitellan knelt beside the girl's body, then gently lifted it from the mud. The limbs were stiff, and it seemed to have little weight. He started back for the ruins, Guy beside him.

"Long ago, when Trajan was Emperor of Rome, I saw . . . there was a goodwife whose sanity twisted. She killed her family in their sleep, then took her own life. That was a little like this, it squeezed my heart more than the bloodiest battlefield."

"So ye have a mind to bury these folk, Master?"

"Yes."

"Even the Jacques?"

"Not the Jacques. Let them do some good at last by feeding the crows." They walked on in silence, the girl's hair hanging to the ground and trailing in the mud. Guy gathered up the hair and walked with it in his hands. "There is smoke over there," Vitellan observed, nodding to the southeast.

Guy squinted into the distance. "Aye, looks to be a hamlet."

"We'll get the others to help us carry these folk back to their house, then cover them with boards and stones. The villeins in that hamlet can dig the graves."

"I doubt that they'll be willing as to help the likes of us, Master. Bein' scarcely a mile distant, I'd say their menfolk were here last night with the Jacques."

"I did not say they'd be willing, Guy."

The people of the hamlet were not alarmed to see five strangers come striding into the place. The country was full of stragglers trying to join up with the main group of Jacques that had just swept past. A dog sensed something odd and began to bark, but nobody raised an alarm. Some of the women and children were disporting before the others in fine robes from the nearby mansion. Those of the men who had not gone off with the Jacquerie were out of sight, still sleeping off the wine of the night before.

The travelers entered an outlying house, leaving two at the door. A moment later they emerged, blood dripping from their swords. They were already entering the second house before the reality of what had happened sank in and the screaming began. Drowsy men stumbled out of houses armed with hoes, scythes, and billhooks, only to be methodically cut down by the well-trained men-at-arms. Those who fled into the fields were shot down or turned back by the four strategically placed archers, and those who tried to hide in their houses were dragged back out and bound.

Vitellan paced before the captives, speaking in French that was all the more terrifying for being slow and broken. There had been over ninety people living in the hamlet that morning, but twenty-six had died before the survivors were seated in the dust before their nine attackers.

"Men with mud or blood on their loins, hanging!" At once a collective groan went up, blending with shrill pleas for mercy. Mal and Guy walked among the captives, slashing away leggings with their knives, culling those marked as guilty. Fifteen villeins soon knelt trembling and whimpering. They ranged from teenagers to the hamlet's elders.

"All others. Men, women, children . . . ah, wash dead nobles, clothe dead nobles. Dig graves. Bury." There was silence at his words, there was sure to be worse to come.

"All take off clothes. Houses, clothes, we burn!" Screams of anguish and pleas erupted, but to no avail. The naked villeins watched as the fifteen men were hanged, then they were driven over to the ruins of the mansion carrying spades, washtubs, and looted clothing while the hamlet burned behind them. Mal, who had trained for a time to be a deacon, conducted a service for the dead.

Within five hours the English party was back on the road, marching briskly and leading their four horses. That night they camped in open woodlands and buried a small amount of looted coin, silver, and jewelry that they had found in the hamlet. They left no marker over the little cache, and drew no map to locate it again.

At that time there was a truce in the Hundred Years War between the English and French, so Vitellan's party could move as freely as the brigands, Free Companies, and Jacquerie would permit in the anarchy of the

French countryside. They passed within sight of Paris, but did not approach the city. There was a dispute going on between the Dauphin and Étienne Marcel, and fighting flared from time to time. In spite of what had happened at the hamlet, the travelers were not looking for trouble.

Their guise was good, that of English men-at-arms going to meet with their lord in Berne, then escort him back through the troubled and dangerous French countryside. Their armor was hardened butt-leather and sewn iron strips over quilt padding: nothing worth stealing, but very effective in a fight. Four were bowmen, five were infantry. As they journeyed, word of what the Jacques were doing was always with them. Houses and castles burned, looting, mass rape, murder, and estates abandoned by nobles who had fled in no more than the clothes that they were wearing. They reached the River Marne, making their way carefully because of a huge force of Jacques said to be in the area. Vitellan rode one of the packhorses most of the time, as he tired easily.

"The late spring weather's to blame for the Jacques," Guy said as they walked. "It's warm, and there's food a-plenty to be had in the countryside. Such a big rabble would starve and die as quick as swallows if this were winter."

"It's early June, aye, so there be a whole summer as to have the Jacques rampagin'," Walt added. Guy had nothing to say to this.

"If we came upon a dozen knights ravishing a peasant girl, would we attack as readily as we did in the hamlet?" asked Mal, who was something of a scholar and had a knack of asking awkward questions.

"Your questions will get ye a brushwood footwarmer one day," muttered Guy, but he did not have an answer.

"If they were knights, I'd tell 'em 'tis wrong," Walt ventured. "If they'd not stop, I'd lose my life shamin' those knights that a commoner be more chivalrous than they."

"And if they were a thousand Jacques ravishing a noblewoman, and there was but one of you?" asked Vitellan. "Would you give your life to shame men who know no shame?"

"I . . . reckon so," Walt decided. "How else could I face my Creator when I die?"

"Would it not be better to go away, recruit a hundred men-at-arms and return to slaughter those evil men, so that they murder and ravish no more than that one woman?"

"Should a thousand sinners die so that one innocent should live?" asked Mal. Guy cursed and swatted at him with the end of his liripipe.

"Aye, that they should," said Walt firmly.

"Then what say the same noble lady had taken a handsome traveler into her house while her husband be off at battle—Guy here, for example." Guy turned to scowl at Mal, but he smiled and continued. "What say she bedded him, but was ravished and killed by a thousand Jacques a day or two later. They are all sinners now, all bound for hellfire if they die unconfessed. Should the Jacques not be allowed to ravish her and cut her throat?"

"Her adultery does bring death upon her by law in some parts," Guy agreed. "But so it should be for each of those Jacques for the sin of ravishin' too!"

"Aye, and you also for mountin' her in t'first place," said Walt solemnly.

"I never mounted anyone but my wife!" snapped Guy, whose wife had died of the Black Death a decade ago, and whose patience with the joke was wearing thin. "I'll not be doin' so in time to come, either."

They were silent for a few dozen steps. Will, who was some distance ahead, stopped on the crest of a hill and waved that all was clear. Vitellan turned to check the bowmen, who were following the horses with Gilbert as rearguard.

"The Jacques should die because she's a noble," Vitellan declared.

"Say you that nobles are different in God's eyes?" asked Mal.

"No, but nobles represent order. Order builds churches, castles, and roads like the one we walk. Order stores grain against famine and allows kings to form armies to protect villages from brigands. I saw England in the ninth century, and it was very like France as it is now. What would you have? The rule of nobles, or the rule of the Jacquerie and Free Companies?"

"But, but if the noblewoman had committed adultery—" began Mal.

"A king who buggers a sheep is still a king! Upon his death he might have trouble talking his way past the Gates of Heaven, but meantime he is still a king."

"I'd have no respect for a king who'd wagtail a sheep," said Walt, shocked by the proposition.

"Walt, when I was young Rome was ruled by Emperor Nero, who was a drunken fornicator. Did all the great Roman Empire throw off the rule of law just because the Emperor set a bad example? Thirteen years before him was the Emperor Caligula, who was as mad as hares in March and a sodomite too."

"T'bugger were not fit ter lead," snarled Guy.

"Eventually he was assassinated, but we Romans put up with a lot from him because he was our leader. Which would you rather have as ruler? An otherwise just king who tups the queen's ladies in waiting, or the Jacques and brigands?"

"He's right, Mal," said Walt. "Nowt but Christ an' Mary walked the earth free of sin. Ravishin' is always evil, but killin' them as leads the land means evil for all."

For once Mal had been played out by an argument. "The French I've seen have been sorrowful bad rulers," he muttered.

"Aye, but give our king a few years and all France will be under good English rule," laughed Guy, and for once the others all agreed.

Will was waiting for them as they reached the crest of the hill. Below was a village of about five hundred, and there seemed to be a disturbance going on. The road led right through its center.

"There's no fighting or burning," Will pointed out. "And no large numbers have passed this way for a few days."

"A wedding, perhaps, or a fair?" asked Vitellan.

"Seems a happy crowd," said Walt, who had acute hearing. "A lot of shouting and laughing, but no screams or clashing of weapons."

"Then we go in," said Vitellan. "If it's a fair we can buy cakes and bread as a break from our dried meat and nuts."

As they reached the outskirts they met a lookout sitting on bundles of brushwood and drinking from a heavy silver goblet set with green stones. Guy scowled to see the goblet and turned to Mal as they approached.

"That cup be looted, and he be a Jacque," he said softly. "I'll talk with him, see what he's about."

Smiling broadly, Guy walked forward and hailed the villein, who sat up and raised the goblet in salute. They began speaking, and the villein got to his feet and pointed over the roofs to a stubby chapel tower. Almost at that moment the chapel bell began to ring. Still smiling, Guy smoothly drew his falchion and drove it underhand into the man's belly, then jerked upward. The villein collapsed to the road, screaming and writhing. Guy wiped the blade on his jerkin, then walked back to the others.

"T'bugger breathed garlic on me," Guy declared. Vitellan looked to the villein, who was trying to stuff torn intestines back into himself and shrieking with agony and horror.

"So there's been a massacre here, too?"

"There's Jacques in the village, about ten score. Sir, ah, Perceval de Boucien and his squire were killed outside the chapel just now. His lady and children are cornered in the stairwell of the chapel's belltower."

" 'Tis bigger than that hamlet," said Guy, looking straight at Mal.

"Master?" implored Mal, looking to Vitellan.

"Advise me," ordered Vitellan.

The ringing of the bell and shouting of the distant crowd were a background to his silence. A thin scream cut through the noise, not loud but quite distinct. Vitellan folded his arms and waited for Mal's reply, as did the others. Behind him the villein bubbled out a last breath and died unheeded.

"Master, there's—Master, say there's not too many for us, please!"

They split into two groups, both taking bundles of brushwood that they lit from the coals of an untended communal oven. They made their way through the back paths of the village, setting fire to houses, woodpiles, and brush fences as they went. As they passed near the chapel they could hear laughter and taunts above the commotion and the ringing of the bell. They re-formed on the main road at the other side, just as the fires were noticed and the first shouts of alarm went up.

Seated awkwardly in front of the horses' packs, Vitellan, Mal, Walt, and Will charged the mob, which was already streaming off to fight the fires. Guy followed on foot and to one side, wearing a villein's jacket draped over his shoulders and without a helmet. The riders ploughed into the crowd before the chapel, laying about them with their swords. Guy caught a glimpse of a headless, battered corpse, then he reached the door where villeins were streaming out in alarm. He gripped the edge and squeezed his way in past the crush.

Within the chapel his eyes took some moments to adjust to the gloom after the bright spring sunlight outside. The stone stairwell was to his right, on the other side of the crowd. They were mainly Jacques, all asking each other what was going on outside. Guy cursed himself for not asking Mal a few more words of French as he skirted the crowd, then guessed at two and began to shout "Chapel burning! Chapel burning!" The panic to get through the door intensified.

A stoutish woman of about forty was holding back a dozen or so remaining Jacques with an oxtongue pike, defending the entrance to a stone stairwell. A boy of about eight was behind her, holding a small axe but petrified with fear. Two Jacques were thrusting severed heads at her on the ends of staves while the others were jabbing with pikes. She was bleeding from several cuts already and her face was streaked with sweat and blood.

Guy calmly removed the villein's jacket, drew his sword and took a handaxe from his belt. He had quietly and methodically stabbed three Jacques in the back before the others realized and shrank back in alarm. Blows from pikestaffs bounced from Guy's butt-leather armor, but the Jacques were wearing only padded surplices. Guy cleared a path to the base of the stairwell, where he dodged a vicious swipe from the woman's oxtongue.

"Friends! Friends! Aht, stupid snaileaters!" he bellowed in English.

"English, I speak it," the woman cried back.

"How many of you?"

"My two girls ring the bell, this boy, that is all."

"Call 'em down, keep together. Throw the pike away, take the boy's axe. Better for close fighting, aim for their faces."

The girls had been dressed as boys, and had had their hair cropped short. By now the chapel was all but cleared of living Jacques, and the woman shepherded the children behind Guy as he led them to the door.

"Stay together as we go through the door," he called. "Don't strike anyone unless they attack, we may not be noticed in the fuss outside. Make for the east."

One of the girls began to whimper, but her mother slapped her ear smartly and she stopped. They went through the door and stumbled over heaped corpses as the sunlight dazzled them. The four riders were fighting in a group over to one side of the square in front of the chapel, and a Jacque captain had managed to get his pikemen into sufficient order to surround them. Guy skirted the fighting with the family behind him, then waved to the concealed bowmen as they got clear. Giles and his men began to methodically shoot into the east side of the circle of Jacques surrounding the riders, and after what seemed an eternity they realized what was happening and began to scatter to either side. Vitellan led the riders through the break, and the bowmen laid down a covering fire as they rode back to them.

Luckily for the travelers the Jacque captain was no fool, and had probably spent time as a soldier. Not knowing how many attackers there were and with the village blazing around him, he ordered his men to form a pike-wall across the main road to protect the other villagers as they fought the fires.

Vitellan looked back and realized that there would be no immediate pursuit. As he tried to lift the boy onto his horse Mal toppled to the road, leaving the back of his horse slick with blood.

"You ride?" Vitellan demanded of the woman in French, and she shouted in English that she could.

"Then mount the horse. Gilbert, get Mal across the horse's neck in front of her. Will, Walt, take the two girls and the boy."

The overloaded horses could barely manage a slow, jarring trot, but even so Guy was so exhausted that he could barely keep up. Mal had a pike wound over the right kidney. He moaned for them to leave him, then vomited down the front leg of the horse. One minute of hard fighting is a strain, five minutes can have even a strong man-at-arms near exhaustion: the battle in the village had lasted over fifteen minutes. Guy managed to jog for a mile before he collapsed. Vitellan ordered his armor stripped and shared among the bowmen, and Gilbert helped Guy up and supported him as they made for a cluster of willow trees where the road touched a curve in the River Marne.

The woman and Mal fell from the saddle in a bloody heap as soon as they stopped. They were hidden by the drooping branches, and the village was marked only by a thick column of smoke behind some low, scrubby hills.

"Have to move on, soon," panted Vitellan, untying a saddle pack, "but . . . horses exhausted. Unpack blankets, all but a day's ration each. Dump the rest in the river."

"Mal can't travel," said Gilbert, pouring the last of his wine over the wound while one of the girls cut bandages from a cape. "He may not last to nightfall."

"We've not even got an hour," wheezed Guy.

"Cut four willow branches. Strap a stretcher between two horses. I've seen the Danes do that."

"That would kill him as surely as riding."

"We can . . . leave him here to die . . . or he can come with us . . . and die." Vitellan's voice was a rasp, and his legs were trembling. "No . . . no other option."

Vitellan collapsed on a grassy bank, hungrily gasping for breath. Although strong, he did not have much endurance. He watched the girls help wash the blood and grime of the battle from his men while the little boy helped the bowmen wrap food and spare gear in blankets weighted with stones, then dump them in the river. Well-trained, well-disciplined children, he thought with approval, then remembered their mother. She was squeezing river water from a cloth onto Guy, who was still gasping loudly for air and feeling his fifty-seven years heavily after running a mile and a half from the village. Vitellan took out a strip of dried meat and began to chew. His stomach was still hurting, but he had forgotten the pain during the events of the morning. When he had chewed what juices he could out of the meat he spat out the pulp, closed his eyes, lay back and drifted away to somewhere quiet and blank.

"Are you wounded, good sir?"

Vitellan opened his eyes to see the woman kneeling beside him. He shook his head.

"I tire easily, I—I have a wasting disease. Nobody can help."

"Good sir, I must humbly thank you with all my heart for saving us from the Jacques. There were hundreds of them, and against them only nine of you." Tears welled in her eyes as she spoke, then ran down her plump cheeks leaving glistening trails in the blood and dust.

"We help as we can," he said, embarrassed, "but this land has gone mad and we are few. What is your name, please?"

"I am Anne, widow of Sir Perceval de Boucien as of this hour. Guy told me that you are Vitellan, from England, and that you are his Master."

Vitellan sat up. "You must wash your face, we must not look as if we have been in recent fighting. Your robes are torn and bloody: how bad are your wounds?"

"Many but slight. My death was to be a long, slow game, they meant to bleed and weaken me."

"You must wear Mal's armor over your robes to hide the rents and blood. Guy! Can you walk?"

"Aye, Master."

"Bring Mal's armor over and show the Lady Anne how to strap it on."

Guy's deathly pale face instantly flushed red. "Master! I couldn't, I, I—"

The undivided attention of everyone was suddenly upon Guy. Even the dying Mal managed to raise his head for a moment.

"Better *your* fingers than those of the Jacques," said Lady Anne with her hands on her hips. Mal began a wheezing rattle of a laugh.

Guy tramped away to gather Mal's scattered butt-leather armor, sword, and shield. He dropped them in the grass before the knight's widow.

"My lady, please to put these on and look the part of a man-at-arms."

"I am sorry for thrusting at you with my pike, and I swear that I shall never eat another snail."

"My lady, I didn't mean . . ." He stood scratching the back of his neck for a moment. "Please to armor up, I'll help—that is, meanin' no lewd intent."

She took his hand and squeezed it in both of hers. Guy blushed beet red again, then reached down for the armor.

In less than a quarter hour they were on the road, with the horses a little restored from the water and grazing. Mal was on a stretcher between two horses walking side by side, with light packs piled to conceal him. The archers had shot most of their arrows in their barrage, and had not been able to recover any before they fled. Smoke continued to rise from the village behind them on the still air of late morning. Nobody came after them, but many villeins came hurrying from the other direction.

"Brigands attacked a village but were beaten off and fled west," Guy called in French under instruction from Lady Anne.

All the while Anne told her story. She and her husband had been fleeing for the town of Meaux with their children Louise, Marie, and Jean. They had taken refuge in the village when one of their former servants had betrayed them to a group of Jacques that had become separated from the main mob. Her husband and his squire had died covering the family's flight to the chapel.

"You fought uncommonly well," said Vitellan.

"That is, for a woman or for a pampered noble's wife, do you mean, sir?" she replied with a smile.

"I have seen women fight as well as Guy says you did, and even better, but only after I'd trained them for many weeks."

She blinked in surprise. "So you English train women to come against us now?"

"No, it was against the Danes when they invaded."

"There are no Danes invading England."

"But five hundred years ago there were."

She stared at him, waiting for the smile that would confess his words to be a joke. The smile never came. She looked to Guy. Guy nodded.

"Do not be alarmed, Lady Anne, you have not been rescued by a madman," Vitellan reassured her. "You had been trapped in the chapel for an hour, you say?"

"Yes. They were toying with me, only giving me many small cuts with their pikes. They could have rushed me at any time, but they knew they had all the time they wanted."

"So your husband taught you to fight like that?"

"Not so, good sir. My father was a baker, and a very rich baker. He owned nine mills and I was his only child. He thought to marry me to a knight, and he had a notion that the wife of a knight need know something of war's arts, along with the more usual women's skills and graces. Nobody could persuade him otherwise, so I was taught something of sword, pike, and archery."

Vitellan rubbed his chin speculatively. "Did it help you to secure a husband?"

"Not at all. Sir Perceval had been captured during the fighting near Caen in 1346, and had lost all of his wealth and estate in the ransom. My father provided an estate near Trakel for my dowry, and the marriage was quickly settled."

"But the Jacques have not threatened Trakel," said Guy.

"We were visiting my father in Beauvais when the Jacquerie began their revolt."

By sunset they were fifteen miles from the village, and they stopped in a wood to rest and eat some of the dried meat that they had kept. Mal had begun bleeding again on the road, and his blood had soaked right through the stretcher and dripped into the dust. He was still conscious by the time they stopped, but very near to death. Gilbert boiled a soup of chopped meat in a helmet, but Mal choked while trying to swallow it.

"Best to die wi' conscience quiet," he said as Guy and Vitellan knelt beside him. "Honored to know you, Master."

"You can't die without Master's permission," said Guy awkwardly.

Mal closed his eyes. "Nobody to read over the dead now, Master. Best make sure that no others die."

"Would that I were such a good leader," said Vitellan.

"Dummart, who's to read over you if you die?" pleaded Guy. "Tighten your straps, Mal, the worst is over."

"Aye, the worst is over. I'll say a good word for all of ye . . . wherever I'm sent."

Lady Anne tended him for a while, and managed to get him to drink some tepid soup and keep it down.

"If he can eat he has a chance," she said to Guy, who had not left his side. "Now he needs sleep."

Some minutes later Mal had fallen asleep and was breathing regularly. Guy began to doze as the others ate and talked, but when he awoke Mal was dead.

They cut makeshift wooden trowels from branches and dug a grave in the soft soil. Vitellan spoke some Latin that he remembered from a Christian burial in the first century, then a few words of some language that none of them understood. Guy wept openly, and the children quietly gathered spring flowers for Mal's grave at the edge of the little fire's glow.

Gilbert had first watch, and Guy ordered the others to get what sleep they could. He was talking with Vitellan about how they might forage for food the next day when Lady Anne came over to them.

"There is no safety in any direction," she said as they sat in the darkness, "but I had heard that the royal family was sheltering at Meaux, on the River Marne. There is a fortress area, called the Market of Meaux, a strong and secure place. Perhaps three hundred great ladies and their children are there, guarded by loyal knights. The town is loyal, too."

"A fortress," Vitellan said doubtfully. "I have seen what the Jacquerie have done to fortified houses. What of the town? Are the people really to be trusted?"

"The mayor and magistrates have sworn to protect the Dauphin's family from dishonor."

"Seems as good as any place in this terrible land," said Guy listlessly.

"Three hundred noblewomen will draw the Jacques like flies to spilled honey," said Vitellan.

"Aye Master, but if the Market be a stout fort it can withstand a siege for months. When winter comes the Jacques will flee the cold to their homes."

"It's the seventh of June, still two weeks before the solstice and half a year away from winter."

"A siege of six months is nothing rare."

Vitellan sat silent in the darkness for some time, making up his mind. "Meaux it shall be," he finally declared. "How far from here would it be, my lady?"

"Two days at today's pace, good sir."

"It's new moon," said Vitellan, looking through the trees to the west where Venus and Saturn hung brilliantly together above the horizon. "It's also near solstice, so the days are long. Mal is gone, so we can make two or three times today's pace. Tell me, if we were on the road before dawn and marched the whole day, stopping only to graze and water the horses, then could we reach Meaux by dusk?"

"Dusk or soon after," replied Lady Anne after thinking for a moment.

"Then we must do that. If the Jacques are converging there, we have to reach the Market of Meaux before it comes under siege."

As Vitellan had hoped, the party was taken for a band of English men-at-arms and their French servants. As he had feared, they encountered larger and larger groups of villeins going in their direction. Nearly all were male, and carried improvised or looted weapons. Lady Anne chatted constantly with Guy and Vitellan, trying to bring their colloquial French to a usable level for the hours ahead.

They managed to get within sight of Meaux by the evening. The fields surrounding the town were covered with Jacques sitting around bonfires, and Will put their number between five and ten thousand. There appeared to be no organization, other than a general focus on Meaux. "Tomorrow the King Bonhomme arrives" was the cry as they passed the carousing groups.

"In a way this is a good sign," observed Vitellan as they walked along the road, waving and returning cheers. "A rabble like this cannot live off the land for long, and there are virtually no armor and supply waggons."

"A short siege after all, Master?" said Guy.

"No more than weeks. As long as they can be kept out of the town and away from its stores they will soon be in search of an easier target. Our problem will be getting through the gates, but I have a few ideas . . . that's odd." He peered ahead to a line of bonfires. "There's quite a group near the gates, and the gates are open."

As they got closer Guy mounted the lead packhorse and gathered the reins of the other three in so that they made a heavy wedge to push through the crowd. "Make way for King Bonhomme's captains, make way for King Bonhomme's captains," he called firmly and ignored questions thrown back to him. They broke through to a clear space between the gates of the town and the crowd of about a thousand Jacques. Four bonfires burned on either side of the road, but it was not clear who had set them. A dozen frightened pikemen of the town militia were standing on the road, barring the way.

"That's bad," Vitellan said as he surveyed the mob.

"They bar the way to the Jacques," said Guy, leaning down from the horse. Vitellan pointed to one side, where a town magistrate was speaking with two Jacque captains. All were smiling and nodding as they conversed.

"They should not even be talking with them. I've faced mobs, you have to be firm. They should close the gates and station archers on the walls."

Having only one man able to speak fluent French was a serious handicap. Vitellan briefed Will on what to say, then they moved forward to near where the Jacque captains were talking to the magistrates. Will strode over and began announcing a message from King Jacque Bonhomme for the mayor of Meaux. This caught them all by surprise, and they turned to listen. The Jacque leaders scratched their heads and frowned, and the magistrate nodded and smiled uncertainly. Then, at a word from the magistrate, the pikemen stood aside to let Vitellan's group enter.

Suddenly a lone Jacque broke free of the crowd and ran for the gates. Immediately the militiamen lowered their pikes and blocked the way.

"Please, please, I am the Countess de Hussontal," she cried, tearing off her cap. Now a dozen Jacques ran forward and seized her while the militia kept their pikes leveled and the magistrate watched in silence with his arms folded.

"Ho! Strip her where can all see!" shouted Vitellan in broken French. Lady Anne gasped in horror as the Jacques roared their approval and the countess was thrown down by her captors. She writhed and screamed as they tore off her clothes with the skill of practice.

"Gather your men, string your bows," Vitellan said to Giles, then he turned to Guy while rummaging in a saddlepack. "Keep the horses together, ride for the gates at my signal."

"But the pikemen—"

"Trust me, they'll break ranks and run," said Vitellan as he hefted an odd black jar about the size of a child's head. "Giles, take the gates with your men, Lady Anne, follow with your children. Hold the gates open. Shoot into the Jacque crowd and shoot anyone in the town who tries to close the gates. The rest of you, run for the countess when I do."

Vitellan strolled across to one of the bonfires, uncoiling a length of string from the jar. The string began to sputter as he dipped it into the flames, then he calmly walked back toward them. He stopped, examining the progress of the fuse as if it were an interesting book, then he hurled the jar just behind the foremost Jacques in the crowd.

The explosion was shocking and shattering, it was the first gunpowder blast that most of them had ever heard. Fragments of iron tore through flesh like jagged arrowheads and pandemonium was instant and complete.

Will backhanded his sword into a Jacque captain's face as Vitellan and the others ran forward and began to cut down the dumbfounded Jacques surrounding the countess. The horses reared in fright and bolted, but Guy turned them for the gates. The combination of the explosion and charging horses was too much for the militiamen, who threw down their pikes and ran. Guy was first through the gates, struggling to control the horses. Lady Anne followed with her children, followed in turn by the bowmen who backed to the gate, firing at the writhing mass of Jacques as they went. Gilbert reached the gates to find Lady Anne standing over a body and brandishing a bloody pike at a half-circle of frightened townsmen holding a huge wooden crossbar.

The countess was bruised and bleeding as Will dragged her to her feet by one arm and pushed her at the gate. "Go! Run for the gate!" he shouted in French.

At that moment the archers fired the last of their arrows. Vitellan shouted to fall back, but by now the Jacques were beginning to rally behind their surviving captain. Pole weapons against swords is a one-sided fight, and Vitellan saw Will fall before him with a pike through one eye. Blades and points began to thud and scrape across the Roman's armor. Two of the bowmen ran forward with the militiamen's fallen pikes, and the Jacques fell back for a moment before the longer weapons. That was all the time they needed to turn and run for the gates. Behind the gates Lady Anne and the other bowmen were holding back the militia and townsmen while the countess and children huddled together.

"Close them, quickly!" shouted Vitellan, and now the militia, townsmen, and travelers worked together to push the gates shut against the Jacques and drop the heavy wooden bar into place. Vitellan collapsed before he could take another step, completely spent. Behind the gate they could hear the mob banging on the heavy wood.

"Fool! Fool!" ranted the magistrate. "We had them listening to us, we might have made a truce. You are all to be arrested."

"What is he saying?" gasped Vitellan to Anne, unable to understand rapidly spoken French. The magistrate continued to shout.

"We are under detention."

At that moment the countess, still naked, stormed forward. Her eyes were blazing with rage and she was shrieking at the top of her voice. Vitellan managed to make out something about pigs, dung, and being flayed alive. The magistrate shrank back, then fumbled with the pin of his cloak—which the countess had apparently demanded.

Giles draped Vitellan's arm around his neck and hoisted him up, then they started down the road. The streets were full of people setting up tables in the streets and carrying baskets of bread and meat. The magistrate followed some distance behind them, shouting increasingly loud abuse as he regained his courage. The pikemen of the militia were behind him, walking in no order, unwilling to obey the magistrate and arrest the intruders.

"Strange, they're preparing for a fair," said Walt.

"The Jacques are to be let in to drink, feast, and do as they will, it's happened in many other towns," said Anne.

"We must get into the Market right away," panted Vitellan urgently. "The Jacques will have all the food and shelter they need for a long siege."

Several streets along they met with Guy, who had managed to stop the horses after smashing into several of the heavily laden tables. Angry townsfolk were gathered around him, but they dispersed as the others arrived. The Market of Meaux was connected to the town by a bridge, being built on land between the river and a canal. The walls were high enough to keep out a mob, even an army, if properly defended. They crossed the bridge to the Market, and the guards beneath the portcullis let them pass as soon as they realized who the women were.

Vitellan passed out, and only woke when the sky was brightening with the dawn of the next day. He was lying on a pallet, covered by a blanket. The Countess of Hussontal was sitting with him, still wearing the magistrate's black cloak.

"I am told that you speak Latin," she said as she gently raised his head and offered him a drink from a battered tin bowl.

"You . . . the woman at the gates," he said, confused, his eyes unfocused.

"Myself. I owe you my life, you charged the Jacques to rescue me."

Her lips began to tremble, but she neither wept nor flung herself upon her rescuer. Vitellan glanced about, and noted that he was lying under the awning of what had probably been a vegetable stall. Lady Anne's daughters Louise and Marie were keeping a crowd of onlookers from pressing too close, yet there was no unseemly pushing and gawking. They were all nobles, and were well mannered—in a way their manners were all that they had left to cling to. Some of them were in disguise, others had fled in whatever finery they had been wearing when the Jacques had advanced.

"I must apologize for calling for you to be stripped, my lady," said Vitellan diplomatically, although he was not in the mood for genteel banter.

"Oh, Sir Vitellan, you may do that whenever you would," she whispered in reply, now beginning to drip tears on his blanket. "I thought my next meeting would be with God, but it was with you instead."

She was a tangle of gratitude, restraint, emotion, and manners, all underlaid by her rank among the French nobility. A code of seemly behavior to observe, Vitellan reminded himself. In the distance, beyond the walls of Meaux, he could hear the shouting of the Jacques.

"I must get up, see to the defenses," he began, wearily pushing the blanket back. The countess took the blanket from his fingers and covered him again, gazing adoringly down at his face.

"Last night, when I was flung down naked in the dust before the eyes of those vile swine . . . I went a little mad, I think. Me, a countess, at the mercy of such men, yet God in His mercy sent you to protect me." Her face was pale and scratched, yet was exquisitely fine-boned and framed by twin cascades of black hair that hung down to brush his hands.

"There is fatigue in your eyes, my lady, you should rest."

"And in *your* eyes there is strangeness beyond words. Your manners, your walk, your very speech, all are stranger than those of the most exotic Moor." She lowered her face close to his. "Lady Anne says that you are older than the Royal House of France, that you met with Christ Himself."

Vitellan shook his head slowly on the cushion and said "No."

This seemed to disappoint her a trifle. She sat up straight, assuming her public posture again. The hour of glorious dreams was past, he was just a brave but mortal man again. Soon they would die, and it would be hideous, obscene—

"It was my father who met Him. Christ died twenty years before I was born."

The countess's composure shattered. She swayed as if about to fall from the pallet, with her mouth hanging open and her eyes protruding like a scribe's caricature of a jongleur. Vitellan took her hand in his and gave it a reassuring squeeze. "Do not be in fear of the Jacques, good lady. I shall defend you with my life, and I have lived a very long time. Now, if you wish to please me you must try to rest." He called to one of Lady Anne's daughters. "Marie, take the countess to some place where she may rest quietly, if you please."

With the countess gone Vitellan sat up and began to buckle on his light armor. Louise brought him a bowl of stew, and as usual he scooped out the solid pieces before drinking any. The longing for solid food tormented him, but his stomach continued to twinge its warnings to be careful. The Duchess of Normandy and the Duchess of Orléans called by to ask after his health, to be followed by a score more noblewomen and their families. It was as if he were a foreign king visiting the French royal court. Many girls, and several of their mothers, left their favors with him, scraps of ribbon and lace to wear into battle.

Guy arrived with the three surviving archers, and they reported on their hasty survey of the Market. There were very few commoners in the

Market, only the three hundred noblewomen and their children defended by a handful of knights and trusted men-at-arms. Everyone in the Market was desperate with fear. They knew that the Meaux mayor and magistrates were preparing to open the town gates to the Jacques.

"Had I known how few fighting men were in the Market I would never have led us here," Vitellan said wearily. "Three archers, you, me, Walt, and a few knights and squires . . . but perhaps I would have anyway. Why cling to life for centuries if only to live without honor?"

Later that morning the town's gates were opened and the Jacques poured into Meaux. The sounds of rowdy feasting soon echoed over the walls of the Market, filling those inside with dread. Vitellan was introduced to the Duke of Orléans, who welcomed him and gave him a tour of the defenses. The duke thought that there might be many loyal men-at-arms out in the town, but unless they could be rallied they would be of no help. There was a good supply of arrows for Vitellan's archers, and although they were shorter than the English type and balanced differently, they were quite adequate at close quarters. Guy set about training some of the women to push siege ladders away from the walls with poles.

The sun had been up for about three hours when there was a rumble of hoofs on the bridge and the rattle of chains raising the portcullis. Vitellan joined the duke in time to greet the Captal de Buch and the Count de Foix as they entered with twelve dozen men. The Jacques had apparently been too intent on their feast to try to stop them entering the town.

The story of Vitellan's three battles with the Jacques were of great interest to the Count de Foix and his cousin. They had been returning from Prussia when they heard of the danger at Meaux, but they had not yet fought against Jacques.

"So you razed a hamlet of a hundred souls with only nine men?" asked the count in Latin as they hastily conferred.

"That was because of complete surprise, and good planning," Vitellan explained. "The village where we rescued Anne de Boucien was harder, but we distracted them by setting the houses afire first. The Jacques are not well led, they break and run when attacked convincingly. The danger comes from such a situation as we had at the gates of Meaux last night, when the press of numbers from behind forces those in front upon you. I lost one man that way, and I was nearly brought down myself."

"My men estimate nine or ten thousand Jacques in the town," said the count.

"Cowardly rabble," muttered the Captal de Buch.

"Yes, a rabble," agreed Vitellan. "And a rabble is not an effective fighting force."

"That means we *can* withstand a siege," declared the Duke of Orléans, slapping his knee and smiling for the first time since Vitellan had met him.

"Not a siege, attack!" said Vitellan with infectious urgency. The duke's smile vanished.

"But Sir, Vitellan de, ah—"

"Durvas."

"Vitellan de Durvas, forgive me, good sir, but ten thousand is a very big rabble. Each of us would have to kill a hundred to clear them away."

"If each of us kills even ten the rest would flee," snorted the Captal de Buch. "Do you have any more of those black powder jars, Sir Vitellan?"

Vitellan blinked in surprise at his new title, but his expression did not change. "I had only the one I used last night, but consider this," he replied, gesturing to the bridge beyond the portcullis where the Jacques were already gathering. "The bridge is narrow and those Jacques out there now are the leaders. Look at them, calling for more to come forward. They want a fight. We now have twenty-five fully equipped knights on horseback and more than a hundred men-at-arms to follow on. The push of Jacques from behind will not allow their leaders to escape if we charge out across the bridge."

"In the first charge we shall cut off the head of the Jacquerie's body!" exclaimed the Count de Foix, and the others cheered with approval.

They began to prepare their horses and armor at once, and soon the Count de Foix and the Captal de Buch sat preening themselves before the desperate yet admiring gaze of the three hundred besieged noblewomen and their children.

"Look at them, the flower of chivalry preparing to defend their ladies' lives and honor," Vitellan said to Guy. "Immortal legends will probably grow out of this day."

"Not as immortal as yourself, Master."

"Shining armor, banners, stern faces, and not one of them is wearing the favors of less than a dozen ladies. It's all I can do not to laugh, but that would spoil the effect."

"You wear at least as many," replied Guy earnestly, not really appreciating the joke.

Vitellan gazed at the onlookers, noticing that many of them looked shabby and bedraggled. They were used to being looked after by servants, and in most cases they would have been fending for themselves for the first time in their lives. So many imploring, adoring faces, he thought, so much trust in so few men. If they should fail, then what? Anne de Boucien already had a dozen girls and women standing with her holding pikes, and Guy would remain behind with the archers and a few other men. Perhaps they could hold out until . . . a miracle. He picked out the Countess de Hussontal, who was now wearing the magistrate's cloak over borrowed clothes. She was looking directly at him, and did not look at all frightened. He bowed a fraction, and several other women and girls waved back. Just then Louise dashed out among the horses and made straight for them. She stopped before Guy.

"Will you wear these?" the girl asked shyly, holding out three ribbons. Guy hesitated.

"Wear them, Guy, or find another master," said Vitellan sternly. He stood watching with his arms folded until the favors of Anne de Boucien and her daughters were tied to Guy's belt.

Louise turned to Vitellan. "This is for you, Sir Vitellan, and the lady begs most ardently that you accept it." It was a strip of red cloth from the lining of the magistrate's cloak, wound about with a braid of black hair. He twined it around his fingers, then lifted it to his lips. The countess cast her eyes down, but did not move otherwise.

"Guy, go now, up to that tower," he ordered. "Signal when a heavy crush of Jacques has built up."

"Aye, Master. Is that a special favor?" he asked suspiciously.

"It was all that a certain lady had to cover her nakedness. William of Ockham would have called it symbolic allegory."

"Hah! I calls it an unseemly suggestion."

"Why Guy, you dirty old man. What would Mal have said?"

"T'bugger would be too busy laughin'. I'd best be climbin' the tower, Master. Good fortune to ye, and try to stay alive. I'd hate to be the Icekeeper as let you die."

"I'll return, Guy, and help you to burn this despicable town."

The Count de Foix rode over to Vitellan as he made ready to mount a packhorse in his butt-leather armor.

"Friend, the ladies are full of concern, they say that you are too ill to fight," he said apologetically. "Please, stay here with the bowmen and a few men-at-arms. The ladies will need a leader as fine as yourself to defend the Market if the worst happens to us."

"Guy can do that," replied Vitellan. "I have to be seen to ride out with you, even if my fate be that of the blind king of Bavaria at the Battle of Crécy. You must understand."

The count reached over and seized his arm, full of admiration. "I do understand, and you are welcome. May God protect you, and all of us."

"When ye will, Master!" Guy called from the tower, then he came down the stone stairs at a run.

Guy, Giles, and the two other bowmen began firing through the portcullis to drive the Jacques back as it was being raised, then the horsemen rode out onto the bridge behind the Count de Foix and the Captal de Buch.

Then these two knights and their company came out to the gate of the market place and issued out under the banners of the Count of Foix and the Duke of Orléans, and the Captal's penon. They set upon those villeins, who were but poorly armed. When the villeins saw these men of war well appareled and issuing out to defend the place, the foremost of them began to recoil back, and the gentlemen pursued them with their spears and swords. When they felt the great strokes they recoiled all at once and fell for haste each on the other. Then all the noble men issued out of the barriers and soon won the place, and entered in among their enemies and beat them down by heaps and slew them like beasts, and chased them all out of the town. They slew so many that they were weary, and drove many others into the river. That day they slew of them more than seven thousand, and none would have escaped if they had followed the chase any further. When these men of arms returned again to the town, they set it afire and burned it clean, with all the villeins of the town that they could close therein, because they took part with the Jacquery. After this discomforture thus done at Meaux the Jacques never assembled again together, for the young Ingram, Lord of Coucy, had about him certain men of war, and they slew them whenever they found them without any mercy.

—*The Cronycle of Syr John Froissart,* Book One (1322–1377), Lord Berners' translation of 1525 (adapted)

The Hussontal castle had been built only recently, and loomed new and clean above the spring-green countryside as the riders approached. Vitellan's first impression was of a building approaching ancient Roman standards. The countess had ordered that the survivors of Vitellan's party were to be her sole escort as she returned. She led the way, riding one of the packhorses. The approach to the drawbridge had been lined with the hanged bodies of some dozens of servants who had collaborated with the Jacques.

"She means to bed you, Master," muttered Guy softly, giving hardly a glance to the battered, bloodied specters that hung to either side of them. "An evil thing."

"As evil as a rampaging Jacque might be?" asked Vitellan, staring after the shapely form of the countess on the horse some way ahead of him.

"Great evil don't excuse lesser evil. Ah, I wish Mal were here. He were a great Christian scholar and a good man, he'd have the words I can't find."

"A great *Jewish* scholar and a good man," Vitellan quietly corrected him.

"Master!" Guy exclaimed. The countess turned around, but Vitellan just smiled and waved. She nodded to him, then turned to glare again at the figures now visible beyond the drawbridge.

"People seem to confide in me," Vitellan explained. "Perhaps it is because they know that I shall soon disappear into time, taking their secrets to safety. Years ago Mal was offered conversion to the way of the Church or death. He tried to live as a Christian and even studied for holy orders, but as it came to pass his true faith was too strong, and so he lived as a Jew in secret."

"But—but he gave such good Christian counsel, he fought bravely, he was my friend."

"And when Christ met his soul in paradise he probably welcomed Mal all the more because he had remained true to what he believed in."

"But the Jews, they spread the Black Death, they sacrifice children to the devil—"

"If you believe that then you'd believe the King is a spotty green cow."

"They, they killed Christ, ye can't deny that!"

"It was Roman soldiers who scourged Him, drove the nails though His flesh and thrust the spear into His side, Guy . . . and I'm a Roman soldier."

"Master, but—"

"Were Mal alive, would you still call him friend now?"

"Master, Master, I—yes! He was my friend, my best friend. Dumfargh, you're as bad as he was with such questions. Next you'll be saying that you're a Jew too."

"Would it matter?"

"No, damn you Master, no!" Guy exclaimed, and the countess glanced around again. Guy lowered his voice. "You're changing me, giving me thoughts that could have me burned at the stake."

"My father was Roman, my mother Egyptian."

Guy turned and spat angrily at the last hanging corpse in their grisly guard of honor. "Why bother to tell me you be not a Jew when ye've just taught me not to care?"

"So that you will not lie awake wondering about it for the rest of your life, Guy. As to whatever might happen between myself and the countess, I want your respect."

"But I want to save you, Master. Guilt will tear you limb from limb, shame will burn your heart to cinders."

"Oh so, *how* would you know, Guy of unshakable virtue?"

"I know because—because the Lady Anne—she—we lay together in the fields the night that Meaux burned!" After forcing the words out one by one Guy scowled sullenly at the ears of his horse.

Vitellan pondered this, composed several replies in his mind, but thought the better of each in turn. "Thank you, Guy, for . . . your concern" was all that he could manage by the time their horses' hooves boomed hollowly on the wood of the drawbridge.

Those servants and guards who had helped the countess and her family to escape stood cheering and flinging petals at the little party. Within the keep stood the count, wearing blood-spattered armor and flanked by thirty of his knights.

The cheering continued as the countess motioned her escort to stop, then she rode on to where the count was standing. He held out a hand to her and they began to speak. Abruptly his face paled and his hand dropped. The onlookers fell silent.

"So you slew a few servants while at the head of thirty knights and all their men," the countess was saying. "These few English rescued me from *nine thousand Jacques* who had stripped me naked and flung me to the ground."

"I was not there! How could I have helped?"

"You were only fifteen miles away, 'assessing the strength of the enemy,' or so the Count de Foix told me in Meaux. He was man enough to ride in and defend three hundred noblewomen and their families. Why were you not at his side?"

"I did not know that you were in Meaux."

"You knew that three hundred of us were at the mercy of the Jacques. Why did you not come to help?"

The count had no answer. He stood looking up at her, silently begging forgiveness that he knew she would not give. When he looked to his knights they were all staring at the ground.

"Get out," hissed his wife.

When the count left the castle he was riding alone. The keep remained in silence, with only the horses snorting and nervously clopping the ground. Presently the countess turned in her saddle.

"Guy." The word echoed briefly from the stone walls and Guy rode forward. She turned back to the knights. "Guy, you will go to Riave, where my brother Raymond is sheltering with my children. If you please, bring them back here safely. Take two English bowmen with you, in case you meet with another Jacque army."

Under Anne de Boucien's instruction Guy had acquired a few dozen words of French by now. He understood enough to know that the knights were being humiliated.

"Yes, ladyship. Brave French knights, want come also?" he asked in slow, tortured French.

Thirty armored arms shot up at once.

"Take them if you will," she said coldly. "And Guy, as you return be pleased to call upon Lady Anne de Boucien at Trakel and give her my compliments. I wish our children to be introduced."

As he rode from the keep at the head of his company of thirty knights Guy glared at Vitellan. The Roman centurion shrugged and shook his head.

A fortnight later Vitellan awoke just before dawn in the bedchamber of the countess. The night had been hot and oppressive, and she was sprawled naked on the bed, a tall woman with very fair skin. Her hips were very slightly broader than had been the ideal in Britannia in the first century, but her breasts were in good proportion and still well shaped, even after three children.

Vitellan turned from her to gaze across the French countryside as it came to life under the splash of color along the horizon. Thirteen centuries earlier he had watched the sun setting from the family villa on the slopes of Vesuvius, never dreaming what his future held. Nearly five hundred years previously, sitting on an overgrown Roman wall, he had watched the sun rising through the mists of Wessex. He had spent the spring night alone, in the open. A local warlord had sent his daughter to lie in his bed and seduce him. It was to be the basis of an alliance against Alfred. Vitellan had been lonely and desperate for affection, or at least warm and willing company. He had had to flee his own bed, and it was then he had decided to again flee even farther, into the future, before petty politics turned his welcome sour in that century.

"You look out to the east," said a voice behind him. "You still think to go to Switzerland and forsake my bed for a tomb of ice."

Vitellan turned back to her. "This is a lovely place," he said listlessly.

"Then stay."

"I do not belong. Too many times I have been valued for being a wondrous traveler from ancient times, rather than a man. I have been hated for it, too. In adversity everyone is together, but it's the peace that is the real test. Now you have peace, of a kind, so I must walk away before I am chased."

"Do I count for anything with you?"

"My beautiful, loving, shapely lady, I have to leave because I care for you so very much. People tolerate us being together because I am still a hero, but that will change. Your children will be scandalized, and your knightly brother Raymond does not consider sensual consummation to be part of courtly love. Guy is due back with Raymond and your children tomorrow, remember?"

"We can go to my summer estate while my children stay here for their education. I could send Raymond to Switzerland to prepare—"

She caught herself, but Vitellan shook his head. He returned to the bed and put an arm around her shoulders.

"Raymond can prepare my way, that is a good idea. In the meantime I shall stay for the summer, at least."

"No more than that? You have such silly fears, Vitellan. I am a countess, I am powerful enough to protect you. Besides, you are a great and good Christian: who would want to hurt you?"

"Good and lovely lady, the world is alive with men who would gladly burn a saint at the stake for a little advancement. As to your power, remember what it was reduced to at the gates of Meaux, and how long it took to fall so far? I have no place in your life, your marriage, or your kingdom. Such a strange and exotic man as me will bring sorrow to you, I understand your people well enough to know that."

"You can't prefer the ice to me!" she shouted indignantly. "What is it that draws you back to be frozen again? The glory of living to be a thousand years old?"

"I am already over a thousand years old."

The countess hung her head, baffled and angry.

"Then what?"

"The search for home, perhaps," he replied wistfully.

"So . . . the Roman Empire fell while you slept, and you hope to sleep until it arises again. You want to abandon France because it is full of barbarians—like *me!*"

The countess had worked herself up to something approaching baffled fury as she spoke. She's most dangerous when she's naked, Vitellan reminded himself.

"Rome never really fell, I learned that soon after I was last unfrozen," he said in the hope of distracting her. "The capital was moved east to Constantinople when barbarians swarmed over the West. Roman rule still flickers on in that bankrupt, overgrown city, but I am not going there in search of Old Rome, my love. Neither am I so foolish to search for it in the future. Your own century has greatness that Rome never achieved, and Rome had barbarities that you would never tolerate. The Rome that scholars dream of never really existed. I should know, I once walked its streets."

"Then why leave?" demanded the countess.

"You want a long life with me, but it is not mine to give."

She frowned for a moment, biting her lip as if making a difficult decision. "If you have no place in my century, then take me with you, let me share your bed of ice as you share my bed now. I'll miss my children, it would wring my heart to leave them, but . . . but life is cheap and they are well provided for. I nearly died at Meaux a month ago, and I might die of the Black Death next month. Love is cruel, my brave and kind centurion, and it makes lovers cruel as well. Take me with you, and we can have a long and happy life together in some century to come."

Vitellan hung his head, then took her hand and kissed her fingertips one by one. Abruptly she snatched her hand back and turned away from him.

"You don't want me to come with you, I can tell," she exclaimed angrily.

"As I said, you want a long life with me but it is not mine to give," he repeated slowly and patiently. "Were we both to be treated with my poisonous elixir and then frozen, we would have very little time together once we were revived. I am dying; I shall be dead within two years at most."

She shrank back reflexively, suddenly fearing that he might be diseased.

"My elixir poisons me," he explained. "Even taken in small doses it is harmful. Because it has not been kept cold as we traveled across France, it has slowly been becoming yet more toxic with each week that has passed. Even though I am accustomed to it, I am slowly dying from its effects, and the damage cannot be reversed. Were you to drink some without being used to it you would die within days, yet even taking it in small doses will kill you slowly. Where do you think that I go early in the morning when I slip away from your bed? I go to vomit up blood. I had only a few years to live in 870 A.D., and by this year of 1358 I have declined further. My stomach has been burned to a ruin by my elixir. If I stay here I shall bring great sorrow and dishonor to you, then I shall die horribly before your eyes. If I am frozen again, I shall remain alive and faithful to you until the day that I die, even if you can no longer touch me. You could confess your sin of adultery with me to a priest and be certain in God's eyes that you would never repeat the sin with me." He raised her chin so that she faced him again, and he tried to smile. "Adorable lady, what more could you ask for in a lover?"

She slid forward and held him tightly. Vitellan could feel tears trickling down his chest, and it was a long time before she spoke again.

"So this is the end?" she asked bleakly.

"No, my darling, no, no. We can have a few months more of glorious happiness on your summer estate, just as you say. Passion is sweeter for a little guilt and guile, after all. When I am returned to the ice, we shall not have to watch each other wither and age. There will be no scandals to tarnish your name and honor, and on the day of your death you will know that I am still alive and faithful to you."

They lay down together again, with nearly horizontal beams of sunlight streaming in through the windows picked out in motes of dust. The summer passed peacefully in that part of France, and the weather was dry, mild and balmy. Vitellan made no secret of his origins, and as a result he attracted many dozens of scholars. He enjoyed talking about life in the Roman Empire at its zenith, and filling in details about great events that were once common knowledge but had somehow been omitted from the historical chronicles. The countess was always in his company, sleeping with him by night, and sitting proudly beside him by day as he enthralled rooms full of learned men with tales of Christ that he had heard from people who had actually met Him. The only secret that Vitellan maintained was that of where and when he would be refrozen for his next great leap through time. It was something that nearly everybody asked about in passing, but nobody cared enough to dwell upon. After all, when great news is being shouted throughout a town, who asks where the crier lives?

Switzerland: 28 December 1358, Anno Domini

As the autumn sun blazed against the towering white peaks of the Berner Alpen, the clear evening sky promised a bitterly cold night. A meltwater stream that fed the headwaters of the Rhône splashed through a deep gorge that guarded the approach to the village of Marlenk, and a single rope and plank bridge was its only link with the road that led north to Berne and south to the St. Gothard Pass and Italy. Marlenk was a cluster of three dozen stone cottages, a large inn, a chapel, and a length of low wall that was more windbreak than fortification.

The sentries of the village militia watched a dozen pilgrims approaching on their way south to Rome. They pitched ragged tents on the wayfarers' green beside the bridge, but only one chose to cross to the guardhouse and enter Marlenk. He was a priest, well spoken and friendly, and carried no weapon but the knife that he used for eating.

Outside Marlenk's inn two grizzled English men-at-arms were cutting firewood in the snow slush. They wore leather jerkins and heavy mittens, and the liripipes of their hoods were wound around their necks against the cold. Supper came soon after sunset at this time of year, and the aroma of roast pork was strong on the air.

"The day's old," observed Lew as the sunlight retreated up the peaks.

"Year's old too, world's old, just like us as is old," complained Guy, trying to balance a skew-cut log on the chopping block. "Our village in England fallin' apart, and such young as is left all want to go to France and fight in the Free Companies."

"More fool they," said Lew, shaking his head before swinging his axe again. "France is full of strange and evil men."

"Aye, the Jacquerie. Fought 'em at Meaux, and in other parts of Brie." Guy spat into the snow.

"I heard they roamed the north killing nobles. I heard they roasted one knight on a spit after killing him, and made his lady and children watch. Then they ravished them, and tried to make them eat his flesh before they killed them too."

"That might have been at Beauvais," said Guy after thinking for a moment. "A few good men-at-arms could have stopped 'em before they'd done such mischief, but France has nonesuch. France is fallin' apart. We're fallin' apart too." He paused for Lew's reply, but when he got none he selected another log from the pile. "It's quiet here in the mountains, then?" he asked with a trace of sarcasm.

"Quiet? We're on a major road." Lew laughed. "And what with the League expandin' there's been no shortage of wars. I've fought in every one since the Confederates defeated Leopold of the Habsburgs near Schwyz in 1315. I've become a good citizen of the cantons so as to live here and do the Master's work."

"So who's to watch over the Master when we're dead?" Guy asked testily. "The young of our own village don't care for tradition. Hah, there's scarcely any young left!"

"That's as why we're here," replied Lew, forever optimistic. "That's why you revived the Master from his sleep, brought him over the salt sea, crossed the Kingdom of France, fought the Jacquerie and climbed up here into the Berner Alpen."

"Cold, bare place."

"I like it. Came here wi' Tom Greenhelm in 1311. I dug the ice for his chambers, even married a wench I rescued near the Grimsel Pass. Ah Guy, we're lucky to see such wonders as these mountains, just as we're lucky to have met the Master."

"Lucky? My bones ache with the cold, and I can't draw breath of God's air as easy as can in England. Lungs hurt, feet hurt, piles hurt, and for what? End of our lives and end of tradition! In a few days the Master leaves us, then where are we?"

"Here in Marlenk. Come spring we'll go down into Obwalden and marry you to a fat widow. What with wars and the plague there's a short-age of husbands. You could have the empty cottage near mine."

"Me? Live on this icicle in the middle of nowhere?"

"Why not? Much commerce and news goes by on that road, and all manner of folk call in here to—ah, see? A traveler on the bridge. Looks to be a priest."

They watched a man in a dark clerical tunic with a pilgrim's badge pay the toll, then come tramping up the path to the village, his iron-shod clogs clinking against the stones. He leaned wearily on his staff, and hailing them in Latin he asked what language they spoke. Lew replied that Latin would suffice. They had both learned it for years in preparation for Vitellan's revival.

"Father Guillaume of Chalon," said the priest, as if he expected them to know him by reputation. After a moment he took the cue from their blank stares. "I'm a scholar, well known in northern France. As I passed through Berne with my fellow pilgrims the bishop there told me a wondrous tale of an English traveler named Vitellan. He'd left a week before us, so we hastened to catch up."

"Ye wish to talk of learned matters to Master Vitellan?" asked Lew.

"Yes, very learned matters. The bishop said that Vitellan is soon to leave again, for places where none of us may follow."

Lew looked to Guy and raised his eyebrows. Guy nodded. Their Master's instructions had been quite clear: he would always be available to talk with scholars. Lew stamped off to his cottage, where Vitellan was staying. The Countess of Hussontal was at the inn, and to avoid unsavory rumors Vitellan now refused to sleep under the same roof as her.

"So what of the Master d'ye know?" asked Guy.

"That he was a Roman soldier, that he fought the Danes with Alfred the Great of England, and that he was born in the time of Christ."

"How much d'ye believe?"

"I keep my mind open. He may be a fraud, he may be a madman. He may be Lazarus, raised from the dead by Christ and now unable to die. He may even be the devil, trying to tempt us."

"He's none o' those," said Guy defensively. "He's slept packed in ice beneath our village in England for most time. On his own reckonin' he'd not have walked the earth and breathed God's air more than thirty-six years out of all his centuries."

"He slept in ice? In England?"

"Aye. We harvested ice in winter to last through summer, but now the young folk don't care for tradition. They want to serve in great castles, or fight in France or even fight in the Holy Land."

"Surely not, there's not been a crusade for ninety years."

"Aht, some Cyprus prince plans a Ninth Crusade once he ascends the throne, but no matter. Our young folk will turn to anything rather than tend the Master's ice. That's why we're here in—ah, what's that new name for the Cantons' League?"

"Switzerland."

"Switzerland, where there be mountains an' rivers of ice all year round and Master Vitellan can sleep without ice harvests."

The priest nodded as if he already understood the wonders being explained.

"How long has your village kept him frozen?"

"Oh, I don't know countin'. Master Vitellan's father met wi' Christ, so that's how old he be."

"But that's thirteen centuries, at least."

"Aye, that sounds to be right. He was unfrozen once, as I knows it, and defeated the Danes. Now our village in England is all but deserted and can't make ice. We planned for it, though, so the Master's been unfrozen again and brought here."

"I don't follow."

"We're all old, we can do nowt but launch the Master one last time, wish him well, then live what lives we have left in fear o' God as the good Christians we be."

The priest frowned. "So your master is not immortal," he said flatly. "While awake he ages as we do, but when he sleeps, he sleeps in ice for centuries."

"Aye, that he does," Guy confirmed, but Father Guillaume was no longer paying him attention. Lew was returning with a man of medium height dressed in a quilted surcoat, war boots and shoulder cape. His face was emaciated, but his features were still recognizably Mediterranean.

Much of the traffic that passed over the Alps between the Italian states and the rest of Europe came by Marlenk, and its people knew of the latest fashions in dress and cuisine even before those who lived in the capitals of the great kingdoms. Marlenk's inn was the focus of the local economy, and although most of its patrons were humble pilgrims and merchants, it was sometimes used by nobles. Tonight there was a French countess, the knight commanding her escort, a great scholar, and an English traveler named Vitellan to whom they all deferred.

Fresh straw was on the floor, and the table was set before the fire and laid with two layers of damask. The serving-trestles were already heavy with pewter plate, although some silver had been put out for the use of the countess. The French knight, Raymond, entered. He surveyed the room, then checked with the guards outside. The sky was clear and the moon full, and he shivered with the implication before returning inside and sending a maid for his sister, the countess. He was a survivor of Poitiers and had an ugly scar on his upper cheek to show for it. To distract eyes from his face he wore a tunic gleaming with Bargello work in silver thread, and a wide hip belt with polished latten plates sewn all around.

The innkeeper, local priest, and captain of the militia passed as the dignitaries of Marlenk, and were waiting by the fire and wearing their best. Vitellan entered with Father Guillaume, and a moment later the countess appeared. She had changed out of her traveling robes already, and was wearing a green sleeveless surcoat with diagonal vermilion striping over a gown with tight, buttoned sleeves. Her hair was netted, and framed by a long silk veil, adding a suggestion of modesty to what was otherwise the height of fashionable dress. The sweet scent of her concealed ambergris pomme-d'embre cut through the lingering reek of the recently evicted cattle and sheep.

While introductions were being made over sheep marrow fritters and goose heart pastries, Lew and Guy crept in with their firewood and began to stoke up the blaze. The innkeeper served wine mulled with his best spices.

"These spices are from further away than our geographers could guess at," he told the knight as he sipped from his goblet.

"But never as far as Master Vitellan's journey," added the countess. The innkeeper waited to see that the others were smiling and nodding before responding with a polite laugh himself.

Over bacon broth Vitellan gave what was by now a well-rehearsed account of how he had obtained a jar of what was now known in his village as either the Frigidarium Elixir or the Oil of Frosts. This allowed him to be frozen without dying. Lew was then called over to recite a couple of dozen verses of an epic describing how the Roman's servants had established the village of Durvonum, now Durvas, in the southwest of England, and how they had harvested ice each winter to keep their master preserved through thirteen hundred English summers. A roast piglet was brought in on a large dish, flanked by capon pastry subtleties in the form of towers that seemed to guard it. Serious conversation trailed off, to be replaced by the soft notes of a slender lap-harp under the fingers of a thin, intense Bohemian itinerant. Vitellan, who could eat no solids, was given more broth.

Father Guillaume of Chalon rapidly proved himself to be an enigma. He knew all the courtesies to be accorded the countess and her knight, yet he displayed brash familiarity as well. Once the piglet had been reduced to bones Vitellan took up his story again, explaining that traditions had begun to break down in his English village at the start of the century. The Icekeeper of the time, Tom Greenhelm, made a decision to move Vitellan to the perennial snows of Switzerland. Tom journeyed there with six others, including the teenage Lew, and they explored and dug at several sites. It was forty-seven years before they had finally excavated a chamber that was suitable. Tom, well over eighty by then, returned to England and had the Master revived. He presented Vitellan with a map sealed in a lead tube that showed where the new Frigidarium was located, then died some days later in his sleep. Guy Foxtread was appointed the new Icekeeper.

"The higher regions of the Berner Alpen are permanently frozen," Vitellan concluded, "so I shall not need villagers to supply my new Frigidarium with ice."

Vitellan had spent many such evenings with the scholars, clergy, and nobles of the time. First they would marvel at how he had preserved himself, then they would move on to subjects closer to their hearts. The clergy would ask about Christ, the apostles, and whatever other saints he might have met; nobles would want to discuss Roman fortifications and fighting arts; scholars would be eager to know if he had read manuscripts that were by now incomplete or lost. The countess sat serene and smiling, saying little but very proud of her unique and brilliant protégé. Guy and Lew sat beside the fire, sipping at the local beer and listening to the harpist. Three men of the escort stood by the door, alert but expecting no trouble.

"I can see weaknesses in your Frigidarium," declared Guillaume.

His voice was sharp, cutting through the pleasantly drowsy mood. Vitellan blinked and sat up. Nobody had ever questioned his Frigidarium's viability before.

"You question that Master Vitellan is who he is?" asked the countess, indignation in her voice. The other conversations died as she spoke.

"Oh no, great lady, not at all," Guillaume replied, now with the breathless eagerness of an experienced debater. "I merely wonder how he solved certain difficult problems."

"Please, name them," urged Vitellan.

"Your new Frigidarium needs no people to maintain the ice, but you still need people to revive you. Who is to do that?"

"Master Vitellan saved me from the Jacques," the countess interjected. "That counts for a lot. My descendants will see to it that he is revived. The map showing the location of the Frigidarium and instructions for reviving him will be kept in my castle. If English peasants could keep the first Frigidarium working for over thirteen centuries, French nobles could do at least as well."

The countess was used to her word being taken as the ultimate verdict in any dispute. It never crossed her mind that Guillaume might not accept it. She failed to notice his strange, eager, even predatory expression.

"I disagree!" he exclaimed, leaning over the table and raising a finger for emphasis. The countess gasped with surprise, but Guillaume went on, even as she opened her mouth. "With the great ritual of ice-gathering to keep Vitellan's memory alive, the English villagers were forced to preserve the revival knowledge as well. People forget more easily if there is no actual work to do. Tradition alone is not enough to sustain a memory."

Vitellan restrained the countess with a discreet gesture, but did not take his eyes from Guillaume.

"I have faith in my good patroness and her descendants. There is a risk, but then merely being alive risks death."

"But this is not just a matter of life and death. You might remain in the ice forever, neither alive nor dead. The Day of Judgment would come."

"So?"

"So study the Bible! The Day of Judgment will not mean the end of the physical world—that has been revealed to us by God. The world will continue to exist, as will the ice of these mountains, as will you in your Frigidarium. For you there will be neither the glories of Heaven nor the torments of Hell: you will be neither alive nor dead for eternity."

Guillaume sat back and folded his arms. His eyes were wide and his lips apart in a shallow smile.

"The year 1000 was thought to herald the Day of Judgment, yet it did not happen. I slept through it inside my Frigidarium."

"You took a chance."

"Passing through Beauvais and Brie when the Jacquerie were on the rampage was taking a chance. Traveling in France at all with the Free Companies pillaging and looting was taking a chance."

"Your Frigidarium could be a gift of the devil. It's a machine to defy the will of God, a blasphemy to be stopped by the might of the Church."

"So what is blasphemy? Christ revealed that even the smallest bird is watched over by God, so I believe that He watches over me as well. If on the Day of Judgment He sends fire to melt the ice around me, my body will truly die and my soul will be judged."

"Would God go to so much trouble? You seem to flatter yourself unduly."

"Now who is talking blasphemy?"

The innkeeper raised an eyebrow to a watchful maidservant, and the argument was interrupted by the sodden trenchers being cleared away. The remains of the piglet were left to be picked at.

"Indeed, indeed, blasphemy is as much politics as theology," conceded Guillaume amid the clatter. "Perhaps my fears are unfounded. Surely a noble French family can do at least as well as your loyal peasants. But tell me, Vitellan, why do you travel thus?"

"You study the past, I study the future. I hope to reach the year 2000 with my next sleep. Perhaps I shall stop there and die in some wonderful castle in the company of the nobles and scholars of that year. Perhaps I shall return to the ice to journey on."

"And what of these times?" asked the countess. "Who will be remembered? What is our most memorable achievement?"

"The English philosopher William of Ockham made such advances in clear thought as have not been seen since the great Greek thinkers like Aristotle. I missed William of Ockham by a mere eight years, such a pity. If the world of the year 2000 is very different it will be because of him. Black powder is the greatest and most terrible invention to come from your times, and it too will mold the future."

The answer disappointed the countess, who turned to her brother for assistance.

"But surely the English longbow is more devastating," Raymond protested. "We French were annihilated by it at Crécy and Poitiers."

"Only because you allowed the English to choose the battlefield," replied Vitellan. "Black powder hand-gonnes demand neither the training nor the strength of a bowman, while the large bombards are more portable and versatile than catapults."

"Such weapons have no place in chivalry," admonished the countess, and Raymond nodded his approval.

"Chivalry is a good and civilizing code, I am not denying that. Black powder is a fact of life, however, and the task of chivalry should be to moderate its use."

A spiced apple tart was brought in, steaming fresh from the oven. While it was being apportioned the serving trestles were spread with honey pastries, roasted nuts in cinnamon, and little bowls of spices to aid digestion. Guillaume's aggression seemed to drain away, much to the company's relief, and they were inclined to humor the abrasive yet perceptive guest.

"Sweet Saracen delights," observed Guillaume. "At least something good came out of the Crusades."

"My cook was a Genoese seaman, he made many voyages to the Mameluke Sultanate," the innkeeper explained.

"So now the sailor lives in the mountains?"

"There was trouble over a lost ship; the mountains seemed better for his health."

"Ah, indeed, we are all fugitives from one thing or another," Guillaume replied, turning back to Vitellan. "May I see the Frigidarium Elixir that keeps you alive while frozen in your time ship?"

Vitellan drew back the dagger-pin closure of his large pouch and took out a bottle wrapped in cloth. He unwrapped enough of the neck to display the viscous, honey-brown fluid inside.

"I drink a little each day now, to accustom my body to it. A full dose all at once would be deadly."

Guillaume peered at it. "Were you to drink it all at once and then be frozen, you'd not die until thawed out centuries later."

"Yes, but why do such a thing?"

"Why indeed . . . but now to your Frigidarium. Suppose that peasants found it, peasants who could not read the revival instructions. They might think you a corpse, and carry your body away for burial in consecrated soil in some warm valley. Your flesh would thaw, the worms would eat you."

Vitellan held up a small lead tube that hung from his neck on a leather thong. "Nobody will find me. Tom hid the Frigidarium well, and the only map of its location is in here. His men were blindfolded when they were taken to dig it, and now Tom himself is dead. In a day or two I shall break the seal, study the map, then give it to the countess before setting off alone to sleep in the ice again."

Guillaume nodded as if satisfied, then reached into his tunic and withdrew something that he showed only to Vitellan and asked, "What might this be?"

"It looks to be a favor, such as a lady might give a knight who is about to fight in a tourney or battle."

Guillaume stood up, then slowly walked around to the front of the table, the side where the food was served from. He stood with his back to the fire.

"I am Jacque Bonhomme, King of the Jacquerie!" he announced. He took a pace back in anticipation of their reaction, but was disappointed. Vitellan's expression did not change, the militia captain and innkeeper looked up to the rafters, and the local priest suddenly took a strong interest in a stain on the tablecloth. Raymond turned to the countess, who gave a slight sneer and folded her arms, as if Guillaume had done something as ill mannered as farting.

"After the burning of Meaux my husband made at least thirty villeins confess to being Jacque Bonhomme under torture," she said coldly. "Many others have admitted to the name to gain notoriety, and all were more convincing than you."

Guillaume gloated for a moment, then smiling broadly he held up a gold bracelet tied with a braid of brunette hair and tossed it among the bones of the piglet on the pewter dish. The countess shrieked as she recognized both hair and bauble, then jammed her fist into her mouth.

"My sister, what is it?" asked Raymond.

She lowered her hand. Blood streamed from the knuckles. "He has Lucretia."

Raymond snatched up his eating dagger even as the countess seized him, and they fell struggling across the table. The trestles collapsed, bringing it crashing down. The knight was restrained with some difficulty by his own men.

"Very wise of the countess," said Guillaume. "My death would mean her daughter's death."

"What do you want?" she asked, her voice contorted by a conflict between fear and contempt.

"Nothing that you can give me, great lady," he replied, while staring straight at Vitellan.

Slowly and deliberately, as if he were picking up the gauntlet of challenge, Vitellan bent over and lifted the braid and bangle from the scattered bones on the floor.

"You have the child and you are dangerous," he said bluntly, "but that does not make you Jacque Bonhomme. How did you abduct her?"

"The good countess sent for a great scholar to instruct her daughter in religion, arts, and the philosophies. A benign and pious man. I met him on the road, spoke with him at length, then sent him to paradise and continued to her castle in his place. When I arrived the countess had departed for the Alps with you, and the count was away helping the Dauphin defend Paris, or so I was told. The servants readily accepted and trusted me, as I was obviously a great scholar—"

"Who are you?" screamed the countess.

"Why, His Royal Majesty Jacque Bonhomme, none other."

"The real King of the Jacques was Guillaume Cale," said Raymond. "Charles of Navarre captured him at Clermont—"

"By unchivalrous treachery!" snarled the priest. "He was put in chains, crowned King of the Jacques with a circlet of red-hot iron, then beheaded." Guillaume paused, gasping for breath as he fought down emotion. "But I was the original Jacque Bonhomme. I was a priest, and a teacher of great repute. A wealthy knight employed me to instruct his children, but after a few months the eldest girl was got with child. The little vixen named me as the father, and it was her word against mine. Noble against cleric! Of course the judgment went against me, but as a sop to my obvious innocence it was arranged that I should escape and flee.

"Ruined, bitter, and a fugitive, I took refuge in the nearby village of St. Leu. I noticed that there was discontent among the villeins, their lot had never been easy. Their work supported everyone, yet they got nothing but crumbs and abuse for their toil. Brigands and the Free Companies stole their livestock, their seed grain, even their cooking pots—and finally the Dauphin sent his nobles to seize supplies for the blockade of Paris.

"That was too much. The nobles had let King John be captured through their cowardice at Poitiers, and now they were fighting among themselves instead of defending their people against the English and brigands. What of their *noblesse oblige?* The nobles felt no obligation to their villeins.

"One day after vespers there was a gathering of angry men in the cemetery. They'd been recently set upon and robbed. A few speakers got up and ranted incoherently against the nobles, then it was my turn. I am a trained orator and well educated, I put ideas behind their resentment, I rallied them. I stood on the earth of a freshly dug grave and shouted that the nobles of France had betrayed the realm, that they were a disgrace and that they should all be killed. I got the men shouting and cheering, they waved pitchforks, pikes, knives, and scythes and called for blood. More and more came over to see what was the fuss. I had, oh, six hundred men hanging on my every word.

"I pointed to the house of a knight who lived not far from town and told the crowd to burn and kill all gentry. They did just that. We killed the knight and his family and burned their place to a shell. More flocked to us, and as the numbers grew, so did my courage. I led my army to the castle of my former student's father. His guards fled at our approach, and we took the place with not much trouble. We tied him to a post and made him watch while his highborn daughters and wife were stripped and held down on the good soil of Beauvais. This time I did sample the charms of my dainty little student, aye, and with all of my loyal villeins cheering. As many villeins as felt inclined then bestrode the women of that family while the knight looked on and screamed himself hoarse. Then we cut their throats. As the castle burned I was proclaimed King of the Jacques, and we went on to burn, loot, kill, aye, and plough the furrow of many a lady of high birth."

The countess turned away, unable to face Guillaume any longer, but she caught sight of the braid and bangle in Vitellan's hand. Her daughter was being held by the very men who had done those atrocities, and for all her rank and authority she was powerless. Black specks gathered and swarmed before her eyes as she fainted. Lew, Guy, and Raymond carried her to a bench against the wall.

"So she doesn't like my story," sneered Guillaume. "Well, what about one by another Guillaume, Guillaume de Jumièges, for example? He wrote of a peasant uprising in Normandy two hundred years ago. Not a violent battle, just honest men throwing off harsh laws. They elected deputies to speak with their duke, but he sent soldiers to scatter them and seize the deputies. He had their hands and feet chopped off and returned them to their villages as a lesson in obedience. Well? Was that any better? I could tell dozens more such tales from the years before and since."

The countess remained insensible. The others said nothing.

"My Jacques were unstoppable. We burned five dozen castles and great houses, we could have gone on to seize the whole of France. Oh, the nobles came in force against us, yet they had no nerve and more villeins flocked to our ranks than they could kill. We began to recruit men with military training, Guillaume Cale and even Étienne Marcel. We had a hundred thousand men . . ." His voice trailed off, and he lowered his gaze to the straw at his feet.

"Yet the invincible Jacquerie were crushed at Meaux," Vitellan concluded for him.

"Silence!" bellowed Guillaume, looking up and clenching his fists. Silence followed. He looked about the room, took a deep breath, then stared coldly at Vitellan. "Mind your tongue, historian of the future. Lucretia's life hangs by my fingertips."

"If you try to leave in a mind to kill her, you will not leave here alive." Vitellan's voice was equally cold and emphatic.

"If the moon touches the peaks before I return she will die in any case. Jean, my deputy, has clear instructions."

"So, we had better ensure that you leave in a good humor. What do you want with me?"

"Meaux, Meaux," he muttered. "You want to know why I need your help, Roman? It's because God's judgment was against me at Meaux. There was a miracle. We had the Dauphin's wife, sister, daughter, and three hundred other noble ladies penned up in the Market of Meaux. The mayor, the magistrates, the citizens all came over to us and opened the town. My Jacques were all ready to do a stout job of ploughing those noblewomen, and they were defended by scarcely ten dozen fighting men. Then . . . it was a miracle, there's no other accounting for it. Twenty-five knights and a mere hundred men-at-arms against nine thousand Jacques, odds of seventy-five to one. They cut down our vanguard on the bridge between the Market and the city, then began to advance. Suddenly men-at-arms who had been cowering in their houses saw what was happening and came rushing down to rally behind them. It was God's judgment, and it was against me."

He looked around the room, almost as if expecting sympathy.

"Hellfire cannot come too quickly for you," said the reviving countess as Raymond helped her to sit up.

"For what? Killing knights, nobles, and their whores? Nobles should protect their villeins, yet you treated us as cattle, then abandoned us to the English Free Companies. Villeins who dared to even whimper were killed or mutilated, their goods pillaged, their wives bent over the nearest wall and bulled, and their daughters carried off to be harlots. Where was your justice for my people?"

"Your people?" shouted the countess. "You are a priest and a scholar. The villeins are not your people, you should minister to them but not become one of them. *We* are your people!"

"Oh ho, so now you want me back? Father Guillaume, Father Guillaume, please come back, it was all a mistake."

"Is Lucretia unharmed?" asked Vitellan, breaking a long, delicately balanced silence.

"Would I damage the walls that keep me safe? Of course she's unharmed. She's been forced to eat good peasant bread and walk the road on her own two feet. She has wind and blisters, nothing more."

"What do you want in exchange for her?"

"The means to escape unpardonable sin and hellfire," Guillaume replied smoothly.

"There is no unpardonable sin," exclaimed the Marlenk priest, trying to sound magnanimous and reassuring. "Let me confess you, give back the girl, then go your way."

"Fool! God performed a miracle to stop me, He sided with the nobles of France. I hate Him for that!" His voice had risen to a scream, but he caught himself. He stood facing them, panting and shivering. "I despise divine justice, but I fear hellfire. I could confess my sins, yet I'm not sorry for them so they cannot be forgiven. Centurion Vitellan, your noble French patrons forced me into sin, so you must help me escape. I want your Frigidarium."

"You—want my Frigidarium? How could that help you?"

Although he was desperate, Guillaume's one means of escape clearly terrified him. His nostrils flared, his eyes protruded like those of a terrified ox before the butcher's stall. At last he took a deep breath and began to explain.

"Were I a pagan Greek, I might have planned to steal Charon's boat and drop the anchor midstream in the River Styx, suspending myself between life and death to escape punishment in the afterlife. Because I am a Christian I don't believe in Charon, yet I have still devised a way to suspend myself between life and death. I'll freeze myself undead in your ice chamber, with nobody knowing my location and nobody to revive me. The Day of Judgment will pass, and my immortal soul will be suspended in ice for eternity. Your Frigidarium will let me cheat God Himself."

The Marlenk priest was appalled. "Blasphemy, heresy!" he cried. "God can see everything, he'll melt the ice. His justice—"

"But God is lazy, and cares nothing for justice. He watches over nobles and ignores ciphers like me until our allotted time is done. He'll not bother to melt all the ice of the Berner Alpen to catch me."

"The elixir will ravage your stomach unless you accustomize your-self to it for months," warned Vitellan. "To drink a full dose means death within days, at most."

"What do I care for a stomach? I'll burn holes in it with your elixir, then freeze myself before death can claim me."

"And your Jacques? Surely they cannot all wish to be frozen for eternity?"

"They think that I'm here to steal an elixir of invisibility from you. I'll take them to the Frigidarium, and when they drink your elixir we'll all be saved from eternal punishment together. My Jacques will never know what a favor I did them."

Vitellan took out the bottle and stared at it. "I do not know the method of making the elixir. What remains in this bottle is the last that I have."

"Then your choice is more difficult. Those Jacques across the ravine have ravished more noblewomen and their daughters than any-one in all the world, Centurion Vitellan. Choose between your Frigi-darium and the girl. A scrap of parchment and a bottle of poison for her virginity and life."

"Ho there Jean, he's back," called the lookout as the figure of the priest appeared in the moonlight.

The Jacques were edgy, and none of them were asleep. They tum-bled out of their tents and stood waiting. There were ten of them, the elite of the Jacques, all surly, confident villeins. Some were armed with axes and two had swords. The rest had bound spear-blades to their pil-grim staffs. Lucretia was hobbled, and tethered to one of the Jacques by a length of rope. She began to whimper as she was hauled after him.

"He's walkin' as brisk as always, so they can't have tortured him," Jean observed as the priest reached the bridge.

"Lord Bonhomme, did ye get the elixir to make men invisible?" called the lookout. The priest held up slim phials in both hands, then reached down hurriedly as the bridge swayed under him.

"Fool!" shouted Jean as he backhanded the lookout across the face.

"He nearly dropped 'em. Shut up and stand back until he's safely over. All of ye!"

The moment that he stepped off the bridge they crowded anxiously around him—but the phials in his hands suddenly became daggers as Vitellan reversed them and plunged one into Jean's throat, then backhanded the other into the lookout's eye. A man holding a spear lunged forward, but the blade only scraped hidden chainmail before Vitellan dropped one dagger to seize the shaft and pull him down onto the other. A sword thudded heavily onto the mail on his back, sending him reeling, yet he lunged forward at the Jacque who was tethered to Lucretia, feinting an overhand blow with the shaft of the spear before stabbing him in the abdomen with his dagger. He ripped upward as the man gave a wheezing shriek, then dropped the dagger and faced the others with the spear.

Now luck came to the Roman's aid. One of the six remaining Jacques backed off too far. He lost his footing and tumbled into the gorge with a piercing, echoing scream. At this the others broke and fled. One ran across the bridge, only to be seized and hurled into the gorge by the sentries. Where the road followed a narrowing of the ravine the rest were cut down by a shower of arrows that lashed across the gap from the hidden Marlenk militia.

Vitellan cut the girl free. She did not move, except to stare from one body to another as if unable to comprehend that her long nightmare could have been ended so quickly.

"Are you the Roman soldier?" she asked in Latin.

Vitellan pushed back the hood and moonlight gleamed on his face.

"Yes, I am Vitellan. And are you Lucretia under all that grime?"

She threw her arms around his neck by way of reply, and did not let go until he had carried her across the bridge to the countess.

Jacque Bonhomme had betrayed everyone. After Vitellan surrendered the sealed map and elixir to him he had cut the lead tube open and studied Tom Greenhelm's directions. Then he left, telling them to stay where they were, and that the girl would be sent across the bridge before it was destroyed to cover their retreat. They waited, but Lucretia did not come. Lew crept out to check with the sentries at the bridge. They reported that nobody had crossed since sunset, and in the moonlight Lew found fresh footprints in the snow leading off into the highlands behind Marlenk.

The moon was nearing the mountain peaks as Vitellan put on his mailshirt and borrowed robes from the Marlenk priest. The Jacques would be expecting a priest to return across the bridge, and after that the odds would be merely ten to one. That was still more than seven times better than the odds when he had faced the Jacquerie at Meaux beside the Count de Foix and the Captal de Buch . . . and the Roman army had trained its officers exceptionally well.

Raymond and his squire helped Vitellan out of his chainmail.

"God be praised that the girl is safe," said the knight. "Yet what a pity that the monster Jacque Bonhomme escaped all punishment by using your Frigidarium."

"He has not escaped God's justice," Vitellan assured him. "Tom Greenhelm worked out an infallible means for my revival in the final Frigidarium that he dug. His men hollowed out a great boulder, lowered it into a deep crevasse in a glacier, then dug the boulder into the wall of the crevasse. Glaciers flow slowly to the lowlands, then melt. The boulder with Jacque Bonhomme inside will be carried down until one day, centuries from now, it is freed of the ice in some warm valley. If the gold coins that were dug into the ice around it do not attract people to revive him, then he will die and rot as the boulder warms. If he is revived, the elixir's hurt to his stomach will kill him anyway. Whatever the path, he will be judged by God. Whether hellfire follows is not for me to say."

"And if the Day of Judgment should come before then?"

"In a thousand years and more it's not happened."

The village militia was assembling to hunt down the Jacque king as Raymond sent his squire back to the inn with the chainmail. Vitellan began walking toward the snowdrifts at the edge of Marlenk, and he beckoned the French knight to follow.

"The countess kissed you with unseemly ardor just now," said Raymond. "She is of a mind to bed you. I—I cannot deny that you have done great deeds for her, yet I must appeal to your honor. Please, respect her rank and position—"

"We shall be behind that snowdrift in a few moments. I want you to help me scoop out a trench in it. I shall take off my robes and lie down naked in the snow. When I stop breathing you must cover me with snow, then fetch Guy and Lew."

Raymond stared in surprise, then shivered at the thought.

"But without your elixir you will die."

"There is elixir in my blood, enough for one more leap through time. I have been sipping at it for some weeks to reaccustom myself to its potency. Here, this is a good place."

"Master Vitellan, this snow will melt in spring."

"But by then Lew and Guy will have hollowed out a proper Frigidarium in some deep ravine and carried my body there. Come now, dig. You can make up some story about me being lost in the hunt for Jacque Bonhomme, and there will be no more Vitellan to tempt the countess to impure love. Return in a year or so. Lew and Guy will give you a map and the instructions to revive me. Give them to Lucretia when the countess is dead. Ask her to establish a tradition to revive me in her family. Never tell the countess where my body is hidden: she may try to have me revived."

It did not take long to scrape out a trench in the newly fallen snow. Vitellan began to disrobe.

"Remember, tell Guy and Lew to dig into a deep, blind ravine, where the ice never melts or moves. Tell them that my will is to be revived in . . . let us make it 2054, when I shall be two thousand years old."

"But Master Vitellan, why not a glacier, so that you may still have a chance should Lucretia's descendants fail you? I'll give Guy gold coins to bury nearby to attract searchers?"

"No! Tom Greenhelm studied glaciers for decades. Their ice splits, distorts, and shatters. Without a hollow boulder to protect my body it would be mangled beyond revival. No, it must be a deep ravine where the ice does not move."

Naked and shivering, Vitellan lay down in the trench.

"Heaven and saints! So-so cold. Quickly, pack snow. All around, every p-part but . . . not my face. N-not yet."

"God forgive me, I'm killing you."

"No! Only . . . sleep. W-when breath and t-talk stop, cover face. T-tell Guy . . ."

"I'll do it. By my life I'll do it. Vitellan? Master Vitellan?"

Every man who could be spared set off after Jacque Bonhomme but his trail was soon lost amid the glaciers, ravines, and ridges of the mountains. The countess fell into an exhausted sleep with her daughter in her arms, and did not awake until nearly noon the following day. By then the weather had closed in, and it was snowing heavily. Two of the Marlenk militia died of exposure before they could return from the hunt. The Marlenk priest recorded the deaths of three searchers.

The Count of Hussontal gathered a small group of fanatical knights together and spent the next nine years raiding the English Free Companies. Several of the small, savage battles that he provoked were against odds of two or three to one, and he did much to weaken the myth of invincibility surrounding the English after the Battle of Poitiers. The countess invited him to return to their estates when she learned that he had lost an eye and had had his right knee shattered by an English mace. Although she had forgiven him, he was unable to do the same for himself. Whenever there was fighting anywhere he would leave for it at once. He was killed by an exploding bombard in 1374.

For a medieval knight Raymond lived uncommonly long. He was there to whisper the truth about Vitellan to the countess on her deathbed, then watch her die at peace. Lucretia had already been told what had happened by then, and she undertook to establish a tradition to revive Vitellan, yet . . . Jacque Bonhomme, Father Guillaume, whatever name he went by, he had been right. Lucretia's great-great-grandson fell from his horse and broke his neck while hunting before the story of the Roman hero had been explained to his own five-year-old son. The parchments and map that Lucretia had placed in the family archives remained undisturbed until the castle was looted and burned in 1795. Both Roman officer and peasant king slept on, oblivious, the latter inching his way toward thaw and death, the former with only a scrap of parchment between him and a headlong plunge into eternity. With the paranoia common to all good Icekeepers, Guy had made a second, secret map to Vitellan's frozen refuge against time.

Guy returned to England, although on his way he called in at the estate of Anne de Boucien. He was delayed for some months, journeying on only after they were married. The new match made Guy the stepfather to Louise, Marie, and Jean, and later the father of two children of his own. Once Jean was old enough to run his father's estate, Lady Anne went to live in Durvas.

Guy became Mayor as well as Icekeeper, and with the money from Anne's French fortunes gradually built the declining village back into a thriving community. Even Raymond's long life paled as an achievement when compared to Guy's death in his nineties. To survive both the Black Death and some of the worst fighting of the Hundred Years War he had had a very strong grip on life.

The secret of Vitellan's resting place was preserved in the second map in the Durvas archives, and the tradition of maintaining the village Frigidarium was revived by new generations of Icekeepers. The climate cooled again, and what later became known as the Little Ice Age ended the long, warm medieval summer. Once more the Durvas Frigidarium had work as storage for frozen meat, although Icekeepers still dreamed wistfully of returning the Master to the stone bench that was always kept respectfully empty. Each new Icekeeper's first duty was a pilgrimage to the Swiss Alps to check that the resting place of the Master was undisturbed.

In the nineteenth century a Durvas engineer was among the first to experiment successfully with refrigeration machines, using new discoveries in gas thermodynamics. Durvas grew first into a large manufacturing center, then into a corporation called the Village. It was bombed during World War II, but was soon rebuilt and went on to grow into a medium-sized city by the end of the twentieth century. The University of Durvas specialized in the study of cryogenics and techniques of suspended animation. As far as the people of Durvas were concerned the very existence of Vitellan had faded into the folktales and ballads that were sung in local pubs and at May and harvest fairs, but for the members of the Village Corporate it was different. Vitellan was in theory their chief executive officer, and the entire legend was explained to each new recruit. He was the Centurion of Durvas, and they were stewards of his rapidly expanding empire.

The story of Jacque Bonhomme had been a slur on the memory of Vitellan, at least as far as Guy Foxtread had been concerned. He saw to it that all records of what had really happened at Marlenk were rewritten to denigrate the King of the Jacquerie. As time passed historians grew uncertain whether the original Jacque Bonhomme had ever existed, or had merely been figurative.

The twenty-first century opened to increasing excitement in the exclusive innermost circle of the Village Corporate, for their secret Master's scheduled revival in 2054 was within the probable lifetimes of even those who were middle-aged. Vitellan would be two thousand years old, and he would inherit a mighty corporation that was more far-flung than Rome's empire had ever been.

the centurion's champion

Durvas, Britain: 12 November 2028, Anno Domini

The Icekeeper of Durvas lay dead in the smoking ruins of the Village Imprint Research Clinic, his chest smashed to bloody pulp and splintered bone by a burst of tumble-shot. The rescue crews ignored his body, and even Lord Wallace gave it no more than a glance as he inspected the shattered pile of rubble and collapsed slabs. Downwash from a sky-grapple's rotors raised swirling dust and smoke like the special effects in a cheap disaster vid.

"Anderson, where is the Master?" demanded Lord Wallace in an oddly thin, high voice when he reached Durvas' corporate marshal.

"Under that," Anderson replied, wild-eyed and breathless, pointing to one of the toppled walls which lay alarmingly level on what had been the clinic floor. "Forty minutes since the attack, and we still have no idea what shape he's in. My guess is that he's flatline."

"By the look of it, he's flat as well," Lord Wallace shouted back above the noise. "That's a seven-ton slab."

Rescue workers were swarming over the slab, attaching woven monofiber cables and pressure claws. The downwash began to increase as the motors of the skygrapple spun up to a new pitch. The slab eased up, then the huge machine heaved its load sideways and dropped it on a nearby lawn. Nobody was watching; everyone was looking at the remains of a trolley that had been crushed to a few inches thickness. There was a darkening blot of blood all around it.

A second skygrapple flew in, lowering a cryogenic chamber on a cable as the medics rushed forward to tend the crushed body.

"Careful, don't move him yet," someone called as they began to attach sensors to scan for life signs.

"Damn you, he's *sure* to be scan-dead!" shouted Anderson. "Just cut the straps and get what's left of him into the cryochamber as fast as possible. Every second you arse around means more brain damage!"

Lord Wallace counted four fairly large fragments of skull being put into the chamber with the main part of the body. His gorge began to rise, but it was through fear and guilt, not the horror of what had happened to Vitellan's body.

"Scrape up every bit of tissue and get it into the chamber," the marshal was shouting to medics, who were more inclined to reach for a fire hose when confronted with such a severely pulverized corpse. It was like collecting the fragments of a shattered champagne glass for restoration, and just as futile.

A tiltfan descended smoothly to the disaster site. Cassion, the clinic's director of surgery, jumped clumsily to the rubble and made his way through the dust to the chamber with Vitellan's body.

"Life signs?" he demanded of Anderson.

"With respect, sir, you've got to be joking," he replied, then hit a stud on the side of the chamber. A hologram of the crushed body took form in the air in front of them. "Over forty minutes like that. All we could do was scrape him off the trolley and force-chill him at once. I'm not even sure if he has enough oil in his tissues for a full freeze."

"He doesn't, but I can fix that," said Cassion.

Lord Wallace was grim-faced. "All right, guard what's left of him on a shoot-to-kill alert, and get it all into the shaft to the Deep Frigidarium. What about my son's cryochamber?"

"It's stored over in South Five," said Anderson. "There's no damage reported from there."

"You had better get his chamber to the Deep Frigidarium as well."

"Right away, Lord Wallace," said Cassion, and he left at once.

Anderson took Lord Wallace's arm as the chamber was lifted away. "The Icekeeper's dead," he told him.

"After what happened here today, it's what he deserves," replied Lord Wallace coldly. "His security's a disgrace, it shouldn't be dignified with the name security. The Luministe agents walked in so easily that I actually felt insulted. Gulden will be the interim Icekeeper," Lord Wallace declared, as if the decision had been ratified by the Village Corporate.

"Gulden? He has only minority support on the Corporate."

"Well *he* had plenty of support and look at what's happened," said Lord Wallace, jerking his thumb toward the body of the Icekeeper. "I know what you're talking about but now we need the *best*, not just a good compromise. Bonhomme's people always recruit the best, that's why all this happened. If it's any consolation to you, I don't like Gulden either."

"So why maintain the Icekeeper position at all? There's no Master now."

"We've had Icekeepers with no Master from 1358 to 2016, I don't see why we should change. The true facts will be kept from the rest of the Corporate, of course."

"Of course," echoed the marshal.

Anderson glanced over the shattered building. It was not the damage that unsettled him so much as the implication of weaknesses that almost certainly existed elsewhere in the organization. What other parts of Village security would collapse so readily after a relatively small shock, he wondered.

Lord Wallace beckoned to a waiting tiltfan to pick them up and it advanced toward them, floating just above the rubble and raising a cloud of dust. All at once Cassion came running across the rubble from South 5, waving his arms.

"They've taken one of the cryochambers!" he shouted. "The one with your son's body."

Paris, France: 6 December 2028, Anno Domini

Warmth and contented lethargy caressed Vitellan, melting memories of the sharp touch of snow on his bare flesh and the intense, blazing stars of a night in the Berner Alpen late in 1358. It took some time for his nerves to accept that there was no more cold and pain, and that this was the end of the great sleep and not the beginning.

His eyes blinked open and came into focus on someone holding . . . he could not identify it, but the man's bearing of alert confidence suggested that he was a warrior. Was it a weapon? There was no blade, and it was too short to be a mace. Perhaps it was a distant descendant of the gonnes that he had seen and used as he had traveled through wartorn France? A hand-held gonne, then, but where was the smoke of its fuse? Could it be that—no, impossible.

Vitellan saw white columns beyond the sky-blue blankets of his bed, and there were two men in dark, finely tailored jackets beneath open white robes with colored, oblong brooches pinned to their chests. Perhaps one of the men was a woman, Vitellan wondered, his or her grooming was subtly softer. They walked away, and the one with the warrior's bearing walked past again, alert for anything unusual. His gaze scanned across Vitellan's face.

"His eyes are open!" the warrior exclaimed, jerking his weapon up to point at the Roman's head. A hand-gonne, there was no doubt of it. Vitellan thought his words familiar, but missed their meaning. Perhaps it was a dialect of French, of which he only had a smattering. There was a patter of approaching footsteps.

"How did he wake so quickly?" asked the woman. "It should not have been for another day."

"The devil gives him strength," said the guard.

The people in front of Vitellan were milling about in confusion, and he was confused as well. He had survived another plunge through time, but this was all so unfamiliar. Where was the bath of warm water? His chest was not at all painful from the pounding to restart his heart and breathing, yet he was alive. How had these villagers revived him without pounding his heart back into action? If it came to that, his stomach was not hurting either. After a decade of pain Vitellan was now quite unsettled by its absence. Sweet scents like the perfumes of a strange pomme-d'embre hung on the air.

The architecture was sharp and clean, the walls were flawless white. Almost . . . Roman! Had civilization returned to the styles of the century of his birth? He was lying in a bed. It was soft yet supportive, the blankets were clean and pale blue, and their weave was very fine. Glowing dots winked on the sides of glossy boxes draped with colored strings and cords. Unfamiliar insects chirped sharply in time with the lights. Have I slept too long, Vitellan wondered?

More people arrived to mill about in front of him. Most wore robes like open white togas over dun-colored jackets and trousers. They have the bearing of senators and their guards, Vitellan speculated. One of the women clothed in white sat on the bed and peered into his eyes while holding up a light that blazed like a speck of the sun.

"Salve," Vitellan whispered. "Quid est—"

"He's speaking Latin," she said, looking up at someone behind him.

"Bonhomme must be told," said a man.

"Bonhomme is in Santiago, he flies back tomorrow. This was not expected."

Vitellan could glean crumbs of meaning from the distant descendant of the French that he had heard in the fourteenth century. Their manner told him a lot more. They were brusque, unfriendly, and suspicious. A horrifying thought crossed the Roman's mind: they kept saying *Bonhomme*. These people might think that he was Jacque Bonhomme. Had the events of . . . God in Heaven, only last night, become a great legend over the centuries that had actually passed? Had he been revived as the monster of St. Leu . . . or had Bonhomme been discovered and revived first, and gone on to start a new uprising of Jacquerie?

The sheets and blankets were stripped back, and Vitellan saw that he was naked. More people came to attach green pads trailing orange cords to his limbs. His muscles began to work involuntarily. Once he got over the initial shock the effect was quite pleasant, something like a long, languid stretch. None of those tending him spoke Latin, but their French had something in common with its fourteenth-century ancestor. By concentrating he began to deduce more and more meaning from what was being spoken around him.

"I have word that Bonhomme is returning," someone said to one of the guards. "His suborbital lands tomorrow afternoon. A squad of his Inner Security will take over at the change of shift and remain until he arrives."

The guard made an unfamiliar gesture, but it had the crispness of a salute. Was Latin as dead as Etruscan by now, Vitellan wondered? No, one of the, the . . . physicians, perhaps, had definitely recognized his first words as Latin. The physicians returned to remove the massaging pads and help him from the bed. At first Vitellan's knees buckled with every step, but his strength returned quickly. Too quickly. His other four revivals had been much worse than this. They kept touching little tubes to his skin, tubes that hissed and left the skin tender. When he finally ate, it was sitting up at a table. The soup was filled with shredded meat and vegetables, yet his stomach did not revolt at the solid pieces or hurt at all. No pain in his stomach . . . he began to take almost sensual pleasure in being free of that pain.

The guard changed as he finished the soup. There were five newcomers, two women and three men. Each carried a gonne, but they had more of the barbarian's swagger than the crisp discipline of the previous guards. Two of these guards followed Vitellan and one of the whiterobed men into a tiled room where he was washed and scoured by a pair of metal arms that protruded from the wall. A hose that moved of its own accord, like a silver snake, drenched him with hot, steaming water. Before being returned to bed Vitellan was dressed in a green robe that was laced up along the back. He sank to the pillows with relief, exhausted with the strain of merely walking and eating. He was strapped to the bed, and the bindings were strangely soft yet unyielding. His arms were left free, but the buckles that opened to the touch of the physicians remained inert to his fingers.

Now Vitellan noticed a new woman among the guards—above average height, but with an easy grace of movement. She had dark, slightly wavy hair in a pageboy style, cut so that it could never cover her eyes. Hers was a big smile, an easy smile, she seemed something of a harlot, but more than that. She blended in by putting people at their ease, rather than by being suspiciously nondescript. Her figure was just a little thin to draw admiring glances, and she wore a pastel-blue skirt—mid-thigh and loose, like that of a Roman youth.

Vitellan wondered if he had met her before. Something about her was comfortingly familiar, yet something else was unsettling as well. She moved too easily, she was too confident. Most of the others left after a few minutes, but the woman and one physician remained behind with a guard.

She was speaking with the physician when she pointed to the guard and seemed to rub at her finger. Something made a loud, muffled clack. A wet, red patch appeared at the center of the man's sternum. His eyes bulged with what might have been horror or disbelief, had he not already been dead from shock. As the physician gaped in horror she struck his neck with the edge of her hand and he collapsed immediately.

The woman scooped up the guard's fallen gonne and clipped something to the handle, then she called to the other guard. Her voice was level, with no alarm at all. As he appeared she fired at his head. It disintegrated with a sound like a heavy book being dropped, and his body collapsed across that of the physician. The girl vanished from Vitellan's field of view. There was a soft sputtering outside the ward.

She returned, now wearing a white coat. He noticed that two fingers of her left hand were bleeding where the nails had been.

"Do as I say when I release you," she whispered in Latin. It was odd, awkward Latin, but Latin nevertheless.

"Are you with Jacque Bonhomme and his followers?" asked Vitellan.

"No, I'm here from Durvas, your village. Will you do as I say?" she demanded.

"Yes, yes."

She pointed a gonne at a box on a trolley by the wall, and it burst into shards and smoke from the stuttering fire. The buckles of Vitellan's straps popped open at once. He felt stiff and fatigued as he sat up, but his rescuer touched a rod to both of his legs. It hissed sharply, and the skin tingled coldly where it had been. The leaden feeling in his muscles melted away within moments.

"A miracle wand!" he exclaimed softly.

She shook her head. "A physician's tool. The, ah, philter in it is not really good for you but we're desperate. You're probably loaded with implants."

"Implants?"

"Mechanisms, engines within your body that call to your enemies through false hairs. Never mind, we'll scrub you when we get out. Quickly, get into that physician's clothes—yes I know he's a mess. Just do it!"

She rolled the dead guard off the physician. Beneath his blood-spattered white coat the man was wearing creaseless checked trousers and a blue striped shirt. His shoes were slightly large for Vitellan, but the woman packed soft paper inside for a tight fit. She was quick and efficient, as if she might have done such a thing every day.

"My name is Lucel Hunter. If we live through the next ten minutes I'll tell you more. Come, do exactly as I say and trust me."

She pressed another tube against his skin. Like the others it hissed, leaving a cold, tingling sensation.

"What is that?"

"A disease to counter, ah, a sleeping potion. Like I said, trust me."

Out in the corridor were three more bodies. Lucel stripped a coat from one. There was a neat red spot between his eyes.

"No holes, no blood, close enough fit. Put it on and button up to hide that blood on the shirt—no, buttons work like this."

Vitellan glanced about fearfully. "I gleaned from their strange French that unseen eyes watch me."

"The unseen eyes have been blinded for a few minutes. I am not alone in this rescue, I have friends who are busy in other rooms."

They had descended three floors by what Lucel called fire stairs when something like a huge bull began to bellow.

"That's an alarm—something like a trumpet. One of my agents in the security center has frozen the doors to your ward, so the guards will be busy trying to break in there for at least another minute."

"Frozen them? With ice?"

"Not ice, and my agent's not human either."

The fire doors were still free as they emerged into the foyer. Lucel had the gonne under her coat.

"Nobody can leave," a guard ordered as they approached the entrance. The words were intelligible to Vitellan, but only just. Through vast glass walls he could see that it was night outside, although lamps on thin, high pillars blazed with a wondrous intensity.

"What is wrong, Monsieur?" asked Lucel. "What is the alarm? We have to go—"

"Just stay here, Madame."

She motioned Vitellan to stand to one side with her, and as the guard turned away she pointed her left thumb at the sliding door and squeezed with the fingers of her free hand. There was another loud clack, followed by a blast like a thunderclap as the door shattered. Lucel led him crunching through crumbly glass, spraying death from her gonne into the nearby guards. As they ran out into the night several of the bystanders produced gonnes of their own and opened fire.

"This way, down that street, stay beside me and keep your head down."

The air was full of sharp crackles and angry wasps seemed to buzz all around them as they ran. People screamed and flung themselves to the ground as Vitellan and Lucel left the square in front of the hospital.

They dashed down progressively darker, narrow streets until she suddenly pushed him through a door. Two men began to strip Vitellan's clothes off. Something roared like a lion, and the room swayed and began to move.

A huge waggon drawn by lions, Vitellan told himself, but it was probably nothing strange for this century. He was given new clothes and helped to dress in the strange fashions with even stranger fasteners. Over to one side Lucel was stripping the skin of her face away. His senses overloaded beyond bearing, Vitellan vomited up his soup.

"Give him a scan and an EMP burst to kill anything obvious," Lucel told the others. "The rest can wait." She switched back to Latin. "Vitellan, we are breaking your invisible chains, but we both need new faces as well. Did you see me strip my face off just now?"

"Yes, amazing, I—"

"And you and I are getting new faces right away. Just do as you're told, and don't struggle."

One of the men held up something like pink baker's dough on a piece of cloth. The face felt like a scalding wet towel being pressed against his skin, and the itching was almost unbearable as it cooled. The men touched up rough edges as the enclosed waggon lurched to a stop and the lions became quiet. The skin beneath the mask still felt numb and heavy, and itched unbearably at the edges.

"Don't touch!" snapped Lucel as his hand came up. "A good face, but it's still soft and easily marred. You'll only have it for an hour. We are at a place called the Gare du Nord, it's a type of port for ships that sail on land."

At the Gare du Nord they walked past signs that included the words EST, CHEMINE DE LEVITATION MAGNETIQUE DE L'EST, and MAGLEV EASTERN LINES, but the words were meaningless to Vitellan. In spite of this the place was more familiar to him than anything that he had seen for the past ten of his waking years. The Rome he had last seen in 79 A.D. was a bustling, crowded jumble of people like this, although the smells and sounds here were sharp, harsh and alien. Numerals and words glowed from murals—and the face of Jacque Bonhomme stared triumphantly down from amazingly uniform rows of portraits!

"The Luministe guards are already watching the lines going west," Lucel said in Latin, "but we're taking a line east."

"Lines?"

" 'Lines of Magnetic Levitation to the East' is the best translation that I can manage. Magnetic means . . . oh never mind, they're sort of roads."

"Roads? What is this place?"

"Think of it as a port for now."

"Roads from a port? I don't understand. What city is this?"

"When you were born it was Lutetia, founded by the Parisii tribe and then taken over by Rome. It is now called Paris."

"Paris . . . I passed within sight of Paris in the late spring. It was nothing like this."

Lucel strode on for a moment, but a puzzled expression showed through the amazingly flexible skin of her mask.

"What was it like when you last saw it?" she asked.

"Much smaller, and there were fewer people about. The Black Death and the wars with England had killed many."

"What year was that?"

"The Christian year of 1358. Nothing is as it was then. I must have slept five or six thousand years for changes like this to have happened."

Lucel shook her head as she produced what she called passport cards from her shoulder bag. She talked to a woman behind a counter, then told Vitellan to look into a distorting mirror for a moment. The woman waved them on, and Lucel led him down what seemed to be long piers. Vitellan kept reminding himself that this was a port. He tried not to gaze at anything for too long, everything was meant to be commonplace to him. They entered a part of a pier that was almost deserted, and hurried along to an opening in a long, gleaming white and blue building with that same word EST painted on its side. They entered a door with curved corners, and Lucel hurried her charge along a narrow corridor with a glowing roof and square windows. She guided him through yet another door, and it slid shut behind them with a soft hiss.

The room was small, but opulently fitted with cushioned seats of something like green kid leather, and there were polished metal fittings that Vitellan did not recognize. A middle-aged man sat waiting inside. As Lucel flopped onto a seat, Vitellan realized that a lamp-studded landscape of amazingly regular and uniform buildings was moving past beyond the window. Each building blazed with light, the very sky was swamped by the light and the stars were not visible.

"Cutting it fine, Lucel."

"We're here and we're breathing. That's all that matters."

"The cabin's secure."

"Well, so the fuck it ought to be. Now get a webcap onto Vitellan here. He's coped with this century pretty well so far, but he'll need an imprint suite if he's going to get much further without drawing attention."

She turned to the Roman and spoke in Latin.

"Vitellan, this man is George Norton."

"I am grateful for your help," Vitellan said, dragging his eyes away from the lights beyond the window.

"How are you finding all this?" Norton asked in passable Latin, his face all neutral speculation. "You were last awake during the Hundred Years War, I believe. Have you had any imprints yet?"

"Imprints?"

"Memories added to your mind to help you learn a skill or language."

"Memories of a language? I don't understand."

Lucel sighed. "It's like sex, you can't really understand it until you've experienced it." She turned back to Norton. "He was pretty bewildered when I took him through the fighting."

She ran her finger along a strip below the window and it clouded into a bright milky white. As she drew her gloves off Vitellan saw that the thumb and two fingers of her left hand were bloody pulp where the nails should have been.

"Just talk, I need to disarm," she said.

Norton and Vitellan remained silent as Lucel pressed her right thumb from the sides. The scarlet nail fell off onto an open handker-chief. "That's the heavy one," she said with relief. She repeated the process with each of the nails on her fingers.

"Those things are like little catapults, Vitellan," Norton explained.

"More like tiny bombards, or even hand-gonnes," observed Vitellan.

"Gonnes—guns! So, you know guns."

"That's right," said Lucel. "The first gunpowder weapons were being used by 1358. Vitellan, these false nails of mine can't be detected by, ah, the guards and their machines, but it hurts to shoot them, as you can see."

Norton took something from a leather bag. "Peppare Gas Action TR," he said as he tossed the weapon onto the seat beside Lucel. "It won't hurt so much to use it."

Lucel went on cleaning and dressing her injured fingers. Vitellan reached over to the gun.

"Leave it," snapped Norton, already pointing another snubnose gun at his head. Vitellan turned and stared at what to him was an in-congruously small weapon. Lucel stretched out her leg and flicked the tip of her toe into Norton's wrist. The gun fell as he yelped with pain.

"It's paralysed," he gasped, convulsively rubbing his right hand.

"Pinched nerve. Give it a few minutes, you'll be fine."

Norton glared at her. "He went for your gun."

"His move was just curiosity. *You* acted like the dangerous amateur that you are."

"But—"

"Pick it up, Vitellan. It can't shoot unless a safety catch is released."

The Roman turned the gun over in his hands. Norton massaged his wrist.

"Get the webcap ready for him," Lucel ordered.

"I can hardly use my hand."

"Well try! All this strange tech must be driving him crazy."

Norton began to unpack luridly colored cables and slick black boxes with rounded edges from his bag.

"A history lesson may help," Lucel said as she stretched a skin-simulation dressing over her thumb. "This is Anno Domini 2028, Vitellan. It's not even seven centuries since you were last frozen."

"But the changes—"

"Yes, I know. A couple of hundred years after you were last awake the world started to change more rapidly than anyone could have imagined. At first people concentrated on getting back to the level of your Roman Empire and the earlier Greek states, then it went way, way further. The most incredible machines and sciences were developed."

"Like this thing we are on? It's like a wagon the size of a ship that moves like lightning."

"That's a good description, amazing for someone straight out of the fourteenth century. You're very adaptable, you know. I thought you might see all of this as magic and miracles."

"At first I was tempted to think that," Vitellan admitted, then he raised a hand to his temple as if he had just remembered something important. "Has Rome—that is, does Constantinople still stand?"

"Constantinople?" echoed Norton.

"The Byzantine Empire's capital," explained Lucel. "In a way it continued Roman rule after Rome itself fell. I'm sorry, Vitellan, it fell to the cannons of an Islamic army in 1453."

Vitellan shook his head and took fast, deep breaths to stifle the emotions welling up in him. Rome's continuity had finally been snuffed out 95 years into his future of yesterday, and 575 years back in his past of today. For him the tragedy was real and sharp, yet it seemed such a foolish thing to grieve about.

"Where are we going?" he asked to distract himself.

"A city called Moscow. After that, we are booked for Japan."

"Moscow. Ah yes, a long way to the northeast. Is it still threatened by the Tartars and Mongols?"

"Not for a long time. We'll be there in a few hours."

"Hours! I was told that the journey takes months. What principle moves this land-ship?"

"Ah, that's a tricky one. It's the principle that makes lodestone align itself to the north."

"Lodestone?" wondered Vitellan wearily. "How will I ever comprehend all this? It will take as many years as I have left to live."

"Not years, only days," Norton said, flexing his fingers. "Our people will, ah, change your brain so that you can understand everything that's going on. We'll start as soon as you're asleep."

"I doubt that I could sleep for many hours."

"No problem," said Norton, touching a tube to his neck. There was a sharp hiss, then Vitellan slumped limp in his seat.

Vitellan slept as the maglev train continued its ice-smooth dash northeast. Norton spread a black webcap wide with splayed fingers and fitted it over the Roman's head. The webcap was linked to an ALD tutor. He patched the leads from the language module to interface a larger metal box with gray plastic casing. After taping the edges of the webcap to Vitellan's skin he methodically pushed several dozen electrostaples into his scalp. He plugged the cable from the webcap into the gray box and checked the readings that flashed up on a small inset screen. Five staples needed reattaching, then the screen returned an array of options in green lettering. He keyed *English for Tourists, Moscow Stopover,* and a customized option named *Modern Streetwise,* all from Microsoft.

"That's it, Lucel, by Moscow he'll have enough savvy to pass immigration," said Norton.

Lucel broke the seal on a plastic pack. "He'll need to profile as an English tourist: face, eyes, and fingerprints. He also needs the implants scrubbed out of his body as well if we're to get to Moscow at all."

"That's a go, I'm ready."

Norton used a hypodermic syringe to inject nano-homers to search Vitellan's body for the pulse-damaged implants and any others that had survived. It would take half an hour for the homers to report. He now held Vitellan's eyes open while Lucel swabbed them with a preparator before bonding on holographic retinal mask overlays. His facial mask peeled off like something out of a surrealist nightmare, and Lucel stuffed it into a jar of solvent where it slowly dissolved while she unfolded a new mask.

Norton's nano-homers began to report on the implants to which they had bonded. Nine electronic implants had been disabled by the EMP coil back in Paris, but another fourteen of the bio-mech type were detected by the homers while Vitellan's new face and fingerprints were being attached. Getting them out would be slow work. Twenty-three injections with a wide-bore needle and micro-grapple would take another two hours. Each implant extracted went into a woven monomolecular matrix case, and they varied in size from coffee bean to pinhead.

Lucel began with the fourteen bio-mechs first, as they were still active. While dropping number eleven into the case Lucel noted that two and five had dissolved and were now just a murky color in the solution.

"Probably just something to slow him down," Norton speculated. Lucel shrugged and began probing for number twelve, which was deep inside the left ear.

"Tricky, tricky," she muttered as she worked.

"We should be doing scans on each of the implants," Norton said as he held up the case and examined the extracted implants and their mock-hair antennas.

"Then you do it. Away from here."

The case jumped from his hands with a dull thud and fell to the floor of the compartment. Norton backed into a corner as Lucel checked a display.

"Implant ten has exploded," Lucel said as she looked down at the case.

She turned back to Vitellan. Norton remained huddled in a corner.

"The chemicals from two and five would have stopped the catalytic timer on the explosive in ten," he said in a thin, detached voice. "We'd isolated it, so pow! How did you know to take it out before these last three?"

"Sheer luck."

"Fucking hell!" he exclaimed, his face looking like wet chalk. "Uncontained it would have killed all three of us."

Barely breathing, Norton stared at the woven filament case on the floor. One internal cell was blackened from containing the blast.

"Get it together, Norton, I need help. The other implants could activate at any time."

Number twelve came free just as the monitor reported that thirteen and fourteen were giving off a slight amount of heat.

"Beacons," said Norton. "Now that implant ten has exploded the Luministes want to track down what's left of the body."

"How long before they activate?"

"Two minutes if they're the old fullerine interlock model, fifty seconds if they're the new Hoichi line."

"Should I cut the antenna hairs?"

"That may trigger an explosion, or a toxin release."

"Then I need two minutes each," she said as she inserted the needle again. "Why do they take so long to switch on? Anyway, why didn't the EMP fry them back in Paris?"

"When dormant they're only nonconductive organic goo and a catalytic timer. They're designed to survive an EMP, then generate organic conductors for their electronics later."

"Damn, then they're going to go off. Fourteen will transmit for at least three minutes before I can pull it. We're in for another fight without any backup—"

"Who's dropped the ball now, Lucel? Just stand back a moment." He held up an EMP generator and looked at his watch. "Forty-seven, forty-eight . . ."

As he fired the generator over each of two crosses on Vitellan's skin, there was a faint crackling sound. Lucel glanced at the display readings.

"They absorbed energy. Something had generated conductors in there."

"Then they were Hoichis," said Norton, perspiration dripping from his chin in spite of his smile. "I nailed them just as their electronics formed up into bioconductors. No need to panic."

"No more than when implant ten blew. Okay, let's get the wreckage of thirteen and fourteen out, it might be toxic."

Thirteen was just below the skin in the outer thigh, fourteen was in the small of his back. Lucel drew them out, working slowly, and visibly more relaxed. Norton locked implant fourteen in the case just before 8:00 P.M., Paris local time. He stared at a monitor as Lucel lay back for a moment's rest.

"The sensor in the case shows that a couple of the other organics were beacon implants," said Norton. "They've just begun transmitting but the Faraday cage in the case is holding the signals. It's a wonder that the explosion didn't take them out. It's a good, tough case."

"That's all the active implants," said Lucel with her eyes closed. "Do you still want to keep them for your techs to play with?"

"I've lost interest," he said as he attached an acid flush to the dock on the side of the case. A twist to the right armed the trigger, a twist to the left released it. The implants dissolved as the acid seeped through the internal membranes.

Lucel touched a dermal ram against her own skin, and was swept back to fully refreshed clarity. She removed the last nine disabled implants from Vitellan at a more leisurely pace, then began to pack up.

"Moscow in fifty," Norton reported as Lucel armed another dermal ram.

"Then I'll take forty."

Vitellan had memories of memories as he sprawled in black nothingness. Enclosed chariots without horses to move them, ships as big as fortresses, silvery birds the size of triremes, and images dancing in colored windows. There were people in their millions rushing about in cities that stretched away to infinity, heavily armored men bouncing like thistledown over gray deserts, and gleaming, angular demons that assembled strange chimeras of machines and jewelry.

He awoke to what nobody had warned him about: the nausea and vertigo of postimprint therapy. Norton sat forward with a dermal ram as the Roman groaned.

"You'll cheer up after this," he said as he touched it to his neck. "How do I sound to you?"

"Like—like an echo."

"That's the imprint working. Notice that we're both speaking in English?"

"Ah . . . yes."

"Imprints are not long-term memory," Lucel said as she sat up and stretched. "At least not unless you use them a lot and have plenty of booster sessions. You have to speak, read, and think English whenever you can for the next three months or most of it will fade. The same applies to the tech and culture in your imprint. Tell me now, what's this?"

"A machine pistol," he replied after an imperceptibly short delay. "Short recoil, tumble-shot."

"How does this train move?"

"Magnetic levitation using superconductors."

"What will you say at immigration in Moscow?"

"I'm David Taylor, a British network analyst with Bristol Composites."

"Why are you in Moscow?"

"For a holiday. I shall be staying with my friends Hal Major and Carmen Bolez at the Holiday Tolstoy."

"Good. Your imprint had some Cyrillic capability as well, to help you with signs and basic Russian. Just relax, nothing is going to be hard."

Vitellan leaned back and closed his eyes. There was a feeling of weightlessness in his head, as if someone else was controlling his body. Americans landed on the moon in 1969, America was discovered by Columbus in 1492, and Columbus was an Italian working for Spain. Antarctica was discovered by the Roman navigator Decius some time late in the fourth century, and a Roman time ship carried several dozen Romans, frozen, into the modern world of 2026. First Bonhomme, now more Romans, he thought. Not only was he of no value in this century, he was not even unique. The Romans had been the rightful owners of his freezing elixir, that was for certain. He also noted that they had been discovered two years ago, but for some reason had not yet been thawed.

"I feel as if I'm falling headlong," he complained. "My head is full of things that I've never learned."

"The secret is not to think about what you know, just use the memories as you need them. When you fought with a sword did you stop to think what your instructor taught you before every move?"

"That would be a good way to get killed."

"Yes, and the same applies here. You have the skills you need to pass immigration as David Taylor, British citizen. Trust me."

Moscow, Russia: 7 December 2028, Anno Domini

It was just on midnight, local time, as the maglev glided slowly through the outskirts of Moscow. Streetlights and security floods lit up angular, drab buildings and bare trees under the season's early snow. Some walls were splashed with gaudy letters and symbols.

"What is Koshchei?" asked Vitellan, testing out his new imprint-based skills on a graffiti word in Cyrillic.

"It's the name of one of the gang conglomerates, it marks a turf border," explained Lucel. "Koshchei the Deathless was a Russian folk-magician who could not be killed because his soul was hidden outside his body. The Koshchei gang has a similar organization, a loose, adaptable structure that is very hard for the police or its rivals to pin down. It was modeled on the old Internet, or so they say."

"Internet? The Internet entry is . . . very confusing."

"The Internet was—look, don't worry about it for now. In a few hours you'll get a cyclopedia imprint with a lexicon overlay. You could go demented trying to collect words at random."

The maglev track was built high above street level, reminding Vitellan of a Roman aqueduct. The suburbs were all yards, cranes, and warehouses near the maglev tracks, scored by streets and freeways sprinkled with light traffic. The cars seemed like dark bread rolls with gleaming eyes. In the distance were higher buildings whose façades were largely in darkness. Vitellan said they looked like the cheap, multistory housing of ancient Rome, and Lucel confirmed that some things had indeed not changed in two millennia. Several buildings were fire-blackened shells encrusted with snow.

"Gang protection dispute," Lucel explained as they passed one.

"Even more like Rome," Vitellan replied.

Moscow immigration was slower than usual, but not difficult to get past. The fighting in Paris had caused a routine tightening in immigration inspections, but Lucel and Norton's weapons and bio-electronic kits had already been removed from the maglev's cabin by a contract agent from the Street Duma gang—who was also on the Vostok Maglev payroll. They booked into a Czarist-revival style hotel built in the late 1990s. Their weapons and other luggage were in the room when they arrived. Norton checked the room for monitors, cycling a portable scanner through all usable frequencies, then probed for passives. The reading was clean, but he still set up a standing-wave cloak to muffle their words to outsiders.

"I'll just step out and take the ambience for an hour or so," said Norton as he packed his gear. "It's only ten P.M., Paris time."

"Stay out of trouble," said Lucel, her eyes wide and face blank.

"So who looks for trouble?"

Vitellan lay down on the bed when he was gone.

"Anything you want from the bags?" Lucel asked as she began to strip.

"How could I?" said Vitellan, feeling desperately far from anything familiar. "I came with nothing."

"Good, because you and I are not coming back here. Norton will have a holiday with two other tourists who will come back here with him. They'll have our faces and names." She pointed to a pile of clothing beside him on the bed. "Change into those, then we'll be out of here."

"I don't understand."

"There's a bit of nightlife near the maglev terminus. Lots of hyped-up passengers are always arriving with their body clocks lagging."

"No, no, I mean that we arrive at a hostelry—ah, hotel—so late at night, then we leave without a moment's rest. That seems to be suspicious."

"We're on the run, Vitellan. When we eventually sleep, it will be in an imprint clinic."

Vitellan sat up. His eyes lingered on Lucel's taut body and unfamiliar underwear as he picked up his own change of clothing. No woman that he had ever known had had a body like that. Strong, hard, somehow shameless. Warrior, assassin, and seductress all in one. Again he broke free and drifted through desperation for some seconds. Less than a day had passed since he had been revived, yet he had faced the world with three faces and three names already.

"Vitellan!"

His head jerked as if cracked like the end of a whip. Lucel sat beside him on the bed, putting an arm around his shoulders and stroking his head.

"Vitellan, just hold together and don't try to think about all this. It *will* slow down, it really will. I promise."

"You can't know what this all feels like," he moaned. "All I have is fragments of understanding."

"That's okay. The imprints you have are just customized from standard Microsoft cards that you can buy anywhere, they're only meant as something to hold on to. Soon we'll have some much fancier work done to your mind, and after that you should feel a lot happier. Come on, I'll take you to a couple of bars to blur our trace."

"Bars—ah, taverns?"

"You've got it. Just look tired and smile a lot, like a typical new arrival. I'll do the rest."

The Lyakhov Clinic overlooked one of the many Gorbachev Parks scattered across Moscow. It was after 2:00 A.M. when Vitellan finally laid his head down to sleep in a small, antiseptic ward. Almost at once Lucel was shaking him awake. As he sat up he saw that winter sunshine was lighting up the room. He had slept like a dead man for many hours.

"Breakfast time, Centurion. How have you liked your first day in the twenty-first century?"

Vitellan shook his head and rubbed his eyes. "Better than an outbreak of Black Death, but almost as dangerous as fighting the Scots."

"Go to the soccer games and you can still fight the Scots—no, don't ask, that was a joke."

Vitellan and Lucel breakfasted in a dingy but pleasant cafeteria on the second floor of the clinic. At first she had to show him how to use forks to eat, as they were not in common use when he had been awake previously. The Roman gazed through the window at the snow-shrouded park as he ate. Cooking fires curled up from a huddle of pipe and plastic hovels near the middle of the park, and two figures swathed in rags and insulation patrolled the paths. They carried guns, he noted.

"Rapid-fire guns, machine guns," said Vitellan, fishing the information out of his hastily applied imprint.

"Ancient AK-47 Kalashnikovs," said Lucel, touching a telefocus on her dataspex. "They'd get a good price from any American tourist collector."

"Are they gangs too?" asked Vitellan.

"Those are snow bears, communes of homeless folk that squat in the parks during winter. The authorities tolerate them because they clean up the trash and patrol the parks. You find them everywhere—France, America, and Britain too."

"A plebeian militia?"

"If you like, yes. They chase off the vandals and perverts better than the police ever could. In return the police leave them alone."

"For all your progress and inventions, the poor are still with you."

"It's called the market economy. The Russians adopted it late last century, thinking that it would give them the good life on a platter. They got quite a surprise."

Vitellan had been admitted to the clinic as Clint Padros, citizen of the USA and tourist. The imprint analyst did a detailed scan for gates and imprints, taking until late in the afternoon. Lucel was present the entire time, unobtrusive but attentive. The sun was down by the time the analyst displayed a suite of diagnostic graphs and figures on a wallscreen, and he whistled at the complexity of the imprint layering on Vitellan's brain.

"These are the coordinates and decrypted keywords of the primary imprint gates and data domains that I have identified," the analyst explained as he gestured to one of the columns. "These in red are protected by blankout loops, so you're going to have to get separate keywords to open them up in an unencrypted form. A deep scan will do that, but it would take time and a lot of money."

"That's quite a lot for one head, but it's not unexpected," Lucel observed with a blank expression.

"We could crack the second-layer encryption, but not in less than a week."

"We can't wait. What's in the gated areas that you can restore easily?"

"Some general living skills—not the sort of thing that people usually gate out. Gates were developed to blank out trauma from accidents, torture, rape, or obsessions. Who would want to blank out . . . look at this here: riding a motorcycle?"

"Well, patch it back in, it may be useful. Anything else? Anything . . . interesting?"

"No bio-implants, but nearly two dozen have been removed within the past twenty-four hours. We have also mapped evidence of a good facial rebuild some years ago, about 2022."

"How are his imprints?"

"He is nearly *all* implants! The last brain I saw with even a thousandth as much layering belonged to a banker from Kiev. He had been imprinted all to hell and beyond to learn Japanese etiquette, language, and culture in a hurry. He's still in therapy, as far as I know."

"But Clint is fine?"

"Fine is . . . optimistic. Functional, perhaps. Beyond that I would be wasting words."

"What about stability? Are the imprints stable?"

"Yes, amazingly so. He would have had to be under continuous imprint therapy for at least six years to get that sort of imprint bonding, though. This is the strangest profile that I have ever seen, it must have cost millions." The imprint analyst folded his arms and sat down in his chair. "I'll be honest. In my opinion he has been in some crazy experiment and you are trying to get some of the damage undone before the compensation hearing begins. Is there big money involved? We do quality work here, and are very discrete. Need I remind you in which country imprint technology was pioneered?"

Lucel took a deep breath and raised her eyes to the ceiling, as if tempted.

"Just do a stabilizing booster for those three little Microsoft imprints that he got a couple of days ago, then layer this full cyclopedia." She handed a card to him across the desk.

The analyst put the card into a reader and brought the index up on the wallscreen. "Yes, no problem at all. Remember, though, if he wants to retain the cyclopedia for more than a fortnight he will have to take a course of stabilizing boosters from a portable unit every day for at least three months."

"Not a worry. I'm very methodical about that sort of thing."

"There is a risk from such haste," said the analyst, spreading his hands wide as if to give all the responsibility to Lucel.

"Just do it, now. We'll stay the night here."

She was staring at the wallscreen, scanning it with the sensors in her dataspex.

Lucel slept in the clinic but left early the next morning while Vitellan was still in imprint treatment. He was unwired by the time she returned in the afternoon with a hired van, paid for with a black market credit key. She drove him to a supermarket parking station only a few blocks away. Hidden in the back of the van she peeled their faces away, swabbed the skin with solvent, then bonded on new faces.

"You are about to go flying," she said as they stepped out of the van.

"Fly, as in an aircraft?"

She nodded as she pulsed the doors locked.

"To Japan?"

"Not this time, that was to throw off the Luministe agents. I decided to pick a Moscow clinic at random from a register and have some imprint work done here instead. Details of your therapy visit will leak out to the data brokers in a day or two, but we'll be long gone by then. You're safe, and I've bounced a message saying just that off a geosat to where we are going."

"Geosat, artificial moon—"

"Stop it! For now, just access the cyclopedia imprint when you need to. Okay? Later I'll teach you imprint embedding techniques."

They left the van and took the elevator to street level. After meandering through a number of streets like late-season tourists they had lunch at a café. Thermal plastic film in a sunflower print pattern was peeling from the wall in places, and the menu seemed to be confined to bread rolls, Coca-Cola, and black coffee. A holoposter above the Cafematic advertised the Australian Gold Coast. The place felt lived-in and smelled stale, but it offered Vitellan something comforting that he could not identify. He wanted to stay longer, but Lucel would not allow it.

She pulsed for an autocab using the black market American Express credit key, bought only an hour earlier from a snow bear. After two minutes a red, driverless wedge caked in grime pulled over to where they were standing and opened its door. They stepped in, and the autocab began driving itself with inhuman precision and alarming speed while Lucel calmly scanned the cabin for bugs.

"How's your English?" she said as she powered off the scanner. "Do you still have that echo effect when listening to what I say?"

Vitellan shook his head. "Not as badly as before. It's not even noticeable unless I concentrate on it."

"The imprinter is an amazing machine. It ran through some basic grammatical rules and a few thousand words while you slept, using Latin as base reference."

"It seems alive and magical, like a sprite."

"No, it's a machine, a machine like a book. You don't read it, but it puts memories into your head."

He considered that for some time, wrestling with concepts alien to all three cultures that he had lived in until now. "Memories? Perhaps memories of what did not happen?"

Lucel whistled. "That's smart thinking, Vitellan. Yes, it can be used for that."

"Then it could make me into someone I am not."

"Yes, although there's more than that involved. The process is illegal and expensive, and nobody has ever tried it—officially, at any rate."

"Most of what has been going on around me seems to be illegal."

"True." She glanced at the expression of apprehension on the mask over his face. He was holding together in spite of an enormous overload of new concepts and sensations, but there was no sense in pushing him harder than was necessary. "Personality distortion is possible in a limited sense, but it can be reversed by the right therapies," she said reassuringly. "Don't worry about it for now."

Vitellan looked out of the window of the autocab. The drab cityscape was unending, and the sunlight was far less flattering than the streetlights had painted it as they arrived on the maglev. He estimated that they had traveled several times the length of ancient Rome in a matter of minutes.

"For the whole of my life a man could not move across the land as fast as this, not even the Emperor himself with all his wealth. Now it seems commonplace."

"You're in for quite a few more shocks, Vitellan, but most are like your new face: just a cosmetic trick that's harmless and reversible—but unsettling if you look in a mirror without being warned."

"A new face. If you can do all this, is anything left of me? Are my own memories real? They seem so clear, yet they have nothing of this world."

"I'll be honest," she said, looking him in the eyes. "Your mind *has* been tampered with, but I can't explain everything to you for now."

Vitellan looked out of the window again. The buildings, cranes, and leafless trees continued to drift past, interspersed with chaotic jumbles of shanty-towns. Brightly glowing signs exhorted him to buy Microsoft Traveler, the New Buran Electric, McDonald's Healthburgers, Sony, Volkov AP Vectors, and Ilyushin. There was a strange uniformity about the cityscape, as if they were traveling in a great circle and passing the same places over and over.

"I wanted to see Japan."

"Why Japan?"

"Just an odd infatuation. Before the cyclopedia imprint was put on me I thought it was a city of India. Now I know that Japan is a group of islands, similar to Britain—but is it like Britain?"

"The clinic where you were to be scanned is in Kagoshima, a city in the south."

"Kah-gow-shima?"

"Yes. It's called the Naples of the East, and is something of a health resort. People lie on the beach covered in black volcanic sand for therapy, that sort of thing. There's a volcano there too."

"Naples, a pretty place. As a teenager I lived near there for five years at Boscoreale, on the slopes of a volcano. My father had left me there with my grandparents after my mother died. When he left the army he lived there himself."

Lucel blinked and sat up, suddenly interested.

"Do you know what happened to Boscoreale, Herculaneum, and Pompeii in the Christian year 79?"

"The terrible eruption? Yes, I saw it from Naples. I had just been visiting my father, and was on my way back to my garrison in Britain. He had inherited the family farm and was settling down to eat, drink, and be comfortably prosperous for the rest of his life."

"So he died in the eruption?"

"Yes, poor man. All those long, dangerous years in the legions, yet he enjoyed mere months as lord of his own little estate. The entire farm was buried under the ash. It seems so recent, to me it was only fifteen years ago."

"Have you read the account of the eruption by Pliny the Younger?"

"No. Is it well known?"

"Very."

"I don't recall it, I'm sorry. There was a Pliny who was admiral of the Mediterranean Fleet. The ash and fumes killed him too. I knew his nephew. A few years later we exchanged letters comparing our memories of what happened that day."

The classics scholar Lucel came to life, eager and hungry.

"I don't believe it! *You* exchanged letters with Pliny the Younger *himself?*"

"If you say so, yes, I suppose that was he. He was a friend of the Emperor."

"Yes! Yes, but what did—do you, I mean, what happened to the letters?"

"My servants kept them for a time. The tradition in my village of Durvas has it that parchments and gold were buried when the law and order of Rome started to break down. I visited the site of my old villa once. The walls were gone. The locals had used them to build a church. It was all grassy mounds, nothing more."

"So you could easily find it again."

"Perhaps, but not easily. It depends on how much the south of Britain has changed since the ninth century."

"The ninth—that's when you were last there? Next you'll say you knew King Arthur."

"Arthur? I've met a Wessex swineherd named Arthur, but no king. Perhaps Artor? Artorius? There was Artorius, a sea chief from, ah, Scotland as you would say. He lived and died while I was sleeping in the ice, so I never knew him."

The autocab turned onto a freeway feeder and began to accelerate through a great paved canyon between drab, uniform buildings. Lucel took a pair of dataspex from her jacket pocket and slipped them over her eyes. Soon she was partly away somewhere, although the dataspex allowed her to see the cab clearly while she was connected to distant databases and infomarts. The lenses were transparent yellow, with a spiral bus cable leading down from one thick arm to a netnode clipped to her belt. It had a dull brown case, and was flecked with gold highlights. The arms of the dataspex passed over induction cell arrays just below the skin behind her ears, and the control came from within her head. The unit at her waist linked into the cab's cordless pickup.

"Are you busy?" Vitellan asked.

"Busy but interruptible. When I do deep surfing the lenses turn black."

"Deep surfing: scanning information networks. So that's what you are doing?"

"Yes. I have a little pet research project to learn a few sensitive things about the Luministes. It's professional. I'm an assassin."

"You move like a trained fighter, but not a soldier. More like a gladiator."

"So I'm a gladiator? Tell me more."

"Your attitude is never far from violence. It is black and white, no colors at all."

"That's all?"

"Perhaps with better language imprints I could say more. Can your memory machines teach me more than they have done already?"

"They can, and will. History imprints are easy. Language is much harder because it imposes a bigger load on the brain. The brain tissue literally heats up, and too much heat will cook it like mince in an oven. You should not have become so fluent with English so quickly, but . . . I'll tell you later, I'm not sure I understand it myself as yet."

"Were you ever given false memories?"

Lucel's lips curled up at the edges. "Once. I had parts of my mind gated."

"Gated?"

"Partitioned off while I was taught skills and memories, taught to be someone else. It was voluntary, and it took three years. I was being taught to be like I am now: competently dangerous."

"What were you like before the imprinting?"

"I was a scholar turned junior tutor. I had a good reputation in my field, and I got laid occasionally by some very pleasant men. I liked my food and my figure was built for comfort. There are vids of me from around 2020. Switch the windows and watch."

Tiny holograms of Lucel in a bikini at some sort of fancy dress party with a 1950s theme appeared in midair between them. She had been not fat so much as well proportioned and healthy. A prime example of the post-AIDS, post-drac, goodlife look popular with young professionals of the time.

"So someone changed and controlled your mind?"

"Not quite. Total mind control is still one of the holy grails of modern brain research. The preferred—and illegal—method is to imprint another personality into redundant areas of the brain with a control gate to let it take over. The imprints don't last forever, unless used continually or renewed and boosted for years. The more renewals you get, the better they stick. Mine were renewed quite a lot, and they weren't from Microsoft, Tensai, Durvas, or any of the other legal companies."

"Why did you have it done?"

"I needed the skills to rescue you, Vitellan. I knew that the Luministes were going to abduct you even before *they* knew it. My imprints were from a particularly potent female terrorist. She sold them for a fortune, I'm told."

"Did my village pay for all this?"

"In a manner of speaking, yes."

The little holographic images winked out and Vitellan sank back into the soft seat of the cab, his arms folded and his head bowed.

"Last month I was traveling through the Swiss Alps, escorted by a French knight and his men-at-arms. Now I wake up to be rescued by a female knight and a squad of machines."

Liquid crystal pigments in Lucel's mask displayed the blush on the skin beneath, and she giggled before she could stop herself.

"Me, a knight! Vitellan, you're a dear man and I'm very flattered. It's the romantic in me, I suppose."

Vitellan sat forward, took her hand in his and kissed it lightly, just as he had kissed the hand of the Countess of Hussontal only three of his days earlier.

"The courtly kiss, just a light brush of the lips and not a big slobber," she observed, then practiced on Vitellan's hand.

It was the lightest of flirtations and quite asexual, Vitellan thought as she released his hand.

"The original warrior-woman who provided your imprints must have been very impressive."

"Yes indeed."

"How did you get along?"

Lucel's eyes narrowed, although her smile remained. "Well enough," she volunteered.

Vitellan settled back in the cab's seat again to assimilate what he had been told into the tangle of memories and imprints that was his mind. Lucel plunged back into the world of infobanks and datafarms through her dataspex.

"Sir Lucel Hunter," she said dreamily. "What a zap. I owe you for that one, Vitellan."

Associations suddenly snapped together in the Roman's mind and he sat bold upright in the seat.

"How—how did you know that the Luministes were going to abduct me even before the senior Luministes knew it?"

"Because it's my business to know," she mumbled distractedly.

"But how, why?"

"I can't explain yet."

"Who are you—really?" demanded Vitellan, exasperated.

"For your own safety I can't tell you that yet. Please accept my word on that, Vitellan."

He watched the buildings continue to blur past, but there was little that he could focus upon to study. He began to doze.

"What was it like in the fourteenth century?" Lucel asked as she powered off her dataspex ten minutes later. Beyond the windows of the cab the Moscow suburbs had given way to farmland beneath deep snow. He shook his head and stretched.

"I was only there from 1356 to 1358. I lived in England for eighteen months, then traveled through France to Switzerland in 1358."

"Thirteen fifty-eight. That's when Bonhomme was frozen. They could tell from the coins and clothing found with him, and from carbon isotope mass spectrometry—that's a dating technique, in case your imprint doesn't cover it."

"Bonhomme. My imprint says he is a religious cult leader. I knew him in 1358."

"What do you know of him?"

"You tell me what *you* know first."

Lucel considered, but did not take long to make up her mind.

"Okay. The airport's getting close, but I'll try. Bonhomme was the third of the ice people to be dug out of the glaciers of the Alps. The first was found in 1991. He was a Neolithic hunter about five thousand years old, but his body had been desiccated by the wind before he had been frozen and he did not have the benefit of your Oil of Frosts. Obviously he was not revivable at all. You were announced, rather than discovered. That was in 2016, when the Village Corporate moved your body from Switzerland back to Durvas. There was so much interest when the public announcement was made that your block of ice had to be put on display in the British Museum for a week. Bonhomme was found in the Alps in 2022. He had also been treated with a type of antifreeze oil, the same as was found in a sample from your frozen flesh."

"Jacque Bonhomme."

"He only calls himself Bonhomme or Goodman."

"He was the leader of the peasants' rising in France in 1358—a bad man, an evil man. He was a renegade priest with great charisma. He stole my Glacier-Frigidarium for the price of a little girl's life."

"Ah, that fits with Bonhomme. Now he's a major cult leader. He could tell millions, maybe billions to jump and they'd do it at once. Ah, the airport's coming up."

Snow-shrouded farm buildings had ceased to blur past beyond the windows. Everything was flat, lacking even trees or fences.

"Where are you taking me?"

"Eventually, to your village, Durvas. It's quite a big place now. The Luministes snatched you from there. I snatched you from the Luministes. I suppose you were shocked by the trail of bodies I left while doing it, but it's a tough world out there, Vitellan."

"I can remember seeing men fight each other to the death in public arenas, and for nothing more than sport. Christians were covered in pitch and burned alive as human torches in the century that I was born. I have seen the remains of a French nobleman who had been burned at the stake, and I helped to bury the womenfolk of his family that the mob had ravished while he burned. Later the king of that mob was crowned with a circlet of red-hot iron by other noblemen. Is your world as tough as that?"

"Sometimes," replied Lucel, but with new respect in her voice. "How many people have you killed—with your own hands?"

"I have killed two hundred and ninety," replied Vitellan. "I keep a running tally as best I can."

"Why?"

"Respect for the dead."

"I've killed seventeen over the last two years," Lucel said calmly, coldly. "The CV agent in my office manager keeps a tally—encrypted, of course."

"Are you really a professional assassin?"

"I'm a contractor, and a weapon. I maintain myself well."

She rolled up her sleeve and flexed the muscles in her arm. They were impressive, with the texture of pore-polymer on steel, and were interfaced to a bypass-boosted nervous system. Other tools of her trade were the ability to withstand most knockout gases and trank darts, and to store oxygen reserves in molecular cages within her body tissues and call on them at will.

"Addictive, this life," she admitted without prompting. "Like becoming a cat after living as a mouse."

"The Frigidarium is the same. Survive the first jump and you want more. I turn two thousand in twenty-six years."

"Happy birthday."

"If everyone did it, the world would be a different place."

"I don't think so. As an amateur historian I think it's the same, century after century: same shit, different flies."

"I first heard that said when Nero was emperor."

"Did you meet him?"

"I saw him in the distance, at the chariot races and the games."

"The games? As with gladiators and lions? I thought you were a Christian, or are the Durvas folktales all wrong?"

"My father sometimes took me to the games to see what happens to Christians who get careless."

"So the lions won?"

"Nearly always. The lions cost money. Christians and *humiliores* were free."

"You will find this a rather godless century after living in the pious Middle Ages."

"I like the principles that Christ taught, but I care nothing for the religions that sprang up in his wake. That sort of talk would have got me burned at the stake in the fourteenth century, of course, so I displayed as much piety as I needed to blend in. To travel through time one has to adapt very quickly."

"And you certainly adapt quickly, Vitellan. If an adaptability imprint could be made from your mind we could lease it to Microsoft to sell to the icehead market. You could be a rich man—but then you're already a rich man."

"Am I really?"

"Oh yes indeed."

Moscow South Orbital was a vast snowfield fed by underground maglev lines and surface freeways from the city and other airports. As the runways were enormous maglev lines in themselves, no other aircraft could use them. Vitellan gazed through the panoramic window of the lounge at the massive angular spearhead shapes that floated at about a man's height above the snow. Sub-Orbital Maglev Spacecraft, or SOMS, the cyclopedia told him. They were held above the ground by superconducting magnets in the runway. During takeoff, the magnets also accelerated the SOMS to hypersonic speed by the end of the runway, where ramjets took over. They were braked by a reverse process when they landed. A dragchute and lightweight skids were included for emergencies, but had not been used in twenty years of SOMS operation.

"Boarding now," said Lucel, taking Vitellan by the arm.

The moving walkway took them along a transparent tube that reared up to the side of a SOMS. Vitellan had an idea of the thing's size from his imprints, but not the experience of approaching something so large.

"Will it never stop growing?" he whispered.

"We're going to America," Lucel explained curtly. "By this machine it's only an hour away,"

America. The man who had visited Hadrian's wall in 160 A.D., when it was a state-of-the-art military installation, began scanning the cyclopedic subset of his imprints.

"By common usage, 'America' is a generic term for the USA," he said after a few moments.

"Sorry, you're right. Try scanning Houston, Texas."

They stepped off the walkway and were greeted by smiling flight attendants. Vitellan glimpsed faint brown streaks on the carbonfiber-ceramic skin of the SOMS, then they were inside a vast, low auditorium of golden brown carpet, dark green seats, and rows of blue overhead lockers. Brown, green, and blue were the flag colors of Ecosphere, the Earth-Nation movement. It was one of several international power groups, and the youngest except for the Luministes.

Vitellan sat down carefully and drew the belt across himself with the caution of a beginner under instruction. Lucel flicked on his tray screen and selected the view from a camera near the nose of the SOMS. Being in business class, they sat isolated in a pair of seats. Other passengers filed briskly aboard. Most were in casual clothes, middle-class Russians escaping the Moscow winter for resort ranches in the American Southwest.

"Anything I can get you?" The attendant spoke Russian with an American accent.

"We're fine, but my friend does not like flying," Lucel explained, and she threw the girl a flicker of a wink. "No fuss, please."

"Oh, I'm sorry. We have a range of mini-imprints that can help."

"No, thank you. It would affect his cricket, and he has a corporate match scheduled."

When she had gone Vitellan turned to Lucel.

"An imprint really would have helped."

"Contact with an imprinter would also have relayed a few important IDs from your brain to the Russian Federal Airlines database. Some things have to be done from experience, and this is one of them."

"Cricket," he said, going straight to his imprints. "Bat and ball game of English origins. Popular in countries of the former British Empire and currently increasing in popularity in the United States—"

Lucel put a finger to her lips. "It's considered geek to vocalize your imprints."

"Really? That was not in my imprints."

A flight safety video played in the top right corner of all tray screens. The SOMS began to turn. Vitellan could see the snowfield rotating before the nose camera, but it was so smooth that he felt no sense of motion. A melodious announcement declared to the cabin, "Prepare for takeoff. Counting down . . . three, two, one." The sudden crush of acceleration was alarming rather than uncomfortable. Lucel switched to the tail camera view a moment before the ramjets cut in, but the airport was only visible for moments. The runway and countryside plunged out of the screen, and were replaced by a white nothingness of cloud, then the mottled gray top of the cloud layer.

Imprints flung reassuring background to Vitellan: the hydrogen-fueled ramjet-rocket hybrid was the best and safest transport technology in history. The tail camera now showed the clouds below through shimmering but smokeless exhaust. There was a dull, rushing rumble and a slight vibration to hint at the power that they were riding, but otherwise the background music from the screen unit was easily audible.

"Once you get over the strangeness this is not so daunting," he remarked, more to himself than to Lucel.

Lucel switched on a local standing-wave cloaker in her breast pocket. "We can talk in private now, and I can tell you that the worst is yet to come."

The transition from ramjet to rocket configuration was no more than a slight lurch, followed by an increase in the G-force pressing them into their seats. Vitellan's screen now showed breaks in the distant cloud, and mountains below that. He became aware that the pressure forcing him back into the seat was lessening. "One minute to Zero-G," the melodious, reassuring voice of the unseen captain announced to the cabin.

"You will feel helpless, as if you are falling out of control," Lucel warned. "Just relax, don't try to fight it."

"My first flight," he said, trying to find words to give majesty to an experience that the other passengers seemed to regard with indifference.

"Not so," Lucel corrected him. "Your frozen body was flown from the Swiss Alps to Durvas in a tiltrotor transport after you had been dug out of the ice. You are, however . . ." She studied a cluster of numerals that she had conjured at the bottom of her screen. "As of now, you are the first citizen of the Roman Empire to fly into space. Congratulations."

She reached over and shook his hand.

"Space?" he asked.

"Sorry, check your imprints."

Vitellan found himself hanging in his straps. Lucel held a plastic card before him, then let it go. It floated before his eyes, there was no longer an up or down. He groped for help among his imprints and found breathing and relaxation exercises. After a few minutes he was unclear whether they really worked, or were just a useful distraction. He began to methodically work through the imprint subset on space.

"We are traveling over the North Pole," Lucel said as she switched his screen back to the nose view. "Then we'll pass above Canada. It will be night below, so you won't see much."

"And Japan?"

"Not this time. We're landing at Houston, an American city. You may have scanned your imprints for it already. When we arrive we can have breakfast. It's time for that in Houston."

Vitellan closed his eyes. Food was very low among his priorities just then. Gradually he adjusted, trying to distract himself by playing with a weightless pen and pad. Lucel brought up a view of space on her back-seat screen, giving them a vista of fathomless blackness and brilliant, steadily gleaming stars. Vitellan felt a slight pang of disappointment as the SOMS bellied through the air, and the sensation of down returned to the floor.

Houston, Texas: 8 December 2028, Anno Domini

The landing was an alarmingly fast approach to an expanse of patch-work lights, yet the SOMS aligned itself precisely with a white strip and was embraced by magnetic buffers that lined the maglev runway. It was before dawn, and the screen showed low, softly contoured terminal buildings bathed in floodlights, and a maglev shuttle track that ran above ground.

"Ladies and gentlemen, welcome to Houston," the captain said in English, then in Russian.

"Watch what you say, I'm putting the cloaker off now," said Lucel. "By the way, we've gone back to this morning."

Vitellan was astounded. "You mean this machine travels backwards through time?"

"No, it just happens to be morning in this part of the world. Check 'time zones' in your imprints."

After the experience of the flight Vitellan was bursting to tell every-one what he felt and what a marvelous thing it had been, but as they left the flight attendants merely smiled at him with the bored politeness that Roman shopkeepers had displayed two millennia ago. The termi-nal was little different from that of Moscow South Orbital, and the ma-glev shuttle traveled too fast for him to see anything more than a dark blur of trees, gardens, and buildings. He looked up to see that Venus,

Jupiter, Mars, and a half-moon were lined up across the sky, as if in a great, triumphant procession. They were a welcome scrap of stability in a world hurtling along like a driverless chariot.

Lucel had intended to keep Vitellan at a ranch near Huntsville, which was to the north and only a few minutes by air taxi. It was also a discreet resort, specializing in the accommodation of those who wished to remain out of sight. She did not contact the ranch until they were in a hired van and clear of the airport terminal. Vitellan listened to the argument with interest.

"Why can't you fly straight out in a tiltfan cab?" came the voice from the descrambler.

"Don't they teach you anything about security? In the city we're one in a million. In the open air we'd get scanned, targeted, and charred about a minute after we locked on to your beacon and began to home in."

Someone whistled at the other end of the connection.

"Lady—look, apart from the resort, this is a ranch. We raise cattle and run a few megawatts of solar cells, and we got enough firepower to hold off a gang of roadspikes or aggressive paparazzi until the law flies in. That's all. If you've got serious bogies after you, you'll need help from a serious team."

"Then have a team flown in," Lucel snapped.

There was a few seconds' silence. "Can you keep on hold till this evening?"

"Can you be more precise?"

"Twenty-one-fifteen, local time. Like I said, if you want Core A security, you have to plan in advance. Trusted contract kev-skins take a few hours to round up."

Lucel broke the connection.

"Looks like we do Houston for the day."

"What is 'do' in this context?"

"Play tourist, once I've contacted some very discreet people about a gun and some street money. We'll visit the Johnson Space Museum, teach you to drive this van in the quieter streets, go to the World Three Mall at sunset and have a fish curry at the Rajah Talmas—or do you want to catch some sleep in the back of the van? It's night back in Moscow, and your body is on Moscow time."

Vitellan did not answer immediately. "That flight that we took," he began, then paused for lack of words.

"The suborbital?" Lucel prompted.

"Yes. To you it is nothing, of no more consequence than . . . than a journey from Ostia to Neapolis by ship."

"I know what you're trying to say, but after another century all this will be just as quaint."

"Your technology and your society move too fast. Don't you appreciate the wonder of what we just did?"

"The unfamiliar is easy to wonder at," Lucel replied after some thought. "*Your* life is a wonder to *me*. You fought in the Hundred Years War, you were a friend of Alfred the Great, and you saw Pompeii destroyed by Vesuvius and exchanged letters with Pliny the Younger. According to Durvas oral tradition, your father even spoke with Jesus Christ and did crowd control at one of his sermons."

"My father spoke no Aramaic, so when Christ spoke to him he didn't—"

"Oh Vitellan, that's not the point." Lucel sighed. "To me your life is a wonder beyond my wildest dreams, but *anyone* can do a suborbital flight for the price of a ticket."

"My life? I was there for some great events in history, that's all. What was the first Mars landing to you?"

That caught Lucel off-guard. "I—it was, well, boring I suppose. Okay, I admit it, to me Mars footfall was just half a dozen anonymous spacesuits jumping about on pink sand. Space travel doesn't interest me, I've never been higher than a suborbital hop."

His argument confounded, Vitellan ran his fingers through his hair and watched the other traffic for a time. Most were fuel cell and solar panel boost models, bisected teardrops like their van. A few were the driverless autocab wedge types that he had traveled in back in Moscow. Old high-rise buildings stood out like sky-blue crystals, while more modern buildings were hidden beneath a dense matting of trees.

"We cleared forests to build cities, now you turn cities into forests," he said with incomprehension. "This century is just too much for me. If I stay awake for the next twenty-six years until 2054, I will probably see more changes than in all my twenty centuries."

"Will you ever stop traveling through time?"

"Everyone asks me that, and I always say perhaps: perhaps I would want something different. I was a hero from a more advanced civilization when I was awake during the Dark Ages and the Hundred Years War. I had arts of fighting to teach and advanced scholarship to revive. In this century—I'm just a helpless curiosity. All of a sudden I am afraid to return to the ice. In a hundred years more I might be so out of place that they will keep me in a cage. I don't know what to do. For the first time in my life I know that I have no value as a centurion, and that my scholarship has only historical worth."

Lucel sensed that they were being tracked as they walked through the World Three Mall, just after sunset. It was an open-air market beside the old Astrodome, and although it was packed with shoppers and tourists she noted an imperceptible pattern in the way that some people around them were moving. For a moment she followed something overhead, her eyes flickering up while she faced a stall and spoke with Vitellan, then she drew her Darington TS-17 smoothly and fired. Nobody in the crowd noticed the soft thump of the shot, but a pigeon that had been flying in lazy circles exploded in a yellow splash of burning fuel and electronics that fell into the market, setting hair, clothes, and stalls' awnings alight. Lucel had the gun pocketed before the screams had even started. She took Vitellan by the arm.

"Hurry. They want you alive, but they'll still hurt."

"Who does? What was that thing?"

"A monitor bionic, built like a bird. It was following our conversation."

"It was a hundred feet away."

"No problem, since about twenty years ago. I wonder how much it caught? You were talking about Roman Empire cooking styles just now—okay, they know who you are. Quickly, in here."

They stepped out of the crowd into a sportswear shop. Lucel knife-handed the sales assistant in the midriff without breaking stride and they hurried into the storage area at the back. She pushed a stack of cartons over behind the inner door, then shot out the lock of the roller door opening onto the delivery lane.

"That'll hold them for ten seconds or so, especially if the shop-keep hits the scream button." As if on cue, a siren began whooping somewhere behind them. "Good boy. We may have an extra twenty seconds now."

They emerged from the lane into the swirling crowd of the mall again. A police tiltfan was already overhead, and many tourists were crowding in to watch what was going on. Lucel slowed to scan the crowd.

"We should be getting away," said Vitellan.

"There will be a vector scan from another monitor bionic looking for bodies moving away from the shop. What I need is—there!"

She squeezed off a shot from the hip, and the left arm of a whipcord-thin Chinese in a hibiscus print shirt shattered at the elbow. He dropped silently, paralyzed with the pain and shock, but those around him shouted and recoiled. They were a team of five, not expecting to be stalked by their quarry. They would withdraw, call in more teams to deal with what they now thought was an opposing team. Lucel and Vitellan stepped into a bar and took the stairs to a balcony.

"Good view from here," she said as they sat down at a table. The open-air balcony was part of the upstairs bistro. "Give it a little longer."

"What are you waiting for?"

"I stuck a distress beacon to a garbage skip over at the entrance to that lane. When it goes off my contacts will know that we need an emergency pickup. With luck our admirers down there will also be totally focused on the skip for a good thirty seconds."

"It's my fault for talking carelessly."

"You've done well to adapt as far as you have," Lucel replied, staring abstractedly at the crowd.

Dirty plates and cutlery remained from the previous diners at the table. Vitellan picked up a steak knife. It had a stiff blade, and was surprisingly sharp. Lucel was counting.

". . . four, three, two, one, now!"

Nothing happened that Vitellan could see or hear, but the police tiltfan suddenly turned and descended. A blaze of yellow speared down at the skip. The mall flashed white and the skip shattered in a concussion that they felt rather than heard. An incandescent ball of fire and smoke erupted out of the crowd, and debris hit the tiltfan. It plunged into the fireball of its own making, its cockpit raked by fragments from its own missile's blast. The explosion of its crash seemed more real than that of its missile, and turbine fragments from the shattered fans scythed through the crowd like monstrous shuriken.

"Shit, maybe they really *are* trying to kill you!" exclaimed Lucel in disbelief at the carnage. She scrambled up from the floor, dragging Vitellan after her. "Come! Every vector on someone's monitor screen will be pointing away from this area now. We'll never be spotted."

"But the beacon—"

"My transmitter was not a beacon to home on, it only alerted my contacts that they have to rendezvous at another prearranged emergency point."

They hurried around the balcony and down the rear stairs. The sirens of real police tiltfans were wailing in the distance, and a scatter of bystanders had already summoned the courage to abandon their cover and flee. The police tiltfans passed overhead, casting cones of light through the smoke. Lucel was wearing her wraparound dataspex again, this time with customized enhancements tuned for layered night vision using infrared and enhanced visible spectrum images. They stopped at the loading bay of a darkened office block, and Lucel pulsed the roller door open from the modec of her dataspex. Beyond was a black rectangle of darkness.

"Quickly, in!"

"I can't see in the dark," Vitellan said as he shuffled forward, groping blindly.

"No need, I'll guide you. This is a transfer point, we won't be here long."

The door rolled down again. Vitellan counted his heartbeats in the darkness and listened to distant sirens. Light leaking from outside outlined a brickwork pattern of stacked boxes. Brooms, grapples, discarded packing . . . Lucel's body heat radiated against his arm through the tears in his shirt, yet her hand was cold on his wrist. He counted three hundred heartbeats.

"I thought the Luministes wanted you alive," Lucel said, as if the attack had somehow been Vitellan's fault.

"Why ask me?"

"Because I was thinking out loud, but no matter. I've made other plans in case those loons at the ranch goofed out."

"So—but do your people know we're here?"

"They'll be driving past every few minutes and polling for us with a tight-beam radio pulse. When I get the pulse we leave and walk to the left, two blocks down to the all-night deli. A dark blue Toyota roachvan will be waiting." An amber spot glowed before her eyes on the dataspex. "There they are! Stay with me now."

She pulsed the roller door up and scanned the outer loading bay. "All clear, no—"

An autonic that was clinging to the right wall fired, hitting Lucel's lower left ribcage with a tumble-round. She collapsed with a percussive wheeze as Vitellan saw a shadow step around the corner and fire something at him with a soft stutter. Darts stung his arms and chest, and he fell facedown over Lucel.

"Scrubbed the girl, tranked daddy," the shadow reported to a wristcomm.

Hands seized Vitellan's body and rolled him over. His right arm flopped over lifelessly—and plunged the steak knife from the bistro into the shadow's throat. The second figure did not realize anything was wrong until his companion collapsed. Vitellan picked up Lucel's gun and squeezed the trigger. Nothing happened. Keyed to her palmchip, cannot fire, the Streetwise imprint suggested within his mind.

Vitellan backed into the loading bay as the second man fired more tranquilizer darts into him. There was no effect. Engineered bacteria administered by Lucel in the Paris hospital had manufactured enzymes in his blood that were neutralizing the tranquilizer. The figure leaped onto the bay, crouching low, arms extended. Vitellan threw the image to his imprint: formal martial arts fighting stance, tae kwon do with commando streetfighter variation. Vitellan felt behind him and seized a broom. He snapped the brush off with his foot. The man lunged, easily deflecting the overhand blow that Vitellan made with the handle—but the Roman gently drew it back in a smooth underloop and jabbed it forward. The handle's splintered end smashed past teeth and lodged in the Luministe's throat. Vitellan stabbed underhand with the steak knife, but the blade hit body armor and snapped. Seizing the man's back collar, the Roman slammed his head into the ferroslab wall and he suddenly went as limp as a dead squid in a fishmonger's basket.

Alert for more attackers, Vitellan picked up Lucel's body. His hands clutched cloth soaked in slick, cooling blood. A black shape on the floor vomited Glucoboost through the gash in his neck and died. The tiny autonic gun-platform clinging to the wall followed Vitellan with its barrel, but it had a bar on shooting at his profile. He turned left outside the loading bay and ran, Lucel's blood pouring down his shirtfront and trousers. Two blocks away a laser scanner from a dark blue Toyota van identified the profile of Vitellan's current mask. The driver gunned the fuel cell engine, and within seconds strong hands bundled Vitellan and Lucel inside.

They were Africans, Nubians perhaps, Vitellan realized as the door slammed shut behind him. He had met Nubians when he had been garrisoned in Egypt, so long ago that America was not even a legend in Roman folktales.

A medic pumped broad-spectrum stabilizing serum laden with nanoware into Lucel with one hand and slapped the skin grapples of a heart pacer down on her chest without bothering to remove her shirt.

"She's dead, I brought her anyway," panted Vitellan, watching with the detached despair of one who had already given up.

"Dead she is, mon, but we'll soon fix that."

They seemed to drive for quite some time. Although there were many turns, there was no sense of being chased. The van finally stopped, and the back doors were opened from outside. Vitellan looked out, one hand on Lucel's cold forehead.

Four guards leveled automatic rifles at them and a man with mutton-chop whiskers walked up, a wide-beam weapons scanner held before him. After some moments he held up his other hand. "All clear," he declared, and medical orderlies swarmed up to take Lucel away. Vitellan stepped from the van, unsteady on his feet and feeling curiously lonely.

The man with the scanner noticed the blood soaking Vitellan's hands and clothing. He pointed and began barking keyword-laden orders. More medics rushed forward, but Vitellan held up his hands.

"Ah, believe it or not, I'm uninjured," he said.

Vitellan and Lucel had been brought to a private medical clinic named SkyPlaz near Hermann Park. It specialized in the treatment of those who could afford designer body enhancements that were unregistered, and hence in a murky class of borderline legality. The whole fourth floor of the block had been reserved for them, with Village credit unwittingly picking up the tab.

Lucel had arranged for a contract security firm run by one of the more respectable of Houston's Afro-gangs to pick them up, and a protection bureau in Taiwan that guaranteed secure and discreet accommodation had booked them into SkyPlaz. Lucel's life had thus been saved by the precautions meant for Vitellan.

In the hour after he had been admitted, Vitellan was given an intensive body scan and toxin flush, and his scratches and dart strikes were bonded and sealed. Although he took a shower and was scrubbed thoroughly by the handlers, he still imagined that he could smell blood as he dried himself. Completely exhausted, he lay on his back on a lounge, wearing sandals and a kimono of white silk painted with leafy green bamboo stems. For comfort it was the closest that he had worn to Roman clothing since the second century. Within moments he was asleep, and he barely noticed himself being lifted from the couch onto a trolley.

Lucel was stabilized and put in a biosupport unit while her damaged skin, ribs, and organs were attended to. Vitellan had his mask removed while his body was scanned for organic implants and his blood filtered for debris and toxins. When he awoke the next day he lay running his hands over his stomach for a long time. There was no pain from his stomach, there had been no pain in his stomach since he woke up in the Luministe hospital in Paris. He was free of pain for the first time in a decade of waking life. How long had he been awake now? Three days? He almost wanted the pain back as a reference point in this chaotic, headlong world of the twenty-first century. His body seemed unfamiliar too. Old scars and marks were gone, and his fingers were longer and more delicate. More cosmetic work, he decided.

By mid-morning the doctors and medical engineers had finished with him and he went to visit Lucel. She was no longer at danger status, but had only been revived sufficiently to be integrated with a trauma attenuation imprinter, and was still hours from being allowed back to full consciousness.

Vitellan ate lunch wearing his bamboo print kimono, watching an afternoon thunderstorm lash against the windows. Managing rice with chopsticks was quite a challenge, and he sprayed a lot of food around while a puzzled waiter watched patiently.

The Roman spent the rest of the day watching Lucel being built back into a viable body. Her face was covered in blue utility gel supporting tubes that went into her mouth and nostrils. It looked as if some surreal jellyfish was feeding on her. The tumble-shots had smashed two ribs, minced some abdominal muscles, and torn her intestines in several places. One had pulverized a kidney as it left her body. Medical utility arms carefully cleaned her skin while computer-linked cameras and scanners assessed what could be salvaged.

Her abdominal cavity was opened, and the small intestine carefully inspected and spliced where the round had flayed it. When the surgical handlers had finished she had lost only a few inches of intestine. The damaged sections of rib were reconstructed with a calcium matrix, while the torn muscles would eventually be replaced by vat-muscle keyed to her antibody signature. One quick spray of gunfire, then all of this to bring her back from the edge of death, Vitellan mused. Lucel's abdominal muscles were hard and well developed, so the handler cut, stapled, and bonded to retain the strength. A small array of damaged tissue built up on a platter beside her in the unit.

While she was unconscious an interactive dialogue between a computer and her nervous system probed for brain damage, but none was found. Although her circulation had ceased for a lethal period, the oxygen reserves built into her tissues had saved her. Arms with electrical stimulators worked her muscles to preserve tone.

It was evening before the surgical handler completed the operation by clamping and bonding Lucel's skin where it had been breached. The gel was slowly sucked out until she lay naked on the contoured surgical table within the biosupport unit. Vitellan noted her black wedge of pubic hair. For some reason he had not thought of her as having pubic hair, like the women and goddesses of many ancient statues. Her breasts were small and firm, they would not get in the way when she was fighting. Perhaps she had had them tailored that way, Vitellan speculated. He decided to check, and under Vitellan's imprinted directions the monitor interface confirmed that her breasts had been altered by surgery. It was a common procedure for combat-career military women, the cyclopedia imprint assured him. Her fallopian tubes had also been clamped off, and there were some other minor surgical enhancements involving her muscles and nervous system. The rest of her physique was the result of hard training, Dr. Baker later confirmed that when he called in to assess the progress of his machines with the patient. That gave Vitellan some reassurance. Physical work still counted for something, so there might be a place for him in this world after all. Baker began to talk to Lucel.

"Glad to have you back, Miz Lucel," the doctor spoke into a mouthpiece that curved around from the frame of his dataspex. Vitellan stared at the body in the unit, but it showed no movement other than that of breathing and the induced muscle contractions.

"Yeah, he's here, he's been watching you most all of the day. Sure, I can do that." Baker removed his dataspex and swiveled around to Vitellan. "We've got a consciousness tap into Mix Lucel, part of the checks for brain damage that we've been doin'."

"But she is not awake," Vitellan said with a gesture to the unit.

"Oh she's home all right, but don't ask how. Just watch, this might make it a little easier for you to get your head around."

He tapped at some studs beneath a display on the side of the unit, and above the transparent bulkhead a green holographic ball the size of an apple formed. "Consciousness being gated now," the female Texan voice of the unit announced. The green ball expanded into an orange, life-size holograph of Lucel's head and neck. It was translucent at first, then it slowly took on human tones and textures. Vitellan stood up, and his face was directly before her eyes as the holographic eyelids blinked. It was the first time that he had seen her face without a mask for more than a few seconds.

"Good to see you up and about, Miz Lucel," said Baker as he stood up. "Now I'll just set the cloaker and leave you two alone."

Lucel's holographic eyes followed Baker until he had closed the door behind him.

"Someone locked on to us," she said to Vitellan, her lips and facial muscles working too perfectly for life.

"Two of them," Vitellan replied. "And some sort of robot with a gun. They shot you."

"I . . . think I was hit in the stomach. Is—is everything all right?"

"I think so. We're in a clinic named SkyPlaz. Your contract gang team brought us here. The gangs seem more reliable than the authorities in this century."

"That's the market economy for you. So, the gang's tac squad in the van rescued us?"

"No, I killed both of the Luministe agents and carried your body to the contract gang's van."

"*You* killed two of the Luministe's enhanced contract lock-ons and rescued *me?*"

"Yes."

"How humiliating."

"You'd rather I hadn't?"

"It's okay. A little humiliation can lift one's game, just like a bit of guilt makes sex more fun."

Her approval sent a warm flush through his bleak feeling of helplessness.

"How did they try to stop you?" she asked after a moment.

Vitellan held up five tiny flighted wedges. "With these. The doctor gave them to me as souvenirs."

"Trank darts. They'd dissolve in your bloodstream for five hours or thereabouts, keeping you asleep for the duration. Luckily I set up your body to be proof against a suite of chemicals like that when we first met. Who's running the shop?"

"In theory, me."

Vitellan began to pace before Lucel's holograph, his arms folded tightly and his head bowed. The insubstantial eyes of the projection followed him. Somewhere beneath the tangle of electronics and medical support equipment, Lucel herself sensed that he was disappointed at being let down by his own people in Durvas.

"I wish you could take over again," he confessed. "How do you feel?"

"Absolutely numb," she admitted as her projection looked down into the biosupport unit. "The real me looks a mess."

"You were hit by three rounds from a little robot gun platform. They nearly cut you in two."

"How long ago?"

"Twenty-four hours. Your bones and intestines were bonded back together by the robot arms in the case below you. I watched."

"Voyeur."

"They put in a new kidney."

"I'd have never guessed."

"You were dead for at least ten minutes. You should have had brain damage, according to my cyclopedia imprint. How did you survive?"

"I've had oxygenation backup built into my tissues in stabilized molecular cages. It's designed to cut in if I stop breathing for more than two minutes. There's autoclamps for severed blood vessels, and a pacer also fires up to force my blood to circulate if my heart stops for more than five seconds. I can take a lot of damage and pull through."

Vitellan had been accessing his imprints as she talked. "Micropumps driving and routing blood by selective arterial contraction, with stabilized molecular cages to store oxygen: the cages were developed from the same stabilized lattices as the covalent lattice explosives."

"You've got it. Vitellan, could you find my dataspex for me?"

"Yes."

"I want you to interface them with the cables going into this thing that I'm being repaired in. I can see the panel from here—I'll talk you through the procedure."

"Whatever you say. Do you want to do more database work?"

"Yes, but I want to check what the spex contain as well. They have a low energy recorder, they've been recording everything going on around them since I was shot."

When he returned from his room the pale holographic head remained in midair above the surgical unit. He plugged flaccid, flat cables into slots and pressed patterns of studs while the holograph head called instructions and passwords across the room. As the connection was established the holograph vanished. The Roman suddenly felt like curling up and going to sleep. Lucel was in charge again so he could relax, yet he was still uneasy about being completely in her power. Her projected head reappeared just in time to find Vitellan yawning and stretching his arms.

"You should be asleep," she said sternly.

"Spoken like an Icekeeper," he replied, lying back in a contour chair with his arms folded and looking at the ceiling monitors. "You remind me of a man named Gentor."

"Get some rest, Vitellan. You've been stalked and attacked by professional—"

"As professional killers they were nothing compared to the Danes, or even a well-trained gladiator. I'm a soldier, and I have survived many battles. Remember that, please, and don't try to seal me up in a box. I don't break easily."

"Is something on your mind?" Lucel's hologram asked, assuming a vulnerable and insecure expression.

I am the Master of the Frigidarium, he reminded himself, I have a right to ask questions about what is done in my name.

"I asked to be revived in the year 2054 of the Christian calendar," he said, now trying to modulate his tone to unthreatening curiosity. "That was to mark two thousand years since my birth. Now I have been revived and it is only 2028. Why was that done?"

"It's a long story. The location of your body in the Alps was preserved in both Durvas and a castle in France after you were frozen. Late in the eighteenth century there was a successful revolution against the nobility of France, and the Hussontal castle was burned to a stone shell. Meantime the village of Durvas had maintained a few ceremonies such as the ice harvest, and even the office of Icekeeper had been filled in an unbroken line all the way back to Guy Foxtread, whom you probably met."

"Yes, I knew him well."

"Fantastic," she breathed through translucent lips. "Anyway, the Durvas people had folktales, traditions, the original Frigidarium, and a copy of the map that had been destroyed in France. The folk in Durvas did not know that the map had been destroyed, however, and they were worried that the French revolutionaries would locate your body and destroy it. The Icekeeper of Durvas decided to revive the care for your frozen body, but he also decided that a more reliable way of making ice was needed. Thus Durvas became a center of refrigeration research.

"It soon became obvious that the map in the Hussontal castle had actually been destroyed, because Durvas spies reported that the castle was set afire during fighting, and was not looted before it burned. The Icekeeper decided that it was still safe to leave you in the Alps, but the refrigeration research was continued—just in case you ever had to be returned to Durvas. The village prospered and grew immensely over the next two centuries. In 2016 a decision was finally made to move your body from Switzerland to England. Greenhouse melting of the alpine ice was given as the official reason, but there was also some doubt about whether Durvas had a legal claim to you or whether the Swiss could claim you as an archeological artifact. The move was thus preemptive and done in secret, but once your body was safely in Durvas there was a general announcement about your existence, and about who and what you are. It caused a sensation worldwide."

"All of that is in my imprints," said Vitellan, unimpressed. "So, I was dug out in 2016, then revived in 2028."

"Yes, although in theory you were meant to stay frozen there until 2054, by your own wish."

"If I was still frozen in some new Durvas Frigidarium, why was I revived early?"

"For the same reason that you were revived in the ninth and fourteenth centuries. There was a crisis, and you were needed."

"Me? Needed? In *this* century? You must be joking."

"No, it's true. Bonhomme was discovered six years after you, but in those six years a strange groundswell of cults had sprung up—in the Americas and Africa, but especially in France. In the same way that some nutty groups look to salvation by aliens from space in UFOs, these people preached salvation by a frozen disciple of Jesus Christ. One group, the Luministes, began sending its own expeditions into the Alps, and in 2022 they were vindicated when Bonhomme was found. He was revived at once. After a stomach transplant and a course of imprint therapy he found himself at the head of a very large and rapidly growing movement. The Luministe administration is the real power behind him, but his pronouncements carry a lot of weight."

"I begin to see. After a year or two the Durvas people wanted to revive their own ice-prophet as a counter to Bonhomme."

"In essence, yes. You were their sleeping superhero, their King Arthur, their Ilya Maromyets—check your imprints later, those two have big entries."

"So, I was unfrozen in Durvas."

"Earlier this year, yes."

"But not revived."

"No."

"But Bonhomme's Luministes had me abducted."

"Yes."

"Then revived me."

"Yes."

"You then rescued me."

"Yes and no. As far as the modern equivalent of your seneschal, Lord Wallace, and everyone else in Durvas is concerned, I am an unknown, expensive contract agent. Durvas has been making inquiries about *you*, however, but the clinic has strict orders not to tell them anything until I am good and ready."

"But Durvas is my village. It only exists to help me travel through time. If I can't trust Durvas people, who can I trust?"

"You could trust me."

"Yes . . . but would it be unreasonable of me to be confused?"

"No."

"All right, then, what is going on?"

"I don't know everything that I need to as yet, and meantime I will not have you doing anything rash out of sheer ignorance. You *are* in serious danger, but you are obviously aware of that."

"So I'm to be kept in ignorance?"

"No, no, that's not what I meant. I tell you what: ask one of the staff for a travel-sim called TourHead, and say that you want to run *Decius Museum, Antarctica*. That should give you more than enough to think about for now."

5

the deciad

According to Baker, the wallscreen was a limited tool for doing research, yet Vitellan liked it for that very reason. It was like watching a play or an oration, so he had a parallel of something like it in his background. He had already tried VR helmets, but found that he disliked them. It was like being someone else, and Vitellan wondered if he would ever adjust to that medium. He lay back on his bed, using a remote control unit to select video footage from newsbases. Nearly all of his searches were on Bonhomme the Prophet. He watched rallies, revival meetings, and airport interviews, and after a dozen major events Vitellan had the gist of Bonhomme's message: beware false prophets, and win back the world for Christianity. The face was the same as Vitellan remembered, as was the manner, but Bonhomme had been heavily imprinted to adjust to the modern world. His meeting with Bonhomme had been only a few days ago at Marlenk, even though now he was on the other side of the world and over six centuries had passed. The soul of Bonhomme was missing in this century. Will I too become someone else so that I can adjust to this century, Vitellan wondered. When he had seen enough, he scrolled down a menu of tourist videos until he found the most recent trip of the *Deciad* time ship.

> Paradise Vistas and Tourhead Distribution present THE DECIAD TIME SHIP. Gregory Pine of *Famewar* and *Shore Street* is your sense-host on a tour of the Roman time ship in Antarctica that features in *The Deciad of Quintus*. See the Roman time travelers lying frozen and still traveling through time before the Awakening Project begins. Date of Recording: 17 May 2028. Running Time: 41 minutes. Adapted for *Wallscreen 8* from *True-VR*.

As Baker had said, it was adapted from dataspex cameras, and translated badly to a wallscreen. The sense-host walked down a dimly lit corridor that still contained the litter of recent construction. Vitellan wondered if that was why they kept it badly lit. At the end his host walked through a pair of sliding doors and into a brightly lit auditorium where about fifty people were already seated. He sat in the front row, and almost at once the guide arrived. She introduced herself as Gina Rossi, Italian by birth and Espanic by adoption. Without another word she opened the book that she carried and began to read:

> This is a tale of the world's end, and of the ships that ran before the flames. The vessels were the very peak of our empire's craft, and they bore the best of our learning and the finest of our citizens.

"So begins the *Deciad*," said the guide, looking up from the slim, leather-bound volume.

"The author, Quintus Flavius, was an educated stonemason. He was quite familiar with the *Aeneid* of Virgil, that epic describing the escape of Troy's last nobles after their city fell to the Greeks. He saw this voyage as a similar epic journey. Perhaps he hoped that his chronicle of the flight from the fall of ancient Rome would become as famous as Virgil's *Aeneid* itself.

"I think you will agree that there is nobody better qualified to tell the story of this great voyage than Quintus himself, so I shall read some more passages from the *Deciad* to set the scene. After that there will be a tour of the chambers and tunnels that he eventually built. The more adventurous among you will also have the option of going for an excursion on the beach outside."

There was a shuffling restlessness in the tour group, mainly from some classics students. Their faces stood out, alert and eager; they were awestruck. They were actually *here* at last, at the very site of the famous *Deciad* epic. Vitellan shared their eager restlessness to get on with the tour. The guide began to read again.

At that time of death and pillage the very gods of Rome herself assembled the best remaining scholars and craftsmen at the fishing port of Larengi, together with five warships and a small body of marines. We saw little of the fighting while in that small port. Our days were peaceful and strange, with the marines learning the use of the tools of masonry while the scholars and craftsmen learned to fight with sword, spear, and bow. Sometimes wounded were brought in from the fighting around Rome, and this reminded us that the Visigoths were abroad. At that time none of us knew why we were there, except that we were to help with some mighty undertaking.

Valerius, a skilled blacksmith, said that the revolts in Africa and Britain proved that the gods were abandoning Rome to decay and ruin. With that we all agreed, being good guildsmen. Our ceremonies and secrets had been suspected of being pagan by the Christian authorities as they closed the temples of the rightful gods and persecuted their followers. Many of our ceremonies were indeed pagan, and quite rightly so. The gods of Rome and the walls of her masons had kept her inviolate for eight hundred years. Who were these cultist

Christian upstarts to tamper with the very foundations of our world?

On the morning of the forty-first day after my arrival in Larengi we were roused long before dawn by the sounds of galloping horses and men shouting. Torches and bonfires flared up as we ran into the street, buckling on our swords and rubbing the sleep from our eyes. Publius, the officer in charge of our training, led us to the docks. There we saw an exhausted horse, its sweat turning to steam as it stood shivering in the cold night air. Its rider was slumped against a wall, a goblet in one hand. He was being questioned by Epictetus, the captain of one of the warships, and by Decius, who was commander over us all.

"You are sure that they come?" Decius asked urgently.

"Commander, all I know is that several riders left as I did, and that I was ordered to ride ahead and say 'Nemesis protect the Gods of Romulus' when I arrived."

"It is quite fantastic," exclaimed Epictetus. "Rome will stand forever. This is some mistake."

"No mistake, sir," gasped the messenger. "I was there. Visigoth freedmen within Rome's walls betrayed the city to Alaric's men."

"This is the end, then," Commander Decius said quietly, before he turned to address us all. "Soldiers, craftsmen, scholars of Rome: prepare to sail at once. Officers of the guard, station your men around the boats. Everyone else, stand by the boats to load and row."

Very soon more riders streamed into the port and made for the beach, where we waited. All were robed and cloaked, but by the bonfires' glare I could tell that many were women. Most were tall and fair to behold, though their eyes were bright with fear. There were no children. Close behind them were pursuing horsemen, and as we struggled to launch the boats the enemy smashed into our thin line of marines.

The fighting was savage and desperate, but the stout marines of Rome held the pursuers back. Arrows poured down on us as we pushed the boats through the shallows. I fell, struck in the leg.

"Save Quintus, the mason!" shouted the commander. "We need him more than a dozen centurions."

In the ruddy light of the bonfires I saw Valerius wading back for me. He took me up in his great arms and with a heave threw me bodily into a boat.

"Rome fallen, Romans fighting Romans. What times are these," the blacksmith growled as he climbed in after me.

"But it's Visigoths that pursue us," I replied.

"The horsemen wore Roman armor, and the arrow in your leg is Roman, Quintus. Perhaps Rome would have her gods fall with her in this night of blood."

At about a quarter mile offshore the warships lay at anchor. Four were dromons, solid and stately, each with two rows of oars, and armed with spidery catapults. The other was a trireme, the *Tenebrae,* sleek and proud, her weapons under cover. One and all, the boats made for the *Tenebrae,* and I could hear the rattle of anchor gear being drawn up as I was hoisted aboard.

"Why flee?" cried a sailor who was staring back at the shore. "If Rome is gone the world's heart is cut out."

"If Rome has had its Trojan horse, then Rome can have its Aeneas, too!" said Valerius, shaking him roughly.

None of us knew this to be our purpose, but all carried hopes that it might be so. At that moment, cold, wet, and in terrible pain, I resolved to chronicle our voyage.

The guide led the group out of the auditorium to an antehall where two quarter-scale models of oared warships sat on aquamarine polymer waves within glass cases. She pointed to the ship on the left.

"This vessel is a dromon, a heavy, slow warship of the late Roman

Empire. Rather than ramming the enemy ships, it fought from a distance with catapults and flamethrowers."

"Flamethrowers?" said a tourist with a veteran's pin on his cap. "I didn't know they had gasoline back then."

"They used a mixture of pitch and sulphur called Greek fire," said one of the students. "It had much the same effect as twentieth-century napalm."

"This other ship is a trireme," said the guide hastily, anxious not to lose control of her tour to the students. "It had three banks of oars, was very fast, and was designed for ramming. It fell out of general use about a century before the *Deciad* was written.

"Quintus mentions several times that the trireme *Tenebrae* seemed new, and it is possible that the ship was built especially for this mission. As you will hear, it was armed with very advanced catapults and was probably the fastest ship on the Mediterranean Sea at that time."

Vitellan smiled at the irony of his own fascination. He was a citizen of the Roman Empire learning about the Empire's future as ancient history.

Several days after the morning of our flight we drew close to the Straits of Gibraltar. Though hardly able to walk, and burning with fever, I still had to work with one of the catapult teams. This was because so many of our marines had been left fighting on the beach to cover our escape.

Very late in the evening our lookout called a warning, and we beheld a great fleet of warships in our path. At once the commander ordered the sails furled and the masts lowered on all ships. All those not sailing the ship or manning the catapults were ordered to the rowing benches. Even the Gods of Romulus strode from their quarters and took up positions at the oars beside the craftsmen, scholars, and surviving marines. Shivering sometimes, burning sometimes, I sat by a forward catapult. Valerius, too, was on this team, his great strength needed for the winding ratchet.

The drumbeat began and our ships formed up, two dromons ahead of us and one on either side. The oars were soon in time, and we made straight for the waiting fleet, attempting no evasion. The catapults were drawn and aligned. These weapons were really half catapult and half ballista, with an iron frame. They shot fused clay pots of Greek fire with prodigious range and accuracy.

I sat ready to light the pots' fuses while Valerius worked at the winding handle. The enemy ships converged on the place where we would meet, and we cried out in amazement to see so many Roman dromons scattered among the barbarian vessels. Our dromons began to fling their fire pots, and many warships halted, drenched in smoky flames. We passed among crippled ships in safety, but many more were speeding to block our path.

Our drummer raised the speed, first to maximum, then to ramming, and the *Tenebrae* easily pulled away from the escorts. The enemy captains had not known that any ship could move so fast, and were not able to close with us or block our path. Our catapults thudded at closer and closer range, and soon the stones and Greek fire of the enemy began to crash down on our own deck. Arrows struck the barricades around us, and we could hear screams from men aboard the burning ships. Our steersman fell with an arrow through his neck, and Decius stood up and seized the steering oar, shouting orders all the while.

Then we were in the clear with the open ocean before us, and though the rear catapults still shot at the swiftest of our pursuers, we were safe. The marines cheered and embraced each other before leaving their stations to put out the fires. At about twelve stadia from the battle we shipped oars and raised the mast again. It was dark by now, and as Valerius helped me to my feet I looked back to the horizon where our trapped escorts fought and burned among the enemy ships.

"Such a fierce battle, yet only a glow now," I said.

"A glow where brave Romans die," replied Valerius. "First the marines give their lives for us, now entire ships doom themselves so that we may flee. We should have stayed to fight."

"They burn that we may escape, my friend. Our mission is worth those lives."

"No mission is worth dishonor," said Valerius grimly. "Better to have no New Rome than to found it in cowardice, betrayal, and flight."

I told myself that Aeneas might have felt thus when he left Dido to her funeral pyre and sailed away to Italy, but the words cut deep. Were Roman virtue and honor too high a price to pay to found a new city?

The guide led the group to a map of Africa just beyond the model ships. It reached halfway to the ceiling, and was labeled in Latin and English. A heavy red line ran from Italy through the western Mediterranean, then down the west coast of Africa.

"The islands referred to in the next passage are the Cape Verde Islands," she explained, pointing to their position on the map with a spotbeam. "The remains of a small Roman garrison have been found there, and the best dating techniques available suggest that it was razed by fire early in the fifth century A.D. Several dozen graves were also found."

This was all a curious mixture of the future Rome and the Rome of the distant past, Vitellan noted yet again. There was also something odd about the guide—she seemed strangely dynamic, larger than life.

"Quintus wrote most of the *Deciad* while the expedition was staying there. The base had been set up by Decius during an earlier expedition as a place for rest and provisioning. He also had three cornships waiting there. These were much better suited to the voyage ahead than the trireme, and some naval historians have said that if Columbus or Cook had been given a Roman cornship to use on their own expeditions, they would have done just as well.

"The next passage deals with part of the voyage to the Cape Verde Islands on the trireme. They were sailing south along the African coast, and had just entered the tropics."

Delirious, near death, I lay oblivious to all around me as we sailed many hundreds of miles. As the fever broke and I revived I noticed how warm and humid the air had become. At first I could see only the blurred outlines of the cabin, and feel the pitch and roll as the warship crashed clumsily through the waves. Then I heard voices behind me. Commander Decius was speaking with a woman.

"The fever has broken, Decius," she said with a low, gentle voice. "He will live to build our chambers, perhaps even to grow old."

"Good, Helica. Very good," he replied in a voice more tender than I had ever heard him use. "One less trouble for us."

"Does the crew still mutter about being near the edge of the world, or that the sun will drop from the sky and destroy us?"

"They do. They are frightened to see it so high overhead."

"Such foolishness, my love, but then they are not like us. Did you reassure them?"

"Yes, many times. They know I have sailed much farther than here already, yet they still talk. Captain Epictetus ignores them and says that sailors understand only wine, buggery, and the cat, but now the wine runs low, and there are few marines to beat obedience into them. As for the other, there are thirty beautiful women aboard this ship, and this is the longest voyage that the crew has ever made."

"Attack us, the Gods of Romulus?" Helica gasped. "They would not dare. They must know better."

I could hear Decius begin to pace slowly, and the creak of the boards beneath his feet.

"What special powers have we?" he said with a sigh. "Our usual lifespan is several times longer than that of most mortals, but that means only that we accumulate more learning and experience. These sailors think that we are just rich nobles, they do not know that our kind guided and governed the Roman Empire for eight hundred years."

"Several lifetimes of training make deadly fighters of we Temporians," replied Helica ominously.

"Indeed, we could kill many in a mutiny, but we need a live crew to sail the ship. In a way it is good that the trireme sails so badly in these rough seas. The caulking of seams and bailing of leaks takes more time with each day that passes."

The commander ceased his pacing, and there was a long silence. I was wondering if they had left when Helica spoke again.

"My love, it pleases me very much to sail with you this time. It pleases me beyond telling."

"Helica, Helica. For years I cursed the waves, wind, and creaking timbers that took me from you, and the thousands of miles between us. Even now I must remind myself not to be lonely as I look out over the water."

"We shall even be together on that greatest of all voyages," she said with a strange eagerness in her voice.

"First we must build the greatest of ships," he said with a laugh. "Tend Quintus well, now. Without his skills there will be no ship, and no escape from this savage world and our enemies."

"And no hope of children for us," she added in a very small voice.

Many days later I was able to sit up, and to speak. I confessed to Helica that I had heard her words to Decius, and I told her that I was very confused.

"My lady, I heard that a great ship is to be built," I said. "I am a mason. I know only walls, arches, and the cutting and fitting of stone."

"So? Did not Rome stand behind walls of stone for many hundreds of years?" Her eyes were wide, sparkling, pulsating, growing.

"All the other artisans, the scholars, even the sailors, talk about founding a new city, just as the Trojans built Rome after their city was betrayed."

"Not a city, Quintus, yet not really a ship as you think of it. You shall design its rooms and corridors, and we Gods of Romulus shall certainly travel in it."

As her eyes grew I no longer felt the motion of the ship. I seemed to fall for a very long time.

"I'm going to skip a rather large part of the text now," said the guide. Vitellan noted that several of the students were looking particularly impatient. "If you want to read the *Deciad* for yourself there are some good translations available in the museum bookshop."

There were sneers, but no interjections. The students probably disagreed with the guide's translation, yet they were quiet.

"The *Tenebrae* reached their garrison in the Cape Verde Islands in spite of the trouble with the crew, and they stayed there for several months. There Quintus completed the drawings and estimates for the chambers that the expedition built, the chambers that we are standing above now. He also wrote about two thirds of the *Deciad* there. Yes? You have a question?"

"I've always wondered why the 'Gods of Romulus' had to run for it in the first place," said a middle-aged woman with a New York accent. "If they'd been controlling the Roman Empire for so long and they had such advanced technology, surely it would be easier to stay and rally their folk against the Visigoths."

There were titters from the students at her question.

"That's almost as big an issue as the fall of Rome itself," the guide replied, and now there were frowns of impatience from those who were hearing the story for the first time and wanted to know how it ended. "Quintus imagines that some malevolent goddess was responsible and he states several times that Juno was attacking the expedition, just as she harassed the Trojans in Virgil's *Aeneid*.

"Recent research suggests that the 'Gods of Romulus' were being defeated by a combination of infertility and attacks from an early Christian sect. Arabic documents were discovered in a Spanish library late last century that describe a cult called the Manneleans, a group of 'heroes' who struck down the last of some unspecified pagan gods just as Rome fell. There is also strong evidence that the Manneleans were led by a renegade from the 'Gods of Romulus' themselves. The eminent authority Professor Storey suggests that Constantine, Theodosius, and even Saint Paul might have been this same man. At any rate, the 'Gods of Romulus' were seen as agents of the devil, and a systematic Mannelean campaign of assassination probably began.

"By itself that may not have been enough, but Quintus mentions a disease similar to gonorrhea that was making many women infertile around that time. Perhaps the Manneleans singled out those who could still conceive, and both the 'Gods' and Rome went into decline. Eventually someone came up with the idea for this voyage to escape the Manneleans."

"But what was the point, if they were infertile?"

"A few of the remaining thirty women probably could conceive, but to do so would invite instant attack from their enemies. By targeting only pregnant women and babies they would hit the group at its most vulnerable point. Decius decided to use technology to escape to where the Manneleans could never follow. As it turned out, the stay at the island garrison was quite eventful, as some Mannelean agents seem to have infiltrated the *Tenebrae*'s crew. There were several murders, and a small battle that took the lives of fifteen men and two 'Gods.' Knowing that his enemies could do great damage if they got as far as the ultimate sanctuary, Decius mustered all those he could trust for yet another secret escape."

One day, a full month before we were due to sail on, the commander ordered all Gods of Romulus and many of the artisans to board the cornships and inspect our quarters, so that we could make suggestions for the final fittings. At this time the ships had only skeleton crews aboard, and very little in the way of stores.

Valerius and myself were the last to be rowed out, but no sooner were we taken aboard than the anchors were raised and the ships began making way under a fair breeze. All at once there was a great shouting on the shore as Juno entered the hearts of many left behind. Some groups began to battle each other, and some even tried to launch the beached trireme, but it was still under repair and many planks were missing from the hull.

Thus did we sail beyond the reach of Juno, long the enemy of Rome and persecutor of both Aeneas and Decius. For all of that day we sailed, and for the following night. At dawn the commander called us together on the flagship, the *Nemesis*. Gods and mortals together, he addressed us.

"People of Rome: Even at our remote island garrison the enemies of the Gods of Romulus reached out their bloodied hands to slay us, but now they are trapped there. Each mortal among you was ordered aboard yesterday because your loyalty was beyond question. Now we shall sail on to complete our work in safety."

At this there was a great murmur among us, and Rentian, one of the senior Gods of Romulus, raised his hand and spoke out.

"Commander, we have three ships to sail, yet hardly the crew and stores for a single one."

"You are right, but all is well," said the commander. "This very morning all stores and crew will be brought aboard the *Nemesis,* and the empty vessels put to the torch. If the estimates done by Quintus the mason are good, this will give us just enough to complete our task."

All at once I felt very fearful. The fate of this voyage, the lives of many Romans, everything depended on my hasty calculations. Yet in spite of all my drawings and designs, I knew nothing of our ultimate purpose. There would be a small labyrinth cut into solid rock, and that was all. No city and no ship.

The next display was a diorama of the island garrison, complete with a battle scene in which tiny figures were frozen in desperate, struggling groups—a disorderly, spontaneous conflict, lacking any of the discipline for which Roman soldiers were famous.

"Decius is now acknowledged to be one of the greatest navigators in history," the guide said as the group crowded around the diorama. The well-trained sense-host of the Paradise Vistas tour vid scanned the displays systematically. Vitellan paused the vid at several items that caught his interest, then let it continue. The guide began speaking again.

"It is hard to believe that without the *Deciad* of Quintus we would know nothing about Decius. The voyages and feats of navigation by Columbus or Erik the Red are nothing compared to what Decius did, yet we had to wait sixteen hundred years to learn about him. He must have been a fantastically charismatic leader to have kept his crew behind him on such long and dangerous voyages.

"From this point on Quintus was only able to keep a rough diary. When you consider what they must have gone through, it's amazing that he was able to write at all."

DAY 91: The skies are almost always gray now, and the smallest of the seas could wash over the very walls of Rome. Each day the wind is colder and stronger, and we all now wear the fur jackets and trousers of the northern barbarians. There is no more muttering that the edge of the world is near, as all of the remaining sailors were with the commander when he came here years ago. On the few clear nights I see strange new constellations that circle a celestial pole with no pole star. Among them is a mighty cross that never sets—surely a sign of the Christian God. Is his domain here? Do the Gods of Romulus come to do battle with him?

DAY 157: Icicles hang from the ropes and fittings, and the clothes of the sailors are stiff with frost. Great islands of floating ice loom all around us so thickly that we must use sweeps to navigate around them. Two steersmen have died of exposure, and there have been some beatings to keep the discipline.

DAY 170: I write on land, but this coast is the most barren, cold, forsaken place ever beheld by mortal eyes. Day and night have merged into one, the birds walk about as men, yet the cattle crawl like worms. Everywhere is ice and rock, with not so much as a single tree, or even a blade of grass. Rentian begged the commander to let us return in summer, but he replied that this *was* summer, and that we had better dig out the first of the chambers quickly, to have shelter in the really bad seasons. Just as Aeneas descended to the Underworld, so have we come here. Stoutest of mortals, Valerius builds a forge and whistles cheerfully.

"Quintus' dating is not always reliable, but we estimate that this Roman landing in Antarctica took place in February 412 A.D. Two of the men buried at the Cape Verde Islands garrison have fingers and toes missing, probably through frostbite, and these graves have been dated to around 390 A.D. They were almost certainly from Decius' first voyage to Antarctica."

By now they had moved on to stand before a map of Antarctica, with the site marked by a red arrow. While the tour group stood staring with indifferent interest, the guide pressed a stud beneath a handrail, and the curtains that covered one entire wall were drawn aside. There was a collective gasp, even from the students. Beyond the triple glazing was a gray, choppy sea, with light snow blowing past on a strong wind. The shingle beach was bare and lifeless, just as it had been when the Romans had landed there. Some of the tourists shivered and rubbed their hands, perhaps in sympathy with Quintus, who had had no more than heavy clothing and a tent for shelter when he wrote those words so long ago.

"I shall read one last passage," the guide announced as she closed the curtains again. "In the year that followed, the expedition dug the chambers that Quintus had designed. It was revealed that they were building a time ship to enable the 'Gods of Romulus' to escape to the future.

"These strange people may or may not have had the longevity that Quintus attributes to them, but they certainly had some advanced scientific techniques. They had discovered a method for suspended animation that involved antifreeze chemicals such as polyhydric alcohols and glycerols. These were probably extracted from snow-dwelling insects such as springtails, midges, and snowflies, and they allowed the human body to be chilled without tissue damage."

If only you knew who would be agreeing with you, thought Vitellan. He paused the vid, then reran her explanation twice. Here was the secret of his own time machine, and here were the people responsible for it. He pondered many seemingly unconnected facts, then keyed the vid to continue.

"The time ship had to be in a place that was always freezing, but was also so very remote that neither the Manneleans nor curious natives could disturb it while the centuries passed. Decius would have found Eskimos in the Arctic lands that he explored, but Antarctica was so very remote that only the finest Roman ships and navigation techniques would have allowed the people of his time to reach it. With Rome fallen to the Visigoths, Antarctica would be as inaccessible as the moon would be to us after some nuclear war."

... and on that final day that saw neither dawn nor dusk, the Gods of Romulus gathered to drink the golden elixir before sailing away into the ages in their time ship. Like Aeneas, Commander Decius lived this year past in the underworld of this land, paying homage to the gods, his very brothers and sisters.

Even as he wiped the last drops of the elixir from his lips, though, his gaze did turn to us, the mortal Romans. Crew of the *Nemesis* and builders of the time ship, we could never sail back through the islands of ice without him to navigate. Sad, wretched, doomed, our plight reached out to his heart.

"These brave, loyal Romans will surely perish without me to guide them back," he cried to the assembled Gods of Romulus, dashing his silver goblet to the shingles. "Friends, you have your time ship and may go in safety to some new age. I wish to stay behind. Too many loyal Romans have died already for us, and it is my will that these at least should grow old under a warm sun."

Then Helica spoke, saying "Decius, my lord. Many years have I been apart from you. Nine decades have I waited since we were married, so how could I now give you up forever? If you would stay in this age so that these brave craftsmen and sailors of Rome might live, then I shall stay too, tending the sick and ever by your side."

Even as we cheered their noble sacrifice, the godling Rentian raised his voice in an angry cry. "This is madness! Decius, Helica, you must come with us. Forsake these wretches. They will lead assassins back here to destroy us as we sleep in the time ship."

Loud and long were his pleadings on that bleak beach, but to no avail. As Decius turned to lead us away, the false Rentian took a lance and flung it full at his back. Had not Valerius pushed him aside and taken the point between his own ribs, we would all have been fated to a cold, lingering death, lost amid storms and islands of towering ice. Only then did Rentian feel remorse, and he ordered choice stores from the time ship itself to be put aboard the *Nemesis* so that the noble blacksmith's death would be atoned for. Then we were sped on our way.

That was our parting—the Gods of Romulus into time, and Decius, Helica, and we mortal Romans into the gray and terrible sea.

The guide closed the book with a snap and declared: "There is no more."

Some of the tourists shifted uneasily, puzzled by the abrupt ending. This was obviously her standard, dramatic way to end the readings from the *Deciad*. It brought the focus back to her with a jolt.

"Late in the Resources War of 2026," she continued, "an Australian hovertank crew found the half-buried remains of a raft made from charred timbers on a pebble beach while conducting a sensor patrol. The nails and metal bands in the timber registered on the tank's instruments, and the crew shoveled away the overlying pebbles to reveal the raft."

The group moved over to an air-conditioned glass case the size of a small room, in which were housed the carefully restored remains of the raft. Some of the charred beams showed the chisel strokes of the Roman shipwright who had originally fashioned them.

"Rentian probably planted some sort of timed incendiary device among the stores that were put aboard the *Nemesis*. This detonated when the ship was well out to sea. Incredibly, Decius somehow survived, built a raft, and reached the Antarctic coast again. We presume that Helica died when the *Nemesis* sank, but no further mention is made of her. The fate of Quintus was another matter. The manuscript of the *Deciad* was found in a lead tube strapped to his body."

In a separate case was a lead cylinder about the size of a wine bottle. The metal was bright where it had recently been cut open at one end, and there were letters and symbols scratched in the lead. The guide translated the message:

"Beware the time ship and Godlings of Romulus. Mark well the tale of Quintus."

Now there was absolute silence. Here were the last written words of the author of the *Deciad*.

Vitellan reran the seconds where his host's eyes stared at a silk rubbing of the words and symbols from the cylinder. Could it be possible that nobody else but he had grasped what Quintus was trying to tell the future? The letters were slightly smaller and neater than those of Quintus in the mockup scroll lying open beside it. Vitellan decided that this should remain his own private secret until he knew more about this century and his own place in it. After another half-dozen reruns and pauses Vitellan finally continued on to where the guide was speaking again.

"We shall never know exactly what happened as the *Nemesis* sank off the coast of Antarctica," she explained. "Perhaps Decius managed to drag Quintus aboard his raft, but the mason died, probably of exposure. When he reached the shore Decius placed his body in a depression on the beach and covered it with the raft.

"Nothing of Decius was ever found. He evidently set out overland to avenge Helica's death but died before reaching the time ship. The hovertank BM 895 took both the manuscript and Quintus' mummified body to Jones Base, but within hours they were caught in an Espanic attack. The hovertank was destroyed with all hands in the fighting. Quintus' body was lost when the administration bunker of the base received a series of direct hits from Espanic percussion-wave missiles. The *Deciad* manuscript survived, and was smuggled out to Australian lines a few days later. It contained enough clues to allow the time ship to be located. After the final treaty to end the war was signed, the Australians sent an expedition to find the site. As you know, the time ship has proved fascinating to tourists, being the greatest archeological find since the tomb of Tutankhamen. It had to be developed quickly as an international museum."

Leaving the group at the exhibits for a moment, the guide returned her copy of the *Deciad* to the lectern. The tourists spent a lot more time with the exhibits, now that the end of the *Deciad* was fresh in their minds. People were nodding and pointing, and Vitellan could even hear snatches of very strangely pronounced Latin in the conversations. After an appropriate interval the guide called for their attention.

"If you will follow me into the elevator now, we shall have a tour of the parts of the time ship open to the public."

The elevator was large and broad, the size of a small room. It descended, then opened into a low-roofed chamber cut out of the rock. Half of it was partitioned off by a double wall of thick glass. Beyond this a tall, well-proportioned man lay on a couch, naked under the fluorescent lights. Beside the couch was a complicated mechanism connected to several vats of liquid and the shutters of two ventilation shafts.

"There are three other rooms like this," said the guide. "The people in them were to awake first, then revive the others manually."

"Why have four rooms?" asked the veteran.

"Multiple redundant systems, like the early spacecraft had. The mechanism in one room has in fact failed because of slow corrosion, but the other three would have functioned properly."

"When?"

"About twenty years from now."

There was a murmur of astonishment. Vitellan wondered what the reaction of the world would have been if the time travelers had revived themselves.

"The timer works by the liquid properties of cold pitch. Pitch is actually a liquid, but flows very slowly if the temperature is lowered to the point that is needed for suspended animation. The designer calculated that after a few centuries enough pitch would drip through a broad funnel to trip a balance arm. That would in turn trigger mechanisms to seal off the cold air vents and start a chemical reaction to ignite a separate vat of pitch and heat the place. The ice encasing the man on the couch would melt, and the spring-and-wax clamps that had kept water out of his lungs while he was being frozen would pop off his nose and mouth. After a measured period, when the body was warm enough, a series of three hundred lead balls would roll down a race. They would strike his chest at about one-second intervals and were meant to start his heart. A second race with heavier balls was meant to work his lungs."

"And they expected this wacky contraption to work?" asked the tourist from New York.

"Actually, it probably would. A chemical analogue of the Romans' elixir had already been synthesized from the body of the Durvas time traveler, so a team in Berkeley conducted experiments using monkeys in a scaled-down version of this type of mechanism. One out of four were revived by the mechanism alone. The Romans had a fighting chance."

"So what does the elixir do?"

"Their bodies are preserved from decay by the cold, but they are not frozen solid—ice formation within individual cells would damage their bodies' tissues. They used a type of antifreeze derived from snow-dwelling insects to get around this problem, so that in theory they could stay frozen forever. In practice, natural radioactivity from their own bodies and the surrounding rocks would slowly damage the DNA of their cells, and after several thousand years of accumulated damage the person would die of cancer soon after being revived. At worst, the symptoms would resemble a massive radiation overdose. They could not have known about radioactivity, however, and were just lucky to have chosen a safe period."

"Hey, wait a minute! That one there—"

"Rentian."

"Whoever he is, he's not frozen in ice."

"It's good that you spotted it, a surprising number of people don't. Look closely, everyone. There's a thin film of thermal pump gel, layered and molded to his skin. First, it makes his body more accessible to scientists doing scans and taking samples; second, it keeps him as stable as ice would in the chamber's freezing air; third, it makes it easier for you to see him than if he were in a block of ice. Now step this way and you can see the real thing."

The group proceeded to the dormitory chambers where most of the sleepers were on display but still in blocks of ice. Over a dozen spaces were ominously empty, and the guide said that there was evidence of fighting among the time travelers after Decius had left. Very significant, Vitellan thought to himself. Other chambers held clothing, food, weapons, and instruments. Everything was well preserved and ready for use; there was even a small prefabricated ship. A model of the assembled ship stood before it. Now the group began to break up, and people wandered off to examine what interested them most.

One of the classics students tried to start up an argument with the guide about her use of "elixir" instead of "philter" in her translation of the *Deciad.*

" 'Elixir' is a word associated with alchemy, it has a European medieval origin," he insisted earnestly.

"English has a European medieval origin as well," replied the guide.

The veteran spoke next. "I still don't see why we have to keep them frozen," he said. "I mean I've heard all that guff about them starting cults and causing trouble like Bonhomme did when he was unfrozen, but I can't believe that a bunch of folk over eighteen hundred years old could take over the world."

"You may be right," said the guide, "but we want to be sure. The revival timer will click over in about twenty years, and the Deciad Management Trust Committee has decided to postpone revival until then. After all, it conforms with their original plans. In the meantime we have yet another frozen time traveler to observe when he is revived. The city of Durvas in England has that time traveler claimed to be a Roman who was awake for two years in the fourteenth century. I actually saw his body when it was on display in the British Museum in 2016. He was due to be unfrozen in 2054 according to Durvas tradition, but the revival has now been brought forward to later this year. Radiocarbon microcore samples of his tissues verify the body's age, so he must be as genuine as Bonhomme or any of these bodies here. If *he* turns out to be less trouble than Bonhomme, then we shall definitely revive these Romans early as well."

The veteran pointed to the model of the ship. "Just imagine if we hadn't found this place. Twenty years from now the Gods of Romulus might have revived and sailed that proto-schooner into Sydney harbor by themselves."

"It's one of my favorite fantasies," the guide replied, cocking her head to one side and folding her arms, "except that they go to Valparaiso for me."

The vid tour ended, and a list of credits scrolled up the wallscreen. To his surprise Vitellan found that the tourists were all actors, and only Gina Rossi was what she was portrayed as: a tour guide. The entire thing, all the spontaneity, everything had been a show.

As bedtime entertainment Lucel could not have made a worse recommendation than the vid. Images of the Deciad Museum and readings from the *Deciad* cascaded through Vitellan's mind all night, and he had questions that nobody in this century was even capable of asking. Answers were, of course, well beyond hope. Vitellan could not fall asleep, and eventually he gave up. Looking for uncomplicated distraction, he accessed the full text of Geoffrey Chaucer's *Canterbury Tales* from a datafarm and lay reading from the wallscreen until dawn.

Lucel's hologram-face was neutral as Vitellan spoke to her the next day. She listened to his impressions of the vid with interest, and was able to field his questions with unexpected authority.

"I've done some research on that first expedition, and I found out that a conscript classics tutor named Max Kerrin was shown the *Deciad* manuscript after it was smuggled out of the Jones Base. He even did a rough translation to assess its worth."

"And the crew of the hovertank?" asked Vitellan. "Did they speak to anyone on the base about their find? Did they even know what they had found?"

"Of course not, none of them knew Latin and they were not archeologists. They probably thought that they had found some modern Espanic wreckage, and that the manuscript might have been coded intelligence. That's why it was smuggled out after the base fell."

"And is anything known of Quintus' body?"

"Nobody survived to tell. The fighting for Jones Base was very heavy, and only a few people in the hospital bunker lived through the first attack. Why are you so interested?"

Vitellan leaned forward, a hand resting on one knee and the other gesturing in the air as if he were conducting the Orchestral hologram tutor.

"Why? They were the first Romans I've seen for six of my years—or 1,867 of yours, and they made the elixir that allowed me to travel through time. It's like an orphan suddenly discovering a book about his parents, except that a lot of the pages have been torn out."

"Well, don't get too excited. They're all dead."

Vitellan's arm flopped to his side, limp.

"Dead?" he echoed. There was something authoritative and final in Lucel's voice, as if the only possible question were how.

"The Resources War finished early in 2026, and an Australian expedition was sent to the time ship after a huge fanfare of media hype. The original recommendation was to revive the Romans at once, then to set the time ship up as a museum. The Luministes had agents infiltrate the staff of the expedition, however. Someone drilled a microshaft into the brains of each Roman sleeper and inserted a bead of thermix the size of a hair follicle. From the outside the bodies look normal, but X rays show serious damage. The Australian government was highly embarrassed that such an archeological sensation in its care had been so terribly damaged, so there was a cover-up while their scientists investigated. It soon became clear that something could be salvaged.

"Three of the bodies were actually still viable. One man and two women were quite a lot smaller than Quintus had rather romantically described them in the *Deciad,* and the Luministes had drilled too deep to plant their thermix—all the way down to the nasal cavity. The bodies were secretly replaced with wax mockups and taken away to the Mawson Institute in Melbourne. There they were unfrozen for reconstructive surgery, but that took a long time because they were badly messed up. Meanwhile a story was published that the Romans were being kept frozen because they might all turn out like Bonhomme, who was still causing a lot of problems internationally. The plan was to present the three survivors to the world around now, then 'discover' that the Luministes had killed the others."

"If they are now all dead, then the Luministes must have been ahead of them," said Vitellan doubtfully.

"They were. A spy named Gina Rossi was appointed to the museum staff, and she worked there for months, slowly getting people's trust and picking up clues. Some months later she turned up at the Mawson Institute posing as a postgraduate student and got right past the outer security before she started firing fingernails like the ones I used back in Paris. She offed thirty guards and staff before she reached the isolation ward, where the last Romans from Antarctica were being kept. There she detonated a copy of the *Deciad*, a copy made of laminated covalent lattice. It took out the Romans, the agent, the lab, another twelve guards, and half the west wall of the Mawson Institute. *Now* do you see why I'm being so careful about your security?"

"She—the guide in that tour vid? She suicided to kill them?"

"She did. All Luministe agents have obsession imprinting as part of their training. Suicide is no problem for them."

Vitellan stood up and stalked across to the unit and stood face to face with Lucel's holograph.

"And you're telling me that the public knows nothing about all this?"

"Until this morning that was the case, but the Australians have just released the results of an investigation into the Luministe attacks. Because there has just been a change of government they have published the entire truth, blamed the previous administration for everything, and screamed bloody murder at the Luministes. The hard-line Luministe nations are insisting that they are innocent, but they applaud the killings and accuse the Temporian Romans of being pagans and agents of Satan. Australia has broken off diplomatic relations with a dozen governments that have condoned the attacks. Check the news, Vitellan, it's the biggest thing since the Japanese landed on Ceres."

Vitellan paced across the room several times, absorbing and assimilating what Lucel had said. Abruptly he sat down and took a pair of voice-key dataspex from his pocket and plugged them into a console. It took him many minutes to navigate to a newsboard archive that Lucel

could have found in seconds, but he eventually found what he was looking for.

"FORTY-TWO STAFF DIE IN MAWSON INSTITUTE TRAGEDY. DAMAGE FROM
SUSPECTED TERRORIST ATTACK ESTIMATED AT 12 MILLION AUSTRALIAN DOL-
LARS."

"It should be dated November third," said Lucel.

"It is November fourth."

"Ah yes, the International Dateline. I was in California doing some
illegal training and it was the previous day. Serves me right for not up-
dating my impressions with an imprint overlay."

"Illegal training?" said Vitellan wearily, sweeping the dataspex off
and dropping them back into his pocket.

"It was to do with rescuing you from the hospital in Paris—"

"What!" Vitellan exploded. "That was nearly a fortnight before the
Luministes abducted me."

"When I am out of this thing I'll explain as much as I can."

"Explain now! You're working for me, I order you to tell me."

"I'll explain nothing until I'm ready."

The holographic head winked out of existence. Vitellan stalked out
of the room, furious. He met Dr. Baker in the corridor.

"How long will the—will Lucel take to heal?" he asked, forcing an
affable tone into his voice.

"The shock from the three rounds that hit her was partly absorbed
by woven monomolecular armor in her clothes. Miz Lucel died in the
sense that you would have defined death up to ten years ago, but she's
coming back fast. In three days she'll be allowed to be conscious for a few
minutes, in a couple more she'll be walking. She was lucky. The Luministes hired serious firepower."

Three or four days, thought Vitellan. Without the interface to her
dataspex and the data networks of the world, she would have no control
over him.

"She was finding it distressing to be awake while her body was so
helpless," Vitellan lied. "Would it be possible to have her, er, unconnected until she is ready to awake?"

"I guess so. You know, people are funny about biosupport units. Some folk like to be a holovid and look down on themselves being cut open, others just don't want to know. Okay, I'll leave her interface switched off until it's time for a physical revival."

Vitellan glowed with the minor triumph. He was learning to take control of his own destiny yet again.

"I'd like to talk to you about having some facilities made available to me," he added casually.

Baker nodded and gestured to a consulting room nearby.

Houston, Texas: 10 December 2028, Anno Domini

Vitellan came up to Caleb Hall's sternum, and the tall, gangly man reminded him of some type of powerful djin from an Eastern folk tale. In a heavy Texan drawl the imprint analyst explained that he had been brought in on contract from a clinic-cartel run by the more upmarket Houston gangs, and had been briefed about what was happening.

"So you want to talk to some folk in Britain, then get me to sort out the facts from the bullshit in what they say?"

"You have it," replied Vitellan. He sat down on the edge of the telepresence couch, hunched over and rubbing his hands together. "On the voice-face link just now . . . Lord Wallace, the head of the Village Corporate, seemed surprised to hear from me. I think that he even doubted who I really was."

"Has he ever met you?" asked Hall. "Have you spoken to him before?"

"He has seen me, yes."

"Hey, I get it, you're a British media personality."

"I . . . have been seen widely on the media, twelve years ago."

"So who are you, man?"

"I'd rather not say. Why would he be so suspicious?"

"With voice profile synthesizers you could sound like most anyone you wanted," Hall explained, sounding surprised that Vitellan was not aware of it. Vitellan looked to Baker.

"About the results on those whole-body scans, Dr. Baker? Are you clear about what I want to know?"

"You want an accurate fix on your physiological age," he said, scratching the back of his head and looking puzzled.

"Yes. If my telepresence session is not over when the results come in, interrupt the session."

"You're the boss."

The telepresence couch contoured itself to the shape of Vitellan's body as he lay back on it. The feeling was oddly sensual, just as Hall had described it. Medical technicians bonded the thin gauze of the dermal interface suit sensors to his skin.

Hall sat watching with amused curiosity.

"If you had a nerve-line interface like mine you wouldn't have to fool about with this museum piece," he pointed out as the technicians slowly and methodically configured the unfamiliar unit.

"I'm a museum piece myself, it makes me feel at home," he replied through the gauze over his lips.

"What do you mean by that, man?"

"Never mind. Look, enough has been done to my head already, so let's just do what keeps me happy."

"Deal. You're the boss."

As patches of the suit became active, Vitellan began to lose the sensations from his nerves. The feeling was like floating in a deep, tepid bath.

Fishbourne, Britain: 11 December 2028, Anno Domini

The linkage with a node in the south of England began as fading into a vague, shadow existence. Vitellan's inner ear tried to tell him that he was lying flat on his back, yet he was standing on a grassy rise beneath a clear sky in late afternoon. A cold wind was blustering through the grass and tugging at his overcoat. An overcoat. The software had dressed him for a cold, windy day outdoors.

Even as he became aware of his own disorientation, the equipment compensated. The first node was to have been at the site of his old villa, but nothing seemed particularly familiar. The land was gently undulating and covered in bushes and new-growth trees. He had known it as farmland, and somehow this revegetation program reminded him of the Dark Ages. A wedge-shaped SOMS rumbled high overhead on its ramjets, hurtling spaceward.

The air to his left solidified into a pillar that resolved itself into a tall, imposingly built but elderly man wearing an overcoat like his and a wide-brimmed hat. The hologram of Lord Wallace introduced itself.

"So this is where my villa used to stand?" Vitellan asked, the dismay obvious in his voice.

"No, this is just for us to focus. The excavation is over this rise. Come, I'll show you."

The word *excavation* should have warned Vitellan of what to expect, but the sight of what his villa had become still came as a shock. They walked their holograms over the low, grassy rise and came upon a dark, oblong scar in the earth, about the area of an arena. The lighter color of regular stone foundations showed an echo of disciplined Roman design that had survived but not triumphed. A team of archeologists was at work with an ultrasonic scanner while robotic excavators patiently dug, mapped and catalogued fragments of Vitellan's past that had escaped the turmoil that had shattered and plundered the villa.

"We are near modern Fishbourne," said Lord Wallace. "The Village Corporate bought the land as soon as the ruins were, ah, discovered. That was two years ago, but the Resources War delayed excavations. Austerity and all that."

Vitellan walked his hologram down an excavated path and stared at the foundations he had never set eyes upon when he had lived there.

Beneath a large plastic weather dome the mosaic of a blue dolphin in green waves was taking shape under the gentle manipulators of terrier-sized robots on arrays of padded legs.

"I try to remember what it used to be like, but this is too much for me," he admitted. "Seeing one's house in ruins is bad enough, but seeing it made as ancient as this is far worse."

"We may be able to help there," said his host. "Jackson, a full simulation if you please," Lord Wallace said to the air before him.

Walls and tiled roofs shimmered into being over the foundations, hedges and carefully manicured bushes grew out of air. A mathematically level lawn was even being cropped by virtual sheep. Sparrows splashed in the shallow water of a gently bubbling fountain. The walls were gleaming with whitewash, and were all as straight as a lance.

"Would you like to go inside?" asked Lord Wallace. Vitellan nodded and followed him down the path and through a door.

Apart from being unnaturally clean, Vitellan could not fault the reconstruction.

"The accuracy of the floor plans and floor mosaics I can understand," said Vitellan as he looked from the dolphin mosaic to a fresco of Diana the Huntress on a nearby wall, "but the furnishings and frescoes should have been impossible. How did you get all that detail right? Even in the ninth century this place was a pile of rubble."

"The science of archeology can deduce a fantastic amount from very little," Lord Wallace replied. "Fragments of tiles and stones found in the soil show what the roofing and walls were like, and subtle discoloration of the soil reveals where bushes and trees once stood in your garden. We have even used chemical tracers to identify odd corners where people used to piss when caught short."

Vitellan gave a start, as if he had been caught in the act of doing just that.

"Why go to so much trouble?"

"Why? You're the Centurion, *our* Centurion."

This was meant to explain everything, but although Vitellan did not find it helpful, he was too distressed and disoriented to argue the point. He had seen this place in its prime barely half a decade ago, yet now it was so very old that even its ghosts had surely faded.

"The Village Corporate is building a replica villa about a mile away," continued Lord Wallace with a brief wave to the northeast. "We thought that it could be a soothing place for you to live after the shock of being revived in this century."

Vitellan fought hard to resist the temptation to run forward and hide from the gaudy tumult of the twenty-first century in the fantastically realistic image.

"I . . . I must admit this is wonderful," he stammered. "I never thought that I'd ever again see Roman buildings as anything more than piles of stones. It's been so long, five years—of *my* life, at least. You say that a solid version of this illusion is being built?"

"The work is scheduled to be completed in four months. The garden was to be given twenty years to grow, and we planned to have people living in the villa for a time to give it a used and comfortable feel by 2054."

Comfort! That was it. A comfortable cage, a museum display case for a museum exhibit, Vitellan realized abruptly. The thought revolted him, and now he just wanted to get out. He shielded the eyes of his hologram from the descending sun as he looked through a door to the northwest.

"There was another villa out across there, as I remember, about three miles away. Do you know of it?"

"Jackson, did you catch that?" Lord Wallace asked the unseen operator, then assimilated the reply for a moment before turning to Vitellan. "A ruined villa was found there in 2019. It has been mapped by ultrasonics and some preliminary trenches have been dug, but it seemed to be nothing special so no serious work has been done as yet. What can you tell us about it?"

"Someone lived there, a girl who . . . who meant a lot to me."

Lord Wallace examined his imprint index for a moment. "No written records exist regarding any villa there. Can you give me a name?"

"No! No, forget that I mentioned it. You were right, it's nothing special."

"Would you like to see the Frigidarium now?"

"More ruins?"

"Oh no, the Frigidarium has never been in ruins."

They faded out of the countryside and were reprojected in the grounds of a large Georgian manor with a walled garden of about ten acres. The late afternoon shadows were long and deep, and the fashionable free-growth garden plan seemed more like overgrown neglect to the Roman's mind. The elderly man was still in a long overcoat, but his wide-brimmed hat was gone. As a hologram Vitellan was nervy and hesitant in his mannerisms, as if the direct line to his mind made it harder for him to hide his real mood. From the background noise of traffic and solar cell film–clad office blocks looming beyond the wall, Vitellan deduced that they were within a city now. The stone building that had been built over the entrance to the Frigidarium in the twelfth century was as he had last seen it in 1358, except for over six centuries of additional weathering. A thick evergreen vine smothered the north face with leaves.

"Not as good as it was when new in 1155, but we looked after it," declared Lord Wallace with pride.

Vitellan shrugged. "I would not know. It was already two centuries old when I last saw it, in 1358. Even then it had not been used in decades. They had been keeping me in a cave in Wales, because snow and ice were more readily available there."

Lord Wallace turned and walked through the iron-bound oak door after gesturing to Vitellan to follow. Vitellan knew that he could walk wherever the hologram projector could reach. He walked for the door, his hands before him. There was slight resistance imposed by the projection software as he passed through, as if he were pushing a heavy curtain. Hall had said that the effect would be disconcerting for a first-time user. Beyond the door Lord Wallace was holding the glowing hologram of a fluorescent lantern.

"This place was used as a store for five hundred years," he explained as he led the way down the familiar stone steps. "It was a terrible irony that after you were moved to Switzerland, the English climate became cold again, and Durvas was once again able to keep the Frigidarium stocked with ice. In 1870 the Village Corporate decided to restore it to the way it was when you had last used it, in the Middle Ages."

"They did good work. This is very close to what I remember."

"Oh no, this is a more recent restoration, done in 1988. The Victorian effort was sheer butchery and bad taste—terracotta cherubs, gargoyles, miniature Greek pillars, all that sort of thing. Fortunately the Durvas archives were not all sent to France and destroyed during the Great Revolution of the 1790s. A few plans and drawings were left, so we had a good idea of the authentic layout."

Vitellan counted ninety-two steps to the little stone anteroom. RUFUS ME FECIT was still inscribed above the massive wooden door and there was a trickle of meltwater running to a collection trough cut into the stone floor. The outer chamber was stacked with French champagne, Australian chardonnay, and Californian genoeisvine, all on oak racks with bar codes burned into the wood.

"I'll enter with you this time," said Vitellan.

They stepped through into freezing air, and the hologram projector even fabricated the condensation of breath that was actually leaving Vitellan's nostrils back in Houston. The blocks of ice were now made in a refrigeration unit behind the main house, and were renewed every month instead of seasonally. The stone platform that had been Vitellan's bed for so long was flanked by ten packing cases. He walked over to look at them.

"Those are the Century Roasts," explained Lord Wallace. "Every ten years we unfreeze and roast a century-old sheep, and put another down in its place. It's a very old custom."

"I do not remember it."

Lord Wallace smiled approvingly.

"Well, for most of us it's very old. The practice was established after you were taken to Switzerland, to try to preserve the tradition of keeping something frozen in this chamber. Everyone in the Village is entitled to a share."

"With two hundred thousand people in Durvas and another fifty thousand working for the Village there can't be much to go around."

"Members of the Village Corporate get a couple of mouthfuls, and the rest is mixed into several tons of mincemeat for soups and pies. True, it's spread rather thinly by the time everyone who wants to partake has done so, but it's the symbolism that's important. It gives us unity."

"When did it begin?"

"It was started back in the fourteenth century by Icekeeper Guy. The roasts were kept in Wales at first, but then the climate cooled and the tradition was brought back to Durvas and this Frigidarium. Until a few years ago—when your body was moved back to Durvas—it was a rustic, eccentric, and, well . . . very *English* custom that inspired unity among our employees. People like tradition and certainty, especially when the world around them is changing so fast."

Vitellan's mind was racing all the while, because he knew that Lord Wallace and his Village Corporate had plans to turn him into some type of prophet from the century that Christ had lived in. The Luministe attack was certainly due to fear of a rival prophet and leader, but perhaps revenge was also part of it. There were many twisted, convoluted agendas to think about. Durvas had changed a lot since Guy had been Icekeeper—and the villagers had changed a lot too.

"A quarter of a million Durvas people," Vitellan said as he stared at the frozen meat. "In 1358 Durvas was dying, yet Guy built it up again, leading to all this. I seem to be always served by people so much better than me."

His host took that as a compliment and gave a little bow, his hand across his chest.

"This must be your only real link with the past," Lord Wallace said proudly as he held the lantern up to the arch of ice blocks lining the roof.

"I designed it and supervised its building with Rufus and Milos, but from then on I only saw it when I went down to be frozen. Revivals were always up in some house in the village. It was not practical to have roaring fires and tubs of water down here."

Lord Wallace squatted down and pointed to a groove in the stone floor. As a hologram his movements were far more agile than with his real body.

"One point that has bothered us for centuries is the meltwater channel. It allows a little of the warmer air from outside into the inner chamber. Why not have the collection trough inside?"

"The amount of water in the collection trough measures the rate of melting without anyone having to open the door and let even more warm air in."

Lord Wallace arched his eyebrows and nodded his approval. "Like everything else Roman, it's wonderfully simple and practical."

"But I've never been afraid of new and improved technology," Vitellan assured him. "Remember that I consented to move to a better model of this time machine in 1358."

He ran his holographic fingers over the rough stone surfaces, noting familiar marks made by a stonemason who had been a contemporary of Christ. Once, when he pushed too hard, his fingers sank right into the stone. "If you were to freeze me again, how would you do it?" Vitellan asked.

"Ah, we have a synthesized version of the Oil of Frosts, based on samples taken from your frozen blood in 2016. As for the location, well perhaps we could build an underground site near one of the lunar poles, with liquid nitrogen storage and a refrigerator powered by a solar collector."

"Lunar—the moon!" exclaimed Vitellan.

"Why not? It's the most sensible place. Oh, and we have identified the toxins present in the Oil of Frosts and separated them from the beneficial components, so your health would not be as badly affected. The Oil has had to be modified for use with the lower temperatures that liquid nitrogen provides, but it is still basically much the same mixture. It would be advisable to spend a couple of years on a diet low in radionucleotide traces to reduce the danger from long-term irradiation from trace radioactivity in the environment, and we would build the components of the new chamber from materials made of stable isotopes."

"What sort of period would that allow me to jump across safely?"

"We did a study of this some years ago and found it to be thirty thousand years, with an error margin of five thousand years."

"So twenty-five thousand years, if one was being conservative?"

"Perhaps even more. You could make your next jump say, five hundred years, and use the improvements in technology that have been developed by then. A million years may not be out of the question, in spite of damage from cosmic rays and natural radioactivity. You would have to be monitored for radiation events by some type of advanced scanner, then injected with nanotech repair bio-mechs targeted on the damage sites when you were revived. Current medical technology would allow you a 140-year lifespan, and assuming that you stay awake for about six months between jumps . . . with luck you *could* get to over two hundred million years. That's assuming you don't have a fatal accident at any stage."

The number was too big for Vitellan, and he was silent for some time as he thought about it. He scanned his imprints for a few facts to cling to, anything to supply a perspective.

"According to my cyclopedia imprint, two hundred million years ago *we* were triconodont mammals the size of rats, eating insects and dinosaur eggs. In less than six hundred years, while I slept frozen in the Alps, the world has changed so much that any pleb can wield the sorts of powers that Roman gods were credited with in the time that I was born."

"But it would be a journey to end them all," said Lord Wallace, his voice colored by the romance and adventure.

"Would it? Suppose for a moment that some proto-shrew had somehow been preserved in a pocket of ice since the late Triassic, and had then been found and revived. How would it feel about life in a cage, with no dinosaur eggs or familiar insects to eat, and no mate?" He gestured to the door. "It was good to see this place again, but can we go now?"

Outside the Frigidarium they were met by two guards dressed rustically in dungaree shirts and moleskin trousers, but carrying quite modern tumble-shot automatics. They had emerged from a neat square of bricks that hinged out of the wall to reveal a long, high tunnel lined with red brick archwork and paving.

"This is new," observed Vitellan.

"It leads back into the manor's cellar," Lord Wallace explained as they turned down the tunnel.

"So that you can get to the wine when it's raining?"

"That too, but it was actually built as an air raid shelter during the Second World War."

Vitellan sorted through imprinted databases for a moment. "Bombs dropped from enemy aircraft, I see. But would the, ah, German airmen have attacked a civilian house?"

"Yes. They bombed our cities to rubble, then we flew over to Germany and bombed their cities a lot worse. This place was not hit, but that was only by luck."

"But what evil had the people of all those cities done to be so terribly punished?"

"Evil had nothing to do with it. It was strategic bombing, to weaken the enemy overall. They were making munitions and general supplies for the war effort, so bombing their cities made it easier to defeat their armies."

In spite of his twenty-first-century memory imprints, Vitellan still had the values of a centurion from the Roman legions. The mass destruction of cities from something as remote as a flying machine offended him, and there was no escaping the fact.

"The pattern of the bricks and brickwork is familiar," Vitellan said as they walked.

"Oh, it's very much in the Roman style. We couldn't have it any other way, that would never do."

As they were walking along the tunnel something faint but insistent called to Vietnam from within himself. At first he thought it an imprint malfunction. They were known to happen, and their effect was described as similar to this. He had something like an itch to think about a memory.

He realized that he was aware of having spoken to Baker, and within the past few seconds. It was a memory without experience, just like an imprint. He had told him that the results of certain tests on his tissues were ready. Dr. Baker had also advised him to return to Houston at once.

"The house itself is the old headquarters of the Village as a corporation," Lord Wallace was saying, "but the functional headquarters of today is wherever the Corporate meets. That's usually at one of the datanode buildings, but this place is still used for ceremonial occasions. The Corporate has been called to meet here in an hour, and I want to show you over the place first."

Vitellan stopped and deliberately made to steady himself against the wall. His hand sank in before the orientation software stopped him and tilted his hologram upright.

"Please, I think I've had enough for now," he said as Lord Wallace turned back. "My real body is tired. Could I come back here later, just before the meeting with the Corporate?"

"Yes, of course. You are the Durvas Centurion. You can do whatever you want."

Houston, Texas: 11 December 2028, Anno Domini

As easily as waking from a dream, Vitellan was back in Houston. The webbing of the couch parted like tearing cobwebs as he sat up.

"Baker?" he asked the form before his unfocused eyes.

"Yeah, that's me. I sent a flagged imprint directly to your brain, rather than the sensory access point at your holograph. That way the message could not be monitored unless someone did a blanket scan."

Vitellan examined the memory of the message that he had neither read nor heard.

"You . . . informed me that I am between twenty-four and twenty-six years old," said Vitellan in a flat voice, fighting down his incredulity.

"That's right."

Again there was a moment of silence, except for the soft rushing of the air conditioning.

"How?"

"It's a summary of a lot of little things, such as wear on your teeth. Just for the record, the scans of your teeth confirm some very classy laser dental work was done on your molars in 2014, 2017, and 2019. There are ceramic fillings with datable trace radioisotopes mixed in for reference purposes."

Vitellan's jaw dropped to say "Impossible!" but he caught himself in time.

"What were the other tests?"

"Bone joint condition, skin conductivity, a whole bag of cellular tests for mutation, telomere erosion, and the buildup of trace environmental pollutants such as dioxin."

"I seem to have scars missing from my body. Have I had plastic surgery?"

"Sure, there's evidence of it. Could you tell us where the scars were?"

"Later." Vitellan put his hands together and pressed his fingertips against his lips. He turned to Hall. "Soon I have to return to the telepresence tour of my Village in Britain. When I get back here from that telepresence session I want a . . . a diagnostic scan of my imprints done. Is that the right term?"

"Sure is."

"After that, I want certain locked memories probed directly. I believe that can be done."

"Big bucks," interjected Baker. "You would have to guarantee the Village to underwrite that sort of work."

"I can do that. How long would it take you to set up the equipment?"

"Get the credit for a deep scan and we can be doing it within, say, four days," said Hall.

Durvas, Britain: 11 December 2028, Anno Domini

Vitellan's historic meeting with the Village Corporate had not been originally planned as a telepresence event, but while the Durvas Centurion had demanded that it be held at once, he also refused to leave the safety of Houston until he was more confident about his own staff. His attitude was quite understandable, given all that had happened to him since his body had been unfrozen.

So this is what it is to be a ghost, he thought as he materialized in the unfamiliar room. It was a high-ceilinged anteroom decorated in a vaguely eighteenth-century style, although the furniture ranged from early Georgian tables to a chunky art deco lounge suite. Vitellan tried to walk, but it was no more effective than treading water.

"Will yourself in the direction you wish to move in, sir," said a software tutor's gentle voice. The sound seemed to enclose him.

He floated over to a wall, where a gold-leaf strip divided coffee cream painted plaster from red wallpaper. He tried to reach out—that same mistake again. Before the tutor came to his aid he extended his sense of touch and felt the texture of the red velvet wallpaper. Looking carefully, he noted that the velvet did not show the impression of a finger as he trailed his senses along it.

"What will the Village Corporate see?" he asked on the auditory band.

"A hologram of yourself dressed as you are in Houston, sir."

Vitellan drifted across to a full-length Victorian mirror in a rosewood frame. A fuzzy green sphere about the size of a melon hung in midair.

"Then why do I look like a green snowball?"

"That is only a position-point hologram, sir. It is for courtesy referencing. Full projection facilities have been installed in the Corporate room only."

So, I obtain a body only as I enter the room, he realized. I enter clumsily, feel a fool, begin the meeting on the back foot. He moved forward and extended arm-equivalent force to the door handle. A rubbery resistance barred his way.

"The Village Corporate is not yet ready to see you, sir," the disembodied voice explained with a blend of patience and regret.

"Inform the Village Corporate that I am to be admitted at once or they can come in here and talk to me as a green position-point snowball. I am going to count to ten," he added without elaborating.

He reached seven. The door opened of its own accord. Vitellan drifted forward, then found himself abruptly anchored in a simulation of his body. It had weight characteristics and could not be willed to float like a wisp of smoke. He held up a hand briefly, as if to satisfy himself with the hologram's quality, then walked forward.

The Village Corporate's boardroom was brightly lit, with spotlights playing down at the space enclosed by a U-shaped table of varnished oak. Each member's place was encrusted with interface studs and navigation pads. There were seventeen members, and all wore white silk knee-length kimonos over business suits. Although the effect was meant to be Roman, it came across as a tasteless combination of smoking jacket and laboratory coat. There were six women, and nobody was under forty, Vitellan noted. Lord Wallace was present as a hologram.

The walls were frescoed with art nouveau images of Durvas history. They featured an early Roman occupation idyll, Alfred of Wessex fighting the Danes, Durvas bowmen in the Hundred Years War, the great revival in the fifteenth century, and the Village's rise as an industrial center during the nineteenth century. Vitellan noticed that the trip through time ended with a Durvas elder shaking hands with a scruffy-looking little man who wore an ill-fitting suit and top hat, and smoked a cigar. An early wide-gauge steam train was belching smoke in the background. A display case full of weapons and ice-compacting equipment covered the remaining space.

"The wall is about due for another extension of the mural," Lord Wallace explained, following Vitellan's gaze.

The Corporate remained standing, stiff and uncertain. Vitellan looked to where the usher was beckoning him, a point at the focus of the U-shaped table. He ignored him and walked toward one of the glass-fronted cabinets.

Upon extending a hand he felt the image stopped at the glass. He made a fist and punched through the glass. Nothing shattered, but there was about the same resistance as a sheet of paper would have offered. He ran his finger along a familiar-looking blade. It was hard and cold to the touch. The sensors in the room's projector could apparently scan through glass.

"I recognize this Saxon half-sword, the one with the two nicks in the blade," he said, almost as if he were talking to himself.

"A fine and prized relic," Lord Wallace explained, breaking ranks with the others and walking over. "It is said to have belonged to the Centurion himself—well, I mean . . ."

Vitellan turned, frowning as if trying to recall something in the very distant past. "Yes, I remember using it in the fighting against the Danes."

That broke the decorum. The rest of the Village Corporate abandoned the table and crowded around to share in this magical moment of reunion, this confirmation that they had indeed served the Centurion well.

"We had it restored very carefully, Centurion," the Durvas conservator assured him, "but someone had butchered the blade by grinding it to a more tapering point."

"Ah yes, it was I who modified it," replied Vitellan. "I preferred the balance of a blade with the long, tapering point of the Roman gladius."

The conservator seemed to shrink before his eyes. Vitellan withdrew his hand and walked his hologram briskly to the table. The Corporate members hurried back as well, but the hologram Vitellan took a short-cut through the table and sat down in Lord Wallace's chair. The usher came running up with a spare chair as the others stood beside their seats. When Lord Wallace's hologram finally sat down the rest took their seats. There was a welcome speech for the Centurion, delivered by the Corporate herald from a carved oak lectern. The text read very strangely, having been carefully sculptured and remolded over many centuries by Durvas elders who had all wished Vitellan to hear *their* words—even though they would not be alive to speak them. After that, Lord Wallace went to the lectern and read from the *Chronicles of Lew and Guy,* written in the Swiss village of Marlenk in 1359 and brought back to Durvas a few years later. The reading was from the later pages, and concentrated on the Centurion's crossing of war-ravaged France and the confrontation with Jacque Bonhomme at Marlenk.

Vitellan frowned during the reading, unsettling those members of the Corporate who noticed. Something was amiss; the Centurion was displeased.

"That was probably written by the Marlenk priest under direction from Lew and Guy," Vitellan commented as Lord Wallace finished. "They would not have written about theology and such matters so very fluently."

As the members of the Corporate realized that the frown was for the long-dead, the mood relaxed as palpably as if a terrorist had placed his machine pistol on the table and raised his hands.

"But Centurion, is it accurate?" asked the Corporate herald, who was sitting up straight with his hands so tightly clasped that his nails were digging into the skin.

"Accurate but limited. Father Guillaume, Jacque Bonhomme, whatever you call him, he was not the sniveling, cowering wretch that this chronicle describes. He was proud, charismatic, cunning, and fairly brave."

"But in the final analysis, a medieval priest," said the chronicler. "How could he possibly run a major religious movement in the twenty-first century, one based on mass media? The chronicle is so specific, Bonhomme was a coward, an inept leader—"

"Not so. I met him only weeks ago, but in the fourteenth century. *I* ought to know."

The chronicler still seemed unhappy, but he said no more. The reality of who Vitellan really was tended to smother his own status as the ultimate authority on the history of Durvas.

"What else can you tell us, Centurion?" asked the marshal, Anderson.

Jacque Bonhomme and his followers were seldom far from Vitellan's thoughts.

"The Jacques did indeed commit atrocities against the nobles, but not on the scale described by Lew, Guy, or other contemporary chroniclers such as Froissart. Most Jacques just wanted to eat the nobility's food and loot their houses. If there were folk weaker than they to victimize, they would do it. I'll not deny that there was a lot of torture, rape, and murder as well, and none of that was excusable, but most of the Jacques were just yokels grasping for riches and pleasures. The nobility were not entirely innocent either, but then is anyone?"

"So who *is* Bonhomme?" asked the chronicler.

"Guillaume of Chalon. He was a priest, and apparently a respected scholar. As Jacque Bonhomme he was a compelling orator, as well as being an exceptional organizer and tactician. He was the right man at the right time, he led the Jacques superbly, and nearly brought down a kingdom with that rabble."

"And he's doing it again!" exclaimed Lord Wallace with theatrical indignation, as if he regarded Bonhomme's success as a personal insult.

"No, he's not."

"What do you mean?"

"The Bonhomme of the Luministes is neither Jacque Bonhomme nor Guillaume of Chalon. Oh, he has the right face and body, and some of Guillaume's memories and motivations, but the man who I have seen in the vids giving orations to prayer meetings and ranting to the media is someone different."

Vitellan looked up and down the arms of the table. Several faces had lost color, others still sat vacantly attentive.

"It must be imprints," said the Corporate treasurer, a woman near the end of the table.

"Undoubtably. He crossed several centuries in a single step, and now he's leading hundreds of millions of Luministes in the twenty-first century. He could never do that without heavy imprinting. I've had terrible trouble adjusting so far, and yet I'm an old hand at awaking in new centuries. This was the first time for Bonhomme."

The chronicler picked up the unintended pun and visibly suppressed a laugh. Lord Wallace looked puzzled. Anderson raised his hand.

"A lot of the therapy used in Bonhomme's revival is public knowledge," the marshal explained. "First he had an imprint to help him with modern French, then they gave him an adaptive overlay to help him adjust to our culture and technology. These have been repeated every few days for six years, so they are part of him now. His charisma showed through very early, and people were impressed, but they probably credited him with greater powers than he really had. In a sense what he can do is unimportant, it's just that people have a reason for following him. He's from the past, so he's as special as if he had stepped out of a UFO. Someone probably realized it the moment that he was successfully revived. There's a lot of evidence that a very carefully crafted campaign was staged to promote him by a worldwide alliance of militant Christian groups that saw his value as a rallying point."

There were murmurs of assent.

"That explains the attempts to kill the Centurion," Lord Wallace added. "Anyone equally special would draw worldwide media attention away from Bonhomme. The Luministes feared him as a rival."

Lord Wallace nodded to the chronicler, who began a holovid documentary projection describing how a Luministe survey team had discovered some fourteenth-century gold coins at the foot of a Swiss glacier in 2022. An artificially shaped boulder was visible within the ice.

The entire operation had been recorded on holovid. The hollowed-out boulder was dug out of the ice by the Luministe archeologists. Bonhomme's body was discovered inside, and it was quickly realized that he had been treated with an antifreeze compound.

The boulder was sliced apart with abrasion jets, and the core of ice carefully melted back to the body. Bonhomme was dressed in his priest's robes, and both body tissue and cloth were carbon dated as fourteenth century. The body temperature was raised to a few degrees above freezing while doctors determined that all the tissues were at a uniform temperature. Ultrasound profiling revealed extensive ulceration and perforation in his stomach, and trauma stabilization gels were applied by microsurgical flexors. His body was warmed further, and his blood replaced by oxygenated synthetic plasma. The body on the contoured bench gradually took on the color of a living human. Brain function, heart, and respiration were all restored before he was given a transfusion of real blood and actually revived.

There was much speculation by both the scientific experts and the media about the shock effect of being revived in a state-of-the-art twenty-first-century hospital. Thus a medieval bedchamber was constructed and furnished with careful attention to detail. The sleeping priest was brought in, still wearing the cranial webcap that was maintaining a controlled coma. Staff who had been given imprints for Latin and medieval French were dressed in fourteenth-century costumes, then the webcap was removed.

Hidden holocameras recorded the awakening as if it were part of a great holovid epic. Bonhomme's eyelids flickered, then he was awake, looking about him in alarm.

"Who are you?"

The first words were a wheezing croak. His throat was inflamed from drinking the Oil of Frosts without accustoming himself to it slowly. A nurse bent over his bed. She had been selected for having an especially good manner with patients.

"You have been frozen for more than six centuries. We are scholars and physicians. We revived you."

Bonhomme remained suspicious. "Do you know who I am?"

"No, you will have to tell us that."

He closed his eyes for a moment. "I am a simple scholar and priest. I did not expect to be asleep so long. Tell me about your kings and popes. Let me . . . let me read your chronicles . . ."

He lapsed into sleep again, already exhausted and overwhelmed by no more than a minute in the distant future. The holovid was stopped. Wallace leaned forward over the table.

"He later said he was a Christian prophet who was escaping persecution by the medieval nobility. When asked where he had got the Oil of Frosts he said that he was a Roman who had met Christ. Christ had given him the Oil of Frosts, then told him to travel through time to preach the True Word, and make sure that His original message was not corrupted."

"Plausible, but a lie," Vitellan commented.

"He also gave his own version of the 1358 peasant rebellion."

"I can guess what he said about that. How fast did he rise to power?"

"Almost as soon as Bonhomme was revived he found himself at the head of the Luministes, a militant Christian revivalist movement. They knew his value as a figurehead, and they promoted him very, very skillfully. He played a very minor part in the building of his own legend at first. His ulcerated stomach had to be replaced and he had to be brought up-to-date with the twenty-first century first. Imprint technology was more primitive back then, so it took several months.

"The trouble began soon enough, though," the chronicler added. "He had immediate appeal for the French, who had been humiliated by three major invasions over the past century and a half."

"I don't follow," said Vitellan.

"It's a very French thing. Once the French attitude used to be 'Monsieur, I am a very civilized man, and if you step over my borders I shall slap your face.' After World War Two it became 'Monsieur, I am a very dangerous psychopath, and if you step over my borders I shall blow your head off and nuke your homeland.' The latter attitude has proved itself for the past eighty-two years, and Bonhomme fitted in with it perfectly. He certainly is a dangerous psycho. There were also wars in Africa, Asia, and South America fought in his name, nasty little wars that the Christian sides always won. Bonhomme began to take a more active part in political life. The major religious leaders might not have liked him, but they recognized that he had given Christianity a boost in popularity on a scale not seen since the great missionary expansions of the nineteenth century. It's six years since his revival now, and a quarter of the world's population is influenced by him to some degree."

"I do not remember him as a good Christian," said Vitellan. "He hated authority and he hated Christianity when I knew him in 1358. He also feared divine retribution for what he had done at the head of the Jacques mob. He even stole my new Frigidarium to escape hellfire."

"Now *that* is consistent," said the marshal. "Luministe nations have put a huge amount of money and effort into medical research disguised as philanthropy—even the Village does a lot of contract work for them. He may want to be refrozen eventually, to escape an appointment with his creator."

"But he's hardly a Christian saint, anyone can see that," said Vitellan with ill-disguised contempt.

"But he *is* a type of crusader," countered Lord Wallace. "You lay frozen during the Crusades, you never saw how easily people can be led by scoundrels."

"I didn't have to witness the Crusades to see that."

"Well then, you should understand Bonhomme's position. He only had to declare himself a Christian to get some Christians following him—he has charisma, after all, and he has a flair for organization and tactics. He nearly destroyed the French nobility at the head of an untrained and badly armed mob in 1358. Now he knows that you are still alive, and *you* could easily become a rival prophet: you're a man whose father met Christ, it says so in our chronicles. You also know who really led the revolt of the Jacques, so you are both a rival and a threat. He wants you dead, and he has access to resources and firepower that could have wiped out the Roman Empire hundreds of times over. The Village can protect you from him, but you must return to us."

"You were not much help last time he sent his people after me," said Vitellan doubtfully. "I was kidnapped from the Village's own research park in Durvas."

"We were infiltrated and caught off-guard," said Lord Wallace defensively. "That will not happen again. It's *war* between the Luministes and the Village now. Bonhomme must be stopped. When will you come back to the safety of Durvas?"

"When I am satisfied about the safety of Durvas. Meantime I want a line of credit opened up to my node in the clinic in Houston. When I have checked certain matters, I shall consult you about when it is safe to return."

"How much credit do you want?" asked Lord Wallace suspiciously.

"That is none of your business. My bills will not break your annual budget, but I want them paid instantly. Do you have any objections?"

"No, Centurion," replied Lord Wallace, but he was clearly unhappy.

Houston, Texas: 15 December 2028, Anno Domini

Vitellan had secretly been fairly confident about the security arrangements in Durvas. The real problem was that the Village Corporate had wanted him to come back to Durvas physically and be their leader, but he had no intention of doing that. Vitellan knew that he was at his best leading groups of a few dozen, but Durvas was now huge, powerful, and daunting. He knew that he had no hope of being more than a figurehead, just as Bonhomme was to the Luministes. A centurion could not run an empire. In Houston, in the SkyPlaz Clinic, he had at least a scrap of real authority, even if it had been bought with the money of the reluctant Village Corporate. Security was, however, not an implausible reason for staying where he was after all that had happened to him. The Corporate agreed to wait for Vitellan, and the Corporate agreed to pay whatever bills he saw fit to incur. Baker and Hall's bills were large, but Vitellan felt less uneasy with them than with anyone else that he knew: he was paying the two specialists, and that seemed like control.

Four days after the telepresence meeting with the Village Corporate, Hall and Baker had their equipment collected and calibrated. As they strapped, bonded, interfaced, and tuned Vitellan in to the quantum-effect scanning gear he felt that it was all strangely familiar, as if he were entering a new type of Frigidarium. Oxygenated blood was fed directly into his circulatory system so that his breathing reflex could be suppressed. He was held totally rigid, it was like being frozen in warm ice and remaining conscious.

Vitellan's impression was of complete darkness, then spears of light touched memories, memories that were all his own. The bloody head of a Dane dangled by the woman who had just been raped by him, the bonfires in front of the gates of Meaux, the creak of ropes aboard a ship approaching Ostia, the chill wind of the northern garrisons . . . everything was confident and clear, it all meshed together.

"That was the voluntary gates," the Texan drawl echoed somewhere in the distance. "How did it look?"

"I did all that," Vitellan thought within the imprisoning blackness, and his words echoed from a distant speaker.

"You did? Even that costume stuff I saw on the monitor screen?"

"Yes."

"Weird. New gates coming up now. This won't be as nice."

The feeling jerked him like a spear through a fish, a perspective he had never seen/felt/believed. It was being not-him. An alien certainty was skewering his very existence.

"Vitellan, how're you doin' there?"

"That was bad."

"Bad as in hurts?"

"Bad as in—bad because it wasn't me. Something picked me up and walked with me for a moment. Not . . . comprehensible. I tried to fight back, but I could not hit anything."

"Oh, you hit it okay, son. Killed it too. That particular gate is all you now—what was left of the guy underneath just lost a big chunk of his remaining brain function to your imprint."

"That can't be right. It was like being swept along in a riptide."

"I'll light him up again. Get in, look around quickly. If I keep the gate open too long your imprints will move into a bigger area. We're killing him a little by even doing this."

Ruins. The host brain had been taken by force, whatever came in was the victor. Vitellan touched memories. Blue sky, green waves, unfamiliar seagulls on a foreshore lawn. They dissolved like ashes as he examined them, only his perspective of the memories remaining.

Dry summer evening heat, driving through a large town or a city. His host was tired, he had been at the wheel of the car for some time. There was also something wrong with the landscape, Vitellan quickly realized. Things were missing that should have been there. He turned into a road that ran beside a beach, the blazing red disk of the sun on the horizon, the roar of an internal combustion engine under the bonnet of a sportscar. Austin Healey Sprite, Mark 3A, he was aware of what it was. There was a metal plaque bolted to the dashboard with the words "Vintage Restorations" and dated 2014. He felt the weight of a hand on his leg as he drove, but his host did not turn to look directly at his passenger. He knew the make of the car, but not his passenger's name! You will remember fragments, bits will be missing but don't fight it, Hall had said. There seemed to be three or four images superimposed, all a fraction of a second apart, and the last was the strongest. A right-hand-drive car, aviation yellow, slowing, parking, a row of dowdy terrace cottages, lurid green patches of lawn. The girl who got out of the car with him was svelte, wearing a green, leaf-pattern cotton dress. She was sweating in the heat. His host found that very alluring.

Vitellan pulled back a fraction, observing rather than being. The girl unlocked the door to a cottage, sunlight streamed down the corridor. They went to the kitchen, sat down and drank rum and Coke with ice. He had two, the girl four, she was proud, yet unhappy too. His body was aroused, this was a seduction. There were Christmas decorations strung from the picture rails, and a tiny tree surrounded by presents in one corner of the breakfast bar. At its summit was a kangaroo wearing a red coat and white whiskers.

After some small talk about their drive in the countryside they walked to the front bedroom hand in hand. He helped her undress, and he was so eager that his hands were shaking. They rolled on the bed naked for a few seconds, then he was astride her, he pushed in hard, almost the length of his shaft in the first thrust. She gasped but did not scream or complain. He ejaculated after a few seconds.

No style, no affection, Vitellan thought to himself. This man could afford to be as inconsiderate as he wished, he had power or privilege—or both. He did not care what people thought about him, least of all his lovers.

"Repeatin' son, if you hear my voice, move toward it. You been down there three hours, fifty-eight minutes. Not safe to stay much longer. Can you hear me? If you hear—"

"I'm back."

"Hey there, just you hold it. Let me get a fix."

"What do I do?"

"Just sit tight. How does that feel?"

"Bad. I can feel the clamp again."

"You're back. Okay, lights coming on now, clamps off."

Vitellan sat up—and passed out. He was lying on a bed wearing a green clinic gown when he awoke. He related the visions and sensations to Hall and Baker, who had been watching them on a monitor screen. They were pleased with the results.

"Four hours," said Vitellan. "I would have said one."

"The pickup was badly attenuated, we had to do a lot of regenerative sweeps."

Vitellan ran his fingers through his hair. "All that meant nothing to me. The memories were not mine, I never drove a car like that, I never got into bed with that woman. Even the city was—all wrong."

"You were on the west coast of some city that has Christmas in summer, and in a country with right-hand-drive cars. That was an Austin Healey Sprite, a 1964 model that was running gasoline, but all the other cars that I noticed were 2020 models or earlier. I saw a billboard ad for *SOMS Honeymoon,* and that was released early in 2022."

2022. Memories of 2022. The host body's owner had been leading a normal life in 2022. Six years were required to fully stabilize a total overlay of another personality, and this was 2028. The implication was that Vitellan's real body had been revived and interfaced with whoever this person might be for six years.

"So who am I?" Vitellan blurted out before he could stop himself. "This is not the body that I was born with."

"Hey there, the real agenda!" exclaimed Baker.

"I want this body identified, and I want to know what has been done to—to make me what I have become."

Hall held up a sheaf of hard copy covered in symbolic imprint delineators.

"No attempt was made to disguise or hide the imprints and gates inside your head," Hall explained. "You really are a thick layer of imprints on a host brain. I've never seen anything like it, you must have spent billions and taken years to get that done. Anyhow, it's all illegal as well. There's some countries where folk could be tied to a post and shot for doing that sort of work on a human brain. In most others they'd be locked up for more years than you're liable to live. How can I say in downspeak—say, you got a cyclopedia tag for the Apollo project?"

"The first human landings on the moon, 1969 to 1972."

"That's it. A quarter-million folk involved, twenty-six billion dollars in old-time money, nearly every switch and wire leading edge. Now imagine that going to the moon is illegal, a capital crime, but someone still manages to pull off a Project Apollo. *That's* what I just saw inside your head: classy work and fully stabilized, really wonderful stuff. Why I never thought I'd live to see that sort of thing done, you know?"

Vitellan had his answer, but it was of no help at all. One thing at a time, he told the maelstrom of questions in his mind.

"Can I find out whose memory fragments are below that overlay of imprints that are me? I want to know whose experiences I just relived."

"We have a bunch of images on disk, so let's find out," said Baker.

*   *   *

Baker used Durvas funds to engage a datavend who wanted to be known as Seishi. He was a slight, self-effacing little ex-Yakuza who had survived to middle age by living his life as a valued tool. He worked for a sieve company in the Christmas Island databoard node. After viewing Vitellan's memories of the sportscar and seduction, he sent out a *help* notice from a bogus client wanting data on Austin Healey Sprites in countries with right-hand drive: Britain, Australia, and New Zealand. The sunset over the water had already narrowed the search down to Melbourne, Adelaide, and Perth—the kangaroo-Santa also suggested Australia. Melbourne seemed to be a good contender at first, being built around a wide bay and having rows of older houses looking out over the water to the west.

Christmas Island returned real estate beachfront property guides, and Vitellan identified a line of single-story terrace houses in South Fremantle, near Perth. This reduced the number of eligible cars to four. Seishi probed further, and noted that one car had belonged to Mark Stannel, an English undergraduate at the University of Western Australia. He had returned to Britain without graduating. A privacy bar cut in there, and he vanished from the records. The other three owners of similar cars were quickly identified and cleared. Seishi checked the university archive database, which was scanned from hard copy and of limited use, but it yielded the subjects that Stannel had studied. These led to student publications that were only in hard copy and not scanned, but Seishi hired an investigator from Ozcover Services to go to the University Library. Within twelve hours an annotated photograph taken at a faculty ball in 2021 appeared on the wallscreen before Vitellan.

The man behind the memories stared from the photograph into Vitellan's face. The jawline was familiar, as was the way he tilted his head back slightly.

"He reminds me of Lord Wallace of Durvas," said Vitellan. "Check if he has a son."

Now it became easy for the datavend, for Robert Wallace was the only son of Lord Wallace. He had been sent to Oxford University but he had made himself a bad name. When he lost control of a car and killed a pedestrian there was a lot of bad publicity that even the Village could not blank out unless . . . Bribes were paid and favors called in. Robert Wallace was given a bond, then he was sent to Perth incognito to get a university degree and blow off steam out of sight.

"The girl that you saw him with was Emeline Dorcas," the datavend reported in a clinical tone. "She was another student at the university, studying economics. She works for a stockbroking firm in Singapore at present. Her parents lived at that house on the beachfront when she was at the university, but they must have been away when she brought you home."

"Not me, they were imprint memories," muttered Vitellan.

"As you say, sir, so shall it be," agreed Seishi, his face blank.

Baker sent Seishi out of the room. Vitellan looked at his hands, then regarded himself in a mirror.

"Just who am I supposed to be?"

"Your body, especially your face, has had extensive cosmetic work," said Baker, scanning the report on his dataspex, "but you know that already."

"Someone has altered my host's face to resemble the Centurion of Durvas, but why and who?"

"Someone with access to a lot of money and clinic tech, that's who."

"It has to be Lord Wallace. He has access to big capital."

Baker closed his eyes and snapped his fingers. "There you go, man!" he exclaimed. "You've got a big future in PI if you want it, Mr V." He leaned over to a voice node. "Seishi, get back in here."

Seishi scanned the datafarms for Robert Wallace, who had been born late in his father's third marriage, in 2002. He gave a running commentary as he probed.

"Robert Wallace features extensively on paparazzi databoards that carry a lot of, ah, soiled news about the rich and famous. In 2022, soon after he returned to Durvas, he dated a young Italian girl and took her to a resort in Portugal for a holiday. She decided that he was not her type on the first night, so he performed date-rape upon her. He also left her to find her own way home. Her father was old Mafia, and a week later a half-kilo of covalent lattice collapsed under Robert's car on the estate of a man named McLaren, near Durvas. He was rushed straight into the Durvas clinic by McLaren, but six years later he is apparently still there."

"Is any of that what you want to know?" Baker asked.

Vitellan slowly sifted through real and imprinted memories, wishing that he could share some of the complexity with Hall and Baker, but not daring to confide in them fully as yet.

"McLaren was a member of the Village Corporate and Icek—well, he died recently. Lord Wallace is a ruthless man, or so Lucel has told me. Perhaps some very illegal experiments in whole-mind overlay were done." He spread his hands wide as he sat there. "Here's the son's body, and overlaid on the brain is me—yet can that be possible? I was told that imprints fade if not renewed."

Vitellan already knew the answer, but in this environment of lies and half-truths, his only weapon was cross-checks.

"Hell son, ordinary memories fade too," said Hall, who had been quietly observing the debate. "It's just that they fade a whole lot slower. Imprints can be 'fixed' by intensive reinforcement sessions, but that's expensive work for something the size of the human mind. The tag for the computing power needed would cost out at hundreds of millions, maybe billions."

Vitellan sat up, but the room seemed to break loose from reality and tumble about an oblique axis. He flopped forward with his elbows on his knees and his face in his hands.

"I need to have another talk with Lord Wallace," he said into his hands. "Get the telepresence gear ready, if you please, and give me a dose of something for this nausea."

Durvas, Britain: 17 December 2028, Anno Domini

The hologram of Lord Wallace lost color in sympathy with his distant body. It gave Vitellan's hologram a curiously blank stare.

"Yes, your body is that of my son," he said simply, then turned and beckoned Vitellan to follow him. They walked down a corridor in silence, stopping at a heavy steel door. Lord Wallace extended a hand which slid smoothly into the electronic lock. It opened with a dull clunk.

"I thought holograms could not move things," said Vitellan.

"There's an internal optical scanner inside," Lord Wallace explained.

In the room beyond was a small electronics laboratory, yet it was somehow too neat, and the equipment was chunkier than Vitellan was used to seeing in this century. This too was a museum.

"We can talk here," Lord Wallace said, and he switched on a link for Vitellan's node.

"Where is my real body?"

"In an intensive care clinic, about a quarter of a mile straight down."

Under the pretense of consulting his cyclopedia imprint, Vitellan took some seconds to assimilate this revelation.

"I would like an explanation, Lord Wallace."

"I can—"

"And I would ask you to remember that I have access to my own sources, and I've not told you all that I know. Be truthful and don't waste our time. Why have I been kept revived but unconscious since 2022? Why was your son interfaced with me while he was being grown and grafted back together after that car bomb shredded him on Icekeeper McLaren's driveway?"

Wallace's composure cracked a little, possibly on cue.

"Centurion, you know what happened after Bonhomme's revival. Massive upheavals, a new crusade for Christianity to put Islam in its place, and vendettas against the rich and powerful. Meantime, *we* had the problem of what to do about *you*. Would you be the same as Bonhomme? We would have *had* to do some psychological tests eventually. Our Village charter states that we must revive you in 2054, and it's the cornerstone of everything that we do. We just wanted a preview of what you were like, using a host that we could control."

Lord Wallace's holograph looked down and frowned, as if he was pained by the topic. Even as Vitellan was tempted to feel sympathy, Hall's warning echoed through his mind: if he's imprinted with Fujitsu Shakespearean 6.2 he will be a brilliant actor.

"Let's not mince words," said Lord Wallace, squaring his shoulders and drawing himself up straight, seeming to steel himself to approach an unpleasant subject. "My son Robert had been an embarrassment for several years. That's a cruel thing for a father to say, but one should not let tragedy gloss over the truth. You know that he received terrible injuries from that car bomb, but did you know that his mind went into shock-induced catatonia?"

Vitellan checked his imprints for the unfamiliar term, annoyed at the delay needed for the retrieval routines and the comprehension algorithms to work. He was obviously a novice with the words and ideas, it was all so humiliating that he wanted to give up and just trust his people. Still, he knew that there was no real alternative to this slow-motion fight with a fast-forward opponent.

"No, most of the gates behind my imprints have not been explored as yet," he replied. It was a smooth, convincing lie. Vitellan had been imprinted with Fujitsu Shakespearean 6.2 that very morning.

"Just as well, the real Robert's mind was . . . hopeless. We thought it—well, we imprinted some of my own memories and attitudes on Robert to try to provide a level of stability for him. It was highly illegal, you understand, but the boy was beyond hope, so my conscience was clear. Only Icekeeper McLaren and I knew the truth. My son was gone, just a vegetable . . . but maybe not forever. It took nearly a year to transfer temporary imprints to test his brain function."

"A year, you say?"

"Yes, and the Resources War was not far off by then. It became hard to scrounge up supercomputer time, and we needed a lot of processing power to do the transfers and imprint fixing. It was so slow because we were doing illegal work, so we had to do almost everything by ourselves—we even invented some new technologies."

"Two men, working alone?" said Vitellan skeptically. "I find that unlikely."

"*You* are the living proof. For example, we had a problem with heat dispersal in Robert's brain, because there was so much neural rewiring going on. We had to cool the arterial blood supply while boosting the oxygenated red cell level."

"All this so that you could check out my emotional stability? You could have done that by just reviving me and having a chat. It would have saved you billions."

Lord Wallace hung his head, obviously disappointed that Vitellan seemed neither to believe him nor share his enthusiasm for the work.

"The Resources War alone cost the world hundreds of times what we spent on your imprinting."

"This is still not credible," Vitellan insisted, rubbing his eyes. "Someone in the Village must have noticed that a lot of investment capital was out of circulation, and that a lot of work was going on that involved my body."

Lord Wallace sighed and shook his head. "No wonder there is such a legend surrounding you, Centurion. You really are fantastically capable and adaptable. Yes, you're right, there was a secret within a secret. Your body also needed medical treatment and extensive surgical procedures. The ice and rocks where you were last frozen had a slightly higher level of background radiation than in most other parts of the Alps— there was a radioactive mineral deposit nearby, pitchblende or something. Over the centuries your frozen cells accumulated tissue damage, and when you were unfrozen you developed tumors and leukemia. The medical work to save you disguised the, the other procedures. All right then, it was not just McLaren and me, but all the other people involved only had a small part of the picture. We disguised it in the general research budget, and oddly enough it paid off. We developed technologies and patents that made Durvas a world leader in imprinting while working on you. The whole exercise may turn in a profit by as early as 2035, according to the Durvas Councillor of Treasury."

Vitellan considered this with care, painstakingly drawing facts out of his imprinted learning, matching them up with other facts, then placing them in a bigger picture. He was oddly annoyed when forced to concede that Lord Wallace was telling a plausible story.

"And if I'd passed the tests, if I was not another Jacque Bonhomme? What then?"

"The real you would have been revived."

"And the me in this body?"

"Centurion, that imprint is not stable, it will fade suddenly after a few weeks. Our idea was to put Robert's body into a comatose state and let the test-imprint of you fade without you regaining consciousness. The real Centurion would not have your memories, but that would not matter."

Vitellan considered this carefully, but did not take long to make up his mind.

"We have a problem, Lord Wallace. I have been awake and active for a month, and now I *do not* want to lose my experiences from that time. It would be like having an alternate 'me' die. Besides, I have had experiences and collected insights that I would have been shielded from as a two thousand-year-old celebrity. You say I passed your tests for . . . whatever you wanted to know."

"Oh yes, better than our wildest hopes."

"But if I failed you'd hardly tell me."

"Centurion—"

"Can you transfer my memories of the past month to my real body?"

"It would be possible to get some of your experiences across and permanently fixed, but the longer you leave it the more you will lose when your overlay in Robert's brain begins to fade. You *must* return to Durvas."

The explanation was convincing, but a long-dead Roman teacher's words returned to Vitellan yet again. Never be completely satisfied with any report, always probe for cracks.

"Durvas security still worries me," he responded doubtfully. "Why was your security so lax for a project worth billions? How did the Luministes get into your research clinic so easily and abduct this body?"

Lord Wallace waved his hands in exasperation and seemed to lose his composure. "Pah, hindsight, the wisdom of fools!" he snapped. "Whoever briefed you did a very one-sided job. Check your imprint cyclopedia for *Challenger,* January 26th, 1986. A billion-dollar American spacecraft and its crew was blown out of the sky for the sake of a couple of rubber rings. History is full of that sort of thing, and people never learn. Back in 1969 a huge Soviet moon rocket exploded because some idiot left a spanner in the fuel system and it fell into a pump. Sheer importance and cost does not proof a project against stupidity."

Vitellan thought back to the Battle of Poitiers and could not help but agree. "Well then, what did happen?" he asked.

"Durvas security was good, but we trusted the Luministes more than we probably should have. We had a lot in common, after all, and had a good business relationship with them. We even did some cooperative work on cryogenic research. Some of their scientists on secondment with us must have been spying. Initially your brain and my son's were connected by a long and expensive data bus, but Icekeeper McLaren began to complain about access delays and data bottlenecks. The Village Corporate eventually gave permission for your body to be brought up to the surface clinic so that a shorter, higher-capacity link could be used. The imprinting arrays were too bulky to take down to the Deep Frigidarium. Maybe it was all a Luministe plot to make you more vulnerable. If so, it worked only too well."

Yet again, Lord Wallace's story continued to be plausible. When the Luministes had attacked and taken the wrong body, they had not been far away from the original. The Roman had not been in the vault, a quarter of a mile below the clinic, he had been on the surface inside the clinic itself. They had detonated a lattice bomb to act as a diversion. The interlocked-slab clinic had partly collapsed, and the wrong body had been taken in the confusion.

"Would you like to see yourself?" Lord Wallace asked, now genial again.

"How difficult would it be?"

"Not hard at all. Merely a switch of your hologram reference point to down into what we call the Deep Frigidarium."

It took Lord Wallace some minutes to arrange a switch to the other projector node. "I happen to be down there with some medical staff just now. Allow me a moment to detach from the telepresence transponder and brief them, then you will be switched down."

Vitellan waited, and after no more than a minute his hologram was switched to a brightly lit chamber with a low ceiling. The real Lord Wallace met him and gestured to the door in a partition. He was more slow on his feet than his holographic projection.

The Roman centurion contemplated his own body lying on a padded bench. Familiar old scars were there, white weals amid new, thin, red and white lines.

"What are those new scars?" Vitellan demanded.

"Ah—oh, those are for various operations. To repair damage done by the antifreeze oil to your stomach, for example. The form that you had been drinking was full of toxins and they were slowly killing you. Other work was to remove tumors, cysts, and part of an arrowhead, and to repair minor injuries from the Luministe attack."

The chest was rising and falling with regular breath, and a monitor followed its pulse.

"Don't be alarmed by what you are about to see," warned Anderson, whom Vitellan recognized from the Village Corporate meeting. "An operator is controlling the movements from a VR board in the next room."

The body's eyes opened, then it raised itself slowly on chalky white arms. A flaccid amber cable trailed from beneath its left ear, as limp as a dead worm. It swung its legs over the edge, but did not attempt to step down to the floor.

"Vocals please," said Anderson.

"This is a sensory test," the body said with the Welsh accent of an unseen operator. "I can hear your words clearly, and can see you standing together. Mr. Anderson has his arms folded. Lord Wallace is also there, and the hologram of an unidentified visitor is present. The hologram needs boosting, it is attenuated enough to see through. The visitor's hologram has his hands behind his back."

Vitellan peered intently at the automation that his body had become. It was not readily familiar. There had been few good mirrors in his pre-twenty-first-century life, and he was not used to seeing himself so clearly. The eyes and head were alert, but they only paralleled the operator's movements.

"What is in the head?" Vitellan asked.

"Your brain, in bypass mode," replied Anderson. "The real Centurion Vitellan will remember nothing of this."

"But I *want* the real Centurion to remember this, and the month past as well. Lord Wallace tells me that I am running out of time. Can a transfer be done before I fade from this host?"

"I say yes," said Anderson. "A restoration could take as long as six months of live body time, but there are leading-edge methods that might work faster. We could imprint selections of your memories onto a dozen volunteers—not enough to hurt them, we would just use redundant capacity in their brains. Each of those would in turn be imprinted and fixed in your real body's brain, and you would be brought to a full revival with your present memories in, say, August next year. I'd stake my career on it."

"That's all very comforting, but *I'm* staking my identity," replied Vitellan. "I'll have to think about what you propose."

Houston, Texas: 17 December 2028, Anno Domini

The telepresence meeting left Vitellan drained mentally, yet physically fresh. He wandered about aimlessly in the SkyPlaz clinic for an hour, unable to make much of what he had just been through. Finally he called Baker and Hall, and asked them to meet him in an executive ward that had been converted to a lounge.

As he had done many times in the ninth and fourteenth centuries, Vitellan told the story of who and what he was. For twenty minutes their side of the conversation was little more than whistles, "Incredible!," and "Hey man!," yet Vitellan thought that they assimilated the wonder of what he was remarkably well. It was a century of wonders, however, so perhaps their attitude to yet another wonder should not have been so very surprising. Hall had also lost a lot of his spontaneity: Vitellan could tell when people were being guarded; he had spent too much time with kings and nobles not to have learned that.

When he had finished recounting what Lord Wallace had just revealed they became more animated.

"What he told you is downspeak, but it's accurate as far as it goes" was Hall's verdict.

"Are you sure? You said it would take me six years to be made into a stable imprint on another brain."

"Oh yeah, that tech's all well known and understood, but from what my scans show, the imprinting has not been going on for six years. You began the overlay treatment in around 2025, so that's only three years. Imprint experiments with capuchin monkeys back in 2020 showed rapid fading to be a problem with big overlays that have not been boosted enough times to bed down."

"So the me in here is fading," Vitellan said, tapping the side of his head.

"Well, yeah, but very slowly right now. The end will be one big rush, then nothing."

Vitellan shook his head and stared at the rose-patterned carpet. "It's like the barbarians moving into the old Roman Empire. They just kept enslaving Roman officials to herd sheep, and pulling down Roman buildings to make their fortresses until Rome's identity died."

Baker blinked, then nodded vigorously. "Sure, that's just like it. Mr. V., the Wallace guy is right, you have no real choice. You either trust him or you fade anyway."

Vitellan did not answer.

"What plans have they got for you?" asked Hall once the silence had stretched uncomfortably long.

"Oh, I'm to be their figurehead leader and provide a focus to take the spotlight away from Bonhomme for a few years. People are vulnerable to novelty, they always have been. That's what makes Bonhomme dangerously special, and that's why I have value as a counter against him."

"And if you want to time-travel again, what then?" asked Baker.

"I'll be injected with glycenal-AT4, that's the new name for Oil of Frosts."

"Yeah, I know. My father was on the team that did the analysis," said Baker. "They won the Hotchkins Award for that."

"Your—yet *you* work in a black market gang clinic?"

"Pop still drives a 2007 Toyota and lives in a rented apartment in Durvas. He even became a British citizen to stay on that research team. He's crazy. I live a whole lot better. Now then, after they freeze you it's off to bed in a vat of radioactively stable liquid nitrogen, right?"

"Yes."

"And that's in the Deep Frigidarium?"

"Temporarily. The Village is planning a new Frigidarium about a mile beneath—well, somewhere hard to reach. It's all very secret for now, but they plan to market it as a high-security body store in decades to come. One-way time travel has potential as big business, or so Wallace told me during one of our talks. Thousands of people have been injected with glycenal-AT4 and had themselves frozen, either to wait for a cure for illness or just see what the next century is like. I'll just be another one of them."

Vitellan stood up and walked to the wall-window. He stood with his hands behind his back, staring out over the flat, green cityscape of Houston for a while.

"Could you stabilize my imprint overlay in here?" Vitellan asked without turning.

"We need big iron, and big iron like that is only available to the likes of you in Durvas. SQUID arrays with thousands of elements, that sort of thing."

"Couldn't you even try?" Vitellan asked.

"Hey there, I can help with what's known and not strictly legal, but real bleeding edge games are not my bag. Durvas is the only place where they can do what you want."

"Could you at least tell me how much time I have until the fading starts?"

"Yeah, no problem. You should notice dropouts in a week. Little things, like, well, the overlay will not be able to reference the cyclopedia imprint properly, even though we give your cyclopedia a boost every day. It can't stick with nothing to stick to. Where was the cyclopedia work done?"

"Moscow."

"Oh yeah? In that case, you could have big dropouts in a day or two. You will be you until the middle of February, but after that—hey there, I can't really say what it will feel like, a human's never had a total overlay until now."

Vitellan turned to see Baker glance to Hall, who was nodding.

"I need to think things through while I'm still me," said Vitellan, stroking his chin and still savoring the novelty of being so incredibly close-shaven.

"You don't have much time, man," said Hall.

"That's my business. In the meantime, Lucel is due out of the medical unit today, and she's going to be angry. I was supposed to give her a line outside, but I didn't."

"Ahhh—but that's cool," said Baker. "Don't you trust her?"

"No. I want her out of here as soon as she can walk. How many weeks until she can do that?"

"Weeks? More like hours. She can get out and get dressed as soon as the cover is raised on her unit."

"Hours!" exclaimed Vitellan. "Impossible. Scars like she has take weeks to heal or they'll tear open."

"Not so. Collagen bonds and braces are holding her muscles and internal organs together, and her skin is bonded with Dermal Clear over the scars. She'll have to get the internal scaffolding stripped out in a couple of weeks, and she isn't going to be winning any races for a while, but she will be walking today."

Vitellan sighed with relief that he hoped came across as amazement.

"Before she revives could you put a tracker implant in her and have her movements monitored?" he asked Baker.

"You're payin' the bills, Mr V. Do you want Durvas told she's still alive?"

"Ah . . . no. They don't know who she is anyway, and neither do I."

"Mr V., you sure learned about not trusting people in a hurry."

Faster than you realize, Vitellan thought to himself. Everyone had been lying to him. Hall had been smoothly contradicting what he had let slip several days ago, Vitellan was sure of it. It had been just after Hall had been probing the memories beneath Vitellan's imprint overlay, and he had been exclaiming in amazement at what he had seen. *Classy work and fully stabilized,* Hall had said.

Houston, Texas: 17 December 2028, Anno Domini

"After all the fuck I've done for you and you had to do that to me!" snapped Lucel furiously as she flung her green hospital gown to the floor and snatched a black sportsbra from the couch where Vitellan was sitting.

"You did not trust *me!*" Vitellan retorted. "I asked you for the truth and all you did was hide it from me!"

"I didn't *know* the truth!" she screamed back. "I had a few clues and theories, I would have told you what I knew once I knew more myself."

"Would have, would have. Words are cheap."

She dressed stiffly, unsteady on her feet as she pulled on her jeans. Vitellan's eyes kept drifting back to the tracery of scars at her midriff beneath the strips of Dermal Clear.

"Would you mind fucking off, I'm trying to get dressed," she suddenly snarled.

Vitellan stood up.

"All right, but you will not see me again. I leave for Durvas tomorrow. I have a lot of imprint therapy to be done there."

"Really? So, after all we've been through, it's bye." She held out her hand. "Just one last warning," she said as they shook hands.

"Yes?"

Her fingers snaked forward and stabbed into a pressure point in his wrist. Pain came as a blue bombflash behind Vitellan's eyes and he dropped to his knees in shock.

"Trust nobody," said Lucel as she pulled a T-shirt emblazoned with LIBENS VOLENS POTENS over her head.

Lucel discharged herself from the clinic within the half hour. She left through the front entrance, and security cameras followed her as she walked from the foyer carrying a shoulder bag with the few personal things that came with her. A gunmetal-blue, roach-profile suncab glided into the field of view, summoned by her call to Transit Southeast. It raised a wing of solar panels and she stepped into the reclining seat. A moment later she was sealed out of sight.

"The job is to Eastwood, not the airport," the security regulator reported to Baker from his screen.

"Not surprised," replied Baker's hologram head from beside him. "How are her implants?"

"Loud and clear."

"Good. Now I want you to post their code profile to this netboard address."

The regulator sat back in surprise at the letters suspended before his face. "Foxhound? That's not a clean shop, that's the undercoat gangs."

"Just do it."

"Okay, okay. Can I patch through to you when the police holos walk in here asking questions?"

"That won't happen."

Lucel left the suncab at the Eastwood Mall, a Latino marketplace. The gangs had taken over the district early in the century, but by 2025 their structures had evolved into warlord-style district councils that provided services and protection, and even attracted business with their economic stability. The crowds were more exotically dressed than in the condo and civil areas of town, and there were more weapons being carried openly, yet the incidence of violence was lower than outsiders realized. A system of truces and alliances kept feuds under control, and what had once been protection money now amounted to something like municipal rates.

The buildings were poorly maintained although the roads were well swept by the pickers, who also collected the garbage. The area was like the gangs themselves, surviving on the by-products of society, a remora that neither harmed nor hindered its host city. Graffiti was left in place, a symbolist newspaper and roadmap on the very buildings themselves. It was not a culture of polish and shine, although exquisite little gardens and courtyards could be glimpsed occasionally through half-open gates.

Most of the people that Lucel passed smelled stale, and the cars were filthy: some external authority was restricting the water supply until a new contract could be agreed to. States within states. There was no mediating body for state/gang disputes and transactions, so they were settled by barter and embargo like medieval fiefdoms. The world had unified internationally only to fragment locally.

Lucel passed the headquarters of the area, which was a squat bunker of concrete blocks streaked with oxides. The blocks were angled upward to deflect the blast of any car bomb, and there were drop-moats and gardens filled with blocks to prevent any vehicle from reaching the walls. The windows were narrow and featured heavy blast shutters. At one end was a stained, pitted area the size of a tennis court, evidence that the bomb-proofing had done its job. Gang-gang confrontations seldom resulted in outright war, but terrorism was a common method of diplomatic pressure.

The crowds swirled around Lucel, people who were fawning yet assertive, respectful yet intrusive. Some begged for spare change while others tried to sell credit and goods. Some of the kids waved and pointed their guns at passersby, but both Lucel and the locals knew better than to flinch or reach for their own weapons: it was only bravado. Lucel was doubly safe, because nobody tried anything with someone wearing dataspex. You never knew where the images were being transmitted, or who was storing them.

A beacon at the focus of her dataspex map guided Lucel until she came to a shop front overhung by rust-caked steel shutters and pulsing electronic warnings to any dataspex sensor within range. Her key interlocked with one of the transceivers and executed an encryption match, then her visor glowed green with an acceptance. She walked through the hologram of a door without breaking stride. Nobody greeted her inside; there were only two rows of booths on either side of a strip of aqua carpet. The color clashed disconcertingly with the flaming red of the booths and the yellow walls and roof. Shanty decor was always ruled by the use of what was at hand.

Shimmering electric inversion fields warned of which booths were occupied as Lucel made a selection and spoke a code from memory. The booth sealed itself into a bank-level security mode, then the connection was made. She noted the lightspeed delay of a satellite link.

"Bonhomme nodal," declared a blank-faced holographic bust that materialized before her.

"FreeView Latin," Lucel replied. "Patch me to Crusader TY03 on my entry code key."

Moments later the holographic face assumed detail. Eager, anxious detail.

"FreeView! It's been a very long time between reports."

"So? Are you giving me a redundancy deal?"

"You were told to report back weekly."

"Lift my cover for the sake of Luministe bureaucracy? That's the best joke I've heard in months."

The hologram froze for moments which extended into more than a minute.

"Very well, give us your report."

"Please?"

"Please."

"You screwed it. The body that you abducted from Durvas was a modern with the Roman's total overlay."

"Total? That would take years, cost millions plus."

"Whatever. The real Roman is back at Durvas and well out of harm's way, as I'd reckon."

"So there's a total overlay of the Roman walking about with some expendable modern's body."

"The modern is Lord Wallace's son. The word is that the overlayed modern is being flown back to Durvas on a private scram."

The hologram froze again, this time for three minutes. Lucel leaned back and began cycling through muscle-tensing patterns. By the time the hologram of the Luministe came back to life there was a sheen of perspiration on her skin.

"Most of what you speculate is in theory feasible but technically front of edge. My advisory pool has done a total project cost estimate at up to ten billion pounds, mostly on processing and data storage: whole brain image transfer and stabilization is not cheap. Why did they do it?"

"Paranoia? Who knows? Durvas has that sort of money, and a lot of the development work is returning profits."

"Ten billion pounds for one Roman's life? The Japanese manned landing on Ceres had a smaller budget."

"Vitellan is more than just a life. He's been a focus, symbol, idol, god, and military savior for the Village for nearly as long as the Christian church has existed. Their dedication has nothing to do with reason or economics."

"What about those closest to the overlay Roman? The white coats in the clinic? Are they vulnerable?"

"Yes and no. They do what he says, but it's only because he has a line of credit from Durvas."

"You're sure of this?"

"Can you do better?"

Areas not controlled by gangs, condos, or civils were to be avoided. The civil police were as concerned with avoiding lawsuits as with keeping order, and without stable infrastructure the flow of information ceased. As Lucel walked into the Blacklight border area the short-range, low-power Village implants in her body groped for bandspace on ill-maintained, overloaded, and vandalized transponders, then were lost to the Foxhound monitors. They went into a holding pattern while they waited for her to emerge into a more reliable part of the city, but she stayed out of contact for two hours. Every fifteen seconds the implants polled for a transponder while drawing power from her body sugars.

"Got her!" the operative contracted from Foxhound by the Village exclaimed as Lucel's implants responded to a poll.

His supervisor was sitting just across the room, lounging in black denim shorts and a T-shirt with the Foxhound logo on the front. Instead of getting up he materialized a holographic head with red skin, horns, and a goatee beard.

"Two hours," he observed. "They could have done anything to the 'plants in two hours."

"None look sick. Going in to suck datafiles, and . . . it looks good. Full audio record."

"Hell 'n shit, how did her friends miss them when she was scanned?" asked the devil-head, its brow furrowing. "Maybe they're some new tech with evasion cycles to fool the field detectors. Maybe they didn't scan her at all—nah, that's shit. What type of 'plant are they—same as before?"

"I can't tell their brand. Signals look the same whether the hardware is junk or gold stamp."

"How about encryption checksums?"

"Ah . . . same. That's a hard one to fake at short notice."

The devil-head added a pair of shoulders and shrugged.

"Okay then, I'll bite. Prepare a presentation for the client. I'll pull back and raise him now."

Vitellan's holograph solidified in what he saw as a featureless room. The Foxhound supervisor appeared, having dressed his hologram in a dark blue combat coverall and holstered rail pistol, trimmed twenty pounds from the waistline, straightened its hair, and dissolved the stubble from its face.

"Where is she?" Vitellan asked.

"In a five-acre compound on Waugh Drive. It's the Yakuza embassy to the local gang cells."

"And what is she doing?"

"Just staying in the grounds. She's lying about in the gardens near the pool, and we're recording a blood sugar boost right now so she's just had a meal. No alcohol, though."

"That would be right, she doesn't drink. Pipe the sound effects from earlier in here."

The Roman's holograph sat in midair with his arms folded. While Lucel had been in the shielded booth, the implants had stored a half hour of speech. As her conversation with the Luministe contact was played back his frown became deeper.

"She betrayed me and now she's settled down for a holiday, courtesy of the enemy," said Vitellan.

"Hey mon, that's women for you."

Vitellan suggested that Baker and he have masks of each other's faces made up for when they went to the airport. They would walk into the chartered scramjet together, then a man with Vitellan's face would leave. A net message to Durvas would be that Baker was flying across to verify that the medical facilities were ready and that his body was unharmed. Durvas agreed, and so did Baker.

"I want privacy on the flight, I want to be by myself," Vitellan insisted as they were driven to the airport in a limo-length suncar. "No movies, no meals."

"That's cool, but why?" asked Baker.

"I need to be with my memories while I still have them. You couldn't understand."

"No, I guess not."

At the airport the SkyPlaz security guards went as far as the access gate. The interior of the scramjet was furnished as first class, and there were only ten seats. Baker gestured to the back of the cabin as they entered. "There's a bar and pantry," he began. Vitellan turned, slowly and casually, then drove his fist straight up into Baker's jaw. Baker collapsed.

Vitellan hurriedly changed clothes with the doctor, then dragged him to a seat and strapped him in. He took three of the trank darts that had been removed from his own skin at the clinic and pressed them into the flesh of Baker's forearm.

"Five hours to sleep, or so the lady said," he muttered to himself as he peeled the Baker-mask from his own face.

The man with Vitellan's face sat in a window seat, head against the bulkhead, apparently asleep. The slight rupturing of mask dermalic under the chin was not visible. Vitellan stuffed the remains of his own mask into an airsick bag and dropped it into a dispenser, then he left the scramjet. He told the ground crew to seal the door and stood watching until the scramjet was moving away from the terminal.

The two security guards were waiting at the gate. They expected to see Baker with Vitellan's face, and so were not alarmed to see Vitellan without a mask. Baker's gloves had been too small for the Roman, so he kept his white hands firmly inside his trouser pockets as they started back for the limo.

"Need a Coke, meet you there," said Vitellan just as a flight call blared out from speakers directly above them. His accent was nothing like that of Baker, but the terminal was noisy and chaotic. The SkyPlaz guards nodded and walked on.

Vitellan took out Baker's wallet and bought a cap, sunshades, and a brownout jacket. He stepped into the washrooms. Another quick change had him transformed again, but as he emerged he could see that the SkyPlaz guards were already back and peering about nervously. As he walked briskly from the terminal he heard the rumble as the chartered scramjet was boosted into the sky on its way to Britain.

Vitellan made for a rank of cabs. Hire scabs, fire caps, he thought, groping for terms in his imprint. Words were missing, others were confused. Facts were scrambled in some places. First moon landing: Juri Gargarin, British astronaut in 1996, reported the imprint, yet Vitellan had realworld memories of accessing it as Neil Armstrong, American astronaut, 1969. A terrifying qualm washed over Vitellan and he panicked. Most of his English vocabulary had vanished, and much of what was left came from his time in the fourteenth century. He would sound like Chaucer's Wife of Bath telling her tale if he spoke to a cab's autonic, and he doubted that the machines would cope with that. He continued on past the rank of cabs in the bright sunshine. Was his imprint really fading, were they all telling the truth after all? Vitellan groped for the fourteenth century, spent vivid seconds at the siege of Meaux, then languid seconds in the arms of the Countess of Hussontal. Imperial Rome was just as clear: the scent of bread baking and olive oil spilled from a broken amphora as he walked past with his father. The symptoms were consistent with what Hall had told him, but . . . the clinic had supposedly been giving him boosters every night to fix the commercial imprints that Lucel had arranged for him. Maybe they had stopped the boosters after selling out to Durvas—or the Luministes. His imprint would be stable, but the commercial imprints would be fading!

He walked out to the public carpark, with no idea of where he was going. How long to fade an imprint less than a month old? In my imprints, maybe, he cursed to himself. Make me look like I'm fading, trick to frighten me. He explored further, found many areas still intact. Memories of real experiences were as clear as ever, everything from the 6th of December stood out as starkly as his memories of Vesuvius erupting. A tall, bearded roadspike in an old-style impact jacket approached him.

"Wheels to your car, mon?" he drawled.

The remains of the Streetwise imprint flashed a warning to Vitellan: MUGGER; ACTIVATE PERSONAL BEACON AND MOVE BACK IN A CONFIDENT MANNER; SUSPECT OFFERS RIDE TO CAR IN LARGE CARPARK THEN DEMANDS WALLET.

"Lost . . . car," Vitellan managed to fight past his tongue.

The roadspike blinked deliberately. "You lose a car or you needin' a cab?"

"Lost. No fly."

"Hey, you missed your flight. Is that it?"

If any security monitor is recording this I can't afford to sound like I just stepped out of the fourteenth century, Vitellan had decided. Only one man in the entire world would talk to a potential mugger in Old English, and the Luministes would be onto his trail at once. Maybe if he slipped in some Latin words he might sound as if he was a modern Italian, Vitellan speculated.

"Losting anger est, profecto."

"Los Angeles! LA, you missed a flight to LA. Is that it?"

Vitellan glanced back to the terminal building. Have to get away, anything. Los Angeles was obviously a place some distance away.

"Los Angeles. You take?"

The roadspike whistled and put his hands on his hips.

"You real or what? That's, say, sixteen hundred miles or more."

Vitellan took out Baker's wallet. The clinic preferred to be paid in untraceable currency, so the wallet bulged with banknotes and unsecured smartcards. The roadspike's eyes widened beneath his black shades.

"Ticket!" said Vitellan firmly.

"Hey mon, you got a ticket with me, no problems," he said, taking Vitellan by the arm and waving at a chrome and solar-gunmetal Harley layback with a gasoline engine. "This here's the wheels."

Fifteen miles away the Doberman carrying Lucel's implants glanced up briefly as a little scramjet streaked across the sky, noisily laboring to gain height.

The North Atlantic: 17 December 2028, Anno Domini

Vitellan's chartered scramjet climbed and went transonic over the Gulf of Mexico, flew west, then turned north for Britain as it reached the Atlantic. As it passed the Newfoundland coast it was at ninety thousand feet and Mach 6, riding its own shockwave. The orbital air traffic control center was having hardware problems at the time, and all atmospheric traffic had been ordered to fit into more generous safety profiles than usual.

Far below, a Boeing Surface Effect Transport the size of a ship was lumbering along at 400 mph, just above the water. A small wedge dropped from its underside and flew clear, hugging the waves at subsonic speeds until it was lost amid the general Atlantic traffic. At two miles distance from the Canadian Navy patrol SET *Janus*, the wedge suddenly dropped its turbines and lanced into the overcast sky on a hydrogen-fluorine rocket. The *Janus* detected the weapon at once and went into red alert automatically. The ELTY targeting control computer reported that the missile had locked on to a small scramjet within three seconds of acquisition by the *Janus*, even before the operator had determined that the threat was not to the Navy SET. At the sixth second she had opened a channel to the scramjet.

"Scramjet, transponder Kappa Delta 174, this is Canadian patrol skimmer *Janus*. You have an intercept locked on. Unknown origin and accelerating. Switch to your AT jammer and evasion override."

"Wha—hell and shit! Incoming confirmed!" replied the alarmed voice of the pilot. "Evasions locked in, jammers live."

The chartered scramjet's computers took milliseconds to calculate the options for escape, then it banked left and went into a shallow dive, dumping fuel into the denser air and raising its Mach number by one. The interceptor continued to close, but now more slowly. The Navy patrol's tracking radar locked on to it and coordinated with an orbital laser platform of the UN Anti-Terrorist Authority.

The scramjet was weaving randomly at hypersonic speeds, leaving twisted contrails as the laser struck the interceptor. The shell disintegrated but the core blasted out with a far higher acceleration, flying blinded by the ionization of its own passage. It shot past the scramjet, missing by less than a hundred feet.

"Clear miss, and—yeah, it's flamed out Kappa Delta, you're safe. Kappa Delta? Hey ELTY, the scramjet's downlink is out."

"Tracking debris," the ELTY targeting computer's voice reported. "ATA platform reporting a second hit."

The operator stared into a hologram scenario, numbly watching two clouds of debris and the free-falling warhead. The warhead suddenly self-destructed, to be replaced by a third red cloud-icon.

"ELTY, report and record the intercept status of the Kappa Delta," she said, afraid of her own words, hugging her arms tightly against her breasts.

"The ATA platform destroyed Kappa Delta 174 with a direct hit from their laser cannon array."

The operator shivered. There was a metallic taste in her mouth, and her body felt numb and clammy.

"ELTY, where did the targeting priority on Kappa Delta originate?"

"Point of origin was the ATA platform."

The operator collapsed with relief across the hologram desk, her head amid the miniaturized symbols of the scenario display, her uniform coverall drenched in her own perspiration. The targeting that had destroyed the scramjet had not originated from the *Janus*—but who had ordered the orbital to fire?

Back in Houston Lucel listened to the audio news as she unpacked in a luxury hotel. A scramjet on charter from United to Wurzel Electrobionics had been destroyed during what appeared to be a terrorist incident. Initial reports were unclear as to whether it had been destroyed by a missile or by the ATA orbital platform in a targeting error. The names of the two pilots and an executive aboard meant nothing to her.

Rural Texas, 18 December 2028, Anno Domini

The roadspike took Vitellan almost due west to Austin, then up onto the Edwards Plateau. They had been riding for several hours when the roadspike called "Shortcut!" over his shoulder, then turned off along a dirt road. It led to an abandoned quarry cut into the side of a hill. The Harley slithered in gravel, then came to a stop. The roadspike lowered the kickstand, then stepped off.

"Los Angeles?" asked Vitellan, stiffly climbing off the seat.

"No mon, but it's the end of the road for you. Savvy?"

A blade snicked clear of its handle, gleaming bright and silver in the sunlight.

"Ah, *humiliores*," said Vitellan, raising a finger and pointing at the roadspike.

The roadspike had wanted a quiet kill; one never knew who might hear a gunshot. He advanced on Vitellan, who backed away slowly. As the roadspike rushed him Vitellan did a spin-dodge and slapped aside the knife-arm that sought him like some chimera of unicorn and cobra. The roadspike stumbled past, then whirled in the dusty gravel, in time to see his victim pick up a length of wood from a smashed pallet. It was about the length of a gladius, and Vitellan hefted it for balance in a disturbingly professional manner.

In a sudden panic the roadspike flung his knife to his other hand and groped in his jacket for his Ruger 9mm, but Vitellan was already closing. A moment later the last centurion of the Roman Empire stood over the body of his would-be murderer. Blood trickled from one of the roadspike's ears, and there was a distinct dent in the skull.

"Fuckwit est," Vitellan said as he looked at the hair and blood on his length of timber, then he dropped it to the gravel and began stripping off his clothes.

Once he was dressed in the roadspike's gear, Vitellan dragged the body over to the quarry wall and triggered a small rockslide to cover it. He stared at the Harley, trying to relate it to the van and his driving lesson on his first day in Houston. Lucel's words were still in his memory: "brake," "clutch," "throttle," and "gears" fell into place as he tinkered and experimented. The sawn-off, pump-action shotgun in the bike's carrier made him pause for a moment, as did the sealpacks of amphetamines and bloodsand taped under the tank. At last he took a deep breath, offered a prayer to the God of Christians, and began trying to start the engine.

Two hours later the bike was dented and covered in dust and Vitellan's jeans and jacket were torn and bloodied . . . but he could ride a motorcycle! Leaving the floor of the quarry scoured with skidmarks, he rode triumphantly out onto the dirt road, waving to a fresh rockslide by the wall and calling "Vale, et grates."

Vitellan had little trouble on the highway, as fragments of memories gated in from what was left of Robert Wallace included road codes. His appearance was intimidating. Covered in dust, blood, and scratches and riding a filthy bike, he was given a very wide berth by the few others on the road. At Fort Stockton he decided that the bike needed fuel and that he needed a map and food. The roadspike had already stopped for gasoline, so Vitellan knew something of the procedure.

Rosamaria Conception very nearly fainted when she saw what had just ridden in from the east and stopped before the pumps. She was alone at the gas station, just minding the place and studying for the next semester's coursework. Imprints had not yet managed to displace old-fashioned study, even in 2028, as students were required to come up with original conclusions about what they studied. She watched as the roadspike fumbled with the pump, struggled with the fuel cap, splashed gasoline over himself and the bike, and finally managed to get some into the tank. He's out on bloodsand, thought Rosamaria as she watched the gasoline overflow and billow in clouds off the hot engine. Her foot caressed the security button. The specter limped across to the office and through the automatic doors.

"Feed bike! Gas!" Vitellan declared, opening his wallet and displaying the contents to Rosamaria. She glanced at the reading on the display.

"That will be $35.80 sir," she said with as much calm as she could manage.

Vitellan offered her a thousand-dollar banknote. Rosamaria swallowed.

"Sir, do you have anything a little smaller please?"

"Small pease? Pease pudding?" asked Vitellan desperately, knowing that he was missing the point completely.

She shook her head. "No, smaller bills. A hundred or something. I don't have enough hard-c change, but if you give me one of those unsec smartcards that would be fine."

Most of the words washed past Vitellan. He knew English, but it was two years of English from the fourteenth century. He had picked up a few modern words in general speech, but his basic infrastructure for modern English had faded with his imprint. He could have bought gasoline from Chaucer, but not from this Texan girl of the twenty-first century. He rubbed a grimy hand over his face.

"Is there nobody on this entire continent who can understand a civilized language?" he sighed to himself in Latin.

"Latin!" exclaimed Rosamaria. "You speak Latin?"

"Why yes, indeed I do," replied Vitellan in Latin, almost collapsing with relief and immediately switching his manner to fourteenth-century courtly charm. "But how do you come to speak such an old language so very beautifully, good lady?"

"Me? Oh, I'm a college student on a break from Flagstaff," she replied, thinking *weirder and weirder* all the while.

"Ah, a student. One should always study and better oneself, it is a very noble pursuit. Now then, how much do I owe for the, ah, gasoline as you call it?"

"Thirty-five dollars eighty."

"Yes, yes, now I see. I thought you were saying thirty-five dollars *and* eighty *dollars.*"

Vitellan glanced around the shop, noting the range of goods with interest.

"Would you be so good as to help me with some other purchases?" he asked.

"That is what I am paid to do," Rosamaria replied, half suspecting that she had fallen into a dream.

Vitellan bought her personal low-speed portable imprint unit, a roadmap, and the imprint disks for Selective American Vernacular, Rough Tours of the West Coast, and Know Your Rights. Rosamaria gave him a canvas backpack that someone had abandoned there months ago, and he added several bottles of soda and cans of meatballs in sauce to his purchases.

It was a quiet day, so she talked to him about English usage and street talk, and answered his questions about survival on the road while he hosed down his bike, washed, and bandaged his cuts.

"That bleeding star on your jacket must be removed if you want to cross gang turf," she advised. "Give it here, I shall pick the threads and put a *T* on your back with gray tape. *T* means you are a transient."

"What is a transient?" asked Vitellan as he shrugged out of the heavy impact jacket.

"Transient means you have been booted out of your gang, and are moving to new territory. Most gangs leave you alone, but if you meet up with psycho-cells . . ." She noticed the Ruger in the inner pocket of the jacket. "Well, you will need to use this persuader."

"Ah yes, I have been meaning to ask you about that. Could you instruct me in its usage?"

"You must be joking! You do not know guns, yet you pack a Ruger and a pump-action. You ride in on roadspike wheels, but you speak Latin like . . . like . . . an alien out of a UFO."

"Aliens and UFOs. My acquaintances tell me that they are literary and mythical."

"Believe me mister, *you* are mythical. You turn up out of nowhere looking like you tried to punch out a bear, but then you start speaking flawless Latin. That's as strange as any UFO story. I hear a lot of UFO stories when I come out here in semester breaks, folk make up wild stories to cut through the boredom. You are different. You do not have a story, yet you talk like you stepped straight out of . . ." She reached behind the counter and held up her copy of the *Deciad*. "Out of this."

"You flatter me," Vitellan replied quietly, raising a bandaged hand to his face and bowing slightly.

Rosamaria took Vitellan through the basics of cleaning, loading, and firing his guns before he handed her five thousand dollars of Baker's money.

"This is too much!" she exclaimed. "Five K for my old imprint deck and some roadgear?"

"You gave freely of what could not be purchased," replied Vitellan, zipping up the jacket. "My regret is that I could not give more."

Rosamaria dashed back into the office as he swung a leg over the Harley and gunned the engine into life. She returned with her trade paperback edition of the *Deciad* and thrust it at him with a heavily chewed pen. Vitellan stared at the book, then looked to Rosamaria.

"My lady, I am not Decius," said Vitellan after thinking for a moment and deducing her probable thoughts.

"But you could not say anything else . . . Please write in it, anything. It is something that *you* can give that cannot be purchased."

Vitellan took the point and killed the engine. He wrote in Latin TO ROSAMARIA, THE FRIEND WHO CAME TO MY AID opposite the title page and returned the book to her, then he took her hand and brushed it with his lips. The spell was shattered as the Harley's engine hammered back into life, and with a final wave Vitellan engaged the gears—then lurched forward, stalled, and nearly overbalanced. Sheepishly he started the engine again, and this time released the clutch more smoothly. He pulled out onto the highway, ventured another wave, swerved wildly, regained control, then opened the throttle and accelerated away. Rosamaria stood hugging the *Deciad* to her breasts and staring down the road after Vitellan long after his bike was out of sight. It was like the wildest, most indulgent of wish-fulfillments, as if she had stepped into a legend just long enough to save the hero and avert tragedy. As she watched the newscasts in the months that followed, however, she could never entirely escape the notion that her fantasy might have actually been real.

6

countess and knight

Hall was based in Northward Civic, but commuted to the SkyPlaz clinic along F59 and S288 every day. The SkyPlaz clinic was on neutral ground between Hermann Park and the Brays Bayou; it was an interface between two economies and legal systems. Some of its floors were legitimate medical suites, others were leased by the gangwards. There was much interchange between floors. Patients, drugs, and equipment moved freely, with no questions asked, and a sophisticated database laundered the accounts to protect both the guilty and guiltier. In SkyPlaz work could be done at other than the prescribed rates, in fact work could be done that could otherwise not be done at all. It was an embassy and marketplace all in one, with excellent security and discretion included. Hall was one of the resources available through SkyPlaz, an MIT graduate whose reputation was international—if not mainstream international. He was part of that "best" that SkyPlaz provided, and as such he was highly valued. This was not always well understood by those outside.

"No word of Baker yet?" Hall asked the hologram of Roarch, the head of his security node. The holographic face suspended above his desk looked tired and worried.

"He was last seen entering the scramjet," Roarch replied.

"Someone came out wearing the right mask, our guys confirmed that under deep scan. We got a security monitor record of the dude with the same mask talking to some roadspike working carpark E. He rode off with him."

"Smells like shit on a shoe. Which spikes was he with?"

"Hellrunners. We got calls out but they're traditionals. They spend a lot of time on civilian turf and they got no comms. It could be tomorrow before we get real words."

Hall glanced to a wallscreen, where a newscast showed shattered debris being skimmed from choppy gray waves by Canadian sailors.

"He could have been aboard the scramjet," said Hall as he turned back to face Roarch's hologram.

"Yeah, but airpost security says only three boarded. Anyhow, why go to that sort of trouble to trash a medical? Jinslash would have done the job for fifty K's."

Hall flung a stylus down on his desk and folded his arms. "Give me a break! Jinslash would have had its ass kicked from here to low orbit by the Ward Lords. They're stupid but not that stupid."

"So we're left with the big who, and I don't like that." A hand appeared beside the holographic face and Roarch chewed a thumbnail. "Like you said, Dr. Hall, there's shit to smell but not to see. Get back here, my man, now. Get all the cards and disks on that Vitellan dude and bring 'em with you. Everything! Do a mask on and take a car—and make sure you got muscle with automatics."

An armored sedan pulled out of SkyPlaz from the outpatient ramp an hour later. Hall had been wearing a mask and his head had been swathed in bandages, but Lucel had other criteria to watch for. Hall's stature, the armed guards, and the fact that a patient in bandages was well enough to carry a heavy tote bag. She pulled her Sundart convertible out into the light traffic and followed the sedan, keeping quite close behind.

Within two blocks the sedan's driver realized that someone was following. He gunned the peroxide engine and engaged the computer-enhanced evasion option to weave through the traffic. Lucel cursed quietly, but her car had all the same pursuit and evasion options and the gap barely widened. They entered a feeder for S288, going north, weaving through the traffic in formation. From the sedan's side window a guard fired a laser at the Sundart's windshield, but the bursts were absorbed by polarity baffles and Lucel was annoyed rather than dazzled. The guard changed to a Ruger GP-100, but Lucel's own dazzle-laser was locked on to him by now. Shielding his eyes, he aimed low, and hit her front right tire.

Lucel's Sundart lurched as she fought for control. Almost at once autoseal polymer repaired the rents and a gas reservoir began to pump the wheel back to operational pressure, but now the sedan was two hundred yards ahead. UniWard was to the right of the freeway.

"Bad turf, anything goes," muttered Lucel as she hunched forward slightly.

As if to agree with her the Sundart's onboard radar blazed a warning of an attack vector from the right: airborne and coming in low. It was a big profile, the size of a tiltfan. An overpass shielded the aircraft's approach as Lucel gained on the sedan. She reached down for a heavy tube trailing flaccid cables that plugged into her radar. Holding it up over the windshield she fired blindly at a space beyond the overpass where the tiltfan would have to fly. The Taipan interceptor swamped the sportscar in exhaust as it streaked to where its target was headed—but someone in the tiltfan had already fired an identical Taipan at the sedan.

The sedan detonated in a fiery teardrop that smeared along S288's bitumen and dispersed into burning shards. The tiltfan's passenger shouted "Hit!" triumphantly just as the horrified pilot cried "Incoming!"

Lucel's Taipan struck amidships, and the covalent lattice in the warhead collapsed right between the rear engine bay and the cabin. The tiltfan sprayed flesh, flames, and composite debris to either side, but it flew on, hanging on the two front fans and slowly descending before hitting a construction site in Broad Acres and exploding. Lucel paused, standing up in her Sundart and confirming that everyone in the sedan was dead. She set her dataspex to scan for a suite of profiles, and within seconds a flashing wireframe centered on a blackened, battered composite case that had been inside Hall's tote bag. She jumped from the car and snatched up the case in a towel.

Another car had stopped by now, and a man had got out.

"Hey, look at that, she's part of a heist," he called. "Stop—"

Lucel shot him in the leg. He collapsed but held on to the driver's-side door, shouting in surprise and pain. His passenger scrabbled in the car's door pannier for a gun as Lucel heaved the case into her Sundart and tumbled in after it.

"Evasive!" shouted Lucel, lying across the seats as shots whined past her. The Sundart added the smoke from its tires to that curling up from the roadway as it steered for the feeder into the matrix of streets that was EastWard.

Twenty minutes later the smoke had dispersed from the Houston sky. Across the city, where the Buffalo Bayou marked the border of EastWard, a hawk floated on the air, flying in the random, soaring curves of a scavenging pattern. There was no suggestion of an attack vector until it was right over a walled compound on Waugh Drive, then the wings folded and it fell like a stone. The explosion was sharp and hollow, showering soil, grass, and shreds of flesh into a nearby swimming pool.

The attack generated a report that was transmitted to the other side of the Atlantic:

> Seeker bion targeted on implants in Luministe agent Lucel Hunter. Successful impact took place at 3.17 PM Houston time in the Nin-gyo compound, Waugh Drive, Houston. Microcamera images from the seeker indicate that the implant carrier was an adult Doberman bitch, and subsequent datafarm sifting indicated that it was part of the compound's security pack, and was designated by the name T-rexette.

Lord Wallace crumpled the hard copy and flung it across the Deep Frigidarium. For a second time the Luministe agent had cheated death and evaded him.

Within three minutes of leaving the freeway Lucel had exchanged her Sundart for a laundered Toyota Earthway electric sedan and sealed Hall's case inside Faraday cage mesh to smother any surviving beacons. By the time her former implants had attracted the seeker bion, she was in a shielded workshop in Eastward, watching a framescreen where a military surplus bomb disposal unit was drilling into Hall's charred metal case.

"Checkin' the air," said the Creole technician as a probe replaced the drill. "Nitrogen, ninety-nine parts, one part argon. Someone's paranoid."

"I want the contents, nothing else," said Lucel.

"Hell lady, you'd sure be a kook if you just wanted the case. Sending in the camera."

A silver cable with a surface like fine scales replaced the gas sensor probe, and an image of the inside of the case filled the framescreen. It was a jumble of paper notes, insulated sample phials and datacards, all stirred together by the explosion that had killed Hall. The back of the lock came into view. There was a red plastic lozenge bonded to the surface.

"Now that's a gas-magnetic Shalis. NorthWard got a batch in from Switzerland two years ago. A magnetic key shuts it down, otherwise it flames the goods if someone forces the lock and lets in oxygen. It's not a problem, a coat of polymer will make it think everything's dandy."

"Or you could cut the case open in a nitrogen atmosphere."

"Sure could, but poly is cheaper . . . hey now, lookey here. Another one on the back hinge. It's white, and, and shit, I never seen that type."

"Like you said, someone's paranoid," Lucel reminded him. "You'd better hurry."

"Think I'll go for poly *and* the N-two flood before I cut."

"Listen to me!" snapped Lucel. "Just use nitrogen, and work fast."

"I'd rather—"

"Do it!"

Once the chamber was flooded with nitrogen the tech made a narrow slit in the case and removed the cards and paper notes with a suction grapple. The phials needed a wider hole, but it took only fourteen minutes from the first drillhole to empty the insulated case.

"No beacons, no sleepers, it's all yours," he said as he took a tray from the chamber's airlock. "If you—holy shit!"

Flame and fumes belched from the incisions in the top of the case, quickly filling the chamber with yellowish-brown smoke.

"So the white one was on a timer," said Lucel as she emptied the tray into her Faraday-cage bag.

"Someone's real seriously paranoid," agree the tech, staring into the opaque smoke.

The River Oaks checkpoint on Westheimer Road was all soft-contour white moldings and lattice-weave barrier pickets, but it had the strength and firepower to stop an old-style tank. To the east of it the suburbs were like a huge, exclusive, high-security condo and the checkpoint was as much to say *your rates at work* to those within as *keep out* to unauthorized drivers.

Lucel's ID was for a wealthy British tourist driving a sensibly downmarket car while outside the exclusive Greenpark independent municipalities. The security guards waved her through with no more than routine facial profile scans. She drove to the hotel where she was staying, which was part of the Greater Galleria Center. The zone where she parked the Toyota was legal, but it would vanish within the hour with no questions asked and no alarm raised.

Lucel scanned her hotel room very carefully before opening the Faraday-cage bag. With her dataspex plugged into a reader she examined the cards in turn. They were mostly scan data on Vitellan, thorough and meticulous scan data. Some of Hall's notes and impressions were there as well, under an encryption that took an hour of commercial processor time to break.

Lucel had began to download data from software agents that she had left to monitor certain network lines. While working for the Luministes in Paris and Durvas, she had also been working for herself, and to an agenda that nobody could have suspected. The software agents cleared their data buffers and reset their address registers to a number of industrial espionage agencies once they had downloaded, giving both Durvas and Luministe systems security staff something to discover and purge before they had supposedly done any damage—and Lucel had plenty of other agents hidden in positions of trust. Both Durvas and Luministe Security would report an intrusion foiled before any data had been collected, so it was a win-win situation for all concerned. The encrypted messages that Lucel assembled had been further disguised by seeming outwardly innocent and unconnected, but once gathered together they interlocked to tell a very different story. That story was now negotiable currency in certain circles.

Lucel approached the SpanTurf blockhouse the following evening. It was a calm, overcast dusk, and the reek from a breakdown in the sewage works just over the Buffalo Bayou was heavy and cloying on the cold air. The streets had a thin sprinkling of cars and pedestrians, about what one might expect for a chilly Houston evening. Stopping before the blockhouse entrance, she spoke to a comm beneath her wrist, then folded her arms and waited. A cell of five youths approached in a wide curve, guns out but held casually. They wore no tag-patches, she noted. Ronin-G kids, out to build reputations, out to get patronage.

"You don't know where you be, slut."

"Yeah, you don't know."

"You got stop here, you stop here a lot."

"You know, stop a lot, you know."

Most of them wanted their say, and they were loud and brash. One had glazed eyes and did not speak at all, he just held his Mexican copy of a Makarova to Lucel's head. The others pushed and pummeled her, but made no attempt to force her to go with them. They were posturing for the monitor cameras in front of the headquarters building. The leader spat in her face. Spittle dripped from the lens of her dataspex.

"I spit you, dirty bitch, but you not worth spittin' on. You owe me a favor, you know? How you gonna pay me back?"

The one with the glazed eyes continued to point the gun at her head.

They know I'm here, they're just watching the show on their screens in there, Lucel decided. They probably even sent these kids to pump the muscle. Sorry boys, nothing personal.

Her head snapped about, deflecting the gun as her elbow came up into the boy's chin, and she was drawing her own gun as she spun and lashed the toe of her boot into the leader's teeth. Guns crackled, Lucel staggered as her armor stopped a bullet high on her chest, then she fired at the neck in an open shirt and the sternum beneath a red T-shirt. Suddenly everything froze, Lucel and the last youth pointing their guns at each other.

"If you so much as move a muscle I'll kill you where you stand," Lucel said firmly. "You're pointing at my tits but I've got armor. *I* have a bead on your *head*. Drop the gun."

He dropped the gun. The doors of the blockhouse slid open and two security guards dashed out into the street. Both carried Mossenberg slide-action combat shotguns. Urine suddenly stained dark at the crotch of the youth's citi-gray slacks as one of the Mossbergs drifted over to take a bead on him. The two other surviving Ronin-Gs got to their feet, dribbling blood and spitting teeth.

Lucel turned to the youth who had been holding a gun to her head. The tumble-shot was steady in her hand.

"You with the eyes," she said coldly. "If some scumbag holds a gun to my head I like to think that he's paying attention. I don't think you were paying attention just then. Are you paying attention now?"

"Yes ma'am, 'deed I am ma'am, I'm sorry ma'am!"

"Well, I don't believe you, I think you need a reminder."

She fired into his left knee. He doubled over, howling, then toppled to the sidewalk. Lucel put a boot on his throat and jammed the barrel into his open mouth.

"Are you paying attention?" His shrieks transmuted into whimpers. "*Now* you're going to pay attention with every step you ever take. Say thank you, ma'am."

Lucel removed the gun from his mouth, but it took him some moments to articulate the words. She turned to the other two.

"You may be thinking payback for your Ronin-G dead, but forget it kiddies. If I *ever* see *any* of your faces *anywhere* I'm going to make sure you take a week to die. You just touched something so fucking big that you wouldn't believe it." She played a burst about their feet and they jumped, then she turned to the guards. "You're late!" she snapped at the blank blastmasks. "All this shit is your fault."

"Lady, we had orders—"

"Shut up and take me in there! Now!"

Lucel would not see Roarch before she was allowed to wash her face. He was scowling at an image on his wallscreen as she entered his office.

"Did you have to mess up those kids so bad?" he asked as the scene replayed on the wall beside him.

"It was a lesson in manners. Good manners are the gateway to the upper classes."

"That's shit."

She shrugged. "The right to spit in my face and point a gun in my ear comes with a very high price tag. Besides, you made it happen by leaving your fucking door shut so long. You wanted me taught what a mean fucker you are, but *you* went to school instead."

Roarch switched to realtime on the wallscreen. The living youths were gone, leaving smears of blood, piss, and vomit. The dead still lay where they had fallen.

"You got a nerve and then some, lady," he said as he powered off the screen. "At least I'll talk to you—none of the Ward Lords wanna hear any sound from you but splat after you torched their doctor."

"Not me. I do know who bought the pipes that hit Hall and Baker, though."

In spite of having a Shakespearean imprint, Roarch forgot himself and blinked in surprise. He recovered quickly.

"We already got all what we want on how Hall and Baker died, ungrateful bitch. *They* patched you back together, then *you* pointed your Luministe iceheads straight at them."

"Not so. I have proof."

"That's shit, I done a lot of scans and filters. The tiltfan was hired through their LA temple. The Go-Bucks were ridin' the contract, and right now they're in so much pain they wish their folks had never screwed."

"So why did I shoot out the tiltfan?"

Roarch hesitated. "Uh, coverin' I guess."

"Now who's talking shit, Roarch? I was trying to get the real hit squad before they locked on to the car. Get a fact! I chased that damn car for two miles without firing a shot, didn't I? I was *trying* to protect *Hall*!"

Roarch snorted, then turned away from her and paced beside his desk. Lucel folded her arms and remained standing.

"The Go-Bucks were paid in clean, mixed bills," she said when it became clear that Roarch was not going to say any more. "I mean shit, the Pope himself could have handed over that stack of bills, but if he said he was a Luministe they would have still believed him."

"How'd you know they were paid in bills?"

"The Yakuza were very helpful after I tipped them about a hit on their datavend, Seishi. They own the franchise that the Go-Bucks work. They also want to taste blood from whoever dropped a half-pound of covalent into their Waugh Drive embassy."

"I heard about that. Shredded the bodytats off a couple of grandsans by the pool. They're sore."

"I've got something else you might like to know about," she admitted, her eyes narrowing. "I can finger who did the World Three Mall attack, *and* provide an audit trail."

Roarch swallowed. World Three Mall had been a showpiece market for gang commerce, cooperation, and responsibility, and the attack by the unidentified crew of the stolen police tiltfan had annihilated more than the lives of 270 people. Years of public relations work and millions of dollars in potential business had been blasted out of existence, so whichever Ward Lord tracked down the culprits at the top of that contract would gain a lot of status.

"Okay, okay, that's an offer too good to refuse," said Roarch, sitting on the edge of his desk and spreading his arms wide. "Who then?"

"Durvas."

"Durvas? As in *the* Village? Now hold on. Durvas was picking up the bills for that Vitellan icehead."

"Durvas had no choice, he was under SkyPlaz security. Check the clinic's records: the contract was to keep Vitellan isolated from everyone, Durvas included. I should know, I wrote it."

Roarch pressed his hands against his head, wanting to believe, yet still unwilling.

"This sounds like so much shit," he muttered, feeling the blood vessels pump against his palms, his mind devoid of a better reply.

"Okay then, I didn't know you take lumps quietly."

"Hey now, I get one, I give ten," shouted Roarch, striding over and waving a finger at her as if he could shoot it. "What's for us to see?"

"I have a set of encrypted strings from the Luministe headquarters in Paris. They contain instructions to the LA Luministe Temple of Pure Light to buy the contracts with old bills."

"You just said they didn't do it."

"Uh, uh. The Luministes did the legwork, but the orders came from Durvas. I had a pattern filter on the Durvas research node, and an algorithm which compares that with outgoing traffic from the Luministe headquarters in Paris—even with encryption. I got a match dating back before Hall was torched, but it took a lot of time and CPU credit to break the message. By then it was late—too late, as it happened. I can tell you about an old man and a dead man, both a long way underground. Security, layouts, equipment, all that sort of thing. Send a payback team, I'll be project leader if you like—"

"Hold it, just hold it!" shouted Roarch, holding his hands over his ears and squeezing his eyes shut. "What do *you* get out of this?"

"The same as you: payback. I'm a mean bitch and I'm into revenge.

Play back the monitor of what just happened on your doorstep if you don't believe me."

Roarch was beginning to feel comfortable with Lucel, and he suspected that she would let him have all the credit for the payback as long as he provided the resources. He sat down and put his feet on his desk, pressing his fingertips together.

"You're incommin' on a deal, mean bitch," he said smoothly, "but I'm curious to know what Durvas did to get *your* gripes so sharp."

"Uh, uh. That's on a need-to-know basis, and there's only one man alive who needs to know."

Durvas, Britain: 25 January 2029, Anno Domini

Anderson stumbled, then seized a railing to steady himself as he cut through the gardens of Durvas University on the way to the shafthead of the Deep Frigidarium. What are the warning signs of a hidden imprint? Blank spots, vertigo, atypical memories. He walked on, thinking carefully about his morning routine. He remembered breakfast in his bathrobe, showering under needles of hot water and being shaved by his new GE grooming unit. After that . . . nothing was missing. He arrived at the shafthead building after what should have been a nine-minute walk. He glanced at his watch. Eight minutes, ten seconds. No unaccounted time in his routine. Perhaps he really was working too hard.

At the shafthead he had the security crew check him with particular care. He stripped completely, then thought the better of his morning routine and had a voluntary enema and stomach pump. Half an hour later Lord Wallace called him as he sat eating a second breakfast of thoroughly scanned food and wearing a security uniform from stores.

"The duty officer says you are putting yourself through Core A-plus-plus security, old boy," said a hologram of Lord Wallace's head hovering just above his plate. "Anything I should know about?"

"I had a dizzy spell on the way over," Anderson replied defensively.

He was the Durvas marshal, the head of the security system. The idea of admitting that he might be a security risk did not come easily.

The hologram bent forward and peered at him carefully. "Anything else? Time unaccounted for, lightheadedness, unfamiliar clothing, odd smells on your breath?"

"Nothing, and the scans are all clear. No implants, no overlay, no obvious imprints, although the microimprint of a trigger would take hours to find."

"What about VCA?"

"Viral Culture Analysis shows nothing out of the catalogue."

"And nanoware?"

"That needs a full blood exchange to do properly, especially if we're looking for a multiphase biological mimic on a random switch cycle. I'd be two hours in the unit, and another to get the results. Still, I could do it."

The little hologram of Lord Wallace brought his fingertips together at the point of his chin. His eyebrows converged slightly with the hint of a frown.

"I need to speak to you soon."

"So? You're doing it now."

"It must be off-comm," the holographic Lord Wallace insisted.

"We've got encryption."

"Encryption's not good enough."

"That serious? All right then, three hours more, that's when I get the all-clear."

"And if they find some harmless anomaly? We might wait days, and I don't have days. *We* don't have days."

"I'd prefer the screening to be finished," said Anderson reluctantly. "It's the proper procedure."

"I *wrote* the procedure, and this can't wait. Look, meet me in the screen room of the Deep Frigidarium. That has total privacy and is as secure as anywhere on earth."

Anderson pushed his plate away and sat back, arms folded and defiant. "Lord Wallace, the last time we bent our own rules some screwy Luministe faction blasted their way in and—"

"I know what they did, better than anyone. You will be behind an armored, blast-proof partition, it will be quite safe."

"You hope. What could be so damn important that we have to take risks again?"

"It is time for Black Prince."

Anderson sat up and put both hands on the table, staring intently at the hologram.

"Black Prince? Are you absolutely sure?"

"There's no other way, Bonhomme's timer is already counting."

The quarter-mile drop to the chamber where Vitellan's body was being kept took less than a minute. Lord Wallace had a suite of offices and living space down there, far beyond the reach of any macro-attack from terrorists. The screen room was nothing more than a narrow cubicle with two chairs separated by a laminate film partition—a deeply inset partition that would not blow out should there be an explosion on one side. Anderson was still wearing the spare security uniform as he entered and sat down. Again he was scanned, but this time it was only ultrasonic resonance, a newly developed check for covalent lattice explosive disguised as bone or muscles. Lord Wallace entered the other side of the cubicle, carrying a holoboard. His face was tight with fury. The gaslift chair depressed slightly as he sat down, Anderson noted. He was no hologram.

"*This* is all that we have to show the world in 2054," Lord Wallace said, coming straight to the point as he thumbed the hologram board into life.

Vitellan's body materialized in the space between them, bisected down the middle by the laminate partition. It was not healthy looking, even to the casual glance. The skin was a murky, soiled white with a chaotic tracery of red hairline scars. His head was hairless, even his eyebrows and lashes were gone.

"Yes, that's how his realware looks," said Anderson. "Not a pretty bear, is he?"

"He's all that we have now," replied Lord Wallace. "I want a complete cosmetic job on him, electrostim workouts on his muscles, and enough sunlamp to get his skin back to the way it was when he came out of the ice."

"But he's a vegetable."

"As I said, he's all we have, and Black Prince *must* be put into operation now if we are to get the credit. Bonhomme's timers will soon fire unless I stop them, and I have no intention of doing that. We can leak data that the Master was revived, ran Black Prince covertly, then was injured and had to be refrozen."

"Good enough for Abe Lincoln, good enough for us," agreed Anderson.

"The Village Corporate and several guards have seen the overlay Master and even spoken with him, so he was known to be revived. The overlay is now at the bottom of the Atlantic, so the body down here is once again the one and only Vitellan. After Black Prince I shall be frozen with him, traveling as his escort, and we shall both be revived in 2054."

Lord Wallace held up a datacard, slowly and reverently, as if it were a powerful magic talisman.

"I have medical advice that fetal brain tissue transplants can restore enough function to the Master's body for him to open his eyes and say a few preprogrammed words like 'I die happy, two thousand years old. I name Lord Wallace, who stood beside me against Jacque Bonhomme, as my successor in the Frigidarium of Durvas.' I shall then name you as my escort through time, William, and we shall both become immortal."

"A berth in a commercial cryochamber would be simpler," sighed Anderson, weighed down by years of subterfuge and plotting. His limbs felt heavy, his joints stiff.

"Bah, do that and you arrive in the future as a nobody with an investment account: no contacts, no friends, and a whole industry dedicated to fleecing yokel time travelers of their capital. If we travel to the future in the Master's place, we have the entire infrastructure of Durvas behind us. We'll arrive in the future as legends, people who fought beside the Master himself."

There was no single trigger within Anderson's microimprint. The faces of Vitellan and Lord Wallace; "2054" spoken with Wallace's vocal profile; the greater air pressure deep in the shaft; even the periodic EMP pulses and ultrasonic resonance sweeps focused on the marshal to destroy any Trojan builder-implants. It was a whole-environment trigger, designed to ensure that Lord Wallace was close by when it activated. Anderson hooked his feet behind the struts of his chair and gripped the edge of the seat as he leaned forward, as if to listen.

The marshal tried to let go, but nothing happened. My bones, they've changed my bones into destabilized covalent lattice, he thought, no longer even in charge of his own breathing. How did the scans miss it? I'm dead, but they've failed. When I explode the laminate will hold, the back of the cubicle will be blown out instead. Lord Wallace is safe . . . William Anderson died, still sitting with a calm, attentive expression on his face.

Multiphase biological nano-mimics in his blood, in an undetectable form when he had been scanned earlier, transformed his blood sugars into energy cells. At the same time they also transmuted his nervous system into organic conductors and semiconductors wired into a tuned circuit and oscillator. The periodic, circuit-destroying EMP pulse from the security unit actually brought it all to life.

The blast of microwave radiation from what had been Anderson was unimpeded by the laminate partition. Lord Wallace felt a sudden flush, but did not recognize what was happening as an attack. By the time he thought of escape, alarms were already whooping. He lurched for the door and hammered his fist against the release button, then collapsed. Anderson's body was bent to focus on Lord Wallace's seat, but it also pointed to the floor near the door, exactly where Lord Wallace now lay. A security team high above at ground level activated a mobile handler, which arrived within a few seconds.

"Don't move him, we need a medic at the controls!"

The words sealed Lord Wallace's fate. His body lay there for another fifteen seconds while the husk of Anderson poured microwave radiation into it, then burned out. The medic assessed Lord Wallace through the handler's sensors, then lifted his body and took it to the very intensive care unit that had treated Vitellan's body just after his skull had been crushed. It was soon apparent that Lord Wallace was beyond the help of even the most advanced therapies of 2029.

Anderson's body had all but dried out, and steam from his tissues filled the cubicle. He was a curved husk, charred black but still gripping the chair and hissing softly. Like all high-tech assassination techniques, this would be its only use. Microwave shielding would be added to laminate screens all around the world by the end of the week as agencies learned of the trick.

The two most senior surviving members of the Village Corporate hurried across the university and into the Durvas Technology Park to a mock art deco building that was the wellhead of the Deep Frigidarium. As they walked, a gaggle of assistants and technicians fluttered around them with oxygen tanks, masks, and items of protective clothing. Guards moved aside, already aware that Durvas had suffered yet another catastrophic intrusion.

"It was a very sophisticated attack," Icekeeper Gulden reported to Lord Wallace's ashen-faced deputy, Dellar. "The marshal was probably abducted during the night and dosed with multiphase nanoware programmed to rebuild parts of him in a second or two on some key or key combination."

"But his wife noticed nothing. Anderson said as much himself, I heard him say that on the monitor tapes when he had a link to Lord Wallace from the shafthead."

"A team from the Durvas clinic is at her house at this very minute with a mobile lab. Initial scans suggest that she was imprinted too, according to what is coming in on my dataspex. Of course she noticed nothing! She couldn't!"

"So the assassins might have been calling in every night for weeks to nanoform him into a pop-mold human death-ray."

"Very likely, Sir Peter."

Like the authorized successor to any absolute dictator, Sir Peter

Dellar had little real experience with the exercise of authority and all its realities. At that moment he also had a very real sense of his mortality as well. Burgess, the new marshal, met them at the entrance to the wellhead, already in protective clothing and carrying his helmet. His hair was soaked with sweat, and he smelled faintly of charred flesh.

"I was just coming to get you," he began breathlessly.

"Well I'm here, brief me as we descend!" snapped Dellar, angry and exasperated with the continual failures of Durvas security. "Gulden said that they turned the marshal into a human microwave dish and murdered Lord Wallace. How did our scanners miss the trigger imprints and implants?"

"Given a few hours we would have found the triggers, but they're tough to isolate and Lord Wallace was impatient to see him. Something about a black prince, it's on a monitor tape, but—"

"Black Prince is a codename for a campaign Lord Wallace was planning with the Centurion against the Luministes, that's all I know about it."

"The Centurion! That's the other—"

"What can you tell me about the microwave weapon?"

"It's not very hard with the right nanotech. The human body is already close to being a chemical power plant driving an electronic network. Rewire it a bit, then key it off at the right time and you have a one-shot microwave cannon. The Centurion—"

"Forget the Centurion, he's safe in Houston, safe from the Luministes and safe from your incompetence!" Dellar shouted.

"The Centurion is down there in an intensive care unit!" Burgess shouted back, stabbing his gloved finger downward. "If you don't know *that* as the deputy head of the Village Corporate then you have no right to flounce about tossing rocks at me when I'm up to my earlobes in sewage. Do I make myself clear?"

The security OIC at the elevator doors would let nobody through without their protective gear being checked and sealed. Dellar was annoyed at the delay, but had become more subdued after the deputy marshal's outburst. Nobody was in a mood to flaunt security and safety regulations after what had just happened.

"How the hell did they know when he'd be staring at Lord Wallace?" Dellar muttered as technicians sealed the seams of his suit.

"I'll write a report when I'm good and ready!" snapped Burgess.

Icekeeper Gulden came to Dellar's rescue.

"For a start, go down a quarter mile to the Deep Frigidarium and the air pressure is greater. That probably keyed the process off and primed other triggers. The screen of the interview chamber down there is transparent to radiofrequency radiation to allow hologram dialogues, and that is the key weakness. On the other hand I'd be surprised if there were less than a thousand other trigger scenarios in the imprint that Anderson was given."

Dellar turned to Burgess. "Deputy Marshal, why didn't your people bring down the shutters as soon as the temperature rise was detected?" he asked with as much diplomacy as he could put into his voice.

Chinless wonder, Burgess thought to himself with detached resignation. "With respect, Sir Peter, the procedure is that Lord Wallace had first right of cutoff. The monitor record shows that Anderson seemed to be just sitting there, listening attentively. Lord Wallace suspected nothing until he began to cook."

At last they were cleared to enter the elevator and descend to the Deep Frigidarium. They dropped the quarter mile in uneasy silence. The air was rated safe as they stepped out of the elevator, but a reek of charred flesh met them as soon as they removed their helmets. Dellar dropped his helmet, seized a railing and retched.

Vitellan's body was lying in a biosupport maintenance unit in the actual vault of the Deep Frigidarium. The unit was running on battery power, and could remain totally isolated for up to a month. There was no master code to open the vault, however: that was shared between Lord Wallace and Anderson. The vault's lock triggered a variety of traps and alarms, including a hydraulic system that flooded the chamber with nerve gas. A team of security technicians and a contract bomb disposal squad were hard at work breaking through the security systems. The engineers who had designed the systems were there too, as telepresence holograms, offering helpful advice.

"Deputy Marshal, it will be dangerous down here when the locks are finally drawn back," the OIC of the team reported to Burgess. "There might be any number of trap devices that we missed. The marshal may have added extra systems that the original designers don't know about."

"Then we'll seal off our protective gear and stand ready," Burgess replied. "I don't want *anyone* else but Sir Peter, the Icekeeper, and me to go near the Master's bio unit."

The vault finally yielded its treasure early in the afternoon. The three executive members of the Village Corporate entered the vault alone and examined it carefully. There was a frozen cadaver in a cryogenic store with a dermal mask and scars applied to make it resemble Vitellan. That surprised them, but it was hardly surprising that a decoy mockup of the Centurion would be kept to fool potential assassins. They unbolted the real Vitellan's biosupport unit from its base and slid it onto a trolley. It was brought to the surface under a shoot-to-kill alert and hurried over to the intensive care facilities of the technology park's research clinic. There Gulden began the first of a series of ultrasonic scans, prior to bringing the body up through a full-consciousness revival. He stopped almost as soon as he had begun.

"The cranium!" he exclaimed. "Nearly half of the cranium is empty!"

It took some time to deduce the truth about the condition of Vitellan's body. It had been skillfully reconstructed after some terrible accident, but it was not until records were brought up from the Deep Frigidarium that the details were filled in. Forty minutes after the explosion a skygrapple had been brought to the scene and lifted the slab, but the body had been unfrozen and biologically active at the time it was crushed. The slab had descended, smashing his head to a bloody mush of brains and broken bone barely three inches thick. Three quarters of an hour after the explosion the body was in a cryogenic chamber and being chilled, but it was a desperate and futile act.

Dellar noticed that the director of surgery's name was on the report, and he sent Burgess to fetch Cassion at once. Burgess reported back that Dr. Cassion had vanished, and that all of his records had been removed or destroyed.

"I want security checks done on the entire Village Corporate," said Dellar between clenched teeth. "Every single member, all seventeen of us."

"I initiated just that from Dr. Cassion's consulting rooms," reported Burgess, "starting with you."

Vitellan would have stood a better chance of surviving a bullet through the brain. A battery of ultrasonic scanners slowly assessed the body's damage. Quite apart from his head injuries, both feet, one arm, his liver, his right lung, and all the ribs on his right side had been crushed so badly that Cassion had been forced to do experiments with anesthetized pigs to develop new techniques for rebuilding severely crushed bones and tissues. While the surrogate Vitellan was watching Lucel being rebuilt in a biosupport unit in Houston, the Roman's real body had been in a similar unit thousands of miles away across the Atlantic. Cassion had managed to work miracles, and using calcium bone matrix grown at the injury sites the skeleton was slowly rebuilt. The soft tissue damage was easy to repair by comparison, and required only a series of grafts and transplants.

Vitellan's head was an order of magnitude more difficult to even begin work upon. Rebuilding the skull was comparatively straightforward, and the upper spinal cord, pituitary, cerebellum, midbrain, and thalamus were not badly traumatized, being deep within the brain. Unfortunately the buffer that had saved them had been the cerebral cortex, which had ruptured and flowed like cream cheese underfoot in places.

It was early in the morning as Gulden concluded his briefing to Dellar and Burgess, and it had more of the sound of a coroner's report than the assessment of a critically ill patient.

"Much of the braincase contains sterile gel encased in a membrane grown from the body's tissues on a vat template," Gulden concluded. "The other brain tissue is in a number of low-temperature storage vats in the Deep Frigidarium."

The time was 4:30 A.M., and the marshal and Icekeeper were looking haggard.

"Where was the main damage to his brain?"

"The cerebrum is forty-seven percent rebuilt, and that portion has been returned to his skull."

"Is that enough for him to be, ah, viable?"

"Yes and no," said Gulden, almost playfully. "There is some control from the brain over body function. The main problem is that even if the skull had been undamaged, the tissue shows signs of massive oxygen starvation—about a half-hour's worth. The previous best was a stockbroker who was revived after eleven minutes facedown in the family spa. He is still alive, and has his self-awareness and some memories—"

"But?"

"But his IQ is down one hundred points."

"So the Master is dead."

"Well . . . nothing is quite so certain. What is left of the cerebrum does show a surprising degree of activity—considering."

"Dammit, a beard will grow on the face of a corpse, but that doesn't mean that it's alive! Is anyone home in that body?"

"The body is biologically alive. The brain is functionally dead. Is that sufficiently blunt?"

"Yes. Marshal, do we have any idea at all when and how this happened to the Centurion?"

"The Icekeeper's tests on the body indicate anytime between late October and late December. We saw the Centurion's realtime holo at that Corporate meeting, so the injuries were probably inflicted in the second half of December."

Dellar clasped his hands behind his back and walked over to the wall of glass laminate that looked out over the city center of Durvas. Distant lights twinkled serenely, in fact nobody in the small city yet knew about the second attack. Durvas Security had a charter that allowed it to handle most police functions, but a full report was due to be filed with London soon, and then all hell would break loose.

"This city, the Village itself worldwide," Dellar said with his back to them, "it's founded on the life of the Roman time traveler. Lord Wallace was only one of his servants, just as I am. Now that I am in the supreme chair, I learn that Vitellan's brain is pulp! It's just twenty-six years short of the two thousandth anniversary of his birth, when he's due to be revived before the world. Why me? Am I to preside over the presentation of this corpse? How can I explain why we can't do what a lot of filthy, hairy barbarians did successfully back in the ninth century?"

The marshal turned to Gulden. Frederick Gulden, like Burgess, had been isolated while a deputy, but far from being intimidated, he came to his new position with fresh ideas and enthusiasm.

"If you will permit me, Sir Peter," said Gulden after clearing his throat. Burgess turned away from the Durvas panorama and glared at him.

"Well, Dr. Gulden, what have you found in the medical database?"

"Many puzzles, sir, but solutions as well. Much of it was obvious, I can't understand why Dr. McLaren didn't—"

"Solutions?" said Burgess hopefully. "As in reviving the Centurion?"

"No, solutions in terms of massive, massive imprint exchange and new fixation techniques. Icekeeper McLaren was part of this conspiracy too, and his research notes show that he was experimenting with a method of imprint buffering that involved double brain imprinting from massive data buffers. His doctorate was in imprint systems analysis, as you must recall, so he was well qualified for such work. You had better sit down before I tell you the rest."

Dellar glared at him. "Cheap dramatics are for interactive soap holodramas. Get to the point."

"Lord Wallace was having a large-scale gating and imprint therapy done on his son."

Dellar sneered. "That's well known, he spent a large part of his personal fortune on the work."

His reaction disappointed Gulden, who snatched up a vid board and glanced at the next item on his list.

"Robert Wallace's comatose body is not accounted for."

"Yet. That may just be security arrangements."

"I'm working on the search," added Burgess.

"So, are there any other bombshells to be uncovered?" Dellar asked Gulden.

"Just one," replied Gulden, keying his vid board to display a report on the wallscreen. It contained scans of a human body with areas enhanced by knots of false color. "One fact that I *can* be sure of is that the body of the Centurion was not at all healthy, even before it was mangled."

His voice was sharp and his words clipped. His pride had been stung, and he was a very proud man.

Dellar blinked. "Few medieval people were ever particularly healthy," he ventured cautiously.

"Quite so, but whatever the cause, that body's immune system is severely depressed. There are strong concentrations of cancer-inhibiting drugs and viral carriers in his bloodstream, and a lot a small tumors. A more thorough scan that I have planned for tomorrow will probably reveal that he had terminal cancer."

"Terminal cancer?" echoed Dellar, his voice drained of intonation.

"I suggest that we send a team to where the Centurion lay from 1358," Gulden continued. "The natural radioactivity in rocks near where he was frozen may have given him accumulated tissue damage during his six hundred years of suspended animation. I am an experienced doctor, and I have seen patients in this sort of condition about four to six years after massive radiation exposure. In my *professional* opinion, Sir Peter, the late Icekeeper McLaren knew that the Centurion was dying, yet kept him unfrozen and comatose for at least five years, maybe six."

"Why?" asked the marshal, when Dellar did no more than press his lips together and stare at the floor.

"Indeed, why?" replied Gulden sharply. "It seems that I am not the only person on the Corporate with little need to know whatever is to be known. The key areas of McLaren's records are so heavily encrypted that it may take months of processing to decode them, but my overall impression is that my predecessor was conducting a massive, massive imprinting experiment with Lord Wallace, Robert Wallace, and the Centurion."

The Icekeeper's final bombshell did indeed make an impression on Sir Peter Dellar. The muscles of his face sagged and he swayed on his feet. Dragging his feet along the carpet, he walked to a chair and flopped down listlessly.

"What do we put in the report to London?" asked Burgess, who was also too weary to think straight by now.

"Lord Wallace and William Anderson can be part of the report, but the Centurion's body has no place there. It was not mentioned as a casualty in any attack, and it was not directly involved in yesterday's intrusion, was it?"

"Are we stalling for time, do we have anything to hope for?" asked Dellar desperately.

"Yes and yes," replied Gulden. "I swear it as the Icekeeper of Durvas."

Atlanta, Georgia: 30 January 2029, Anno Domini

Bonhomme had been in a strangely exhilarated mood for some hours. His handlers were pleased, as the great prophet from the past had just endured a week of black moods of despair and had refused to speak to anyone. Public appearances had been canceled, and the media were making their inevitable speculations. Paparazzi were loitering in increasing numbers with their high-tech cameras and intrusion drones, a sure sign that a scandal was suspected.

"I shall need a gun today," Bonhomme declared as casually and brightly as if ordering a white shirt. "Have it keyed to my palmprint so that I may shoot it, and it must shoot bullets that *annihilate*."

The gun was fetched, and Bonhomme fired several test shots from the Lanther tumble-shot into the wall of his hotel suite. They tore gaping, jagged holes in the plaster and he declared himself satisfied. His startled handlers had witnessed stranger behavior from him, however, and they thought little of it as a Luministe security team swept them away to an Atlanta stadium and the massed eyes, holonodes, and cameras waiting there. The gun would be part of some brilliant lesson in faith, they told each other. They were not wrong.

Across the continent, on a Los Angeles sidewalk, Vitellan sat hunched over his handheld television. The scratched LED screen was only inches from his nose and Bonhomme's words were a tinny cackle in his earpiece, with no overtones or bass. He was standing on a wide, white podium of marble, holding a short-recoil Lanther TS in one hand and gesturing with the other.

"And to me is said 'Give us a sign,' just as was said to Christ in the time that I was born. I say unto you, have faith! Do you have faith?"

A vast rumble of voices echoed back, "We have faith!"

"Do you see the light?" the prophet from the past cried.

"We see the light" overloaded Vitellan's earpiece.

Bonhomme held the gun aloft. The crowd was silent at once.

"Our good lord Jesus Christ did give a sign, as you will recall from the Gospels. He died, and he rose from the dead after three days. I will give you just such a sign, in His very name. Do you believe?"

"We believe!"

"Then stay, keep a vigil for three days with me. Keep my body undisturbed where it falls, call cameras to stay, for on the third day from this moment I shall get to my feet and stand before you.

"Will you help me witness to the world?"

"We will help you!"

"Do you believe?"

"We believe!"

Bonhomme raised the gun to his right temple in a smooth, sweeping gesture and fired. His head burst, and he collapsed to the marble.

Vitellan gasped, then swore in Latin and Old English. The subsequent screams and rioting went on for some minutes, but the Luministes had good crowd control at their rallies and Bonhomme's body lay undisturbed where it had fallen. The vigil began for the miracle on the third day.

Durvas, Britain: 2 February 2029, Anno Domini

An emergency sitting of the Village Corporate of Durvas confirmed Dellar as their new chief executive, and Burgess as the new marshal. Burgess was puzzled as he walked back to his office. He had been the deputy marshal during two massive security breaches, yet these had apparently been overlooked in the voting.

As was to be expected, the dashpad in what was now his office was flashing for attention. He ordered it into display mode and piped it through to his desk hologram projector. A cartoon billboard materialized in midair and he filtered the messages. Lucel's name stood out as he paged through a score of reports. Informants had tentatively placed her everywhere from Antarctica to Finland. He stopped at a display form that profiled a suspect landing at Gatwick Airport. She was a nightmare, Burgess fumed as he worked. With her the Luministes could hit Durvas at will, the Centurion's city would never be more than a spear carrier in the world's history—he caught himself and straightened, clenched fists sliding along his desk with a loud squeaking. Never give up, he told himself. Fight back, get out of your office, disguise your movements, be a real agent again.

"Beatrix, come in here for a moment," he said to the pickup that shimmered at the left-hand corner of his desk. The oak panel door to his left swung open.

"Book me on a flight to the Canary Islands tomorrow, Bea. Spread the word discreetly that I need a holiday—"

"So will Beatrix, when she wakes up."

The marshal's head jerked around, and he instantly noted both Lucel's mocking smile and a rail pistol.

"Just stand up slowly and walk around to one of those giltwood chairs," she ordered.

"I've already pressed the security pedal, the guards are on their way."

"Then I suggest you piss them off again—if you want to hear about how Lord Wallace was imprinting himself on the Centurion."

Burgess goggled at her, then looked down at the rail pistol again. If she had wanted him dead, he would be dead by now.

"Security! Kill that alert," he snapped to his desk manager, then ordered the desk to switch into dormant mode. He walked warily around to where Lucel had already seated herself.

"Were you behind that attack on the Deep Frigidarium?" he asked, his teeth barely moving.

"As it happens, not quite. I offered, but was turned down."

"Then who? Was it the Luministes?"

"No."

"We are running out of interested parties, Ms. Hunter."

"The Houston Ward Lords and the American branch of the Yakuza both had a grudge. Two of their best doctors and several hundred other folk of varying rank were killed under Durvas orders. Lord Wallace was covering some very suspicious tracks. He was being a little clumsy about it, though: America is not his turf, and he did not realize how easy it is to antagonize some very dangerous and resourceful people."

"Impossible," said the marshal smugly. "Anything like that would have come through me first."

"Wrong. Lord Wallace arranged it himself, merely by applying money. He bought contract hit squads through the Luministe accounts."

"Impossible," the marshal sighed again, confident that she was lying.

"I'm a Luministe agent—and traitor," she admitted. "I was in a position to know, *and* I was able to give the Ward Lords and the Yakuza a very convincing audit trail."

She suddenly smiled broadly, as if she had just taught a very important lesson to a very slow child. The marshal's calm had vanished, but he was unable to articulate his fury.

"They paid me a fortune," Lucel continued, "yet all that I had wanted to do in the first place was kill Lord Wallace. Kooky world, don't you think?"

"Who the hell are you really working for?" shouted the marshal, standing up and knocking his chair over. "The Luministes?"

"No. *I* am working for Vitellan, the Eternal Centurion of Durvas. True, I have made use of the Luministes for a long time. They're awfully earnest, just like all other religious folk that I've met."

The marshal picked up his chair and sat down again. He squeezed his eyes shut and gripped the armrests so tightly that the joints creaked.

"Lady, I'm rather strung out and probably in a fairly psychotic state just now. Just stop these fucking riddles and come to the point. Why are you here?"

"Whatever I say, you are not going to believe me," Lucel declared coyly, settling back in her chair and crossing her legs. "As soon as I've said my piece it will be *splat!*" She fired the rail pistol with a sharp clack. It struck a charcoal portrait of the late Lord Wallace squarely between the eyes.

"Hey! That's a Breugon original, it cost a hundred thousand—"

"Compared to what his Lordship did to Vitellan, that's nothing. Dr. Gulden, you can come in now!" she called.

Gulden entered with the missing director of surgery, Cassion. The Icekeeper was holding a command remote and Cassion was wearing a penal control collar.

"Dr. Cassion and I had a little talk with the Icekeeper last night," Lucel began to explain, but Burgess shouted her down.

"Gulden! You knew about this, you sat through an *entire* meeting of the Village Corporate without telling me anything!"

"My loyalty is to the Centurion, not you," said Gulden tersely.

"The point is that the Icekeeper of Durvas thinks that I am worth a fair hearing," Lucel cut in as Burgess was drawing breath. "Dr. Cassion, would you say your piece, please?"

The director of surgery seemed uninjured, yet he was pale and haggard. When he spoke the stress was evident in his voice.

"Marshal, what she says . . . is true," he said slowly. Burgess waited, but Cassion just stood staring blankly, his eyes slightly crossed.

"Dr. Cassion will be available for further consultations after your interview with Ms. Hunter," Gulden finally added. "Come on, Doctor, walkies."

The marshal watched as the Icekeeper escorted Gulden from the room, and Lucel could hear the grinding of his teeth from where she was sitting.

"Don't think too badly of Dr. Gulden," she said as she pocketed her rail pistol. "I approached the Icekeeper first because he would guarantee me a fair hearing if it involved Vitellan's safety. Icekeepers are like that."

"What? I'm marshal, damn you, Vitellan's safety is my life's work—"

"Marshals are merely vigilant where Vitellan is concerned. Icekeepers are psychopathic. Now, bear with me for one more riddle. Who organized the attack on the Durvas clinic last November?"

"The Luministes, I suppose, but you're probably going to tell me I'm wrong so do it now."

"Yes, you're wrong. The Luministes only did the attacking; Icekeeper McLaren did the organizing."

Burgess gasped so hard that he breathed some of his own saliva. He flopped back in his chair coughing, with the heels of his palms pressed into his eyes. When he spoke again his voice was barely a whisper. "Are you going to tell me any details, or do you want to play more humiliation games? I can have security send in a whip and a leather cat suit if it makes you happier."

Lucel giggled, then shrugged. "Sounds like fun, but this is meant to be a business meeting. As you know, some of the Corporate wanted Vitellan kept frozen until the appointed year of 2054, others wanted him revived to help with the crisis of the Luministes. Six years ago an agreement was reached to revive his bodily functions without consciousness, primarily for surgical work. He was carrying a lot of battle injuries, and had been drinking a degraded, caustic version of the Oil of Frosts for a long time."

"I was not on the Corporate then, but I know about that decision. Whenever the Centurion was to be actually awakened, it was to be in perfect health: no pain, no infections, and no parasites. The surgery and healing took a few weeks, then he was refrozen."

Burgess clasped his fingers beneath his chin, waiting for Lucel to fall into the trap.

"He was not refrozen," said Lucel.

"Damn!" he snarled, looked away from her.

"Sorry?"

"Nothing, go on."

"McLaren refroze a cadaver of identical build with a mask bonded onto his face and dermal mockup scars in all the right places. Lord Wallace, Cassion, Anderson, and McLaren had set up a tight little team of systems medics and agents from outside Durvas. Over six years McLaren imprinted Lord Wallace's whole consciousness on the Centurion's brain, leaving only gate-access memories so that his total overlay could mimic being the Centurion. If it had not been for the Luministe raid he would have his own life functions terminated during a final imprinting session, and been awakened as the Centurion himself. Don't worry about reviving Vitellan's crushed body, Marshal, it's only a stale version of Lord Wallace."

Burgess treated her horrifying revelations with grudging acceptance. She knew so much about what should have been secret that this story was probably true as well. He was eager to know more, in spite of himself.

"So what about that Luministe imposter that he paraded in front of us at the Village Corporate meeting last December?" he asked.

"I'm coming to that. Lord Wallace had everything sewn up, but there was only one thing that he did not understand: the fanatical loyalty of the Durvas Icekeepers. Any of the other ten dozen Durvas Icekeepers would have shouted the truth from the manor's chimneypots, but for some reason McLaren kept quiet and helped. I don't know why, but it *must* have been something to do with Vitellan's welfare. Can you help here—and please, no tricks."

Air hissed between the marshal's teeth as he drew breath. He took his time, thought carefully, looked to a portrait of Icekeeper Guy Foxtread for inspiration, then decided that he had no alternative. He had to share information with Lucel Hunter.

"I probably need my head read for telling you this, but . . . the Centurion's body was frozen near rocks of relatively high natural radiation in 1358. That did a lot of damage to his tissues over six centuries, and Icekeeper Gulden tells me that McLaren and Dr. Cassion probably had quite a battle to keep his body alive from 2022 to the first Luministe attack."

Lucel sat forward eagerly. "Yes, yes! *The good Icekeeper.*"

"Good Icekeeper? He was bloody awful, he was the first traitor in 120 appointments—"

"No, just the opposite. McLaren was behind the entire scheme, he probably planned it back in 2016 when he first realized that Vitellan would die of cancer only a few years after being unfrozen. Lord Wallace was his stooge. While his Lordship was being imprinted on Vitellan, the same resources were being used to imprint Vitellan onto Robert Wallace. McLaren was sending Vitellan to safety, into a young body in near-perfect health. I've done some rough calculations, and they show that two total overlays would cost only about five percent more than one—if done together. The difference is noise. I doubt that our late peer knew the truth about Vitellan's condition until after McLaren died. What else can you tell me?"

"The imprinting cost a lot. There are vast amounts of credit missing from the Durvas books, billions. We are not bankrupt, but our economic health will be delicate for at least a decade. The money has been hard to trace, but it appears to have gone to medical and CPU service wholesalers. Whole-brain imprinting would account for it. How lucky for McLaren that Robert Wallace was at hand, and in a comatose state."

"I'd bet anything that McLaren staged the car bombing and had the boy drugged and abducted to the clinic—where he was sedated and mocked up to look braindead. Recent scans of Robert's body show only cosmetic surgery. His personality was murdered to become a host for Vitellan's mind."

Burgess whistled. "Icekeepers are dangerous where the Centurion's welfare is concerned, that's a Durvas tradition, but this is the worst example of it that I've ever seen. All the Icekeepers I've known have been a bit strange, maybe it's in the job outline."

"Maybe I'd make a good Icekeeper," Lucel responded. "You male chauvinists have never appointed a woman in two thousand years. Anyway, by November both overlays were complete, but Vitellan's body was close to death. McLaren contacted the local Luministe operative—me—and said that if we were quick we could abduct Bonhomme's greatest potential rival. We acted without authority and attacked. If we'd asked for authority it would have been refused because Lord Wallace was pulling the Luministe strings all along, but we were not to know that—officially."

"I—ah, go on."

"There's a funny thing about that attack. We did not let off the bomb that brought down the building and crushed Vitellan's body—"

"So that's when it happened!"

"Yes, and it must have been McLaren destroying evidence. I do know one thing for a fact: McLaren did not intend us to take Robert's body. That was just an accident. My group leader was confused, she thought she had abducted the Centurion. My own role in this was . . . covert. There was a lot of confused and secret dealing with the body of the Centurion in Durvas, and I found that the best way to keep tabs was to work for the enemy. I wanted Vitellan safe, so I rescued him from the Luministe hospital in Paris. Knowing all that I did, though, I was reluctant to return him to Durvas."

"So, the pieces are fitting into place with the exception of you, Ms. Lucel Hunter. Who are you? What is your interest in all this?"

"Ah, now that would be telling."

Burgess got up from the chair and walked across to his desk. He waved a recorder into life, then realized that Lucel was still there and might not approve. He killed the recorder with another wave.

"So what now?" he asked.

Lucel stood up and took the rail pistol from her jacket, then walked across to the portrait of Guy. She loaded another shot into the magazine while looking up at Vitellan's old friend and servant, then put the gun away.

"I had to make sure that your standard of care was back up to the standard of 1358," she said with a gesture to the portrait. "The Centurion is alive, as a total overlay on a host brain."

"So, the overlay was the man I met at a meeting of the Corporate. Nice chap, very charismatic and sensible, I thought. Nevertheless, I repeat: what now? The Village has failed him, Lord Wallace failed him, I failed him, every stupid bastard in Durvas employment has failed him. Only Icekeeper McLaren and you haven't failed him, and I'm surprised that you even bothered to come here and talk to us. We're no use to Vitellan."

Lucel leaned against the desk and shook her head. "Try asking why I'm here again."

Burgess exhaled loudly. "If the Centurion is alive . . . you would probably want the resources of the Village to protect him. That's fairly silly of you, given our track record, but—"

"Precisely!" cried Lucel, turning and smashing a fist down on his desk. "If Vitellan is to come back here, there must be *no* petty power struggles and disputes, *every single file and database* must be opened and decrypted, every account must be scrutinized. Durvas betrayed Vitellan, now Durvas must make it up to him."

"Now just a minute, I had no part in any of that!" the marshal exclaimed angrily.

"Maybe not, but the Village Corporate needs to be restructured so that secret plots cannot *ever* happen again. There is more at stake than just Vitellan."

"Allow me to congratulate you on your nomination to the Village Corporate of Durvas," Burgess responded.

"I—I'll take that seriously, Mr. Burgess," responded Lucel, caught off-guard.

"It was *meant* to be taken seriously, Ms. Hunter."

Los Angeles: 18 February 2029, Anno Domini

Lucel sauntered slowly down the soiled, stained concrete LA sidewalk. A drab bundle of rage held up a grimy foam cup without raising his head as she passed.

"Spare change lady?" he asked in a servile wheeze.

"Stop waving that filthy thing at me and get to your feet, Vitellan."

Vitellan looked up, suspicious and alert. His left hand slid to a well-maintained Ruger under his jacket.

"You makin' mistake, lady."

"My dataspex show the IR profile of that gun under your coat. You will notice that my hands are on my hips and not anywhere near a weapon. Come on, I know it's you."

"How?"

"You've got an implant."

"Lie. Try again."

"Ah, shit. Look, okay, I'm sorry about before. Your camo is good, I couldn't have picked it, except that you have an implant."

"Not so," said Vitellan. "Had scanning. Cost of ninety dollars at Angelo's EM and Pulse."

"Angelo would not have found mine. I implanted it as a biosleeper on the way to Moscow."

"Where?"

"Remember when I pinched the nerve in your wrist, back in the clinic in Houston? It set off an enzyme-clocked timer. It cycles every few hours with randomly timed activations and a preset frequency progression. The implant forms up into conductors and circuits, pumps out a couple of pulses, then closes down and dissolves its conductors. You could catch it in a scan shop if you were lucky, but you'd have to be *very* lucky. I found you nine days after you made a break at the airport in Houston—that was clever, I was impressed."

By now perhaps two dozen other homeless men and women were shambling slowly over, converging toward them. Lucel noticed glints here and there from beneath the drab overcoats and ragged blankets of the sun bears. They stopped, in a semicircle of five groups: each group could target Lucel without hitting another sun bear in the background.

" 'Bout time you moved on, lady."

A polite but firm voice, all authority with none of the bravado of the gang cells. The speaker's coat hung open, displaying a worn but clean MK-760 that was old enough to have seen action in the Vietnam War.

Lucel looked back to Vitellan. "Well?"

"She's okay," he said as he slowly, stiffly got to his feet. He nudged a bundle with his foot. "Div my gear."

"You sure she's cool, Vince?" asked the sun bear with the submachine gun.

"If not, be back. You lead, Wes."

Lucel had parked her hire van around the corner. A sun bear cell lounged nearby, alert but looking at ease. One raised his thumb to Lucel as she pulsed the wing doors open, and she nodded back. Vitellan laughed softly as they drove away.

"*You* hire *my* sun bears to guard *your* car," he said without prompting.

"I just don't believe you, Vitellan. I let you out of my sight for a day or two and you skip town and set up as a street gang leader in LA."

"Like Cutty Wren gang in Londinium. I had dealings with them. Black market for conversion of booty into sesterces."

"Oh, great. Ancient Rome can even teach LA gangs how to operate better."

"Where we going?"

"To get you a shower and some decent clothes, then give you a suite of imprints to—"

"No. Don't want evasion imprint shit. I liked with sun bears. Was safe. Full story now or stop, go back."

Lucel had stopped at a traffic light. She hunched over the steering wheel, squeezing until her knuckles turned white.

"I'm sorry, I'm sorry, I'm sorry. The Luministes know that you are still alive, and my cover as a Luministe double agent is gone. Their agents are still after you."

The lights changed and Lucel drove off. Vitellan noticed that she kept glancing at a cream and gold box Velcroed to the carpet in front of the power select. All of its displays glowed a steady green.

"You spoil my cover. Why?"

"Because they were close behind. They found a crushed roadspike in the quarry. Your work?"

"My work."

"They've switched their search to LA. That is all I know, but they are on to you, make no mistake about that."

"I repeat, where are going?"

"Where are *we* going, don't forget your subjects and objects. We're going to a motel about fifteen miles from here by freeway. Did you learn English without an imprinter?"

"Used—I used imprinter minimally. Dangerous to depend."

"On them."

Vitellan watched the LA streetscape pass, his eyes blank.

"Of everyone, you not lie. Conceal truth, yes, but lie, no. Apologies required."

"Think nothing of it. Whooo! You have a great whiff going."

"Profession," said Vitellan proudly. "Good sun bear."

"I thought I'd lost you when the ramjet took off. I was all set to get to Luministes to hold the attack when I saw Baker's security guards dashing about and looking worried. That was when I knew you had managed something on your own. How did you get all the way here? You were spotted leaving the airport carpark with a roadspike."

"Killed roadspike in quarry. Self-defense."

"Not guilty on that charge. Go on."

"Stole, ah, his bike and guns. Hard to talk and . . . be mobile. Imprints you did faded. SkyPlaz doctors tampered with unit, maybe. Lord Wallace had bribed them. Perhaps."

"No perhaps, I saw his records after he died."

"He died?"

"He died. It's a messy story, I'll tell you later. He bribed Hall and Baker to give you blank imprint boosters so that you would think you were experiencing large-scale imprint attenuation symptoms. They weren't bad folk, but they got theirs. Hall is char on a Houston roadway and Baker is at the bottom of the North Atlantic food chain right now. How did you learn to ride roadspike wheels?"

"Crashed and fell off until stable. Rode to Los Angeles. Very hard going."

"Hard going? I'll say. Sixteen hundred miles plus, and the PsychoSpikes hang out near El Paso. How did you cope with them?"

"Killed two, lost patience. Or is it lost patience, killed two?"

"No matter, I'm impressed. You say you did it all with your commercial imprints faded out?"

"Yes. Very exciting—it was."

At the motel Lucel examined Vitellan's Ruger. It was clean and smelled of oil. The slide moved smoothly and the magazine held its full fifteen rounds.

"This is a P-85 combat pistol, it's about forty years old," she called to him. "Did you kill the PsychoSpikes with it?"

"Shotgun I used for that. Always dispense—no, discard weapon after killing."

"I was about to suggest just that. Would you prefer me to speak in Latin?"

"English, okay. What now?"

"I'll give you imprints for better English and the cyclopedia imprint."

"No. Imprints betray me."

"Not so, Vitellan. Your doctors betrayed you, the imprints are just a tool. You need English, you really do. Every time you open your mouth you draw attention to yourself."

"*No!* Speak English like Chaucer telling *Canterbury Tales* if not make deliberate mistakes. Train myself to make mistakes. Luministes not dumb. Assassins vector on man with fourteenth-century accent. Stand out like balls on dog unless make mistakes. Work damn hard to speak English badly!"

"Yes, now that I think about it, even after the imprint Norton gave you on the maglev your English was perfect but your accent was very unusual. A real Old English accent. Fascinating."

"Get point?"

"Yes, but . . . I could arrange an English imprint customized to overlay an American accent."

"Accent? You sure?"

"Positive. Most imprints teach words only. Accents are very expensive, so most people don't bother. How would you like to sound like a Californian?"

"Maybe . . . but no cyclopedia."

"Deal! You seem to have picked up enough modern living not to need Streetwise or a cyclopedia anymore. I'll disable your implant and give us both masks, then we'll do Disneyland and Knott's Berry Farm, together, like lovers. I'm using you for bait, Vitellan. The Luministe assassin behind my own suite of terrorist imprints is after you. I want to lure her here, then force her to become visible."

"What lovers doing, ah, . . . damnshit, what English for *feriatus?*"

" 'On vacation' is American usage, 'on holiday' if you're British. You were saying?"

"Never mind, too hard. Take imprint, talk later."

Vitellan lay down to take the vocabulary and grammar imprint while Lucel ordered a fashionable outfit to fit his size and downloaded an accent imprint. Several hours later the imprints were sufficiently stable for a few days of use, and he stripped off the last of his sun bear clothing and took a long, hot shower. He emerged wearing a towel around his waist and drying his hair with another. Lucel noticed several new scars, all roughly stapled but healed.

Lucel was lying across the double bed, propped on one elbow. The expression on her face puzzled Vitellan, it did not fit his image of Lucel Hunter. The top three buttons of her blouse were undone, and even though he had seen her naked in the surgical unit at SkyPlaz, his eyes were still drawn to the V of burgundy polygloss over white skin. She was a big-boned but lean girl, almost all muscle and no fat. He kept wondering why she disturbed him now. Perhaps it was her motivation, rather than her appearance.

"I've got a feeling that you're going to make some more helpful suggestions about what modern lovers do on vacation," he said with a newly imprinted American accent.

"I've been looking forward to being lovers *feriatus* with you for a long time, Vitellan."

For all that they had been through, Vitellan had somehow never suspected that seduction would ever feature in their relationship. He had seen professional warriors as dedicated as Lucel in past centuries, and they tended to be suspicious of sex. To them it was a distraction and a vulnerability, to be treated as a mechanical release if indulged in at all. He also had his own emotional baggage to carry from 1358.

"Mixing business with pleasure . . ." He shook his head. "It's dangerous. You are beautiful, Lucel, without doubt. But . . ."

"But?"

"But dalliance is what it would be. I—ah, hurt my heart badly in 1358. I was forced to leave a loving, beautiful woman because I would . . . what are the words? I would bring disgrace upon her."

"The Countess de Hussontal," said Lucel, expressionless.

"Yes. You must have imprint of *Durvas Chronicles,* of course."

"No, I studied the *Chronicles* when I was a little girl in 2008, before imprinting had been invented and before you had been 'announced.' I am impressed with you, as always. You are still being faithful to a woman whose very grave is little more than a mound of earth and broken marble."

Vitellan sat on the other side of the bed and put his hand over Lucel's.

"Then you must understand. My lover of 1358 is still alive to me, I saw her only a few months ago."

Lucel's fingers twisted around and stroked the palm of Vitellan's hand. The first affection she has shown to me, he thought, but he began to slowly withdraw his hand. She firmly but gently grasped him by the wrist.

"Vitellan, chéri, I have been faithful to you as well," she said, staring straight into his unblinking eyes. "I have been waiting six hundred and seventy years to see you again."

The motel suite had been designed for lovers in search of privacy, whatever their circumstances. There was no danger, as Lucel's contract security was on patrol, and she had five other rooms booked in the motel, all with decoy couples passing the hours in much the same way as she and Vitellan. They did not emerge as the afternoon became evening, and the tickets to Disneyland lay unused in Lucel's pocket.

When they did talk, Lucel told him of how the 1358 Countess of Hussontal had unwittingly started a tradition of love for her frozen rescuer on her deathbed. Her brother had finally confessed that Vitellan had not been killed in the hunt for Jacque Bonhomme, but safely frozen in one of Tom Greenhelm's earlier experimental ice chambers. She had in turn told her daughter Louise, whom Vitellan had rescued. For a time both the men and women of the Hussontals had shared the secret of Vitellan's existence and resting place, but when one of the men had died without passing on the family secret to his son, the women decided upon silence henceforth. Jealousy involving the frozen man in the Alps had already surfaced several times and soured three marriages.

The oral tradition of Vitellan's story had thus been passed down through the Hussontal family's women in spite of wars, invasions, revolutions, and changes in society. The family had been genetically predisposed to girls, and there had been many daughters to carry the story through the centuries. Women marrying into the family turned out to be just as enthusiastic for the ancient hero of Meaux and Marlenk. Some had merely passed the story of their ancestors' hero down to their own daughters without feeling any real affection for him, others had cherished him as an exiled lover who was still alive somewhere. Some even told their husbands, but the tale never seemed to catch the imagination of the men. The French map to Vitellan's sanctuary was preserved in the family library's archives, but it was burned in the revolution that burst upon France in 1789. Through the following seventy years of exile the women of the Hussontal family preserved their secret story while living in Italy, Scotland, and England. They even tried to obtain a copy of the map held in Durvas, but the Icekeeper of the time made it clear to the Hussontal exiles that they had failed as primary keepers of Vitellan's trust, and that Durvas had now taken back the honor of watching over the Master. The Hussontals had fled the French Revolution with a large part of their fortune, however, and they invested wisely and prospered during their decades abroad.

"The family returned to France in 1858," Lucel whispered as they lay together in the darkness and the unsleeping rumble of Los Angeles continued outside. "The women of the time organized themselves to return separately, as a secret pilgrimage. A grandmother, mother, and two daughters started off from Durvas in spring, and rode in a carriage to Dover, then took a steamboat to Calais. They had an early camera, and I have the pictures in a card in my slacks."

"I'd like to see them . . . tomorrow," mumbled Vitellan dreamily.

"They traveled past Paris, followed the River Marne for a while, and even spent a night in Meaux."

"It was burned."

"It's been rebuilt. They stopped at the site of the Hussontal family castle where two of their menfolk had already returned to buy back parts of the old estate and the ruins of the castle. In early winter the whole family traveled on to Marlenk in Switzerland for what was supposedly a holiday."

"Have I really been a party to six centuries of simulated adultery?" asked Vitellan.

Lucel rolled on top of him, pinning his arms as if to prevent him from escaping. He could not help but notice how similar her mannerisms were to those of his original Countess of Hussontal, and he wondered if it was something genetic. With his cyclopedia faded, his knowledge of genetics was patchy.

"Think of us as the backup infrastructure of your time boat," she said gravely. "As it turned out, you needed a backup."

"Your personal dedication to me begins to make sense now."

"It nearly didn't happen. My mother was a dedicated feminist and never breathed a word of your story to me. She told my grandmother that she did not want me to be a slave to some sexist tradition of emotional enslavement and that I should be free to choose my own destiny. My grandmother decided that freedom to choose my destiny included the story of a frozen man in the Swiss mountains, and a couple of days after I got my first Internet account—for my seventh birthday as I recall—Grandmama sent me nearly half a megabyte of unsolicited family history that she had typed with her . . . what did they call them, word processor I think. Of course I was an unreconstructed romantic even at that tender age, so the tradition survived yet another generation. I was just a teenager when you were dug out of the Swiss ice and moved back to England, and ah, but I was thrilled and devastated, all at once. I filed past when your body was on display for a week in the British museum before being returned to Durvas. You were just a blur in the ice, but it was *you*. I kept buying tickets and going past with the crowds, I took vids of you time and again. I knew that I might even meet you if I lived to 2054, but I would be in my sixties by then and probably not very alluring. Perhaps my own daughter might come to love you, but then my own daughter might turn out like my mother and not give a hoot. I considered not having children, trying to charm you myself in 2054, yet there would be thirty years between us. Would you want me? Ah, it tore me apart, I was a very, very romantic young girl.

"When the Luministe cult started I was one of the first to join. You were the only sleeper that they could possibly be talking about in all that preaching about a prophet from the past, and if I was an important Luministe I would be important to you when you woke in 2054. Then Bonhomme was discovered, and the Luministes embraced him as their prophet. I knew the truth about him from the Hussontal traditions, but I was only one voice and nobody would have listened. Suddenly it dawned on me that you might be revived early to fight yet again with the evil leader of the Jacques. If that happened you would need a dedicated spy who was trusted completely by the enemy.

"I volunteered to train as a Luministe assassination agent and spy. I trained hard, and had combat enhancement surgery and implants, in fact I became so good that the Luministes paid for me to be given two years of stabilized imprints from the great and notorious terrorist Vanda Louise Mattel."

A light began to flash on her dataspex on the bedside table. Lucel checked it, then spoke a few words of code.

"All's well," she reported.

"What was that?"

"I have two contract cells watching this place. They don't know about each other, and both groups are reporting that we are being watched but not threatened."

"So we are in danger."

"You specifically."

"From other imprint pupils of Mattel?"

"There was only one other, a girl named Gina Rossi. She led the hit on the Antarctic time ship, and was killed when she blew up the Mawson Institute. No, the vector incoming is Mattel herself: as cunning, ruthless, and deadly as the devil on steroids."

"I've studied modern terrorist techniques, Lucel. Many groups, including the Luministes, use imprint gating to give assassins obsessive, blind dedication to their missions. Their assassins simply *can't* turn traitor. Did they do that to you?"

"Yes, but there was a catch: I had already turned traitor. They fixated me on killing all false prophets from the past, but I did not regard you as a false prophet." She rolled off him and lay on her back with her hands clasped behind her head. "I knew about imprints, and imprints can be adjusted with certain meditation techniques before they are bedded down. When the treatment had finished, my first priority was to keep you safe, but I was also vectored on killing 'false prophets from the past'—Jacque Bonhomme, as far as I was concerned. One day I would have done just that, but he beat me to it and did the job himself."

Vitellan sat up in bed and looked at the radio-clock display. It was 4:47 A.M.

"You have a plan, and it involves me as bait," he said, his throat dry and his voice flat.

"Yes, it involves you flying out to Australia in about three hours," replied Lucel, reaching up and rubbing a hand along his back. "It's called a filter tactic: draw the enemy to a specific location, then run fast. Their warhead unit reacts fast, too fast, blows cover and gets targeted by us. You will leave here with a girl from one of my decoy couples, her name's Jilly Stevenson. You and Jilly will take a SOMS to Melbourne and play tourist, okay?"

"But—"

"Just do it. No buts. Play the part with her: hold hands, kiss, buy each other little presents, sleep together, and make sure that you screw her! Okay? I don't want any hotel staff changing the sheets next morning and reporting to some contract gang cell that the honeymooners who were oh-so-cute in public were not doing it in private. This is war, Vitellan, and this is how you have to fight."

"If we live through this, my countess, knight, and lover, remind me to explain the symbol on the *Deciad* scroll to you. It is so simple, yet behind it is something wonderful."

"Why not now? We have a little more time."

"Because one should avoid fighting a war on more than one front," he whispered, his voice trailing away as if the very words fatigued him.

Jilly and Vitellan set off in an autocab before sunrise, negotiated their way through the airport's baggage check-in and boarding security scans, then boarded a SOMS. She was a little shorter than Lucel, and quite a lot thinner. She said that she had won several gymnastics competitions while at school, and now taught aerobics when not doing contract work. As they settled into their seats she activated a portable cloaker.

"Good work, but you're looking too cool," Jilly said, looking Vitellan in the eyes. "Drop a Latin word, look a bit confused now and then. You're meant to be bait, okay?"

"Yeah, okay," replied Vitellan, unsure of how to react or feel. "I'm new at this."

"It shows," replied Jilly. "Maybe it's why she chose you."

Melbourne, Australia: 20 February 2029, Anno Domini

They landed in Melbourne's evening, but with their body clocks ready for a morning's sightseeing. After booking into a Southbank hotel they had dinner and strolled beside the river in the balmy air of late summer. The waters of the river were black and placid, hardly reflecting any high-lights from the glittering lights of the city.

Jilly was dressed in cheek-shorts, a scoopneck T-shirt, and jogger sandals. Her nipples stood out beneath the white cloth, both casting conical shadows. Vitellan's tracksuit was made of the same light airtrack hemp and cotton, and he felt cool and exposed, as if he were naked. His thoughts tumbled along in a giddy dance: I'm holding hands with a complete stranger in a city that should not have existed in my lifetime, and very soon we'll be fornicating in a hotel room as high as the clouds. Sheer desire drenched him like warm drizzle, and he noticed that Jilly's fingers were kneading against his.

"What was our hotel?" he asked, even though he had been absorb-ing every detail of the riverside plaza and could have returned to the hotel blindfolded.

"The Centenary South," she replied at once. Eagerness, Vitellan wondered? "Do you want to go back?"

"Well . . . we've been out being seen for two hours."

"And you can't wait to prove that we're into good, healthy con-summation?"

"Now that you mention it, no, I can't."

"Hey, then let's do it, that's what we're paid for."

She slid an arm around his waist and stepped in front of him, then pressed her lips against his and thrust her tongue between his teeth. A party boat passed on the river, and the revelers cheered and shone torches on them as they stood rubbing their thighs together.

"I suppose it was built in 2000," Vitellan said to cover his embarrassment as they entered the hotel foyer.

"Yeah, guess so."

"Big party year."

"I thought it sucked," Jilly said, her voice suddenly sharp. "My dad's business crashed when the change-of-year prefix screwed his computer database. By the time he was back in action the competition had moved in on his customers."

The doorlock clacked free to a wave of the desk card. Jilly reached in and switched on the light as Vitellan pushed the door open. The door clunked shut behind them, a firm, secure commitment of what was to come.

They stared at each other across a few feet of Center-red carpet while the cream quilt of the double bed gleamed in the recessed halogen lighting.

"Hey, is this hard work or what?" Jilly giggled, then raised each foot in turn and unbuckled her sandals.

Vitellan responded by removing his tracksuit top. Jilly whistled at his roughly stapled scars.

"Been a bad little boy," Vitellan explained.

"Hell, I can show you mine," she said as she pulled her top up over her head to reveal taut, conical breasts with large dark nipples. She put her hands on her waist and thrust a hip at Vitellan. "But mine ain't scars."

Vitellan was still trying to shake his tracksuit pants free of his feet as they coupled across the bed. Jilly was all long nails, grappling legs, teeth and giggles. She shrieked and laughed at their reflections in the ceiling mirror while Vitellan wondered how Lucel would react to the lurid evidence that he had followed her orders to the very letter. Jilly had excellent stamina, and did not tire for a long time. She insisted on staying underneath so that she could watch their images in the mirror.

It was the evening of the next day when Vitellan awoke from a fit-ful doze, his body insisting that it was time for bed but with moonlight streaming in through the windows. Jilly was in the shower already, preparing for a night on the town with him. There were spots of blood on the sheets, all from the cuts that her false nails had made on Vitellan's back. A detached nail lay among the sheets. Vitellan grinned ruefully, picked it up and tossed it across to where Jilly's gossamer-fine UV body-suit lay across a chair. The fabric stiffened for a moment as the nail landed, then sagged.

Vitellan blinked. Lucel had clothes that did that! The fabric was normally flexible, but stiffened like a thin shell of steel when struck sharply. It was enough to stop a knife or a fist, and would take the kick out of most conventional low-velocity bullets as well. His heart thump-ing, he stood up and took a pen from the commdesk. Holding it like a dagger he stabbed down, overhand. The gossamer fabric snapped rigid, then relaxed. The point of the pen had made only a tiny impression. He picked up the false nail and turned it over. It was heavy, and there were little grooves and flanges underneath. A Luministe weapon, a very, very exclusive Luministe weapon. Jilly was a girl who looked barely out of her teens, yet let slip that she remembered the millennium year. Lucel had said that she was imprinted with Vanda Mattel's tacticals, so Vanda Mat-tel would think like Lucel . . . or try to outthink her. Successfully. Too successfully.

Jilly/Vanda was in the shower with nine explosive nails on her hands, so attack was out. Vitellan pulled on his tracksuit pants and top, checked for his wallet, then slipped on his joggers and pressed the Vel-cro straps down. Battle tactics, his subconscious whispered at him. He picked up the gossamer armor-suit and jogger sandals. Should run with them, but they might have a beacon built in, he thought, but no dataspex, she probably has them in the shower, making contact about what Lucel was doing. Too bad, no certainties. He opened the door. It would click distinctly when the hydraulics closed it. He opened it all the way, then let go and ran.

Vitellan took the fire escape. He pounded down, four steps at a time, jumping six to the landings, counting floors. A door clacked open high above him, then boomed closed again. Was she coming or—express mode in the elevator, she probably had a key for it. Know the battlefield. First floor has a lounge and balcony overlooking the Southbank plaza. Vitellan slammed the release bar down on the first-floor fire door and ran for the balcony bar. An alarm began blaring as he entered, and the doors to the open-air balcony automatically shut and locked. Vitellan flung Mattel's bodysuit and sandals aside, swept the glasses from a granite top table and tried to lift it. The table was bolted down. Hands seized him.

"What the fuck do you think—"

Vitellan drove his elbow back into the man's nose and wrenched at the tabletop again. The filigree alloy base snapped. He flung the marble top at a glass panel and it burst in a hailstorm of glass pellets. Vitellan crunched through the debris out onto the balcony and vaulted the stone railing. He had expected the twelve-foot drop but not the pedestrian who broke his fall. Vitellan limped away past concrete and tile tubs of palms and cycads. Up on the bridge, blue and red lights were flashing and people were hurrying about. He began limping for the edge of the river when a passing jogger in a dark blue tracksuit exploded with a sound like a heavy rock dropped into an iced-over pond. Vitellan ran, dove into the darkened water, then doubled back and swam along beside the embankment. Somewhere behind him an explosion reverberated through the water. He surfaced to breathe then dove again, crossing the river in the shelter of the arches of Princess Bridge.

When he emerged from the water on the northeast side of the bridge Vitellan was dripping water but still fully clothed and wearing his joggers. Sweat from a hard run, nobody should notice, he thought hopefully. He climbed the steps to Swanston Street. Police lights were flashing, people were milling to watch whatever was going on and speculating about the explosions. He walked quickly down to a T-intersection facing a mall. Cars were waiting for the lights to change—

and at the front was an Australian version of a roadspike on a Harley-Davidson. "No problemo," Vitellan said under his breath as he walked out across the road and between the cars.

The roadspike's jacket had INCOMING LOSERS stenciled on the back. Vitellan caught him from behind in a headlock and used his weight to twist his victim and the bike over to crash to the roadway. With a kick to the roadspike's face that he hoped would be adequate, Vitellan turned and wrenched the still-idling Harley upright, gunned the engine and engaged the gears. He roared off against the red light and a traffic camera flashed to record the violation.

"Fucking bastard!" bellowed out behind him, and something heavy and painful struck his right shoulder.

With little traffic sense and some confusion about what side of the road Australians drove on, Vitellan made a difficult and unpredictable quarry for the police as he entered the Swanston Street Mall and weaved his way among the screaming pedestrians and clanging green tramcars. Police ran to bar his way, then scattered as he charged them. Laser-lit fountains, trees hung with fairy lights, buskers, and even a Morris dancing troupe passed in a surreal stream of light and music.

"Morris dancing, last saw that in May 1358," he said to himself as he passed the floodlit museum. "Museum, statues of Saint Joan on a gelding and Saint George on a stallion out front, museum means end of the mall, one mile more and there's a big university and I hope that tourist imprint knew what it was telling me."

Sirens seemed to be everywhere as Vitellan pulled into the grounds of the University of Melbourne and ran the Harley into a stand of bushes. As he limped away into the maze of buildings and gardens he realized that a short knife was lodged in his shoulder. With some effort he managed to reach around and pull it out. His shoulder was throbbing more noticeably now, and it hurt like fire to move his arm but he hefted the knife gratefully.

"At least I'm armed, and at least I'm left-handed," he tried to reassure himself as he limped across a lawn. "And she can't track me—oh shit!"

He realized that Vanda was sure to have put a beacon on him, if only through blind paranoia. Where to hide a beacon? Tracksuit? Shoes? He entered an underground carpark, ignoring a challenge from the automated security system. After three cars he saw an unzipped tote bag with jogging gear visible. The butt of the roadspike's knife shattered the window, and he limped out into the darkness again with at least five different alarms blaring and shrieking behind him. He stripped and changed into the stolen gear amid dense bushes near the library while university security guards ran about with torches. The tracksuit and joggers were slightly big, but still a passable fit. He noticed the lights of the guards were moving away to the east. That was where he had abandoned his stolen bike; they had probably found it and were waiting for him to try to use it to escape. Vitellan dropped the bag in the loading bay of a building in the Faculty of Medicine, then broke a laminate plastic slat from a packing case and crawled back to wait behind a garbage skip.

Leave bait, stalk the stalker: he repeated the words to himself as he tied a strip of cloth to the end of the slat. It had roughly the weight and dimensions of a pilum, he noticed as he tied the knife to the other end. Vanda Mattel has seven of those explosive nails left. Two had been expended and one was in his pocket, in the tracksuit. He hurried back to the bag and retrieved the false fingernail. Back behind the skip he untied the knife from his improvised pilum as he struggled to recall a demonstration that Lucel had given him as they rode the maglev to Moscow. Squeeze the sides together until it clicks, then push down in the middle until it clicks again. That arms it. Push down in the middle a second time to disarm. To launch . . . to launch? No matter, no launch was required. He cut a groove in the end of the slat, armed the nail and jammed it in. Now he was ready to fight.

Vitellan waited. The knife wound in his back ached insistently, but had stopped bleeding. The city beyond the university seemed to be alive with sirens, and police drones whispered overhead several times. The last surviving centurion of Imperial Rome cowered beneath flattened cardboard and foamed plastic packing, his infrared image smothered from both the drones and Mattel's dataspex. Vanda Mattel. Not an hour ago they had been in bed together, he could scarcely believe it. He fingered the lovebites on his neck. His fingers touched something soft beneath the skin. A little cyst? A little cyst, just below one of the lovebites.

With his heart pounding Vitellan slowly drew the point of the roadspike's knife along the skin of his neck. Blood was sticky on his fingers as he ignored the pain and probed. A small, soft bead came away, and it had a fine hair protruding.

Had she suspected all along, or did she just want to be sure of finding her green sidekick if he goofed off? Vitellan flicked the bead across the loading bay and beneath another garbage skip on high wheels. Nothing happened. He waited. The skip was close, too close. He wanted to move to somewhere further away, but that was too risky. He wondered if Mattel had already homed in on him, and was already watching—

A shattering blast lifted the skip into the air, and it crashed down again, half across the pile where Vitellan was buried. Shredded plastic and a snowstorm of foam packing eddied down on the still summer air. Security dogs barked somewhere and footsteps padded across a gravel walkway. Vitellan's ears were ringing, he was buried and blinded by rubbish. The improvised pilum was nowhere at hand, but he still had the knife. Footsteps padded through foamed plastic, the Luministe agent was inspecting her work, probably puzzled and wary at the lack of Centurion splattered all over the loading bay. Six of those ballistic fingernails were left to her. Unlike the set that Lucel had used in Paris, all of Mattel's nails were explosive. A foot came down cautiously beside his concealed arm.

Vitellan swept Mattel off balance, then burst from his cover and sprawled over her, stabbing down into her back with his knife. The knife bounced back—another coverall of that damned gossamer mesh, he realized. Mattel squirmed around, catching him a glancing blow with her fist. Vitellan closed again. Stay too close for her to use her nails, his instincts told him. She head-butted, and he reeled back. Her head was covered in a mesh-armor mask which stiffened to protect her from any sharp blow and felt like solid rock to Vitellan. She put a foot against him and pushed him free, then click, click, she armed a thumbnail. Vitellan grasped a length of plastic laminate and flung it as Mattel fired. The nail flew high and blasted brick rubble from a wall, showering Vitellan with fragments. He fell heavily, losing his knife. Mattel armed the other thumbnail and began to back away to fire. Vitellan staggered after her with another piece of laminate, thrashing at her hands as she tried to fire the thumbnail, keeping them apart. She seized the end of the laminate strip in both hands, flicked a foot up into Vitellan's jaw, then pulled the plastic laminate toward herself as his grip slackened. She pulled too hard. The fingers of her right hand were curled around the end of the length of laminate as it thudded into her lower chest. Her armed thumbnail was protruding slightly.

Even the terrorist's armor mesh could not withstand the explosion that resulted as the covalent lattice within the thumbnail collapsed. Mattel was blown in two, but was held together like a burst rag doll by the mesh at her back. Vitellan was flung back ten feet into a pile of packing and cardboard, and was unconscious when the police arrived. He was still unconscious when the death of a notorious terrorist was credited to him on the night's newscasts. Lucel arrived on the first available SOMS flight from Los Angeles. Vitellan did not regain consciousness until the next afternoon.

"You are recovering well, and you have a visitor."

It was a soft, firm voice in the blackness, and Vitellan suspected that it belonged to a medical software agent.

"Am I seriously hurt?" he replied in his thoughts.

"Your condition is not rated as serious, but you can only be allowed to full consciousness as a holographic projection. Will you accept that option?"

"Who is my visitor?"

"Lucelene de Hussontal, she said to tell you."

"Yes, yes, I'll be a projection."

He found himself floating out-of-body as a holographic bust above his intensive care unit. Lucel was sitting at a console nearby, examining newscast images of the scene of Vanda Mattel's death.

"Lucel."

Her head jerked around as if she did not expect him to appear so quickly.

"Vitellan!" she exclaimed, jumping to her feet. "How the hell did you kill her—I mean, are you all right?"

"I don't know, and probably not, in that order," he replied. "Am I alive? Death seems so hard to pin down in this century."

"You have a concussion and very minor brain damage, but that can be fixed by some imprint therapy and neural gating. In decreasing order of importance you also have a hairline fracture of the skull, perforated eardrums, knife wounds to the shoulder and throat, nine broken bones, and eleven lovebites to the chest and neck."

Vitellan's holographic lips hung open, and his translucent green jaw worked without producing words. Lucel folded her arms and smiled. She shook her head.

"No hard feelings, Vitellan. Nobody likes competition, but like I said, it was war. In war, anything goes and by the way, we won."

"Was Jilly—I mean, was she your teacher?" he asked, tactfully fishing for another subject.

"Vanda? Yes, she was, she really was. She must have thought I was sending you two here as a scheme to check Melbourne for some showdown. Maybe she thought the Mawson Institute was involved. We'll never know now."

"The Mawson Institute was partly destroyed last November."

"Yes, but they had a disaster contingency site set up somewhere south of the city. The switchup computers of their network were online within fifteen minutes of the blast. The surviving staff took a bit longer to come out of hospital and trauma counseling, but the place is open for business again."

The hologram head turned about, as Vitellan examined his surroundings.

"How long will I be like this?"

"Another four days, just to be safe. Meantime you can go anywhere by telepresence, you're wired into the network. The Durvas Icekeeper wants to speak with you, and the Village Corporate can be trusted now. You're safe."

"Safe? What about the Luministes?"

"Have you been following the newscasts on Bonhomme?"

"Until a few minutes ago I was not in a fit condition to do the news."

"And before that you were otherwise preoccupied—sorry, I couldn't resist that. Bonhomme still lies where he fell, and it's five days now. The Luministes are having something of a theological crisis."

Lucel explained Icekeeper McLaren's role in the whole complex affair, how he had founded the Luministes with Lord Wallace, stolen billions in research funding, effectively murdered Robert Wallace, and been responsible for countless other acts of terrorism.

"And all of this so that he could transfer my mind from a dying body into that of Robert Wallace?" asked Vitellan.

"That was apparently his sole motive. He was the most brilliant, resourceful, fanatical, dangerous, and loyal Icekeeper in the history of Durvas."

"He would have got along well with a man named Gentor, but I— I would not have sanctioned any of what he did for me. I would rather that my Icekeepers were all like Guy Foxtread."

"The 1358 appointment," said Lucel automatically. "For what it's worth, Icekeeper Gulden is the current appointment, and he seems to be as steady and reasonable as you could wish."

The holographic face frowned.

"A steady and reasonable Icekeeper? A pious and holy devil would be more believable."

Bonhomme had not arisen on the third day after he had shot himself. Blood congealed and darkened where it had splattered and spilled. Nobody approached the corpse on his own orders, and the Luministe security guards enforced those orders strictly. Telecameras showed insects moving about on the exposed tissue, and the eyes of the world watched as they fed and laid their eggs. Luministe clergy misted insecticide over the corpse, but refused to approach it. After six days there had been no resurrection, and even the media began to lose interest. After ten days the signs of decay were embarrassingly obvious, and the Luministe Supreme College of Light met to pronounce on what to do. The crowd in the Atlanta stadium had dwindled, and the substantial police presence was wound down to a token force. The College proclaimed that Bonhomme may have meant fifty days, that he had mispronounced "fifty" as "three." The faithful maintained their vigil. The mayor, coroner, chief of police, and owners of the stadium disagreed. Oddly enough it was a group of armed sports fans that finally liberated the stadium in a vigilante action that was probably sanctioned from within the government. There was a brief but bloody exchange of gunfire around the corpse. When the authorities were finally able to reach the remains of Bonhomme, the decay was fairly advanced—aided by the heat from the powerful lamps trained down on it. The coroner pronounced him dead by his own hand.

As Bonhomme was being scraped off the stadium floor, Vitellan was discharged from the Royal Melbourne Hospital. He was unsteady on his feet as he and Lucel strolled hand in hand along the Southbank complex beside the Yarra River some hours later. It was another hot evening of late summer, and thoughts of how he had strolled there with Jilly/Vanda only days earlier scuttled back into his mind as fast as he could crush them. The place where her thumbnail-missile had blasted the jogger had been scrubbed clean, but the marks stood out and people stopped to point as they strolled past. Lucel had booked them into the penthouse suite of the same hotel whose bar window he had escaped through, and kept suggesting that he must be getting tired all through the evening.

Vitellan had been sharp with medications and enforced rest, however, and even after two hours of intimacy with Lucel on the huge circular bed he was still wide awake.

"That was important to me," she said as she lay with an arm draped over him in musky dampness beneath the sheets. "I want to have a time to remember when you are all mine, even if it's only a day or two."

Vitellan pulled her close, and she clung to him gratefully.

"I don't understand. Why only a day or two?"

"You have a secure Village again, and Icekeeper Gulden can be trusted. You've been exchanging a lot of encrypted traffic with him, I notice. Do—do you want to return to the ice? There are still twenty-six years to go before you turn two thousand years old."

"Do *you* want me asleep and frozen?"

"No. Who do you think I am, an Icekeeper?"

Vitellan laughed, and Lucel joined him in spite of her mood.

"I wish to stay awake, perhaps for many years. I should have stayed with your grandmother of twenty-eight generations ago, but leaving her seemed to be the right thing to do, for her own sake. I want to stay with you now."

"Because I give her back to you?" whispered Lucel, pressing her head against his.

"Because you give love back to me, Lucel."

"Love. I'm a lot to put up with for just love."

"Peace, too, belonging, companionship, a friend, a worthy opponent, a teacher—"

"A lover who doesn't bite?"

"That too. To me, I'm back in the summer of 1358 in France, lying in a castle bedchamber, but this time there is no reason to flee. I really do want to stay with you."

They were up at dawn the next morning, but they stayed in the spa bath for an hour before having an early breakfast sent up to the suite. The current fashion in leisure wear was cutaway designs over tinted UV bodygauze, but they were both carrying scars that would attract stares, so they opted for white aircell tracksuits.

"We look odd, young heads on old fashions," Lucel remarked as they waited for a tram beside Princess Bridge.

"If I wore the appropriate fashion, I'd be in a toga and sandals," Vitellan reminded her.

Melbourne's center was an enormous pedestrian mall, patched with lawn, fountains, gardens, and sculptures. In a bizarre reversal of its former role, the central business district had become an exclusive residential and tourist area, from which people commuted or telecommuted to work. People ate out, more often than not, and restaurants were everywhere. Vitellan paused before Deciad Grills, noting that it was open for business, and that the owner's name was Greek. Inside, it was fitted out in molded fiberglass to resemble the interior of the Temporian time ship. The symbol from the Quintus scroll was above the door and on every menu.

"Have you ever wondered about this?" Vitellan asked as he and Lucel sat waiting for their coffee to arrive.

"Symbols from the *Deciad* cover of Quintus. You mentioned it back in LA."

"An ancient mason's code, you would call it a triangulation. One point is the symbol for mason, another is the symbol for tunnel. They are each at the points of a set of dividers."

"Quintus and the Temporian time ship. Only two points for a triangulation?"

"It's a riddle, like the symbols over the door to my Frigidarium. A grave without a corpse, and a corpse without a grave. Rufus, my mason of the first century, explained it to me. The Frigidarium is not a grave nor was my body a corpse. The riddle is that I was still alive, although buried."

"And there is a 'riddle' here, too?"

"Yes."

"The sides of the triangle are not defined, only the base," she said, stroking her chin. "What do we have for the third point?"

"The hinge of the dividers. Remember, the Temporian time ship had fifteen more cells for frozen bodies than occupants."

"There were divisions among them, there is evidence of fighting within the chambers," said Lucel, still unconcerned rather than puzzled. "Some must have died and been dumped into the sea for the seals and skuas to eat."

"Without the hinge, the dividers are useless. Without Decius, what are the Temporians? The time ship is built like a fort, it cannot be entered without proper tools. Suppose Decius had returned to find fifteen of his supporters expelled, huddled outside and slowly freezing to death. They had all drunk the Oil of Frosts, they could all be frozen and revived. There is a small range of mountains at the hinge-point: some of the ice there may be nonglacial and suitable for preserving bodies. Decius might have returned to the raft to scratch these symbols on the Quintus scroll's casing, then led his people inland to scrape out—"

"A time ship!" exclaimed Lucel, immediately wide-eyed. "Another Temporian time ship!"

Vitellan put a finger to his lips as a waiter arrived with their coffees. He was wearing a cotton toga, which was admirably suited to the Melbourne summer.

"Have you ever been to the time ship?" Vitellan asked him.

"No, but the owner has. He renamed this place Deciad Grills last year after he got back from Antarctica."

"Nice decor," remarked Lucel.

"Yeah, it gets the crowds in, but I hope he lets us wear suits instead of these bloody togas in winter."

When he was gone Lucel stabbed at the *Deciad* symbol urgently and lowered her voice.

"We'll have to check this at once, Vitellan," said Lucel urgently. "At least some of those Romans may have survived."

"I told Durvas some days ago, over the telepresence net. They are planning a joint expedition with the Mawson Institute."

"You told everyone but me?" exclaimed Lucel. The waiter looked around, then hastily returned to folding paper napkins.

"Lucel, Lucel, please," said Vitellan soothingly. "I have been looking forward to a few quiet days with you for so very long. Last night we talked about each other and our plans and love for hours. If you had known about the second Temporian time ship, could you have talked about anything else?"

Lucel drew a deep, sharp breath, then gulped a mouthful of coffee.

"Yes, I see. Sensible." Her words were remote, neutral.

Vitellan put a hand on her cheek, then looked into her eyes and kissed her. The change is there, I can see it, he thought sadly to himself.

Antarctica: 9 March 2029, Anno Domini

Antarctica was still a rugged place for tourists to visit. Lucel and Vitellan dashed from the SOMS through a snowstorm to a waiting ice-transit, and from there the journey to the Hotel Temporian took longer than the suborbital flight from Australia to Antarctica. They spent the period that was designated night in the hotel, although Lucel wanted to go straight out to the excavation site.

"Neither of us are archeologists," said Vitellan wearily as he lay sprawled across the bed, still wearing insulatives.

"I don't trust the Luministes, you know what they did to the Temporians in the original time ship," Lucel said sharply as she paced the green carpet. "We'll have to be on guard this time."

"No bodies have been found as yet, so there is nothing to guard," grumbled Vitellan. "When we have something to look at, then we go there. Agreed?"

They slept badly. Lucel was restless, and she kept Vitellan awake for much of the time. By the breakfast call there was word from the excavation site that promising ultrasound profiles had been detected, but excavation would take at least five hours more. Vitellan suggested a tour of the Temporian time ship.

"I don't believe you, Vitellan!" muttered Lucel, grating her teeth and shredding her napkin. "These people have traveled sixteen centuries. They're Romans like you, yet you don't seem to care!"

"I care," said Vitellan with a disarming shrug. "When they are revived I want to be there, but just now they are frozen bodies, and that's nothing new for me. I've been one myself for long enough."

Lucel and Vitellan did not take the official tour of the museum, but went straight down to the caverns of the time ship itself. There were no others down there as they walked the ancient passages. It was better presented than Vitellan remembered from his virtual tour, but that card had been made many months ago. As the designer of another time ship, Vitellan took a keen interest in the technology. Lucel remained a curious mixture of boredom and nervous energy. Vitellan paid particular attention to the frozen, murdered bodies.

"The evidence of the intrusion has been cleaned up," Lucel explained as Vitellan bent over to examine the ice in which one of the bodies lay. "The holes in the ice Gina Rossi drilled have been filled. The damage that she did is all within their brains."

"Considerate of her to leave them as good museum exhibits," said Vitellan as he straightened.

They took the elevator back up to the museum and went to the coffee shop. A panoramic window looked out over the frozen sea, and everything was still and crisp.

"The weather's good, that will help the diggers," said Lucel as they sat drinking their coffee.

Vitellan agreed, then looked across at a group photograph on the wall. He noted the date, and that it was of the museum staff. A case with one of the frozen Temporians was the centerpiece of the photograph.

"Is Gina there?" asked Vitellan, pointing to the wall. "I think I remember her from the vid, the one near the center."

"Ah, yes, the one standing to the left of the case."

Vitellan stared at the photograph, then nodded slowly.

"Of course, I have—"

"Just a moment!" exclaimed Lucel, suddenly staring at something on her dataspex. "They've found them! All together, seventeen Temporians. They're separating and extracting them now!"

Lucel already had a tiltfan fitted out and ready for the flight inland. Vitellan went with her to the hangars and sat patiently in the observer's seat while she hurried through the preflight check, then began bringing the motors up to operational temperature.

"They're not going to run away," said Vitellan as she revved up the fans and the machine lurched into the air.

"I can't understand why you're so calm," she retorted.

The tiltfan entered the coldlock of the hangar. Double doors slid shut behind it, double doors in front opened onto blinding Antarctic whiteness, then they surged out on four columns of air. The tiltfan quickly gained height in the clear, cold air, and Vitellan looked ahead to a cluster of hills. Almost at once Lucel began the descent. The site of the time raft was marked by a scatter of red tiltfans and tents, and two spidery ice-cutting handlers stood idle beside a geometrically regular gash in the blind valley's ice. Vitellan noted a row of oblong blocks covered in yellow insulative near one of the cranes, and Lucel steered the tiltfan for these as they came in to land.

Each of the blocks of ice containing the Temporians' bodies was on a pallet. Vitellan walked across the compacted snow past two deferential guards to one of the pallets and lifted a corner of the yellow insulative. He stared at something dark and indistinct beneath the surface of the frozen block, then went across to the edge of the excavation. Lucel joined him as he stood staring into the remains of the time raft.

"I've ordered that the pallets be loaded into my tiltfan at once," she reported.

Vitellan turned to see an articulated handler lift a pallet with firm but gentle efficiency and stamp across to the tiltfan.

"How many trips will you make?" Vitellan asked as he watched.

"Just one. You don't seem very interested, Vitellan. There are cameras recording all this, you know. You're part of this too, people want to share your feelings in this moment."

"I think my feelings are fairly obvious," he said as he turned away again.

Lucel stood beside him for a moment, unsettled by his strangely detached mood, then she strode over to the tiltfan and waited there as the last of the pallets were loaded aboard. She was revving up the engines and preparing to leave when Vitellan finally came back.

"You have to stay here and examine the site and reports," she said, barring his way to the cabin.

"Do I?" he asked. "What I've seen already is enough. I'm just a tourist."

"Please, love, the tiltfan is heavily loaded as it is. I mean it's safe, but I'd rather you went back in one that's not so close to the limit."

"If that's the case we should split the load. I don't want you in danger," he said as she walked him to the hatch.

"Vitellan, I know what I'm doing!" she shouted impatiently. "Now please go and see Gulden. He wants to show you how the last man awake, probably Decius, rigged a snowdrop to cover himself. He also thinks that one of the women may turn out to be Helica."

Vitellan shrugged, then turned and walked clear to where Icekeeper Gulden was waiting with his team of archeologists. They said nothing but exchanged nods and watched as Lucel's tiltfan lifted sluggishly from the ice and slowly gained height. Now Gulden and Vitellan walked straight to a smaller tiltfan that was revving up, and they strapped in beside four armed security guards. Still not a word was exchanged. The second tiltfan surged into the air and rose clear of the low, desolate peaks. Ahead of them Lucel's tiltfan was a tiny red hyphen against the blue sky, high above the ice. A puff of smoke burst abruptly about the distant aircraft, something flew clear, then a roiling ball of fire blossomed in midair. Debris rained down to the ice, followed by a parachute of red and white concentric circles. The second tiltfan descended, pacing the parachute until Lucel landed in a puff of powdery snow. Vitellan jumped to the surface with Gulden as Lucel was unbuckling her harness. The guards followed.

"Vitellan, how did you get here so quickly?" she panted.

"Roman efficiency," he replied tersely.

Lucel nervously brushed at the snow on her parka. "I only just managed to eject in time, there was a bomb aboard. Some Luministe leftover cell must have detonated it remotely."

Vitellan and Gulden drew their rail pistols together.

"Vitellan?" she gasped, spreading her hands wide rather than raising them.

"Don't move, Lucel, don't make this harder than it needs to be," he warned.

"Vitellan, you've lost your senses, I—"

Gulden fired as she began to reach for Vitellan, and she convulsed as a covalat-edge, charged needle tore through the monomolecular mesh bodysuit beneath her clothing and raked her nervous system with pain. Vitellan fired another, then Gulden fired again. Lucel toppled to the snow, as rigid with shock as a bronze statue. The Icekeeper took a web-cap from his pocket and pulled back the hood from Lucel's head as Vitellan covered him. A few seconds later she was safely in an induced coma, and the guards lifted her into the tiltfan.

"You were right," said Vitellan as he and Gulden stood watching.

"I am not proud of being right," Gulden replied, the rail pistol still in his hand, "but the Luministe records that I de-encrypted were accurate. Her mind is still focused by those obsession imprints that she was given. 'Kill all false prophets from the past, and kill all time travelers except the true prophet,' they say. She might have been able to tinker with the vectors so that you are the true 'prophet' instead of Bonhomme, but the Temporian Romans have no such protection. It's not Lucel's fault, they had not been discovered in 2024 when the imprint work was begun on her."

"Are they safe?"

"Safe?" exclaimed Gulden indignantly. "You ask the Icekeeper of Durvas if frozen bodies in his care are safe?"

Vitellan was used to dealing with Icekeepers.

"Well, are they?"

"Our ultrasonics have located seventeen profiles, all about a hundred yards from our dummy trench. Now that my worst fears about Lucel are confirmed and she is under control, we can start the real work. Do you want to be there for the real excavation, Centurion?"

"It will be a great moment, and I seem to be drawn to great historic moments. Yes, but let us get Lucel safely away from here first."

Durvas, Britain: 19 April 2029, Anno Domini

An official announcement was made that the Centurion of Durvas had been revived successfully for medical checks, but apart from some limited interviews he was kept distant from the journalists and their cameras. The media people did not mind unduly. As was expected, events in Antarctica tended to dominate the networks: news of the find of a second Antarctic time ship had been released. It was hyped up like the landing of a UFO. The Temporian Romans would be ambassadors from an advanced but alien society, and their effect on human society would be studied as as an example of "first contact." They also presented an opportunity to study how humans adjusted to really long-term time travel, travel so extreme that no familiar societies were left when they were revived.

"They are a vaccine," explained Gulden as he and Vitellan walked in the garden of Gulden's hobby farm. Spring had taken a firm hold, and the background greenery was swamped with flowers.

"And what is the disease?" asked Vitellan.

Gulden gestured to the sky above.

"Read any history of first contact between civilizations. Even if those in power on the weaker side are able to fight back, there are always those who turn traitor and support the invaders. They are the Luministes in the picture, they sell their own people into submission to gain power under the invader. Our world needs practice in dealing with such times and changes. The Temporians have no power, no weapons, no home world to give them backing, so they are safe enough. The next shipload of intelligent aliens may not be without such backing."

The commnode cheeped on Gulden's wrist. He held his hand up, then slipped his dataspex onto his face. After only moments he removed them and turned to Vitellan.

"That's the Durvas Clinic. You're needed there."

"Lucel?"

"Yes. Come this way, I have a tiltfan ready over there behind the barn."

The tiltfan lifted with a deep, authoritative hum of engines, and Gulden brought it up to a transit corridor level before setting the pilot beacon and selecting the coordinates for the Durvas clinic. He did not switch to autopilot. The act of piloting was something to hide behind while he talked with the memories of a man born nearly twenty centuries earlier.

"There is practically no hope for Lucel," Gulden said as he stared through the windscreen at the English countryside four hundred feet below. "The paranoia against all but her chosen time traveler, you, has been imprinted too deeply, and on too many levels."

Vitellan drummed his fingers on the shockcell padding beside his seat, staring down at the patchwork of fields and tracery of roads.

"McLaren could transfer my mind to another brain, yet you can't undo a mere obsession? Is that what you are saying?"

"Yes."

"Please explain, I find that unbelievable."

Gulden waved his right hand in a little circle. "Were I to botch the landing at the Durvas Imprint Clinic and hit a wall very hard, how much do you think it would cost to restore this tiltfan?"

Vitellan consulted the cyclopedia imprint. "It sells for a quarter million pounds, so . . . perhaps a third of that?"

Gulden laughed softly. "Three or four *times* that, Vitellan. Surprised?"

"Yes!"

"I'll explain. Tiltfan components are stamped out very efficiently in the factories, but a mangled wreck has to be bent back straight again, then panelbeaten until the dents are gone. Torn sections have to be welded, missing bits have to be replaced or filled with bondfiber, and many parts just have to be discarded altogether and replaced. It's intensive work, and expensive work. After a serious accident it's easier to salvage what parts have survived, break up the rest for recycling, and buy a new tiltfan."

"But Lucel is not injured."

"She is riddled with gates and stabilized imprints. We have removed one, but it took a lot of sweat. The rest would take longer than her expected lifetime to clear. We could take whole blocks out, filter them for anything suspicious, then return them as an imprint."

"Then do it."

"The risk is that we shall remove too much of the legitimate Lucel. A lot of gate-pattern memories are the real her, and after six years of therapy you would be left with a pale reflection of what was once Lucel. Something like a shy nine-year-old, someone who would grow into a woman again, but almost certainly a different woman from the one you knew."

Within minutes the tiltfan was descending into a pattern of landing lights on the roof of the Imprint Clinic. Vitellan and Gulden descended to the maximum security ward where Lucel was being held. She was drowsy with sedation, but fighting to keep herself sharp.

"They give me no lines or news," she said as she sat with her head on Vitellan's shoulder. "Information is my life, Vitellan. I can't go on like this."

"You're in the middle of heavy imprint therapy. You must be kept calm and relaxed."

"But why bother with this therapy? I understand what was done to me, I know that I have keys to attack any frozen time traveler other than you, but now there are none left. I'm safe to be with."

"But there are thousands of modern people in cryogenic storage."

"My imprints don't cover them, they have to be from the distant past."

Vitellan said nothing. Lucel began to pace the ward, her arms folded behind her back.

"If I need therapy, it can only be because the frozen Temporian Romans have survived," she concluded quickly. "You probably colluded with Gulden and set up an elaborate hoax to test my reactions. If you had to do that, then it must be because there are other time travelers. If I must still be restrained, it must be because the blocks of ice on the tiltfan contained wax dummies or modern cadavers. The real Decius and his companions are probably still in the ice."

Vitellan sat on her bed, hunched over and hopeless. "What do you want me to say?" he asked.

"Nothing. When I let the Luministes do this to me, I thought that only you and Bonhomme would be involved. With all these others around . . . I'll continue to have obsessions to vector on them. I am only in control now because you have not confirmed that the others are still alive. Imprint therapy is the only answer, Vitellan. I may not be totally in control, but I'm no fool."

They stood together and kissed. Lucel stared into Vitellan's eyes, and seemed to peer into his thoughts.

"This feels like good-bye, you seem so sad," she protested.

"Gulden says the procedure is dangerous," he admitted, his words halting. "You may wake up . . . not quite yourself. He was quite blunt about the risks."

Lucel clenched her fists, and muscles rippled impressively along her forearms.

"I shall not say good-bye, Vitellan. You fought for your identity and won, so I can do it too. I'll be back as me, just you wait."

When she was fully sedated Gulden brought a touchboard to Vitellan as he sat watching Lucel's sleeping body through a window. As the procedure commenced there was nothing physical to see, and as the hours passed there was nothing more for Vitellan to do but watch the steady rise and fall of his lover's chest. When Gulden finally approached him he was not smiling.

"It's worse than I could have imagined," the Icekeeper reported. "Some sort of irreversible random placement has been used, something developed privately that we have no documentation on."

"Couldn't you do anything?"

"We did indeed repair some gating, but it barely scratched the surface. Now I need a decision on how to proceed, and an authorization to do so. One way is to begin removing the gates and imprints individually and hope that a faster technique is soon developed. Another is to try filtering blocks and reimprinting Lucel with herself. That will take no more than six years, but she will not awake the same woman. The third course is to keep her confined . . ."

Vitellan gazed at her sleeping body and shook his head.

"She is very resourceful. Sooner or later she will escape and begin stalking the Temporian Romans, nothing is more certain. The fourth course is to kill her."

"I never said—"

"Of course not, but someone had to say it. There is also a fifth way to cure her."

"Another way? This is my specialty, I doubt that I have missed any alternatives."

"She can be frozen until all the Romans are dead, so she would awake in a world where there are no triggers to make her dangerous. Anyway, in a few decades there may be imprint techniques that can reverse the Luministe imprinting in a matter of weeks, rather than years."

"You are talking about fifty years, or even more."

"Hah, a mere trifle. In the meantime Durvas can set up a research foundation to develop techniques for repairing such imprint damage. As Centurion of Durvas, I hereby order it."

A refinement of what was once known as Oil of Frosts was administered to Lucel before she was revived. Vitellan watched from the observation room, then came in as she opened her eyes. He was wearing a clinic gown himself.

"It failed," said Lucel.

"I haven't said a word," replied Vitellan.

"No, but you are wearing an Alpha-level security badge, and you only need to wear one of those when visiting an extremely dangerous patient. If I'm still dangerous, then Gulden and his team failed."

"You are right, of course," Vitellan admitted. "Dr. Gulden has just given me the results of the exploratory scan. Wait fifty years, or a hundred, and a therapy will be developed to reverse your obsessions and vector keys. You will have to be frozen until then."

Lucel turned away from him and stared at the wall.

"You were right to snatch a few days of playing lovers with me, Vitellan. Dammit, I'm like a race car, tuned up to all hell but burned out after only a couple of hours of competition. Was it all worth it?"

"Was I worth it?"

"If you were not, nobody else is."

"That's not an answer."

"It was not meant to be."

Vitellan sat on the edge of the bed and put his arm around her shoulders. She turned back and flung her arms around him at once.

"It's said that adjusting to a new century is a real bitch," Lucel whispered.

"Who said that?"

"Some Roman I know, a real charmer. He's had a lot of experience."

"Good, good. He'll be there to help out when you wake up."

"What?" she cried.

Lucel sat up and seized Vitellan by the shoulders, her bloodshot eyes bulging with incredulity as she looked him up and down.

"Yes, the gown, the, the . . . You *would* do it, you really would."

She hugged him again, convulsively. He stroked her hair, his eyes closed and his mind blank, savoring the minutes that would soon slow into years.

"You need to key a legal release into the bedside console," Vitellan began, but Lucel reached out and batted out a pattern before he could say any more.

"How long have we got?" she asked.

"A minute, an hour, a day if you like. You have to stay in here, of course, but where you stay, I stay."

"It's a cage, cages suck. I wouldn't make my best friend stay in a cage and you're my best friend."

"It doesn't have to be so frantic, Lucel."

"Yes it does. Don't underestimate me, Vitellan, I know what I am. I know that there might be surviving travelers from Imperial Rome out there. We've been through all this before. Maybe I blew up a tiltfan loaded with frozen wax dummies, maybe it was all a hoax to activate the psycho circuits in my head to show what I can do." She placed a finger on his lips as he parted them to speak. "Don't tell me anything, lover. Right?"

"Right," Vitellan agreed.

Gulden watched as the two bodies were lowered into the cryogenic chambers together. Fumes billowed from the liquid nitrogen, and one by one the sensor ikons on a wallscreen beside him turned from red to green. Covers glided into place, sealed, then locked.

The 121st Icekeeper of Durvas sighed with relief. The Master was safely frozen again, after a most harrowing few months in the world outside.

"A close call, Master," Gulden whispered. "Ah, Icekeeper McLaren was so loyal. It grieves me that the truth about what he did for you cannot be shouted to the world's media and turned into another Durvas legend. He shook the world to keep you alive, Master. The older you grow, the fiercer does our loyalty become."

He touched a key, and the guard circuits switched to automatic-live. The lights dimmed in the Deep Frigidarium.

"I am honored to have known you, but I am glad that you will sleep for most of my tenure. We love you, Master, but we fear the madness that fires us to protect you."

Some minutes later Gulden was back on the surface, chatting with Dellar and Burgess in an overgrown garden that was full of spring blooms and birdsong. They had stopped before the twelfth-century building that guarded the entrance to the original Frigidarium.

"So they're both down now," said Dellar. "The Master and his true love."

"Repulsive woman, I don't know what he sees in her," muttered Burgess.

"We had better start planning for the revival of 2054," warned Dellar.

"He will not want to stay awake long if Lucel remains frozen, Sir Peter," Gulden replied confidently.

"And Lucel? You had all the Luministe obsession gates scrubbed out of her mind?"

"Yes, it was easy. Just after she was sedated for freezing I gave her an imprint explaining everything. The most she can do to me at the time she is revived is jump up and down on my grave."

"Five of those Temporian Roman sleepers have just been revived, including Decius himself, " Dellar remarked, as if he expected Gulden to be following his thoughts.

"I know, I've been following the interviews with them. They said they were part of a secret bureaucracy of time travelers that ran the Roman Empire, and nearly every government on Earth has been sending urgent requests for more information. These men and women from our past might end up changing our world more than the crew of a UFO could hope to. It's like First Contact, in fact in a sense it really is First Contact."

"All of a sudden the Durvas time traveler is old news," said Burgess wistfully.

"Yes, isn't it wonderful!" exclaimed Gulden his elation undisguised. "All those psychologists had been queuing up to study the Master as soon as we hinted at an early revival, but now they're off to study the Temporians."

"They had a point," Dellar reminded him. "Now that time-jumping is to be part of our lifestyle we need to see how people like Vitellan managed to adjust to awakenings in new centuries. Until recently he was priceless for that reason."

"Ah, but now nobody cares about us freezing him again," said Gulden. "The Romans from Antarctica are even older than our Master, and they can teach us an actual science of administration by time travel."

"Are you absolutely positive Lucel is safe?" asked Burgess. "If any of the Temporian Romans decide to be refrozen, then she could cause a lot of trouble in the future if her treatment is incomplete."

"Trust me, Lucel is now harmless," replied Gulden. "I worked from the original imprint maps when I reversed what had been done to her. The Luministe imprint analysts left an encrypted README imprint in her mind explaining what they had done, and I had the encryption key from McLaren's records in the Deep Frigidarium. When Lucel and Vitellan are eventually revived together, they can look forward to many happy years with each other."

Sir Peter Dellar sighed with relief and satisfaction. He was concerned for the Master's welfare, but he also wanted him to be happy. Gulden had engineered a win-win outcome.

"So when will that joint revival be, Dr. Gulden?" Dellar asked.

"Not during my lifetime, Sir Peter. I want it written in the *Village Corporate Chronicles* that the Master remained safe and secure during my tenure as the Icekeeper of Durvas, and that is most likely to be the case if he is frozen."

B+T
8/98